FORTRESS OF CROWS

Knights Templar Thrillers
Book Two

Daniel Colter

SAPERE
BOOKS

FORTRESS OF CROWS

Published by Sapere Books.

24 Trafalgar Road, Ilkley, LS29 8HH

saperebooks.com

ISBN: 978-0-85495-081-2

To Kitty and Gene Peters, and to Barbara and Lieutenant Colonel Bill Adams

ACKNOWLEDGEMENTS

An army of folks helped. Full marks to the crew at Sapere Books — top-notch work as always, and thank you for giving a daft American a chance. Special thanks to Cindy Burch, "President of the Daniel Colter Fanclub;" to Kirsten Kohlwey, for the interview and article; and to fellow Sapere author Alistair Forrest, for your encouragement and enthusiasm. And to my wife Melissa, for giving an ear while I blather on about things archaic, esoteric, or inane; putting an artist's eye on the cover; and knowing when to provide encouragement. Couldn't have done it without you.

Thank you all so much.

PART 1

CHAPTER 1

June, the year of our Lord 1186

"Riders coming!"

Hooves drummed down the road that led to the ruined town and the horsemen strummed shafts as they came, slewed in a spray of gravel, then twisted to shoot over a shoulder as they rode clear. The Templars sent bolts — too few, too late.

"Did you trigger an empty crossbow?" Finnláech of Struan asked his sergeant, Waylon, at his side.

"Aye. Out of bolts. Thought the sound might make them flinch."

"Give, even when you have nothing left to give," Lugh, a second sergeant, said in a fatherly, mocking tone. "Such simple advice."

"Simple? Nothing is simple," Finn muttered.

They said the mission would be easy. Collect a gentlewoman. Escort her to Acre. Return to Jerusalem. But here was Finn, huddled in a war-wasted hovel, not having an easy day.

Finn dragged off helmet and coif to run a hand through sweaty black hair. His hair was short, jagged, because it had been cut with a knife. He was tall, but not awkwardly so, face angular and scarred from cheek to jaw. Patina darkened his mail; the robe covering it was dirty and threadbare.

The setting sun was coming on as fire. Hues of red and orange screamed their last defiance to the gathering shades of grey and blue. Finn's battle mate, Rollo, was slumped against a mudbrick wall and within a moment his head bobbed in and out of sleep. His bearded and battered face bathed in a ray of amber light, making it oddly comforting. Finn's other knights, Hector and Serlo, were clustered nearby.

Finn studied the ground for the hundredth time. Crumbling walls. Skeletons of houses. Windows leering like sockets in a fire-charred skull. All razed by the traitor Templar, Robert of Saint Albans.

Their simple day turned bad on the road to Jerusalem, a pilgrim track Finn had ridden countless times. Black-clad men swirled out of the hills with murder in their eyes. His banner fought free. On failing horses, he spotted this wasted place and scuttled in, then spent the day fending off probing attacks and feints to draw them from cover. The dregs of those fights lay around him, already fly-bitten and reeking.

Out of habit, Finn tried to spit but sputtered instead. Waylon gave a quick handshake and tossed a canteen. He snatched it, downed the surviving water, then flung back the empty. "That the last?"

A clipped nod was his answer.

Lugh flashed a brittle smile. "Eejits going to dismount now … wait until dark and come at us on foot, eh? *Fils a putain.*"

Finn ignored the sergeants' favourite curse, tugged his helmet on and poked his head from behind the wall. Another stood to his right. A whistle and Hector's lupine face peeked out. 'All good,' Hector mouthed. A roofless house sat behind the walls. Serlo sat inside, guarding *Le Paquet*. His meaty hand stuck out from a window with a thumbs up. There was a crack at his ear and Finn flinched back from the shaft that almost filled his eye.

Waylon pulled and loosed and dropped back, laughing. "Stung his arse good."

"Save it for when they come," Finn said in a dull voice.

And come they would. Two score haunted the rocky ground. Their tormentors were tribals, most likely, but some wielded *tirkesh*, beautifully recurved bows capable of sticking a man from four hundred paces.

"Think he got through?" Lugh ran a hand over the side of his shaved head. The hair he left on top made him look like a gigantic cockerel — giving the too-obvious byname, Rooster.

Finn twitched a shoulder to say, *If any man can, it's Elias.* Elias was a Turc, a native scout, as sneaky as a cat and silent as a spider. Finn had sent him to fetch help. If it didn't come soon they would have to fight free or die trying.

"They're moving," Waylon hissed, bringing Finn's meandering mind home.

Finn tugged off his helmet and coif. Daring another lean around the wall, he cupped a hand to his ear and gave a measured head turn. Not a sound.

Finn eased back. Jerol toed Rollo awake.

"You wake me too early, Uncle," Rollo growled at his sergeant, so named for his advanced age. "Aye, you hear them, sneaking about like rats in a cellar. But they'll not come until —"

"There." Waylon listened through a hole in the wall, his head plastered against it.

Nothing. The silence dragged out.

Then the lonely *hoo* of an owl. Many cultures consider the birds bad omens. They were quiet in flight, unnaturally so, and glided the dark with barely a rustle. Some say owls carry souls to the afterlife. Finn found the notion comical. For him the call was lulling, and if owls toiled with the recently departed, well, at least they worked for a living.

"Back home folk mistake owls for the banshee," Rooster said, to himself as much the others. "But I saw the banshee, I did. The nasty bitch —"

The rattle of rock on metal cut his story short.

Hector bawled, "They come!"

Finn scamper-crawled to the opening that once held a door. Dark eyes peered between the rim of a shield and helmet. Then a hiss and a thump. An arrow point, not there a moment before, gleamed in the cloth-backed wood. With a swipe of his sword, he snapped the shaft at the board face, and as shadows flitted in, staggered up on stiff legs to meet them.

A man charged out of the gloom, sword gleaming along his draw arm, teeth white in a tangled black beard. Finn swayed from the cut and let the fool overreach, then casually kidney-stabbed him as he blundered and flailed. A hard yank freed the blade and he whirled to the front.

A flash of silver and Finn used the shield to slap aside a stab. Rollo's axe dropped, close enough the rush of air rustled Finn's hair as it passed, and the stabber groaned and fell. Another man ran in. Waylon's bow twanged and a shaft whizzed between Finn and Rollo. The man lurched to a stop, patted his chest with a confused scowl, then went down in an awkward fall.

"Passed clean through!" Waylon laughed demonically.

Black-clad men swirled like rabid dogs. Shadows shifted in swarms and the dark was full of ringing steel and curses and shrieks.

Hector parried a sword and stabbed its owner in the chest. The stabbed man ploughed on, slicing wicked sharp edges through himself, crazed to get at the man at the other end. He crumpled as the knight planted a boot and wrenched the blade free.

There was a dull thud as Rollo hooked his axe edge over a shield and levered the board down. Jerol leaned and drove a blade through the exposed man with a wet slither.

"I'm out," Waylon yelled, and sent his last shaft. Rooster sliced and got back a crimson spray, then shuffled backward to cover Waylon as he scooped up his falchion and shield.

A crunch, like an axe chopping green wood, and Rollo's rasping laugh. "Thought you'd sneak in, dumb arse?"

A cleaved man toppled from the darkness at Finn's side.

Didn't see him coming in…

There was rustling ahead and a figure loomed from the dark thrusting at his face. He twisted away and cut back. The man ducked, chanting in Arabic, and came up with a slash aimed to drop Finn's guts at his feet. Finn took the slash on his board and thrust quick as a stoat takes a rat. The man made a gurgling sound, perhaps intended as a curse, then staggered and fell.

The dying man was handsome, with striking hazel eyes. Finn felt a twinge and thought it odd to regret killing a comely man but not a homely man.

"Too many," Rollo bellowed. "Back! Form a shield wall."

The handsome man gargled his last. A dupe tried to step over the corpse and Finn stabbed, quick as an adder, into an exposed thigh. The dupe hopped, bumbled into another, and they both went over in a whirling clatter. Another slide back and Finn felt the wall at his back, brothers at his elbows.

Arrows flicked from behind in a sudden deluge. A shadow hitched up on his toes before dropping to his knees. Another *whoofed* as fletching sprouted in his chest. Hooves thumped. Shadows rode through the maze of walls — leaning and loosing, leaning and loosing.

"Elias!" Rollo yelled, and Finn glimpsed the Turc's devil grin as he spurred past.

"On the wall behind you!" Lugh called out.

And Finn went down, slammed by a body and wrapped in arms. His head smashed into the ground. Stars exploded behind his eyes. A brief memory — him, stripping his helmet after hearing the owl. *Perhaps they are a bad omen after all...*

Fingers dug into his chin, trying to leverage his head up for a kiss of steel. Garlic-tinged breath filled his nostrils and brought him back from the daze. With a frantic heave Finn groped behind and felt coarse hair. He wrapped a hand in beard and yanked it from side-to-side, like a terrier fighting a rat. The rat took the beard-yanking well, twitching arms his only reply, then something hot and wet slathered Finn's neck. The weight toppled off; a black-clad man flopped and twitched next to him.

Rooster crouched at his side, a blood-smeared *qama* in his hand, grinning over the dead man. "Having a wee wrestle, I see, but is now the time to play in the dirt?"

Rollo grasped a hand and heaved Finn to his feet. He began picking rock from the side of Finn's gouged head.

"Forgot to wear a helmet ... do this often? Fighting, I mean."

"Piss off." Finn slapped away Rollo's fingers. He drooped over, hands on knees, as blood dripped from his head to his beard and pooled between his boots. He stared at the crimson mud while letting the burn of the fight fade. The quiver in his arms eased and he lifted his gaze to Elias's ugly face.

"Ever tire of me rescuing your pathetic arse?" Elias's voice was harsh, his taunt more so.

Finn ignored the mockery and straightened up to take stock. The enemy lay stuck with shafts or stabbed or hacked. Most of his men were standing, though he counted three fewer sergeants. A cringe, a curse, then he signed the cross to atone for the cursing. He sucked in a breath and let it out. *Men die. It happens.*

Finn raised a brow at Elias.

"Rode for Nablus," Elias answered, "to fetch knights, but found Turcs coming in from a scout. Thought about grabbing a nap and saving you tomorrow. But time is of the essence, I says to myself, so I came with the Turcs." He made a guttural wheezing sound meant to be a laugh. "No knights in shining armour for you."

Finn replied with a scowl and took a few stumbling steps. "Serlo," he said, concern rising in his parchment-dry voice, "the relic hunter, *Le Paquet?*"

Serlo wheeled toward Finn, flipping his blade, sending ruby droplets dancing from the fuller. "*Le Paquet —*"

"Has a name." The voice was a woman's. "You know it, so why do you refuse to speak it?"

An inquisitor Finn knew said men belittle feared things by giving them mocking bynames. And so it was with *Le Paquet*, named Emma of Cherbourg at birth. Baret, her guard, was short and thick as an ox, his once-dark hair shading to grey.

Brothers scuttled away from Emma as though she spewed contagion. Rollo feigned interest in a dead enemy and moved off to examine the corpse, Serlo in tow. Finn stood dangerously alone. He had sworn the vow of chastity years ago, been celibate so long it was now as natural as breathing, his body numb to the struggle. Now temptation stood before him exuding the sweet scents of rose, myrrh, and marjoram infused in almond oil.

"Does the Order not provide you with helmets?" She waved vaguely at Finn's bloodied head. "To prevent such injuries?"

Finn shrugged, trying to appear unbothered by her teasing, and kept his gaze on Baret's wide face and grey brows. *If I'm busy, perhaps she'll leave.* He began barking commands to break the run of his nerves. "Elias, round up spare mounts. Waylon, check if the Blackrobes left water."

The commands were obvious and men already on the tasks rolled their eyes.

Finn tore a strip of cloth from a dead man and used it to clean Oathkeeper, his sword of watered steel, dabbed at the wicked-sharp edges, wiped down the fuller. Once clean, he propped her against the wall, marvelling at the cold grey lines in the steel, the swirling blue whorls, so like the ink on his shoulders and chest.

A rustling made him turn. Emma leaned to dab at his head with a water-wetted cloth. Finn flinched back and swiped at her hand, afraid to touch it, afraid to let it touch him. He stayed frozen in a lean, staring past her like a scolded dog, and she let the hand drop.

"You are frightened."

Finn's gaze defied his mind and leapt to her eyes. "I fear nothing."

"You fear a woman's hand."

Finn blinked, tempted to lie, and glanced away. "The Rule," he muttered over a shoulder and turned back, reciting: "It is a dangerous thing for any religious man to look upon a woman. None of you may kiss a woman, neither mother, sister, aunt, nor widow, and should avoid the embraces of women, by which men have perished many times."

The words felt silly as they tumbled out, but despite their warning, he found his gaze locked on her eyes, blue as a mountain lake. Sun kisses marked her nose and cheek. She had hair the colour of wet cinnamon, the rarest of spices, and large, protruding ears for such a petite woman.

"Fascinating how mere words rule one's life," she said with a theatrical grimace. "But not so much as a peck for your mother?"

"No. Nor for a sister." He glanced at Rollo, pretending to examine a *suif* taken from a dead enemy and eavesdropping. "I met Rollo's sister once," Finn said, then with growing speed, "and I feared her. God's truth. Taller than Rollo. Thicker beard too. Quick to anger and vicious in her rebukes."

Rollo made a huffing sound to imply he did not appreciate critique of his sister's appearance and Emma laughed. Finn stared at her full red lips and was saddened when she hid them behind a fist.

"I have been told Templars never jest. Yet I am confident I just heard one. None will believe me, I fear."

"Not a jest. Rollo's sister is a beast."

Emma's peered over a knuckle, eyes sparkling with mischief. "Is it true that Templars sleep fully clothed — boots, belts, and all?"

Finn nodded slowly, not liking the drift of it.

"You are never without clothes?"

"Can be … to wash."

"Bathing is a virtuous habit. I am dirty from the road and lusty for a hot bath. And I find bathing works best when one is … without clothes."

Sweat trickled down Finn's back like a spring runoff but his tongue was bone dry.

Emma grinned cruelly. "Learning brightens my day. Might I ask another question, sir?"

Finn nodded and cast about desperately for aid. A slightly sympathetic smile poked at the corner of Baret's mouth.

"You are not allowed to embrace women, nor be in their company. Yet Brothers are constant companions. Two men share sleeping space. Two men swap a bowl." Emma paused, bit at a lip, then stabbed home in a soft purr, "Are all things done between two men?"

A thick, "No," was all he managed.

"Seems odd, is all."

Finn stared flinty-eyed and her grin died.

"Lanfrid will be growing worried, I expect," she said, mostly for want of conversation.

Finn's brow shot up. "You know the Commander of Acre?"

"My husband, Adrien, is his brother — birth brother, I mean. I am sister-in-law to your Order, one might say." She added a silken smile to soften the scowl on Finn's face.

Finn had assumed the Order was escorting a noblewoman on pilgrimage. But he guarded family. Important family. *Why do those above take perverse delight in keeping field brothers in the dark?*

"You are kin." His voice was piqued for, again, Finn was given the skeleton of a task. He must add the meat.

She inclined a head to say, *Indeed I am.*

A sergeant came up with horses and Finn glared at the man, then Baret, as if they were guilty for all that had gone wrong. He scooped up Oathkeeper and slid steel into sheath. "If you will excuse me, *Sister*, I must check on our progress."

Finn gave Emma a stiff-neck bow and strode off, barking more needless commands.

"Of course, and my thanks, *Brother*," she said to his back.

The hills of Samaria were desolate, never a place of beauty, even in the blush of spring. They trundled a stretch of road bordered by twisted, skeletal trees and time-cracked slabs of limestone.

"This must be about where the Jew got the straw beat out of him." Rollo had a captured *saif* propped in the crook of his arm and idly stroked the metal handle with a thumb. "What man can't defend himself? And what Samaritan would help a Jew? They hate each other."

"Your knowledge of scriptures never ceases to amaze," Finn said in a bland tone. "The point is that a man was moved to care for an enemy. And we should follow his example."

"Follow the example of a weakling?" Rollo snorted and tipped the *saif* toward Finn.

"Looks sharp. Careful you don't cut yourself."

"Sharp ... and expensive. Watered steel. Like Oathkeeper. Doesn't it seem odd a Ragarse would carry such a blade?"

"He snuffed its owner. Now he carries it ... carried it, I should say." Finn had found Oathkeeper in the Order's armoury, abandoned, unloved, and married the blade to Frankish fittings. She was a wicked thing, ever sharp and thirsty.

"Could be. But while you mocked my sister I poked about the dead. Two of them carried watered steel, each marked with a bird." Rollo flourished a hand over the *saif's* metal handle to show a stooping hawk etched into the grip. The pommel curved into a bird's beak. "All wearing black. Quiet — none of the usual *la-la-la* chanting."

Finn pursed his lips. Rollo was not a complete fool. At least not about this. Watered steel was wielded only by those that could afford it — and not many could. The Blackrobes were disciplined and persistent. Tribal men trill harsh chants to fire their souls and freeze their enemies; these were quiet as Serlo.

Rollo tapped the handle in a rhythmic tic.

"Stooping bird..." The design teased Finn's memory, though the foggy thing wavered just outside his grasp. He half-twisted to gaze behind, where Emma rode beside Baret. She flashed him a silky smile.

After a time, Rollo slid the *saif* into its sheath and glowered at Finn from the corner of an eye. "Be warned, you turd-mouthed Scot, I'll tell Gunnor of your mockery. And you know how angry she can get."

"Can't say which worries me more — mysterious enemies stalking us or a thrashing from your sister."

"You *should* fear her. And Gunnor does not have a beard."

"I oversold that part. All the rest was true." Finn waited a heartbeat before adding, "Though you must admit she has the beginnings of a healthy face pelt."

"Rotten bastard, I'll…"

A lone figure appeared at the road edge. Where a moment before there was nothing now stood a hunched creature, clothed in a ragged robe, a hood shading its face. Elias should have seen the hooded one, as should have the Turcs guarding their flanks. None had.

The hood raised and a knobby hand planted a walking staff in the road.

Finn leaned to Hector. "We'll play the good Samaritan. Keep the banner moving. Be ready."

He reined in Fagan, his destrier, a few steps short. Vulpine eyes shined within the hood. The face was like wrinkled leather. Grime filled every crease and fold. Gender was buried somewhere in the aged countenance.

"God's blessings, Father," Finn said.

"Five warriors to greet an old *woman*." The crone's voice proved as leathery as her face. She jabbed the staff like a spear. "'O, see the fearsome Templars!"

Finn slid off his wide-brimmed hat to run a hand through sweat-tangled hair. His glance swept the rocks behind her. "Why are you alone, Mother? These hills are —"

She made an exaggerated snorting sound, like a pig on feed, and cackled. "I smell fear — and murder! Cain, murderer of his brother, I smell you."

Finn glanced at Rollo, who gave a shrug saying, *Mad — best to ride on.*

The crone's leer showed brown, snaggled teeth. She poked the stick at Finn. "What have you done? Hmm? The voice of your brother's blood cries to me from the ground. And now you are cursed from the ground, which opened its mouth to receive your brother's blood, shed by your hand. You shall be a fugitive for eternity, a wanderer of hell and all the dark places between."

A chill walked up Finn's neck. Unwanted memories bloomed — the light fleeing Robert's eyes, his dying breath rich with herbs from his last supper and willow bark for the pain in his leg. The Apostate, long ago his bowl mate, once his brother, but now sent to the boneyard by Finn's hand. He slid the hat back on and tugged it down.

"God be with you, Mother."

Finn heel-tapped Fagan away and fought the urge to sign the cross.

"Cain said to the Lord, my punishment is greater than I can bear."

Finn plodded on, trying to distance himself from the mad, leathery voice.

"Finnláech of Struan, murderer, you are marked in the book of dead. You escape us, for now," the crone made a feral hissing sound, "but death comes!"

With a curse, Finn kneed Fagan around, tugging at Oathkeeper.

But the crone had vanished — gone like a downy seed on the wind.

Sergeants spurred into the rocky jumble hunting her. After a time, they came back empty-handed, cursing and muttering in their beards.

Rollo pursed his scarred lips. "Just a madwoman."

Finn shook his head. "A madwoman who spoke my name." *And spoke of what I've done…*

CHAPTER 2

Acre was a pearl bedded in the shell of Outremer. The city sprawled over a finger of land jutting from the coast. A sparkling bay provided safe harbour and a bustling port.

She held faded remnants of many people. Jews. Romans. Arabs. Persians. Each held sway here at one time or another. Now Christians held her. Acre was a lifeline between Christendom and Outremer. Pilgrims disembarked here, most walking the lopsided stagger of a landlubber grown accustomed to a swaying ship's deck and trying to unlearn it. A throng of human jackals — guides-for-hire, hucksters, cutpurses, pimps — all vied for the pilgrim's coin.

Emma was delivered. Now they lounged outside the Order's fortress eating baked fish. A lazy sea slushed and lapped nearby. The fortress was in the city's south-west section and abutted the sea. A Templar House was here. And the Commander of Acre's residence. Barracks. Storerooms. Even a prison for wayward brothers. Crenelated walls, more than a dozen strides thick, wrapped the buildings in a stoney embrace. An aged symbol — a triangular shield with an upside-down T in the top half — had been carved in the lintel, branding the place as Templar ground.

Finn gazed on the golden lions topping the guard tower, pondering where the coin to pay for them came from and why the gaudy things were there in the first place. The bowl he shared with Rollo sat in his lap, still swimming with fish.

"Hand it over." Rollo wagged his fingers at their bowl. "Snaggletooth ruin your hunger?"

"And the men who attacked us. They are the same, I think."

25

"You think, aye?" Rollo shook his head at the obvious, then spooned a hunk of fish.

"The stooping bird insignia nags me. I've seen it somewhere." Though Finn would not say it, Emma's blue eyes also nagged at him.

"I know a man who might help." Hector reclined against the wall, his angular face hidden in the shade. "He is learned about many things — history, cultures, heraldry."

Finn shifted to Hector with a raised palm. "Lead on."

"Aye. But just the two of us. The man is surly by nature, vicious by choice. Best to keep the number of potential victims small."

"How ominous." Then Finn saw resignation on Hector's face and nodded at it. "As you will, Brother."

Hector was a learned man who enjoyed war, as skilled at reciting Latin as wielding a blade. Finn relied on Hector's mind as much as his sword.

Hector eased out of the shade. "The bird motif bothers me too." He tossed something and kept talking as the thing spun through the air. "Pulled this off the rabid swordsman I ran through."

Finn snatched the thing and opened his palm to see a pendant swaying on a sweat-stained cord. It had started life as a silver coin but, at some point, had been holed and was now living a second life as a pendant.

It showed a stooping hawk.

Finn and Hector strolled the Templar Tunnel. It began under the Templar House and ran east before daylighting at the port. Access to the port was vital; secretive travel from ship-to-fortress more so. The passage extended more than two hundred paces, the lower half carved from bedrock stone, the upper half from hand-hewn ashlars in a half-barrel vault. Midway, they passed the guardroom, where sergeants stood near a lever that could drop a portcullis to seal the warren against outsiders.

They emerged through a metal door, nodded at the guard, then breathed deeply of the salty air. Three war galleys rocked at the wharves before them — Venetian made and flying the skull and crossbones flag of the Templar fleet. A stone tower spiralled up on an island in the bay; a lighted beacon at the top guided ships to safe harbour.

Finn eyed the tower.

"Christians first arriving here thought they were at the city of Ekron," said Hector, "where the deity was Ba'al-zebub, which means the Lord of Flies. The tower was in disrepair, filled with refuse, and one assumes rife with flies. Thus, they named it, the Tower of Flies."

"You're a fountain of knowledge."

"A true scholar," Hector muttered.

The quay was a hive of activity. Barrels and bales were bustled from ships by cursing seamen. They passed the reeking fish market, where nut-brown men sparkled with the dried scales of their catch. Then the Venetian Quarter, where silk-clad merchants lounged under shaded porticos, sipping wine from ornate glass cups. Past the Templar church containing the Holy Trough, in which Jesus bathed, and at the Hospital of Saint John a turn into the city's heart.

Acre was gaining distinction for scholarship — scholars in Christendom even addressed religious enquiries to 'the scholars of Acre.' A scriptorium had taken root where squinting monks brought to life illuminated manuscripts.

Finn loathed the city. Tight cobbled streets choked him; the stench of close-packed humanity watered his eyes and the ruckus tortured his ears. Hector loved the place. Urban life fed his soul. His face, lean and browned by the sun, paled noticeably as they entered the stern ambiance of the Scriptorium's halls. He was thin-lipped and scowling by the time they found what they sought.

Hector bowed and said something in his native Catalan.

They stood before a tonsured head hunched over an inclined table. The head looked like it had not moved from the table in years. Pigeonholes lined the wall from floor to ceiling; each hole brimmed with tattered parchments and scrolls. The head hoisted up to show a face with sharp cheekbones, light brown eyes, and a proud nose. The resemblance to Hector was uncanny. The monk's face twisted into a rictus of annoyance, which turned quickly to disappointment, and then disgust.

The monk set aside a quill to stroke his beard. It was a colossal thing, falling in a cascade to the frayed rope belting his waist. He continued stroking, the habit done often enough the grey hairs at his chin were streaked black from the passage of ink-stained fingers.

A thick silence drew out.

Hector tried anew. "Good to see you, Uncle Pascual."

"Should you not be off riding down heathens? Perhaps burning a city?"

"Fresh out of cities to burn at the moment, and in the meantime, I have a question."

"Trying to remember the Lord's prayer, *minyó*?" Pascual used the Catalan word for boy, and not affectionately.

Hector ignored the slight and slid the pendant from his haversack. It dropped to the table with a clatter. "I also found a *saif* etched with the bird."

Pascual scowled and plucked up the cord. He squinted at the swaying pendant, then wrapped it in his palm and fixed his scowl on Hector.

"It is not too late to renounce all this sword-waving silliness. Life awaits you here."

"We have talked of this before, Uncle. I have a life. With the Templars." Hector shook a weary head. "God gifted me courage. Speed. Grit. And bade me use these to defend his people."

Pascual rolled his eyes. "You are like your father. A man who loves to run with his hair on fire and most alive when in peril." He jabbed an ink-stained finger at his nephew. "And you always will be, I fear, despite my best efforts."

Hector stared, too worn from the old gripes to chew them over again.

The pendant swung free and Pascual studied it a moment. "A *Hajal*," he pronounced in a bored voice.

"*Hajal?*"

"Cotton in your ears, *minyó?*"

"I see it is a bird, Uncle. But what is its meaning?"

"I thought there were no simpletons in the family line. Now I worry." Pascual was enjoying the game of ridicule. He gave an overly dramatic sigh. "Not just *a Hajal*, but *the Hajal*. A bird of prey, and a rare one, like the offspring of a mating between falcon and eagle."

"All this from just a pendant?" Finn asked.

Pascual shifted his eyes, but not his head, to gaze at Finn for the first time. "Who are you? A Norman?"

"Brother Finn. A Scot."

The old monk had already climbed to his feet, and after a shuffling turn, began rummaging through the pigeonholes. "Here? No, that's Ibn al-'Awwām's treaty on botany. This? No,

Timothesus of Gaza contributed, but did not author." He muttered in Catalan but switched to mutter fluently in Latin. Arabic. Greek. Back to Latin.

Finn raised a brow. Hector gave a half-shrug to say, *You can pick your friends, but not your family.*

"Ha!" Pascual turned, and with exaggerated care, laid down a leather-bound book.

"A copy of the Kitāb al-Ḥayawān. The Book of Animals. Compiled by al-Jāḥiẓ. Though some of his works are inventions or wild exaggerations. See here." Pascual tapped at a drawing of a beast with a ridiculously long neck, a head like a horse with two short horns, and splotched tan and brown fur. "Mythological creature, mayhap … certainly the frivolous invention of a trickster."

The monk lifted pages with reverence. They showed a menagerie of birds, beasts, and fishes, each drawn meticulously. Most were enlivened by gold, green, red, and the rare splash of blue. Arabic scrolled below each. Pascual's hairy brows arched in triumph and a finger dropped to the page.

"The *Hajal.*"

They followed Pascual's ink-stained finger, which marked a stooping bird the twin of the one on the pendant. The drawn bird was streaked with colour, and little slashes in the air near it to show motion, but otherwise the artisan of the coin and *saifs* had practically traced the drawn bird to inspire his own work.

Hector leaned over the Arabic caption. "The *Hajal.* Found only in the mountains of Syria. Stoops on prey from above. Rare."

"God sends a miracle — a knight able to read and make thought into words." Pascual flared his rheumy eyes, as though eagerly awaiting a second miracle. "And what else lives only in the mountains of Syria, *minyo*?"

Hector declined the bait.

"A knight should know his foes." Pascual's eyes cinched in disappointed reproach, then he spoke in a stage whisper. "Nizari Ismailis inhabit the mountains of Syria. The *Hajal* is their sigil — their coat-of-arms. The bird haunts the peaks and strikes unseen from above. As do they."

Mention of the Nizaris brought a flinch from Finn and Hector.

"Some call Nizaris *Batini,* people of the esoteric teachings, or *Ta'limiyyah*, people of the secret teachings. They formed as a sect of Ismailism, itself a branch of Shia Islam. There are three sects of Ismailism, and of them the Nizaris are the most vicious bird." The old monk sifted his mental stores, stroking his beard as he did. "The Nizaris grew into an enigmatic society of killers built on hierarchy, like you Templars. The lowest are *Lasiqs*, the Adherents — also called *Fida'i*, meaning self-sacrificing agent."

"Assassins … the hashish eaters?" Finn asked.

"Hashish eater is japery." Pascual harrumphed. "*Al-Ḥashāshīn*, from whence the jape stems, is a linguistic mutilation. Muslim enemies use it to demean Nizaris as drug-addled fanatics. But there is no mention of *al-Ḥashāshīn* in the Persian sources. Nor of hash use. Islam would not permit it." He gave a dismissive wave. "Hassan-i Sabbah, their founder, called his disciples *Asāsīyūn*, or people faithful to the foundation. Any fool should discern from *Asāsīyūn* grew *assassin*." Pascual took a breath and ploughed on. "The *Fida'i'n* are demons. They train for war and are equipped for war — meaning *Fida'i'n* warriors carried the *saif* and pendant."

Hector and Finn nodded in time.

"Rashid ad-Din Sinan is now Grand Headmaster. The Old Man of the Mountain, he is called. Rumour says he can read thoughts. Control a man's will. Levitate, even." Pascual was back to stroking his beard. "His fanatics are trained for murder. Mimicry. Disguise. Assassins are secreted in every court of the land — Christian and Muslim."

"The Old Man and one of his minions were paid to stalk us." Finn spoke softly, almost to himself. "Shabh. She knifed several and fled into the city."

"Not likely. Nizaris are not paid killers. Nor would a Nizari flee. They are expected to die, in public, for all to see. Death is their purpose, their devotion a message of terror."

Finn gaped at the old monk as the import of his words settled. Shabh hunted Finn for coin — Robert's coin. The traitor confessed as much. *So why does she hunt me now?*

"Nizari mothers do not mourn a dead son — they shed tears for the coward that comes home." Pascual fixed his glare on Hector, then Finn. His ink-streaked beard was split by a soft smile. "Templar and Nizari share much. Each kill only for faith. They look to gain paradise by destroying or dying. Each wear white with red to symbolize purity and blood. And is it not ironic two religions espousing love are rife with devotees willing to commit murder?"

Finn ignored the critique. "How do we proceed?"

"That is for you to decide." Pascual was back to obstinance. "Though a clever man, if one could be found, might conclude he wronged the Old Man or one of his lackeys went rogue. My wager would be on the second, for if you insulted the Old Man you would no longer be among the living."

Finn and Hector stared.

"*Ergo?*" Pascual prompted.

"Therefore, one should seek answers on the mountain," Hector said.

"From the Old Man himself." Pascual picked up the quill and made a show of dipping it in the inkwell. He made a flicking gesture with his free hand. "You have your answer. Run along now, *minyó*, so I may carry on with what was otherwise a productive day."

Hector's face quivered like a fly-bit horse. He opened his mouth to say something, maybe a speech sketched earlier. But Pascual's contempt was plain for who they were — God's killers, but killers all the same.

"God bless and keep you, Uncle," Hector murmured.

An unscholarly snort was his answer. Hector and Finn shuffled into the hall.

"Walk carefully, Brothers." Pascual's words echoed down the corridor. "Nizaris are a wicked species of bird."

"Shabh?" Rollo leaned back, hands clasped on top of his head in a pose of angry resignation. "Women and war are a poor mix. They are too fierce. Take it too far."

Shabh means ghost, and it was an apt name, for she haunted Finn.

Finn told Rollo and Serlo what they learned from Pascual. Shabh had not been doing the bidding of the Old Man. No *Fida'i'n* would take coin to kill. No *Fida'i'n* would run. Robert paid her, and with him enjoying hell it seems her hunt warped into some sort of blood feud. The old crone on the road was Shabh. Sniffing Finn over. Taunting him.

Hector chuckled and shifted to Finn. "You make friends easily and keep them so long. I envy you. I do."

Rollo waved aside the jumble of ghosts, assassins, *Fida'i'n*. They were all the same to him — enemies. "Wee shites try my patience. The Old Man has answers. Where do we find him?"

"He wanders between their mountaintop fortresses. Never spends more than a few nights in any place." Hector began deftly rolling the pendant over his scarred knuckles, left to right and back, in a meditative tic. "Not a man for unannounced social calls."

"We need to find him." Finn spoke to himself as much as the others. "Do what we do best when threatened. Go on the hunt."

"You do not know what you say. With reason, the Nizari call their lairs *dar al-hijra*, or place of refuge." The pendant rolled over Hector's knuckles in a blur. "Masyaf is the Nizari capital in Syria. Castles dot the Nosairi Mountains. The Harim Mountains. Jabal Ansariyya. Each is garrisoned with *Fida'i'n*, each is provisioned, and none are reached by a casual stroll." His brothers' focus was drifting and Hector finished on a rising note. "Point is, it is impossible to see the Old Man if he does not want to be seen."

Finn's voice crackled with anger. "I don't care how sneaky he is. I don't care how high his door. We'll find a way."

The pendant slicked off Hector's knuckle and clattered to the stones. "You forget who we are." He plucked at the red cross on his cappa. "We are not free to fight whomever angers us, whenever the fancy takes us."

Finn's temper flared from ember to flame, but Hector's words were a splash of cold. "She knifed Domnal. Hugues. Three sergeants," he said, trying to rekindle the flame.

"She did." Hector's short-lived grin said, *And what can we do about it?*

Finn sucked in a long, calming breath, then bent to scoop the pendant and flip it back to Hector. "Aye, without orders what can we do?"

"Ask." Serlo kept his fair hair shaved. You could see the seams that made up his skull. He rarely spoke but spoke useful words when he did.

"Ask?"

"To meet the Old Man."

Finn stared a moment, then snapped his fingers. "The bribe is due soon."

The Old Man paid the Templars a tribute to leave him be. In 1173 he petitioned Almaric, King of Jerusalem, to drop the payment in return for concessions. But Templars attacked their envoy, ending talks by force, thus keeping Templar bread in Templar ovens. Almaric raged. But too late. The deal was dead. The bribe alive.

"And we know a brother who could put us at the payment place, where we could request an audience with the Old Man," said Hector, finishing the thought.

"Jean," said Finn.

Jean of Provence had ridden with Finn as his second. After the fight for Jerusalem, Jean was promoted to Commander of La Fève, a castle in the northern Jezreel Valley. From La Fève, Templars patrolled the area, and the castle, though modest, served as a supply hub. Jean's meticulous nature was well-served there and, as Commander, he was responsible for receiving the Old Man's bribe and transferring it to the Order's coffers.

"Won't happen," Rollo said. "God's bones, just the thought of bending a rule would break old Cackhand out in hives.' Rollo used his favourite byname for Jean — slang for a left-handed person, who used that same hand to clean their arse.

'Besides, going after the Old Man, and on the sly, would put us in the oubliette or out on penance."

"Brothers."

Finn turned to a young, dark-haired sergeant. The man took in the four knights, gaze settling briefly on each in turn, before landing on Rollo. "Brother Finn, I carry a message."

Rollo snatched the parchment and handed it to Finn, who passed it to Hector.

The sergeant tracked the parchment's travels and bowed his head to Hector. "My apologies, Brother Finn. I was to look for a surly brother with a scarred face."

"I'm Finn." He shrugged in reply to the sergeant's confused scowl. "Surly, scarred faces describe everyone here."

"You are summoned." Hector rolled the parchment and tossed it back. "By the Commander. Now."

CHAPTER 3

"Did you learn anything?" Lanfrid of Ribeauvillé stood at a window and gazed out at the sea.

"Alas, no." Emma sipped at her wine and grimaced. *Tart, the grapes weren't ripe.* "The Scriptorium is a wonder. Truly. But alas the monks were … not helpful."

She had spent days perusing dusty tomes. She sought confirmation from primary sources. Many wonderous works were housed there, including, to her surprise, an exquisite copy of *The Shahnameh*, the epic poem by Ferdowsi. She could have devoted weeks to the task, if not for the scowling monks. A woman in their midst was scandalous.

"But you believe it genuine?" Lanfrid asked.

"I do. Our field agent also believes so."

"And who will translate?"

"Timothy of Yorkshire."

"A king's fate rests with an English sod," Lanfrid said. "And where is the sod now?"

"Tiberias. Adrien and Watt are with him."

"And you will stay out of harm's way, letting Adrien handle the transfer?"

"As we have discussed."

"A gentlewoman should not be dealing with ruffians. I pray you reconsider."

Emma fought the urge to roll her eyes and instead gave her practiced reply. "It is too risky for me to not be there. You know Adrien. And you know what we seek. I will go as far as Tiberias, as agreed. Adrien and Watt will make the exchange at Arbela."

"If word got out the Templars paid a woman…" Lanfrid let the thought trail off.

"Do not fret, brother-in-law, for I will be escorted night and day by the Order's best." Emma set down the glass and waved at the sergeant to take it away. "The Council has backed out of deals before. Will you make the purchase?"

"If it is what you claim. And if our assessor confirms its validity."

"I hear a lot of 'ifs'." Before Lanfrid replied, she asked, "And what of my escort?"

"A goodwill gesture." Lanfrid eased an arse cheek to the windowsill. "Brother Finn is fearless. Sharp-minded too. He was tasked with slaying the Apostate, Robert of Saint Albans, a quest finished with much bloodshed. Brothers say he hunted the man to the door of Damascus. Finn owns a reputation for these sorts of … unusual tasks."

"I know of the tales. But what I meant was, will he do as commanded?"

"Templars always do. Or they are no longer a Templar." Lanfrid tipped a finger at the sergeant, who leaned across the table to hand Emma a folded parchment.

"New commands, to be given to Finn in the event the translations provide a trail."

Emma tapped the parchment on the table. "We will have a trail."

Finn stewed outside the Commander's quarters, pacing the hall in short passes. Anxiety had a way of sneaking into his thoughts and setting up camp — as it was doing now.

Rollo lazed against the wall using a clasp knife to clean under a nail. He spoke without glancing up. "The unwise man is awake all night, worrying. When morning rises, he is restless still, his burden the same as before."

"You've recited those wise words many a time."

"And yet you fret."

"Something is afoot." Finn slumped against the stone wall opposite Rollo. "The voices nag at times like these but seldom say anything useful."

"Tell the voices to shut their maws. Always works for me."

The young sergeant peeked out of the door. "Commander Lanfrid requests you, Brother."

Inside, Finn took in the chambers — spacious but spare. Persian rugs carpeted the floor. A much-battered oak table filled the space. His gaze found Emma, sitting across the table, and he flinched at her smile.

Lanfrid stood at the window, basking in a lone ray of sunlight. The Commander was remarkably bland and Finn struggled to define him. The hairs of his Pauline tonsure were neither dark nor light, his body neither slight nor imposing. Lively eyes said his mind was not bland.

Finn bowed a head.

"Greetings, Brother," Lanfrid said. He regarded Finn with something bordering admiration. "I must say, it is an honour to meet you. You have a reputation with the blade."

"God gave me speed, Commander."

"And a vicious heart." Lanfrid raised a hand to a flagon on the table. "Wine? From my personal store. Imported from Burgundy. I think you will find it an excellent vintage."

Emma flared her eyes and gave a near imperceptible headshake.

"My thanks, Commander, but no." Finn stood rigid, noting Lanfrid's undue cordiality with a brother of inferior rank.

Awkwardness hung in the air until Lanfrid spoke. "I hear you tussled with brigands."

"Not brigands, Commander. There is reason to think they were Nizari *Fida'i'n*."

"How unusual. I will send a report to the Temple. Patrols should be increased along the Via Superior. Pilgrims must be protected." Lanfrid's words sounded flat, as though humouring a war-addled knight imagining enemy lurking behind every bush. He brightened. "To the business at hand — your orders are changed. You are now directed to escort Emma to Tiberias. Her husband, my brother Adrien, awaits her. Then you will accompany him to Arbela."

Finn glanced at Emma and back to Lanfrid. "Arbela?"

"To Arbela," Lanfrid confirmed.

Emma smiled as if to say passage to Arbela were an everyday thing.

The town of Arbela sat on top of Mount Arbel. A series of caves, also called Arbela, pocked the cliffs nearby. Half-remembered histories prodded Finn. The caves served as hideouts for Jewish rebels fighting Roman invaders. A great slaughter happened. Fathers knifed their families rather than let them be taken. Others leaped to their deaths.

"Adrien has business dealings there." Lanfrid shrugged to say, *What can one do about such worldly things?* "You are to take Adrien's command, should the situation require … flexibility. And you are to safeguard Emma and Adrien with your life. Arbela is a haven for unsavoury characters, thus one endures a slight risk travelling there."

Slight risk? The area is rife with bandits, rapists, and murderers, as well as rebels and warring religious sects. Riding into such a hostile land was a task Finn would rather avoid.

"Does the Master know we are being redirected?"

"He does. I have his writ. Do you wish to read it?"

Finn gave a quick headshake.

Gerard de Ridefort was the Templar Grand Master, elected after an unexpected illness claimed Arnaud de Torroge. Elections were no easy thing and Gerard, to the surprise of many, came out of the chambers wearing the Master's mantle. Finn was not surprised — if thrown to the wolves, Gerard was the type to return leading the pack. He came to Outremer an adventurer, a sword seeking a lord. He found a home with the Order. Then made himself master of it.

Lanfrid took the pitcher and poured himself a cup. His knuckles were delicate, like round white pearls. "You seem troubled, Brother. The command is simple."

Simple? Nothing in Outremer is simple. The escort to Acre, also said to be easy, had swept him into a hard fight. Now he was directed to ride into a hotbed of zealots and brigands. "I am…" Finn was not sure. Flattered? Angered? Bothered? "Honoured by the responsibility."

Emma offered a quick tilt of the head.

"Baret will stay at Emma's side. Malik," Lanfrid pointed his glass at the sergeant, "will accompany you. He was born and raised near Tiberias and will provide local expertise."

Finn took in the brother. Dark as a Saracen. A lean face and an arrogant air. Something in the man was irritating, or familiar — which, Finn could not decide. Still gazing at Malik, he spoke to Lanfrid. "He can handle himself in a pinch?"

"Aye. From my personal guard." The Commander took a nip of wine and sighed like he tasted heavenly nectar. His countenance soured. "Brother Finn, I must emphasize the importance of this task — you must protect Adrien and Emma with your life."

"With my life." Finn gave Emma a slight nod. "Is there more?"

Lanfrid and Emma shared a look. Something passed between them — a glimmer and it was gone. "No. Simple, as I said."

Finn had been a knight for years. A road Templar, a field Templar, not some pearl-knuckled parchment-pusher serving behind stone walls. He had not stayed alive by ignoring his instincts — he made that error once and nearly died. And now, in this sunlit chamber, the scent of buried bones filled his nose. He eyed the pair of them, their bland smiles and forced calm, and asked the obvious rather than what teased his nose. "When do we depart?"

"At first light. For now, escort Emma to her villa."

"We are doing this."

The words came from Malik and were equal parts thrill and angst. Finn did not answer but bobbed his head, for now the nagging voices boiled in his head like an untended pot.

Finn and Rollo stepped from the fortress to the cobbled stone. They waited for Emma, thumbs hooked in their belts, and from habit scanned the streets with ever-moving eyes. Two children shuffled over — waifs with dirty faces, wearing dirty rags, and holding out dirty palms. "I'm sworn to poverty," Finn said, and the waifs, not speakers of French, swapped dumb smiles. He fished in his alms bag, came out with a fistful of dried apple slices, then shared them. The waifs beamed and stuffed their cheeks like squirrels storing away nuts.

"You'll set a pack of them on us," Rollo said.

Finn ignored the grumbling and ruffled the hair of the smaller waif. Knights, according to the Rule, were to give charity, usually food left over from meals. To most it was a chore. Not Finn. He enjoyed the simple honesty of children —

and teasing them. Templars often had squires, lads on the verge of manhood, but Finn found their youthful arrogance bothersome. Strange what a year or two can do to attitude and manner.

Emma strolled out and dipped a chin to say, *Ready*. Finn mimed at the waifs to hold up their palms, then upended the contents of his purse into their grubby hands.

Finn and Rollo led out, Baret and Malik trailed, Emma tucked into their midst. A breeze filtered past, and with it the hairs on Finn's neck raised like the back of a boar. Raising hairs told him unseen eyes raked him. His vigilance — some would say paranoia — had intensified since the roadside meeting with the crone.

He scanned the windows. The doors. The street. A donkey laden with a basket of fish trundled by; a lad trailed with a switch. A hawker called his wares from a distant street. Two veiled women scurried past, copper bangles on their arms tinkling. Beggars slumbered under the eaves. Nothing nefarious — as far as his eyes reported.

Day was running to evening. The western sky blazed with streaks of vermillion, red, blue. Shadows stretched long and would soon merge into the dark. Finn loitered at the first cross-street to get his bearings. Acre was a maze; main streets were mapped in his head but the countless side alleys still mystified him.

Malik spoke up. "Three streets further on, then the street on the left. Takes you through the Genoese Quarter. A shortcut to the gentlewoman's villa, which is near the bathhouses."

Unseen eyes still pricked and Finn gave a visible shiver.

"Someone walk over your grave?" Rollo asked.

Finn tugged Oathkeeper, let her ride up a few finger lengths, and slide back. A blade resting too long in its scabbard can

43

form a seal to the locket, which hinders its draw. His left hand rode the hilt of his long knife. Rollo carried an arming sword and dagger and did the same.

Finn checked over a shoulder with just a slight twist of the head. He used the corners of his eyes, where night vision lived, and his gaze was ever moving. Three streets and the left turn. The street proved an alley, dark and narrow as a crypt. Boot strikes echoed on cobbles.

As they strode into the gloom, it struck Finn odd that Malik knew of Emma's lodging without, he assumed, the sergeant ever having gone there. Finn's back tingled and he resisted the urge to glance behind — but when it came, it came from the front.

A figure stepped from a dark alcove ahead. Then four more. Moonlight glinted on steel, held low, points down, as street toughs wield a cudgel. They wore scarves over their faces; only their eyes showed. Two strolled forward with unhurried menace.

"Gut them like fish," one of the toughs said.

"Come and dance, bastard!" Rollo roared in reply.

Finn spared a glance over his shoulder to confirm what he already knew — three more enemy. Baret and Malik faced them, Emma between Finn and Baret.

There were shuffling steps as a man rushed in, cut high with his right arm and punched low with his left.

Finn ducked the cut and shunted the thrust aside. Steel slid off Oathkeeper's flat with a screeching wail. He leant and stabbed from the outside with the knife. A momentary hitch — crackling ribs as they sundered. He twisted and yanked the blade. A gasp and a curse. Steel clattered on stone. The man reeled away clutching his side.

Another shoved past the reeling man. He was garbed head-to-toe in black, body as long and skinny as a spider's leg, and feral eyes gleamed over his scarf.

Black Man held a long blade in line with his hip, elbow straight, and a dagger near his left cheek. The two points almost touched — *this one has played with blades a time or two*. Finn glimpsed black brows, flinty eyes, a flash of silver chopping down. Black Man flowed from a high cut to a low slice and Finn shimmied sideways. Metal clanged on stone where his boot had been.

"Quick for an arse-humper," Black Man snarled.

From the corner of an eye, Finn glimpsed Rollo grapple his man, elbow lock him, sweep his feet. He followed with a swift stab down. Rollo crouched straight, eyes up, and thus saw the next shape coming in. He flowed up graceful as a dancer to meet it.

Black Man took a step back then came on in a blur — a left-hand cut paired with a stab at the groin. Finn dipped a shoulder to let the cut hiss past and deflected the stab with the long knife — and felt a burn on his forearm. He crab-shuffled forward and stabbed, too late, then caught Black Man's riposte with the long knife.

The two slid back, took stock of each other, then pounced.

Black Man raised into a dropping cut aimed at Finn's neck. Finn slipped inside to stab at an eye. The two came face to face, four blades locked high in a tangled X. Rotten teeth and garlic-tinged fish battered Finn's nose. Black Man tried to knee Finn in the cullions. A bony knee thunked his thigh and Finn head-butted for his nose but hit his chin.

They broke away — Black Man spitting, Finn hopping back.

Rollo weaved sword and dagger in a blur. He was grinning, humming tunelessly, as a man came in. A slash, a stab, a scream, and Rollo kicked the stabbed man to the cobbles. "Come and dance, come and dance!"

Another man took the invite. Rollo bounced side-to-side on the balls of his feet, then slashed at a face with the sword and stabbed with the dagger. The dagger bit and the man cursed.

Black Man took stock. His cronies lay twitching or standing and bleeding. He scowled at what he saw then gave a shrill whistle. "Go!"

"Is Maman calling you to supper?" Finn said, taunting.

Black Man scuttled back, then paused to give a mocking bow with sword and dagger crossed over his chest. "We'll play another time, my lovely."

They slipped into the dark and Finn let them go.

He checked over a shoulder — Emma's eyes were round as coins.

Rollo shuffled in a circle, taking in the carnage. "I sent two on. Poked a hole in a third." He stared at Finn. "Were you going to hump yours or kill him?"

"I got one. The other knew his way around the pointy end of a sword."

Rollo gave a dismissive, *Tssh.* "The legendary swordsman, Finnláech of Struan, bested by a stink-breath cutpurse…" His words trailed off as his gaze found Malik, reclined against a wall and panting. "None? You didn't even bloody one?"

The sergeant glared but held on to whatever retort tempted his tongue.

"You led us into a trap," Finn growled at Malik.

"Didn't…" Malik panted. "Just a shortcut."

"How'd you know the way to Emma's villa?"

"Walked … the gentlewoman … last night."

Baret wiped sweat from his brow with the back of his wrist. "He did. With me. We walked this same alley, foolishly, and it's my error for not seeing the danger in habit." He stared at Finn a moment and growled, "For God's sake man, Malik is not the enemy."

Finn's glare was hot enough to start a fire. He held it a long minute before offering Malik the cold, warning grin of a wolf. "Keep your eyes and ears open. Everywhere. All the time. Remember you're a Templar and someone always wants to cut your throat."

Malik gave a terse tip of the head to acknowledge the reprimand.

Something in Malik's face riled Finn. Arrogance? Contempt? Locals, like Malik, thought themselves civilized. Franks were bad guests likely to steal their silver and hump their daughters, then leave muddy boot prints on the carpet while leaving.

"You should try breathing exercises, Brother Finn," Baret said, trying to ease the tension. "I'm told they remedy fits of anger."

"Tried it. Others too — counting prayer beads, breaking imaginary sticks. None of them make a difference."

CHAPTER 4

The walls of Emma's villa stood before them.

The metal door creaked open after a series of coded knocks. A valet peaked out, the light of a torch framing his messy hair in a halo.

"Trouble?" the man asked, after sighting Finn's bleeding arm.

Emma's stare answered the obvious question. "Bring food and drink."

A fire burned in a stone-lined pit in the courtyard. Spring days were warm in Acre but nights were chilly. Servants brought mullet baked with olive oil and lemon, flatbread, spiced olives, water, and wine. They ate as flames rose from the pit; sparks spiralled into the night sky.

Hector and Serlo arrived. Sergeants and squires and Turcs lugged in their kits.

Uncle Jerol crouched at Finn's side and tipped the cut arm to the firelight. "Long but neat. No sutures needed." The sergeant fussed in a haversack, then without warning doused the wound.

Finn blurted a curse.

"Wine, oregano, garlic, and vinegar." Jerol smirked, taking perverse pleasure in Finn's pain, then began wrapping the arm.

"Can I borrow some?" Waylon flared his eyes and jigged a thumb at Rooster. "I'm asking for a shy friend; he has a rash on his cock."

"Pour a tot for Waylon's ma — she gave it to me."

Finn cleared his throat and tilted a head toward Emma.

Rooster and Waylon cringed and Emma said, "No offense taken. Though I wonder when and why Waylon gawked at Lugh's spindle?"

Surprised laughter, and as it echoed in the courtyard, Emma scooted her chair closer to the flames. Her *barbette* had come off, and the hat attached to it. Now she was unplucking her *crespine* hair net. An ivory pin came free. Gently, almost reverently, she nestled it in her lap. It was shiny and long, with a knobby end carved to resemble a seated man.

Emma tracked Finn's gaze and seemed to read his mind. "It is a monkey, not a man."

Rollo had an odd fascination with monkeys and squinted at the carving. "Well done. Looks like Uncle around the eyes and mouth. Aged like Uncle too."

"Boil your arse," Jerol grumbled.

"Roman made. Recovered from ruins near Tiberias." Emma took the pin and re-made her hair. "Monkeys are revered by many cultures. Reviled by others. Some say they guide souls to the afterlife or offer mischief. The Holy Book does not mention them," she gave a quick eye flare, "at least as far as I have been told."

She chattered on. "The Roman playwright Plautus used monkeys to call out many Roman institutions as base imitations, distortions even, of Greek institutions. For Plautus, monkeys were to men as Romans were to Greeks. Monkeys also entertained the masses in the colosseum. Writings describe them dressed as men-at-arms and driving tiny chariots pulled by goats."

Hector raised a brow at Finn. It was a rare woman that could read. A rarer one still that wrung hidden meaning from Roman plays. Learning is an expensive endeavour, and one fathers do not waste on daughters bound to be married.

Rollo had drifted off during the discourse but brightened at the notion of monkeys-at-arms. "Monkeys driving a chariot," he said, and grinned.

Emma bent to cover her legs with a blanket. A charm medallion swung free, hanging from her neck on a silver chain. Finn glimpsed Mary holding the baby Jesus. The medallion, like the hairpin, was an age-worn relic.

"Holy relics — now there's a jest for you. Pig toes sold as saint's fingers. Grease-stained napkins venerated as mandylions. Amphoras of the Virgin's breast milk. Why, I've seen enough nails to crucify a hundred Jesuses." Finn's eyes flared with false drama. "But blind belief in relics is more humorous still, don't you agree?"

She stared, too surprised by his rebuke to give her practiced reply.

He carried on as if he had not expected one. "An old friend of mine, an inquisitor, if you would believe it, once said, 'Faith is not born from miracles; your faith is the miracle.' And I'd wager he was right."

"You do not revere relics?"

"I respect the tradition, if that is your meaning." Finn spoke with care, for a Templar not revering relics was scandalous. "Devotion leads to veneration of anything deemed holy. Demand for curios outstrip supply. Prices rise. Forgeries abound. Graves are looted. Indulgences are bought. And in the end greed fouls whatever good might come from veneration."

"There are ways to discern. Real relics emit a pleasing aroma when rubbed, much like sandalwood. And research can sift the genuine from the false."

"If you say." Finn smiled at her stoney face. "Though no doubt folk also wish the stories to be true and that, with a bit of faith, persuades them they are. The True Cross once moved me to tears. How can a soul not be warmed by a thing Jesus touched? Yet with time, and upon reflection, I find my faith does not need such fuel."

"Templars are rumoured to possess holy artefacts." Emma had taken on a defiant air, perhaps appalled to find herself debating relics with, among all folk, a Templar knight. "Some say the Order was founded as a deception, a ruse to recover the Ark of the Covenant from Solomon's Temple, and to find the Holy Grail."

"Men rumour many things, some of which prove true. But I know nothing of the Ark, nor the Grail." Finn gave a sad headshake. "Perhaps I am unworthy of seeing them?"

Finn stared into the fire, seeking a portent in the pulsing embers. Finding none, he glanced up, and the glow dancing over his scarred face made a grim sight. "It's plain we ride on a fool's errand. What awaits us at Arbela?"

"My husband's business."

"Arbela is a den of murderers and fanatics. One does not rush headlong into dangerous ground just for business."

"What woman would not risk all for her beloved?"

"Love is a strong lure, yet I don't see in you a woman driven to folly. Though admittedly you are savvier than I regarding matters of the heart."

Emma studied her hands, splayed in her lap. The fingers were shadowed and skeletal. In a wooden tone she whispered, "Indeed. Love can drive one to folly."

Silence stretched out as Finn watched her. "You ask me to risk the lives of my brothers in what I suspect is a vainglorious pursuit," he said. "The least you can do is tell me its true nature."

Emma flinched and looked up to stare into his dark eyes.

Finn gave the ghost of a smile. "Falsehoods nag me. I can't abide them. And if I don't know the game, how can I play it well?"

"You must find me a wretched thing."

"I've known worse. A man I once considered a brother left me for dead. I've learned not to judge a … person," he had almost said man, "until having walked a day in their shoes."

She studied Finn's eyes, perhaps seeking empathy. "I… Adrien … we are relic masters."

"Bone dealers."

Finn spat the words and she cringed from his venom.

"Bone dealer is an ugly name — we are brokers. Our agents seek relics. We facilitate the seeking. Arrange the buying."

Bone dealers abounded in Outremer. Wealthy men or church men, which often were the same, requested items through a chain of intermediaries stretching from England to Outremer. People like Adrien pumped their network of cronies to fill the orders. Coin flowed, first to acquire the relic, then from the pilgrims that came to venerate it. Every church held the bones of at least one martyr. A thorn from Christ's crown. The Holy Lance that pierced his side. Even the foreskin from Jesus's circumcision.

"And?" Finn pressed.

"And a relic has been discovered in the caves of Arbela. Our agent arranged a transaction with the man who found it."

"Lanfrid is buying it?"

"Your Order is buying it. The Grand Master assigned the task to Lanfrid — and you. You are to provide protection and force."

Finn spat into the fire with a hiss. Sordid details hid in his orders — as always. Dragging them to daylight was vexing but seeing clearer was a salve.

"What relic do we seek?"

"The Copper Scroll."

"Copper Scroll?" Finn had not heard of it, and he thought he had heard of them all. "Does it hold magic words, this scroll?"

Emma frowned at the derision. "There are rumoured to be three scrolls, each a copy of the other. They date to around the time of Salome Alexandra, also called Alexandra of Jerusalem, and one of only two women to ever rule over Judea."

"The Master wants it for the archives, for the Scriptorium," Finn said slowly.

"That. And other things." Emma jigged her head side-to-side. "The scroll is invaluable for many reasons."

Finn gave a nod, glanced at Hector, who shrugged to say, *Beyond me.*

"And what of the Nizaris?" Finn asked. "Why do they stalk you?"

"I know nothing of them."

Her reply had been swift and sure and calm.

"The men in the alley?"

"Competition." Emma and Baret shared a glance. "Paulus," Emma said. "It can be none other. Born in Genoa. Merchant by day, soulless thug by night. Guilty of theft, extortion, murder. Rumour has it he knifed his brother over a deal gone sour."

Baret nodded. "The masked swordsman was Paulus's henchman, Beau. A Frenchman. I am told Beau means 'beauty' but his mother must have owned a good sense of irony, for he is as ugly as a goat's arse. Folk call him *Le Scélérat* — the Evildoer. Remorseless. And a rare blade master."

"*Le Scélérat,*" Finn repeated, then fixed Rollo with a *Told you so*, look.

Rollo waved it off with a lazy hand. "Does Paulus know what we seek, or was he settling grudges?"

"Aye, to both," Baret said. "He has many informers and many grudges."

"Will he come at us again?"

"Doubtful," Emma said. "Genoese are ocean folk. Riding a horse would be torture for Paulus, thus he is loath to leave Acre, which doubtless is why they came at us before we left the city. Eliminate us and the Copper Scroll is theirs for the plucking. Paulus has a client wringing hands for the thing — just as I do."

Finn eased back and his chair creaked. Sounds. Sights. Smells. They had a way of dredging up memories at the strangest of times and he remembered a dark one now. Robert … sitting in a chair, like this one, and Finn's thrust punching through the Apostate to cut into the wood behind. The Holy Father sent Finn to exterminate the man. And he had. Memories were often ugly. Past deeds more so.

A relic hunt promises more ugliness.

Templars were accused of the odious practice and he, like most of his brothers, wanted nothing to do with it. Relic-mongering stained the Order's reputation yet now, inexplicably, the Order funded such an ignoble enterprise. He wanted to believe in the Copper Scroll. He did. But experience told him relics caused more grief than good.

He gazed at Rollo, Hector, and Serlo. They gazed back, none overjoyed by the prospect but none offering complaint. They would follow him to hell.

His gaze landed on Emma.

"You will seek the scroll?" she asked.

Finn rubbed his scarred face. The others waited.

He wanted to return to the road, to what he was and came here to be — a field Templar. But he had sworn an oath of obedience to the Order. The oath was all. Breaking it would break him. In the end, he had no recourse but to comply with a command, however idiotic it may be. And the fool's errand gave a temporary reprieve from the boredom of daily prayer and that, at least, made the venture worthwhile.

"Aye. We'll seek the scroll." Finn flurried the sign of the cross. "And may God protect us from what we find."

Gulls wheeled and screeched overhead. The rising sun lit their way. As they wound their way through cobbled streets, Finn pondered the past and the future. He was not tied to his deeds like a donkey to a cart. He learned from missteps and strived to better his ways. What lay ahead might offer dark things or might be sent to aid his betterment. Or both of these. A mild thrill coursed his veins at the thought, and he breathed out, glad to be leaving the city.

"Paulus," Emma hissed, bringing Finn from his musings.

The man's residence was at the edge of the Genoese quarter, astride the road to the Land Gate, and they must pass it to leave the city. The house faced the harbour and was a massive affair, all stone and colonnades and windows. Two figures sat on the veranda. A table was set with fruit and bread and wine. A scabbarded sword too.

Finn studied the pair as they plodded closer, clutching their wine. Paulus and Beau; the first was resplendent in red and yellow silk robes; the second ominous in a black doublet, black hose, and black knee-length boots. The Frenchman was hideous. A pock-marked face with thin lips and narrow-set eyes. Ugly enough to frighten children — and his sneer said he revelled in it. The Genoese, though, was a beauty. Wide shoulders and lean body. Blessed with high cheeks and a sharp jaw. Eyes like lapis lazuli. They made an odd pair.

"Why, there rides Emma of Cherbourg." Paulus ran a hand over his hair, slicked to his head with scented oil, before waving the same hand invitingly. "Please, break bread with us."

"How kind, though I must decline." Emma frowned in mock apology. "We are headed to the road and must get an early start."

"Shame. Where are you headed, my dear?"

"To Jerusalem. To pray at the Holy Sepulchre. We will take in the fresh air along the way." Emma patted her horse's neck. "You should leave the city now and then. Spend time in the countryside. It would do you good."

Paulus's handsome face soured. "But I would have to ride a horse."

"That is the usual mode of travel outside the city."

"Acre is home, but out there," Paulus fanned a hand toward the landward side of the city, "is wilderness. I would be lost within hours, I confess, and would die of thirst and hunger."

"All the more reason for you to travel."

Paulus quirked a head to say, *Well played, my dear.* He waved his wine glass at the Templars and laden horses. "All this to keep you from losing your way, or to aid your prayers? Forgive my ignorance, for the complexities of sight-seeing and prayer elude me."

"Bandits necessitate such measures, I am afraid. As you know."

Paulus smiled to say he did indeed know a few such rough men. "And where is Adrien?"

"Conducting business in Jaffe."

"Not what I hear."

Emma said nothing. Paulus sipped wine.

Beau tapped his glass against a crooked tooth, then tipped the glass at Finn. "Have we met?" Finn stared and Beau answered himself. "I think we have — at one of Master Paulus's establishments. You Templars do enjoy a good whore."

Finn played along. "We've met. But in an alley. Not a brothel. You wore a scarf over your hideous face to, I presume, avoid nauseating our stomachs. I commend you for considering the well-being of others."

"Your jests make me laugh," Beau said, unsmiling. "But you are mistaken. I would never wear a scarf. Too crude."

"Crude? Like your attack in the alley?"

Beau gaped in mock indignation. "That sounds like an accusation." He flashed crooked teeth in something between a snarl and a smile. "Be warned — such allegations insult my honour, and honour must be maintained."

Finn carried on the ritual dance of threat and counter-threat. "I'm no philosopher, mind you, but surely you need to possess honour before it can be insulted."

"Ah. Now you've done it. Angered me." Beau grasped the sword handle and tugged the blade free a finger width. "See this? Someday I'll teach you manners with it." He slammed the blade home. "And a bloody lesson it will be."

Finn's gaze flicked from the sword to Beau's face. "Why not now, my lovely?"

Beau, his past night's words turned on him, grabbed for the sword. Paulus's hand stilled him.

"Now, now, old friend. You've had your fun." Paulus ran a hand over oil-slick sideburns, then sniffed his palm. He nailed his iridescent gaze on Emma; it lingered uncomfortably before darting to the harbour. "Time got away from me," he said.

"You must excuse me, my dear. Comrades have arrived and I must play the host."

Finn shifted in the saddle to track Paulus's gaze. Something was peeking over the stone jetty bordering the harbour. Two canvas triangles climbed, tipped, and slewed along just beyond the rock line. Then a ship edged its way around the jetty. She was a pretty thing, sharp and sleek and bright, as most Genoese ships are.

Emma heel-tapped her mount forward and offered Paulus a dip of the head in passing. After a moment she said, "Must you provoke the beast? *Le Scélérat* sought cause to fuel his wrath and you gave it."

"Harmless fun," Finn said. He waved a dismissive hand. "Paulus will never leave Acre, as you said, and I'll not suffer the toad again."

CHAPTER 5

The fields and farms of the coastal plain were a pleasant change from Acre's cobbled streets. The air, salty in the city, became dry and warm and dusty.

"She rides like a Bedouin." Rollo gazed over a shoulder.

Emma sat easy, flowing with the horse's gait rather than being battered by it. She held a soft rein, or looped the reins around the pommel and led with her knees. She dressed like a Bedouin too, in layers of gauzy blue, and a casual glance failed to note the woman buried there.

Finn said nothing.

"You're talkative today." Rollo smirked. "Something on your mind?"

Still Finn said nothing. Inexplicably, Emma swathed in robes, face covered, made her more alluring than if she were riding naked. He tried for misdirection.

"I'm wondering how long it took your sister to grow a beard."

Rollo's laugh was a deep rumble. "Not my sister's beard you're pondering, I'd wager."

Baret rode at Emma's side and led a mule with a wooden chest strapped to its crupper.

Finn tried for more misdirection. "What do you suppose is in the chest?"

Rollo laughed again and Finn retreated to silence. He fixated on their route to corral his errant thoughts.

The road from Acre to Tiberias was a Roman left-over. Mile-marker stones called out a traveller's progress. Stone pavers covered the road in sickly-yellow splotches — here for a mile but gone the next. No doubt many a local farmhouse was floored with Roman roads. Several towns dotted the way. The first of note, Saforie, loomed in the distance. The town sat on a hill overlooking the crossroad of the Acre to Tiberias Road and the Via Maris.

"Saforie was wealthy during Roman rule. Still is. Called the Mosaic City for all the fancy tile decor." Hector prattled on. "Saforie bears several names. Jews call it Zippori, meaning 'bird,' because of its perch overlooking the Beth-Netofa Valley. Nazareth is but a short ride —"

"Fascinating." Finn tugged the lower fold of his *shemagh* to spit.

Rollo gave an exaggerated sigh. "Serlo doesn't speak and Hector doesn't shut up."

Elias and Yousef waited in the road ahead.

Finn reined Fagan in, head-to-tail with Elias's Arab. "What's the word?"

"Lots of folk in town. Templars too — Jean is there."

"Jean?"

They found him on the western summit, where the Christians live. Jean stood in the Citadel's shade, the tower's crenelations cast in shadow around him like the teeth of a gigantic skeleton. Brother Maeldoi was there, and two other knights and a score of sergeants and Turcs.

Templars took pride in grubbiness. Field brothers were marked by threadbare, patched cappas and dark, tarnished mail. Not Jean. His banner was a lesson in neatness — cappas clean and wrinkle-free. Hair cropped short. Beards trimmed. Horses groomed.

"What pretty ponies," Rollo said. "Even their hooves are polished."

Finn strode up, arms thrown wide. "Brother!"

"Brother," said Jean with equal warmth. They embraced with hearty slaps on the back. Dust puffs drifted from Finn in a column of light.

Jean shifted his gaze to Rollo. His lips tightened. "Rollo."

"Cackhand."

Finn embraced Maeldoi, known as Mael, then pushed him to arm's length to study his face. "The chin healed, God be praised, and with but the faintest mark."

Mael laughed. The knight had taken an executioner's knife, Shabh's knife, intended for Finn. The blade carved a deep gulley in his skin — now hairless and puckered and pink.

Finn turned back to Jean. "Shouldn't you be in La Fēve pushing parchments … perhaps requisitioning new cappas?"

Jean's grin faded. "We are escorting Lord Guy."

"Guy of Lusignan? Why do you treat with that arse? And why is the arse near Tiberias? This is Raymond's land. Given the chance, he'd hoist Guy by his cods, then set him on fire."

Jean glanced away from the deluge of questions.

Guy had wandered to Outremer on pilgrimage to cleanse a murder, and in the process somehow managed to get himself married to King Baldwin's sister, Sybilla. Guy had been in line to assume the crown — until his incompetence reared an ugly head. Baldwin shifted course, denied Guy's succession, and anointed his seven-year-old nephew, Baldwin of Montferrat. Raymond, Count of Tripoli, Prince of Galilee, became regent. Joselin of Courtenay became the boy's guardian.

Finn remembered standing before the Leper King, head tipped in more than a nod but less than a bow, neither cowed nor defiant. He proffered his council. Baldwin took it and, in the end, the Kingdom of Jerusalem was saved from the Sultan's cruel hand.

The king had died not long after, God bless his soul, and Finn was there when they raised the boy king. Young Baldwin was small and frail. From Nablus they carried him to the Church of the Holy Sepulchre and therein, and with much pomp and burning of incense, dressed him in robes too big for his body and placed a crown too heavy for his head.

Young Baldwin proved as sickly as old Baldwin, and his weakness drifted on the breeze for nobles to scent. Plots and counter-plots bred like lice and would-be kings jostled for the throne. The scheming disgusted Finn and years past he abandoned care of devious nobles, for they shared a knack for destroying whatever they touched.

Finn ran a palm over his scarred face. "Talk to me, Jean."

The conflict between loyalty to brother and loyalty to orders fought on Jean's face. He was incapable of lying — the mere contemplation of it would put him on his prayer bones reciting paternosters until dawn.

"Master Gerard swore me to secrecy."

"Jean ... it's me, Finn. Your old bowl mate."

Cogs turned behind Jean's eyes as he considered a range of replies. He settled on the one he was willing to share and began speaking in a wooden voice. "I am to assist Guy. Escort him from Jerusalem. We stopped at Nablus. Sebastia. Jenin. Nazareth. Now on to Saforie."

"Sneaking into Raymond's lands... Guy is a fool or he packs a large pair of stones."

Jean continued in the wooden voice. "We will ride to Acre. And Jaffa. And Ascalon."

"Prominent men live along the route, though few of them would enjoy time with the arse; what's he about?"

A muggy silence drew out. Jean's eyes said, *I will speak no more.*

Finn laughed at the Frenchman's misery. "Ah, Jean, some things never change. You among them. You're unbendable."

"Brother Jean!" a voice shrilled. "Business is done. Off to our lodgings." The voice's owner strode from the Citadel. He was tall, with brown hair curling around a diamond-shaped face and eyes like jade buttons. A jewel-encrusted sword hung at his hip. Calf-skin gloves were tucked into a crisp, crimson-coloured belt.

Three well-coifed knights trailed, and a black-clad priest with an equally black tonsure.

Mael leaned to Finn's ear. "Lord Guy."

The Frenchman wore blue and white silk embroidered with a red lion. His boots, Finn noted with disgust, were grossly pointed at the toe and hand-made to fit each foot like a glove.

"The old fool dithers and wrings his hands." Guy gazed at the Citadel and spoke to the fops parading as knights. He glanced around, expecting an audience to gather but carried on without one. "He will regret this. I am the future. Me."

Jean spoke. "Lord Guy, may I introduce brothers Finn of Struan and Rollo of Caen?"

Guy whirled back to favour Finn and Rollo with his attention. "Finn of Struan … killer of the Apostate? Destroyer of Ahmad al-Taqi?"

"Arse, I was there too," Rollo said from the side of a mouth.

Finn grinned at Rollo and dipped a head at Guy. "Blessings, Lord Guy."

"Well met, Brother. Your name is known to us. Meeting such a notorious brother is an honour." Guy's tone said it was not. "What brings you to Saforie?"

"Escorting nobles, a task which is the bane of all Templars." Finn pasted on a soft smile.

Guy tilted a head, trying to decide if he had been slighted, and Finn spoke on.

"Have you met the new king, Lord?"

Guy shrugged. "Of course. Feeble. Sickly. I pray for his health."

"We all pray," the priest said with the same lack of enthusiasm. "I pray nightly God grant the king health and wisdom beyond his years."

"God is generous. He also discerns our heart." Finn dipped a head and spoke from under lowered brows.

"Pray the king brings peace and prosperity," Guy continued as though Finn had not spoken. He stroked his clean-shaven chin in mock concern. "Prayer can work miracles, I hear. And if prayer fails, more able, experienced men await to lend their counsel."

Await to take the reins, you mean. Guy was weak, in soul, not body, and his words petty. Finn met the man's eyes, then his gaze dropped to the boots. *The king thought to leave his kingdom to an arse in pointed boots…*

Guy tracked Finn's gaze and raised up with a glare, not liking what he saw in Finn's scarred face. He dipped a head in mockery.

"Wish I could spend more time in your illustrious company, Brother. Perhaps you might recount the hunt of Robert of Saint Albans or one of your other kills? But alas, I have more pressing matters to attend."

The last light of the sun died, putting them all in shadow.

"I will not keep you from your plans, Lord Guy," Finn said. "Whatever they may be."

"I will say no more." Jean held up a hand to ward off an approaching Finn.

"Peace, Brother. I grew bored the moment Guy opened his wine hole. The game he plays is trivial, for he is trivial."

Jean said nothing, forked fingers into his destrier's mane. The horse was a dun with bright eyes. Morning light streaked the sky with bands of pale red and purple. A night with the arse must have been torture for a pious brother like Jean.

"Come to say your goodbyes?"

Finn sucked in a breath and gusted it out. "You know when and where the Old Man's bribe will be given. I want to be there. And you can arrange it."

Jean's eyes narrowed. "Why?"

"To discuss Shabh. I promise not to harm him."

Jean raised a brow to say, *Couldn't if you tried.* "Seeking the Master's permission is the only way, and there is no way he will grant you an audience with the Old Man. You know the Rule. The process. The hierarchy. I cannot help you around them."

"Cannot, or will not?"

Jean shifted to stare at the villa's door, as though willing Guy to stagger out and rescue him from Finn's harrying.

"I'd wager the arse isn't as keen on punctuality as you are. Probably cropsick too."

Jean kept his gaze on the door. "You are dear to me, Finn, as a brother-in-arms and a spiritual brother. But I cannot grant things that are not in my authority." He shifted his pale eyes to Finn's black eyes. "Nor can I keep you from waiting on the Road to Masyaf three weeks hence, nor would I know if you found the Old Man's envoy travelling there. Thus the Master cannot hold me accountable for the actions of a wayward brother."

Finn clapped a hand on Jean's shoulder. "So good not to have spoken with you, Brother."

It had not been an easy day. The ride from Saforie to Tiberias was pleasant enough. Morning began chilly but as the sun climbed the day turned warm. They passed Tur'an, a fit and lively place. Emma bought honeyed almonds from roadside vendors. Ragged children pestered them with a babble of words and grins and laughter.

A storm brewed in Finn's head, despite the day's pleasantries. Being busy had kept the demon of worry at bay, but with time at hand it flared to life. Finn mediated in rhythm to Fagan's plodding hooves. Shabh. The Old Man. The Copper Scroll. And what was Guy about? Finn had told Jean he did not care, which was not exactly true. The nagging worries bit in turn until they blurred into one stinging bite.

"Chatted with Brother Mael. Told him our burden. Know what he told me?" Rollo answered his own question. "He said Lanfrid and Adrien had an older brother." He paused a heartbeat. "Isnard."

Finn twisted in the saddle to fix Rollo with a shocked stare.

"Aye. That Isnard."

Isnard of Ribeauvillé had been Under Marshal before rising to the rank of Draper. Brother Rumour said the stress of sorting all those swords and cloaks and belts proved too much. Arithmetic rattled his mind until it gradually broke it. Or perhaps he had always been mad? One day Isnard was found in the stables eating horse manure because, he claimed, it contained oats needing to be inventoried. And besides, everyone agreed oats, especially those grown in sandy soil, were laced with veins of pure gold.

"Pray we don't ever find Adrien eating oats," Finn said, and Rollo nodded sombrely.

They rode into Tiberias, capital of the Principality of Galilee. Count Raymond's fortress of sun-white stone towered over the city. To their right, the Sea of Galilee shone velvety blue in the midday sun. The lake bears many names. Yam Kinneret. Lake Gennesaret. Romans called it the Sea of Tiberias, and this is the name Franks use. Locals simply call it, The Lake. Tiberias sprawled along the lake's western shore. Piers rocked in soft waves. Fishing and a brisk trade in salted fish brought the city wealth. The city had grown around hot springs believed to cure maladies, so diseased pilgrims, and their coin, came to wash in the curing waters.

Rollo sniffed like a dog. His lip curled. "Bathhouses."

"I find it odd you recognize the smell," Finn said. "Mayhap soap is ingrained in one as a babe and, even after the passage of years, can still be recalled by men who never use it?"

"Ah. Soap jests. See how I laugh."

Ahead, Baret led the way to Adrien's villa, weaving his horse through streets bustling with folk. A dirty lad ran at Finn's stirrup, jabbering and pandering sweat meats. Vendors called from their stalls. A knot of Raymond's men, wearing red and yellow livery, lounged in the shade of a tavern's porch. One, a burly redhead, hefted a cup in mock salute.

Crowds thinned as they came into an area with low villas lining the way. Some were walled, some were not, but the courtyards of all hung with gardens watered by tinkling fountains. Baret jigged a finger at a stone wall to their left, then hopped off his horse and after three quick strides rapped at a metal door. The door creaked open and Baret said something.

They waited, horses hoofing impatiently at the cobbled road.

"We are weary and dusty. God's bones, tell him to open the door," said Emma.

Finn hoisted a brow at the blasphemy. Emma twitched a shoulder in reply.

Baret pushed away from the door with a sour face. "Adrien is in Arbela."

"What?" Emma's gaze went skyward. "When?"

"Three days past. Took Watt and Botan."

"Timothy?"

"In the villa. Sleeping off the grape."

Emma blasphemed again.

Finn stayed silent. Experience taught silence was best when anger owns one's thoughts. The faint cries of vendors wafted down the street. Somewhere a dog barked. Pots clattered in the neighbouring villa.

"Well then," Emma said, "let us get squared away and decide what is next."

Finn leaned close to her. "Adrien changed the plan and trundled up the hill solo. What comes next will not be easy."

"I am aware."

"Why are you here?"

"We have a deal, as you know. I carry payment. In the box."

"Baret could carry it."

She was quiet, tempted to ignore him, then snapped a reply. "Our business has not been profitable lately. Adrien possesses a knack for making things harder than need be. Another loss would be ruinous. I am here to ensure ruin is avoided."

Sudden insight hit and brought a snort from Finn. Emma was the mastermind. She, the humble, obedient wife, had been directing affairs from afar. It would not be proper for a woman to make deals. The only problem was, directing from afar had not been working lately, so here she was.

Emma continued, "I assume Adrien thought to gain the scroll through wit. Perhaps barter. But, as you say, what comes next will not be easy."

'Put your ear into the breeze and listen,' Finn had said.

Certes … but it can't hurt to enjoy a drink while listening.

Lugh found a battered table in the Drunken Apostle, the tavern they had passed near Emma's villa. The building was a stuttered, leaning affair of crumbling brick and decaying wood. Sun-brown fishermen glared from the edges of the room. Hawk-faced Jews sipped tea and argued with dramatic hand flails and an endless parade of eye rolls and flared eyebrows. Waylon and Jerol sat across from Lugh, holding out cups.

A sweaty man poured from an equally sweaty pitcher. "What brings you to Tiberias?"

"Fish," Lugh said.

"We love fish," Waylon added helpfully.

Sweaty Man paused mid-pour to squint at the Englishman. "Aye. Anyone can see that."

And what does the squinting fool see? Hard, scarred men, down on their luck, battered pommels at their hips. Certainly not fish merchants. Lugh's brown teeth flashed in a casual grin before he ploughed on with the lie.

"Any other fish lovers arrive, besides us?"

"A few."

Lugh plucked a coin from his belt. He held it up for approval before handing it over.

"Fighting men arrived yesterday," Sweaty Man said, "not that you fishmongers care about fighting men, eh?"

Another coin appeared in Lugh's fingers and Sweaty Man nodded. "Rough-looking natives mixed with Freelances. Their leader was an ugly bastard; face like a goat's arsehole."

"How many?"

"More than a score."

Lugh digested, then tossed the coin. "We heard some fool from Acre … Adrune … Adriole … Adrien!" he said with a snap of the finger, "went up to Arbela?"

"Couldn't say. But if he did, he ain't coming down, least not without help."

A shadow blocked the open door. Boots thumped across the floor. "You're at our table," the shadow growled. "Piss off."

Lugh glanced up at a burly redhead. Thick arms crossed over the yellow and red livery of Count Raymond. A battered sword hung from a leather belt. Four more like the first shuffled behind.

Jerol's hand glided off the table. Waylon showed his gap-toothed smile.

"Something funny?" the redhead said. He got no answer and scowled. "We're Raymond's men, and you'd do well to take note, turd-faces. Now shove off." He moved a meaty hand to the sword pommel and rested it there.

The scuffle and scrape of chairs as the fishermen and Jews snatched up their cups and moved their debates outside. Sweaty Man gave a warning glare.

"We're settled here. Take another." Waylon waved a hand over the now empty room. "There are many to choose from."

"Don't like those tables. Like this one."

Waylon shook his head in mock sadness. "Wrong answer."

Lugh smiled, clapped a hand on Waylon's shoulder. "My friend is English, you see, and needs no excuse to fight. He's mad for it." He smiled again, though the friendliness was gone. "I'm fond of it myself. And a table is as good a reason as any to spill your guts."

Something feral crept into Lugh's eyes.

The redhead sensed it and licked his lips, nervous now his usual game of fright had failed. "We are five, you are three," he said.

Lugh chattered on as though the man had not spoken. "We'll have a race, my English friend and I, to drop your guts. Then the arse next to you." He pointed at the man now standing beside the redhead. "His mouth looks like an arsehole."

"Hey now," Arse-mouth said, hand drifting to his hilt.

Waylon flapped his fingers. "Waddle off, before your guts are piled at your feet."

The redhead licked his lips again and palmed the pommel. His mind churned for a suitable retort — and given another day might have dredged one up.

"Christ's bones, enough chatter." Jerol surged up and slammed his sword pommel into the redhead's cods.

For such a big man, he fell with a surprisingly small whimper.

Arse-mouth landed a fist on Jerol's head, sending him to a knee.

Lugh smashed his cup against Arse-mouth's head, then milled the cup's now broken and jagged edge.

"Mouth like an arsehole!" Lugh laughed as the man staggered back, hand plastered to his head. He trailed, and when Arse-mouth lowered the hand to stare at a bloody palm, thumped him in the eye with a fist. Arse-mouth's head snapped back and he went down.

Lugh whirled to find Waylon had another pinned on the boards, knee on a neck, and was rhythmically punching his face.

Waylon looked up with a manic grin. "Fun!"

"You're a mad bastard!" Lugh laughed.

Jerol stood over another, the splintered leg of a stool in a fist. The ruins of the stool scattered around the man's head.

The fight drained from the last man like air from a punctured lung. He showed empty palms. "Table is yours, lads. All yours."

"You can have it. Too much noise in here for me." Jerol dropped the stool leg on the unconscious man, scooped a cup from the floor, and strolled to the counter to fill it from a jug. He swirled the cup and took a swig. "As a lad, I was taught half of the fight is looking like you are bored with the prospect of it, but if you must go to knuckles, save the chatter and just fight the bastards."

Sweaty Man shook his head. "Fish merchants…"

Lugh slapped a coin on the counter as he strolled past. "For the stool." He laughed to himself. "Save the chatter and just fight the bastards."

CHAPTER 6

"Any trouble at the tavern?" Finn gazed at Lugh's split knuckle.

"Got in a wee tussle."

"Anyone die?"

"Don't think so. Uncle busted a man's bollocks — actually busted them, I mean."

Finn rubbed his eyes and breathed out. "Did you learn anything?"

"A cup makes a good weapon, in a pinch. Who knew?"

Finn stared, not impressed, and with a sigh Lugh rolled out what they had learned.

"Men-at-arms and ruffians. Led by an ugly man. Must be *Le Scélérat.*" Finn pursed his lips in thought. "The ship Paulus was waiting for, in Acre, must have transported Freelances."

"You doubted he'd leave the city," Rollo said, and Baret raised his palms in apology.

They stood on a tower of the Templar *casale* outside the city. The *casale* was a villa surrounded by a low wall and two towers. A scatter of Templar-run farms sprawled around it. Emma's villa was vulnerable, the *casale* a better refuge, so here they were. Brother Nadal of Luchon was the Commander. He was an old salt. A veteran of Montgisard. But fading in vigour.

Hector said, "Seems unlikely a tavern owner wouldn't have heard of Adrien going up the hill, especially when the tavern is but a stone's throw from the man's villa. The vintner is in cahoots with the bandits, takes a cut in return for feeding them ripe targets."

"Oldest con the world over. But now the bandits are tipped someone is asking after Adrien." Finn propped an arm on the parapet and gazed at Mount Arbela. "They'll be waiting and they have leverage. Which makes this a pain in the arse."

Nadal eased to Finn's side. "None but bad folk go up there. Too much history. Too much darkness." He grew tight-lipped, shook his head. "I've seen things. Lights glowing in the caves. Strange floating orbs. Restless spirits, I suppose, from all those Jews slain by the Romans."

Finn was silent.

"Every so often the count sends men to scour out the rough folk. We lend a hand. But after a time, the ruffians filter back, and we start over again." Nadal puffed out a ragged breath. "Been a while since we scoured it out. Certain you want to go there?"

"No choice — have to save the fool."

Emma glared.

"I will not go to Arbela again. Not for all the blessings in heaven. But I can loan you blackcoats, if you vow to bring them back whole." Nadal gave a humourless chuckle. "Though you will likely break that vow, which means I will be responsible for your sin."

Finn spoke over a shoulder. "Malik, you're from these parts. Thoughts?"

The sergeant appeared at his side. "Backtrack toward Saforie. Come at the town from the backside of the hill. It is a short ride — maybe a morning? Folk will flee to the caves before they fight. They're brigands; we're Templars."

Malik tilted a head to make sure he had Finn's attention. "Arbela the town is an easy nut to crack. But Arbela the caves have a harder shell. Locals call them *Qala'at Qa'aqa*, the Fortress of Crows. Accessed by a goat trail. Stairs hacked out to allow internal access between the caves. Some are multi-level. Cisterns for water. Stores of food…" he tailed off, then finished with force. "Getting into the Fortress of Crows will cost lives. Best to avoid that."

Hector shook his head. "Josephus Flavius recounts Herod the Great's purge of Jewish rebels in the Galilee. The last of them hid in the caves. The Romans built war contraptions at the cliff edge. Lowered legionaries suspended in cages to rain fire arrows into the caves. Then climbed in to snuff the survivors. Tricky, no doubt, but what a man has done another can do."

"Wouldn't want to be one of the dogs hanging in a cage," Malik said.

"*Audentes fortuna iuvat*," Hector countered. "Fortune favours the bold."

"Arse, no one understands what you say," Rollo muttered.

He hated not knowing what was being spoken, be it Latin, Arabic, or some other tongue, but could not be bothered to learn them either. Hector had, for years now, goaded him with Latin and he flashed Rollo a wide grin.

"Who leads at Arbela?" Finn asked Nadal.

"The boss is … is … his name eludes me. It will come in a moment." Nadal gave a quick headshake. "He follows the bandit code. Kill what you want, keep what you kill. Took the town by force and cunning." He clicked a finger. "Gaspar — his name is Gaspar. An Armenian."

"He'll have Adrien by the scruff," Malik said, "and if it were me, I'd keep the scroll tucked up in a cave until the coin is piled at my feet."

Finn stared at the sergeant, still not warming to the man, then grudgingly nodded to acknowledge he had it right.

"I say we do the usual — thump some heads, rescue Adrien, kill Gaspar." Rollo raised and fluttered his hands as if luxuriating in the applause of an invisible crowd.

"Just make sure you get the rescuing and the killing right," said Emma.

Soft laughter, though Finn could see Emma's eyes might not agree with her words.

A squire scurried up the stairs and handed Nadal a scrap of parchment. Nadal scanned it, flared his eyes, then spoke to the waiting faces. "Gaspar has sent word — the price is doubled, bring payment forthwith, and Adrien is 'enjoying himself immensely,' whatever that means."

"Doubled…" Emma cursed softly, then added something about Adrien and a fool.

Finn hung his head like a mendicant in meditation. After a time, he raised up to study the mountain. The sun was falling, swathing it in darkness, and as he watched an orange orb sprang to life. Then another. The orbs jigged an eerie number on the dark mountainside.

"History makes ghosts," Finn said, "always so many ghosts."

The others waited.

The wooden chest was stacked against the wall and Finn nodded at it. "Does it hold what I think?"

"It does," said Emma.

"Then we'd be fools to lug it up the mountain." Finn turned to Hector. "Romans built contraptions of war, you said?"

Birds held Finn's gaze. Ravens and crows and rooks swooped above the scrub. Higher up, black crosses circled on rigid wings, waiting their turn.

"Not good," Finn said.

"Could be a dead animal," said Rollo.

"Could be." Something told Finn it was not. He nudged Fagan on.

The trail zig-zagged up through the scrub. Random piles of rocks dotted the hillside. They passed a shrine — a slab of rock painted with the Virgin and baby Jesus, each rendered with earnest simplicity in a folkish style. The nubs of votive candles arrayed in neat rows. A beaded necklace and tattered ribbons in a range of hues draped the stone.

Further on, they found Elias and Yousef, lounging in the shade of a dwarf oak.

"Didn't die here," said Elias. "Did him somewhere else and dragged the body here."

Finn shifted his gazed to the rusty-red husk of what had been a man.

He was on a pole planted in the trail. A lone vulture sat stupidly at the dead man's feet. Shining metal in his eye holes marked where he was nailed. Clothes were torn and streaked with brown stains. A boot was missing, the exposed foot stripped to the bone. Teeth leered grotesquely. A hunk of dried meat decorated the wood; experience told Finn it was a tongue.

"Shades of Darbsak, eh?" Elias laughed, a sound as monstrous as the sight on the pole. "Though I suppose a good jest is a good jest wherever its spoken."

Baret nudged his mount forward. The vulture waddled, and the waddle gained steam until he leaped into awkward, flapping flight. Flies swirled in a humming cloud and he fanned them in vain, then sucked in a breath and leaned uncomfortably close. He came back spitting a fly.

"Botan. His mouth always got the better of him — and did a final time, it appears."

"You sure?" asked Finn.

Baret nodded once. "No sign of Watt. Doubtless with Adrien … or on a pole somewhere." He glanced at Elias. "Your man said, 'shades of Darbsak'?"

"Spent some time at Darbsak when I wasn't on good terms with the Master. Banishment as a form of penance, was the idea." Finn quirked his head in a gesture that could have meant anything. "When not chasing tribal goat thieves, we fought Armenian rebels, and they were fond of leaving messages. When they laid hands on our Turcs — no easy task — they'd carve out eyes and tongues to say, 'No eyes to spy, no tongues to inform'."

"We sent messages too," Elias said. "We'd cut and cram to say, 'Bugger yourself'."

"The subtleties of war," Finn said, and Baret grimaced.

Finn took in his men — Rollo, Lugh, Waylon, Uncle Jerol, and Malik. Hector was elsewhere. Serlo was in Tiberias with Emma with strict instructions she was not to leave the Templar *casale*, nor be alone other than for the call of nature.

Elias reclined on an elbow. "Don't glance about like idiots when I say this, but they surround us."

"One under every rock," said Yousef.

Finn swept the area from the corners of his eyes with a deliberate, low sweep. Nothing. "How many?"

"More than a few."

"I'm not much for subtleties, but I'd wager the bird food says we aren't welcome." Rollo spit the foul air. "And I also wager we don't care."

"We don't." Finn's gaze meandered the rising track, and where it disappeared, a pall of smoke marked a town. He twitched a finger toward it. "On to trouble."

Trouble came from the rocks as they climbed.

Three men materialized in the trail, bows in their hands, arrows snugged to strings. They wore ragged leather armour on their chests and rags on their heads. A fourth sauntered forth armed with a nasty sneer. "Are you lost, brothers?" he asked.

Finn held up hands to show empty palms. "We seek our friend. And a chat with Gaspar."

Slithering and shuffling sounds behind, and Finn scanned over a shoulder to see a rabble hemming them in. Several held bows or crossbows. Most hefted spears. They were a mixed lot. Syrians. Lebanese. Jews. Armenians. Even a Frank or two.

Rollo glared at a youth levelling a rusty spear. "Keep pointing that stick at me, *little boy*, and I'll take it and shove it up your —"

"Peace, Brother Rollo," Finn said. He gave a warning stare before turning back to the sneering man. He had the legs of a stork and wore a rusty mail shirt hanging a size too large. A leather square patched the spot covering where a man's heart would be.

"And you are?" Finn asked.

"Shanks." He swept an arm down the trail. "Your friend is in the boss's place. He's in one piece, more or less."

The rough men trailed them, gliding through the rocks with long-practiced familiarity. Arbela proved a crude place — stone homes, narrow lanes, swirling dust. A lone synagogue stood at the end of a street. Mangy dogs yapped and snapped at the horse's hooves. An eagle soared high above it all, coursing the updrafts on broad, rigid wings.

Good omen, thought Finn.

A two-storey tavern stood at the edge of town. In its shade sat a watering trough, and next to it a long tethering post. Along the balcony, a row of women spat and hissed and signed hexes. Several yanked open yellow dress tops, bared their pale breasts and shook them in mockery.

"Well now, look at those beauties," Rollo said. "Seems we're welcome after all."

"The boss's ladies, and the boss's place," Malik said.

"What's inside?" Finn asked Malik. He stared at the sergeant. "It's plain you've spent time here."

Malik blinked for a moment, then fixed Finn with a sour stare. "Bar on the left. Window opposite. One man serving. A wench or two helping."

"Which way do the doors swing?"

"In."

"Second door?"

"At the back."

"Where will Gaspar be?"

"Back corner, holding court. Keeps a handful of scowlers around him at all times."

Self-made lords like Gaspar dotted the land from Christendom to Outremer. Backwaters, like Arbela, give the Gaspars of the world room to carve out a kingdom. And from atop their throne of shite, they bleed folk dry until another comes along and claims the shite-throne for their own. Finn had rubbed elbows with the type. Crafty. Vicious. Would sell their own ma for a coin. Arrogance and greed were their weaknesses.

Living humbly and simply were strength.

Most folk root themselves in wealth — matters of the soul get buried in mountains of things. The less you have the less you need, he found, and having little gave time to meditate on what matters. Finn owned two things — Oathkeeper and the long knife, which had been his fathers. All other things were burned the night he joined the Order, and in the fire and smoke he found freedom.

How one lives each day will decide if they live a full life or die hollow.

Finn slid from Fagan and tilted a head at Baret and Lugh to say, *Come with*, then held a fist to Rollo to say, *Hold here; but come in hard if you hear a ruckus.*

He sauntered toward the door.

Shanks said, "Mouse, earn your cheese."

Mouse ambled over to block Finn's way. For a mouse, he was a mountain of a man, taller than Rollo by a head. A shaggy mop of black hair topped his head and he had black ropes for eyebrows. Bones were braided into his beard and they tinkled as he moved. Mouse and Rollo glared like bulls sizing each other up, then Mouse winked at Rollo and spoke to Finn.

"No blades. Wouldn't want accidents, would we?" Mouse's *lingua franca* was thick with an Armenian accent.

Finn pulled Oathkeeper and the long knife and handed them to Waylon. He stepped forward only to be stopped by a meaty paw on the chest.

Mouse's smile showed a surprising number of straight, white teeth. "Don't make me hoist you by the heels and shake the others loose."

Finn slipped a *sgian dubh* from each boot and another from the cord around his neck.

"Arsehole?" Mouse's grin widened. "I hear you monks like stuffing things in there."

"You mistake me for an Armenian," Finn said with a bland grin.

"Funny man. After this is over, funny man, I'll skin your fingers," Mouse flicked a bone woven into his beard, "and put you next to Loris — he's lonely."

Mouse's voice never thickened with anger, nor did his smile falter, and he was all the more disturbing for it. Finn put on a plain face and pushed past Mouse. A sudden hush fell as he stood blinking, letting his eyes adjust to the gloom.

The beamed ceiling was low and blackened from many an oily lamp. The stench of rank wine and sweat was as stifling as the heat. At the far end were three men, one lounging in an x-frame chair. A nude, black-haired beauty stood behind, fanning the seated man with a palm leaf. Her breasts and belly and hands were painted with whorls and flowers; the henna designs gave her the look of an exotic bird.

Eight men ringed the bar or tables — some natives, others Franks, but all scarred and scowling. Finn did not honour them with his gaze; they battered him with theirs.

Finn strolled down the room, Baret and Lugh thumping along at his heels.

Baret whispered, "Adrien is on the right."

Up close, Adrien was like his brother Lanfrid — pale and frail and bland. Considering the distress he had caused, he was a letdown, and in him Finn saw only a fool needing rescue from himself. A cheek was purpled. A lip split. And his neck bruised by marks similar to fingers in size and shape. Finn nodded amicably, despite his misgivings, and Adrien returned a gesture somewhere between a smile and a flinch.

Mouse and Shanks ambled over to stand behind the lounging man.

The lounging man braced his head on a fist and settled into the chair's cushion. He wore blue, baggy trousers and a silk shirt with a richly embroidered collar. A caftan covered the shirt. Red leather boots beautified his feet. Above a bushy moustache glared the eyes of a jackal — hungry and cunning and mean.

A wiry man stood at the lounging man's side. "Welcome," he said in a voice that was anything but welcoming. His hands were tucked into the sleeves of a voluminous robe, and he extracted one to gesture at the lounging man. "This is Lord Gaspar. I am his servant, Ingbald."

Finn raised a hand, palm out, in a sign of peace. "May God be with you and bless you."

Ingbald translated into Armenian. Gaspar gave a languid wave that needed no interpretation, though Ingbald gave one anyway.

"God is not with Lord Gaspar, nor does he care for His blessings." Ingbald dipped his chin to better stare down his nose. "Speak to me. Do not address his lordship directly."

Finn held the laugh bubbling in his throat.

Gaspar reached to the table at his side and plucked up an ornate glass cup. A gold ring gleamed on a little finger, and Finn had no doubt Lugh was wondering if he could free the bauble without cutting the finger off. He sipped tea, and fixed his jackal gaze on Finn.

"Lord Gaspar would like to know the meaning of your visit?" prompted Ingbald.

Finn played along. "We seek our friend," he nodded at Adrien, "lost, but now found. And we come to make the payment, for the scroll, as agreed."

Ingbald translated.

The nude woman was dozing off, the palm leaf coming dangerously close to slapping her lord's head until Mouse said something that brought her back to life. Gaspar set aside the cup and stroked his luxurious moustache, then broke into an animated speech.

Ingbald gave a nod and wince or two, then translated, "Lord Gaspar says the old deal is dead. No doubt you received his note? Your friend came to cozen us. To acquire a thing of value for a pittance. He is a deceiver. A cheat. And because of his baseness, and poor business manners, Lord Gaspar has increased the price. He wishes it otherwise. But if the new price is not met, sadly, he will sell the thing to another."

"I did not cheat. I merely —"

Mouse leaned and slapped Adrien on the back of the head. His silky hair billowed in the breeze of the strike.

Finn glared at Mouse, marking him for later, then rubbed a finger along his lip. He spoke directly to Gaspar in Armenian. "Ingbald left out the part where you said, 'Templars are catamites. Fanatics. Swindlers. They'd chase gold into the depths of hell itself.'"

Ingbald quailed. Gaspar's eyes cinched to flinty slits.

"Aye, I speak your heathen language. Learned it while fighting your countrymen. It was easy — learning Armenian and killing Armenians, both." Eight blades hissed from their scabbards. Finn ignored them. "I'll share another thing I learned — how the Romans sacked your caves. I studied their masterpiece. They began by —"

Shanks surged with bared teeth but Gaspar's upraised hand checked him. He regarded Finn as if seeing him for the first time. Ingbald's gaze bounced between his lord and Finn.

"You speak Armenian well." Gaspar set down the cup, tapped a finger on its lip, then sighed in apparent disappointment. "How unfortunate Templars pollute my homeland. Fortunate for you, I will ignore slander to Armenia. This time. But know this — speak ill of my people again and you will die."

Finn's lip quirked in amusement.

"A man offended me weeks past. Mouse skinned him. He took three days to pass. His screams became a bother." Gaspar propped an elbow on the chair and stabbed a finger at Finn. "Mouse will hum a happy tune while he adds you to his bone collection. No doubt he could draw a skinning out another a day or two, as well?"

"Five days would be easy, Lord," Mouse rumbled.

Gaspar glared, then nodded once, as though conceding an understanding had been reached. "Let us begin again," he said. "I have Adrien. I have the scroll. The fool stands before you but the scroll is in the caves. Try to take it and it will be destroyed. Then the fool's bones go into Mouse's beard, next to yours."

Gaspar licked a fingertip and used it to smooth an errant eyebrow. "But I am not unreasonable. Like any good businessman, I place profit before pleasure. Pay double. Pay today. And the scroll is yours. As a gesture of goodwill, the fool can keep his fingers."

Adrien sucked in a breath — either at the prospect of losing his fingers or at the new price. Perhaps both.

"You brought the coin, I assume?" Gaspar squinted past Finn, as if expecting to see a litter of coin being wrestled in by sweating, grunting servants.

Finn shook his head. Grinned wickedly. "I bring death."

Gaspar's brows raised. The scowlers murmured. Finn talked on.

"Romans sacked Arbela, as I said." Finn gazed to the smoky ceiling, remembering the history. "They built contraptions to lower men to the caves and from them rained fire arrows. Legionaries climbed in to finish the butcher's work. Fathers slayed their children to save them from slavery. Others jumped to their deaths. The cliffs were smeared with…" He trailed off. "Well, no need to delve into gory details. Suffice it to say I found history informative. No doubt you found the same."

Gaspar's face said he had.

"Your women and children are hiding in the caves. Fled there the moment we started up the hill, no?"

"Your threats are empty. I hold the strong here." Gaspar made of show of grinning at Ingbald, then at Finn. "Perhaps you are mad?"

"I am. And I'll kill you as fast as…" Finn snapped a finger. "Everyone will die. Men and women. Chickens and dogs. Then we'll raze the town. Burn it. Salt it. Memories and ghosts will be all that remain."

Gaspar said nothing.

"You will be the first to die, this I vow." Finn's nostrils flared like a wolf on the hunt. Then he ran a hand over the cross on his chest. "Or," he twitched up a finger, "you can honour the original deal. Death or life. Your choice."

"You are mad," Gaspar said again, this time in a whisper.

"Give me Adrien and the scroll and this madman won't kill you."

"I've considered better deals."

"You won't hear a better one today."

"The scroll will be destroyed, fool. Then what will you do?"

"Wash your blood from my hands and report the scroll was a myth. Most relic hunts are. No doubt the Master will commend me for burning out a nest of vermin — might even promote me." Finn circled a hand in a dismissive gesture. "So, you see, I win either way."

Gaspar shifted and fingered his moustache.

Sounds crept in. A cup scraped over a table. The sluggish whoosh of the fan. A laugh outside. And as Finn waited, his black gaze burned into Gaspar's, and there he saw doubt.

A sweaty man hustled in and bowed before Gaspar.

"Lord, I am —"

"I know you. Speak and get out. And don't steal anything as you leave."

"Steal? I —"

"Out with it. Then out with you."

The man made a pouty face before blurting, "Templars on the trail, Lord."

"Say again?"

"Templars. More of them. More than we can fight." The man sucked in a breath. "They're carrying wood beams, pulleys, other things. Raymond's men are digging in at the base of the hill with those things that fling stones."

"Trebuchets. They're called trebuchets." Finn mimed throwing a stone with a flick of his forearm. "They'll fling fire pots into the caves. Romans didn't think of that nasty trick."

Women and children hid in the caves — the Fortress of Crows would become a tomb. A low murmur arose, like the hum of a kicked beehive, and Gaspar eased forward. A flick of his fingers sent the nude woman scurrying, painted breasts asway.

"The pots hold Greek Fire. The stuff splatters everywhere. Seeps into every nook. Burns hot as hellfire scooped from the Devil's Lake." Finn barked a short, mad laugh. "When a lad, the town preacher said it would burn sinners to charred nubs and when the pots fly, I think, 'hellfire has come'."

The murmur rose until someone hissed, "Kill him!"

Finn paid no attention to their ire and carried on. "Odd quirk too — a pot in the mouth of a cave sucks out the air. As many folk will suffocate as will burn."

The murmur fell. Finn waited until the sizzling of the oil lamps was the only sound.

"We'll give hell time to cool before lowering men into what remains of the Fortress of Crows." Finn tilted his scarred face at Gaspar. "That's what the gear coming up the trail is for."

Gaspar stroked his moustache with trembling fingers, though his eyes blazed.

Finn eased a step closer and spoke soft. "Did you assume I came here to horse trade? I didn't. I came to give life. Or to take it."

Gaspar slumped in his chair and his words were petulant, when at last he spoke.

"You claimed to come in peace."

"Peace is a fickle thing, I've found. Here a moment and then gone."

Gaspar stared up at the smoky rafters. "I believe we suffered a miscommunication," he said, and fixed his gaze on Finn anew. "Most unfortunate. So. Upon reflection, I have decided our previous deal is suitable, given the fluidity of things. Three hundred silver, plus thirty Saracen gold bezants. None debased. None clipped."

"Aye, just as agreed," Adrien gusted out, beaming like an idiot.

"Wise choice, *Lord* Gaspar," Finn said, gracing Gaspar with his imagined title. "Lugh, if you would be so kind, tell Brother Rollo reason rules the day."

Lugh hustled outside and Finn spoke in a flat tone. "There remains one more item — Botan, the man posted on the trail. He was Adrien's man. Beloved by many. Mourned by all. An unfortunate tragedy, likely the work of bandits, or perhaps rogues who misheard your command of safe passage?"

Gaspar waited with narrowed eyes.

Finn interlaced his fingers and bowed his head in a sombre pose. "I have no doubt you will find the culprits and hang them. And no doubt you also agree to withholding thirty of the silver as recompense for the man's widow?"

Gaspar grunted a sudden, "Ha! Profiting over a man's death!" He shifted his jackal's gaze to Ingbald. "Templars — told you they would chase gold into the depths of hell itself."

CHAPTER 7

They stood at the cliff's edge near a solitary carob tree. The wind battered Finn but the view went on forever. The Sea of Galilee was a shimmering blue dollop surrounded by green cultivated fields. The Horns of Hattin, twin peaks of a long-dead volcano, peaked over the south-west skyline. Closer, Mount Nitai faced Arbela like a stone twin — flat-topped and steep-faced. Between them ran the narrow Arbel Valley.

"Would you really have killed everyone?" Baret asked.

"Not the dogs," Finn said. "Nothing purer than the soul of a dog."

Baret smiled dumbly, unsure if Finn jested but too worried for the truth to prod.

Finn gazed down and his gut lurched at the drop — three hundred feet or more to the grey rock below. Scree sloped to level ground. Men scurried like metal-clad ants, hauling beams and clearing brush to make platforms. Finn nodded to Jerol, who waved a black and white flag, the signal to stand down.

Beams piled at the cliff edge, along with ropes, pulleys, and metal brackets. Sergeants had lugged the gear up under Hector's direction; now they mingled nearby, sweating and rolling tired shoulders.

"The ingenuity of the Romans. Seen in person." Baret nudged a beam with his boot toe. "How does it work?"

"It doesn't." Finn tore his gaze away from the scenery and turned it on Baret. "The beams came from an abandoned villa. The rope and pulley borrowed from the Templar wellhouse. Don't know what the brackets are for, but they look convincing, no?"

"And below?"

"More of the same. Apparently, Raymond's sergeant-at-arms and three of his mates were laid low in a recent tavern scrum. Most unfortunate. But Hector found one of his knights. The man leads a rabble of tradesmen, fishermen, and vagrants, all wearing the count's livery. They have been paid a day's wage to look busy. A score of our sergeants lend a hand."

Baret covered his grin with fingers. "Well played."

"Bartering with thieves doesn't fit my disposition. Nor does fighting in caves."

"A close look at the pile, by someone with a practical eye, and we will be undone," Hector said. "Then we'll have a hard fight on our hands."

Rollo grinned. "We'll have a fun fight, you mean."

Eons ago an aged trail had been hacked into the cliff face, expanding cracks and fissures put there by God's hand. Mouse went down it and Finn marvelled at the man's agility, like a huge, two-legged mountain goat. The man-goat scampered down until disappearing into a yawning hole in the cliff face. Gaspar and Ingbald waited at the trailhead, conversing in low, animated voices snatched away by the wind.

Adrien and his man, Watt, lingered nearby. Watt had a warped nose and a ruddy face topped by thinning sandy hair. He had been handsome when young but time, hard luck, and a fist or two had all taken their turn.

Something glinted on Adrien's little finger — Gaspar's gold ring, no doubt stolen from the hostage and now returned to its rightful owner. The ring was set with an oat-coloured stone — agate, most likely. Adrien twisted the ring in a measured, brooding tic.

"Lord Gaspar asks where is the payment?"

Finn turned to Ingbald, but ignored his question. "You were a priest."

Ingbald flinched. "Am I that obvious?"

"You bow your head when not speaking and stuff hands into your sleeves, like every inky-fingered scribbler I've known. I wager a peak at your scalp would find scars from scraping the tonsure. Why are you here, Brother?"

"Habit gives one away," Ingbald said. He dropped his chin, then looked up with a sigh. "Why am I here? Because God is love but God does not accept all kinds of love. Gaspar does. He is not a man given to considering another's sins, nor passing judgment on their nature. Every lord, even self-made lords, needs a learned advisor."

Finn nodded and Ingbald asked again, "Lord Gaspar asks where is the payment."

Over Ingbald's shoulder, Finn's gaze tracked Shanks, shuffling around the beams and rubbing his chin. He squatted to run a hand over a beam. He studied a bracket, fingers on his chin, then raised suddenly. "Lord Gaspar!"

Finn caught Waylon's eye and tilted a head toward the pile.

In three quick steps Waylon was there.

"Hush now," he crooned, flashing his gap-toothed smile. "Be quiet while the high rankers conduct business." Waylon slipped a hand to Shanks's shoulder, and still wearing the smile, kneed him in the bollocks.

Shanks dropped to his knees with a groan, and before toppling to his face, Lugh and Jerol grabbed him under the arms and dragged him behind the pile.

"So?" prodded Ingbald, oblivious to it all.

"God will provide," said Finn in a mysterious voice.

A moment later, Mouse clambered up, a leather bag wrapped in a meaty hand. Gaspar met him.

Finn shifted closer. "Show it."

A nod from Gaspar and Mouse reached into the bag and withdrew the scroll. It was green — aged copper — and rolled like a small, layered bedroll.

Mouse swung the scroll out and over the edge.

"Now, Mouse, let's not be a sore loser." Finn's voice was calm but his heart hammered in his chest.

"Throw it and I'll throw you after it," Rollo said, to which Mouse grinned defiance.

"At my word, Mouse will drop it, and a fall like that will break it to a thousand pieces. Only coin will save it." Gaspar threw out his arms and made a half circle. "But I see none."

Finn waved Hector over, slipped a hand into the knight's haversack, and hefted out a clinking sack. He tossed it to Gaspar. "A quarter of the gold."

"Quarter of —" Gaspar was open-mouthed and red-faced.

"Did you think we'd haul a fortune into a den of…" Finn lingered, then gave a crisp smile. He plucked a parchment from his cappa sleeve and waved it. "The remainder is here."

Gaspar snatched the parchment and handed it to Ingbald. The man ran a finger over the red wax seal — two knights riding one horse — then cracked it open and began reading. Gaspar's face was a medley of fear, insolence, and hate.

"A contract agreeing to pay the remaining sum, Lord. For security, it is written in code. See here," Ingbald tilted the parchment to show Gaspar the chicken-scratch writings. "Carry this to the Templar *casale* near Tiberias and they will hand over the payment."

Gaspar's glare darted to Ingbald, then to Finn. "If this is a trick…"

"Not a trick, Lord," Ingbald said. "Templars invented contracts. I myself have written them. Despite other failings, they are honest in their dealings. I assure you."

Finn dipped a sombre chin. "Templars never deceive, Lord Gaspar."

"It's called a fighting withdrawal," Finn said. "Do it right, we live. Do it wrong, we die."

"Why me?" Waylon said.

"Because you're good with a bow. Or at least not bad."

"I'm cursed with ability. What'd I do to anger the Almighty?"

"You jest about cocks and rashes while in the company of ladies," said Lugh. "Mother Mary can't be pleased and she has Jesus's ear."

"I still question where you got the rash, Rooster," Waylon grumbled.

Finn stared until he had the blackcoat's attention. "It's easy — if pressed, give them feathers. Fall back until you bump into us. And only a handful of them carry bows."

The Turc, Nik, snorted. "Bows? More like sticks with strings. Doubt they'd take a rabbit."

"See?" Finn climbed on Fagan, then leaned to grip Waylon on a shoulder. "Besides, Nik and Yousef will hold your hand."

"Never fear, English. You're a child at play." Nik patted his bow. "But I'm a master."

Rollo slipped a boot in a stirrup. "If you see Mouse, make sure to put a feather in his fat arse."

"I don't carry enough shafts to put that ox down." Waylon kneed his bow to string it, transforming it from a drab, c-shaped stick to a beautiful, recurving implement of death. "Shanks, no problem. I'll feather his skinny arse."

They had left Shanks groaning behind a pile of rocks and started down the trail. It was going well enough until a distant roar said the scheme was discovered, likely when Shanks came to. Now bandits shadowed them. The beams and ropes, no longer needed, were tossed aside to speed their escape.

The trail went down, parallel to the cliff, then angled away. Eventually the track dropped into a narrow valley, which in turn opened on the shore of Lake Tiberias, and the Templar fortress lay to the west of town.

Baret's query echoed in Finn's head, *Would you really have killed everyone?*

Would I? Not dogs. Never children. Nor women, I think, unless there is good cause. But after that… People die in war. Orphans are made. But he was keenly aware that, with the passage of time, his sensitivity to such losses lessened. And, more worrying, the notion no longer sickened as it once had.

"Elias."

Rollo's voice snapped Finn back to the present. The Turc waited in the trail, and as Finn came close Elias gave a sour grin.

"Spied some rough-looking bastards hiding. They've set crossbows where the trail drops into the valley."

"Gaspar's men?"

"No. These know what they're about. Freelances, I'd wager."

"Beau. Must be. How many?"

"More than us."

Finn glanced at Rollo, who gave his usual advice.

"Ride them down, I say. Make them pay for pissing with us."

Distant yells echoed from behind. Not long after a sergeant came up the line, empty crossbow slung over a shoulder. "Gaspar's churls are rushing our rear. We drove them back.

The Turcs feathered some, but they're forming up for another try."

Rollo laughed. "Freelances ahead. Churls behind. Hard fight either way."

Years in Outremer dulled a man's conscience. The death of innocents was not something Finn sought, but it happened, and he did not lose as much sleep as he should. The passage of time also taught prudence. He no longer ploughed headfirst into a fight simply for the joy in it. Various events lessened his bloodlust. Once, Finn fled an army of raiders, and the humiliation of forsaking innocent folk still burned in his heart. Afterwards, Brother Jakelin de Mailly had advised, 'Think of your men. Pick your spots.' Jakelin was one of the Order's famed knights, a man Finn esteemed beyond measure, and his counsel brought a measure of comfort.

"Better to fight Gaspar's men," Hector said, and signed the cross. "Most of them are untrained. We will lose a few but Gaspar will lose more."

Finn drooped his head and rubbed the bridge of his nose. The sound of fighting picked up, closer now. Someone screamed in pain. A garbled command. War chants in Armenian.

Finn turned to Elias. "Freelances block the only way out, you say?"

Elias nodded.

"What about that way?" Finn jigged a thumb toward the cliff edge.

A grin spread Elias's face and it widened as the idea bloomed. "Not as steep here, eh? Now that we aren't on top of a mountain…"

Rollo stared a moment, then swore. "Can't we just do a fighting withdrawal?"

CHAPTER 8

"Impress us with your wit." Finn hefted the scroll on the table and nodded to Timothy of Yorkshire.

"Should be entertaining," Rollo said.

Timothy smirked. "And what do you do for entertainment, o' knight?"

"Kill smart mouths like you," Rollo snarled, then jutted his scarred face close to the scholar. "It's my trade. Birds fly. Fish swim. I fight."

Timothy wisely bit back the retort tempting his tongue.

The ride down was rough, but as Elias had said, less steep than the top of a mountain. They led their mounts, goaded them hoof-by-hoof, and took their time picking their way down a goat trail. Thus Beau's ambuscade was avoided. Gaspar's toughs pecked at their heels. The rear guard sent shafts. Moved. Held. Did it all again. In the end Gaspar, realizing he had been duped but not understanding why, gave up the half-hearted chase.

Three blackcoats took wounds. One rolled an ankle. None were dead. Rollo was denied his trade and his good mood injured.

Finn offered Rollo a bone. "We'll return and kill Gaspar another day. Mouse too. Maybe for your birthday. What do say, Brother?"

Rollo ignored the bone, still unable to speak to Finn, much less look at him.

Finn, from the corner of an eye, watched Adrien slink near the table. He hovered over the scroll, mumbling and bobbing his head, though only he knew if it was holy rapture or something immoral. Neither was a cheering notion.

Timothy shooed Adrien aside and motioned his colleague, Yosi, to come close. The man was a Yemenite Jew with dark eyes and wavy hair. The scholars took a collective breath and began rolling the scroll open, working in crisp and coordinated moves until it was spread over the table. Several pieces fell free. Flat rocks were placed at the corners of the largest piece. The inside was hammered copper. Parchment thin. Red-brown with a sheen of green patina. Rows of exotic words incised the metal.

"The scroll … I never dreamed to see it." Timothy gave a lingering sigh, as if just arrived to heaven but disappointed by the view. "Much is fragmentary, sadly, and pieces are missing."

"How do you know?" Hector asked.

Timothy stared at Hector, then Finn, then mumbled, "I sobered up for these fools?" He carried on in a measured voice, "I know because ragged edges say so. Orphan words hang to the side of the text, which tells me there was more than one column of text, and that column is missing. This is eight or nine hundred years old. Ancient copper would be fused. Too brittle to open without sundering it in the process — which is what some fool did."

Finn eyed the fragments of scroll, then the scholar.

The man was short, bulbous above, with two sticks below, and how the sticks held up the bulb was a mystery for another day. He had a ruddy face with a veiny nose and hooded eyes. A mess of fair, thinning hair topped it all. He was a scholar of renown. Well-studied and far-travelled. Rome. Paris. Leon. Even as far as Iceland. Recent years landed him in Acre.

Wine vapours wafted from his pores as Finn came close. "While you're in our company, you'll stay sober," he warned, then leaned back from the man's rank breath.

Timothy arched a mysterious brow. "*In vino veritas.*"

Finn had no idea what that meant but nodded in stern agreement.

"Most religious scrolls are written on animal skin or papyrus. Why the cost and time of engraving copper?" Hector thought aloud but Timothy answered.

"Because it contains details needing to be preserved for eternity, or thereabouts, anyway. Copper was used for safekeeping vital records — public law, temple records, administrative documents. Discharge orders of Roman legionaries were often in copper. Which tells us, first, the scroll was important and, second, not directly religious in nature."

Hector opened his mouth and Timothy held up a hand for silence.

Finn stole a glance at Emma. Her headscarf was draped around her neck and she stared at the scroll while idly rubbing an earlobe. His gaze wandered over her sizable ears, and found them oddly endearing. She glanced up and he looked away.

After a while, Timothy said, "Jewish rebels hid the original, or originals, from non-believers. Likely during the Bar Kokhba revolt. Maybe the first Jewish-Roman war. Yet the writing style is curious. Similar to Mishnaic Hebrew, an old form of Hebrew. Yosi is the expert there." He nodded at the Jew, then to himself. "Perhaps written by the Essenes."

"Essenes?" Finn asked.

"Essenes were a sect — an apocalyptic sect of Judaism, to be precise. Ascetics. Separatists. They abandoned Jerusalem to protest worldliness and made a life in the wastes, near the Dead Sea. There, they kept vigil for a Messiah — or *Messiahs*, I should say. The Lord would return in wrath to build a new kingdom for the Jews, they said, like the Kingdom of Solomon."

Timothy, now warmed to the task, ploughed on.

"Essenes preached apocalyptic times — the war of the son of light against the sons of darkness. They were obsessed with preserving knowledge that formed the foundation of what we Christians call the Old Testament, or what I call the First Testament. Rumour is they stashed centuries of teachings in caves. I pray this hoard, or hoards, of writing is found someday."

"Some future scholar will find them, dig them from their hiding places," Finn murmured, though all eyes were on the scroll. "The future sage will hold the writings in his hands and marvel at the ingenuity of ancient folk. For only man, among all of God's creatures, has the cleverness to scribble words on parchment."

"Bah." Rollo had come to Finn's side and stared at the scroll with a bemused eye. "Bedouins will find it. They get their grubby paws on everything. But myths will persist about the Templars, of the sacred bloodlines we never protected, the secret rituals we didn't practice, and the relics we never possessed. Future scholars? They'll mock the notion such things were real — and mock those who obsessed over them."

"Including us?"

"Especially us."

There was silence, except for the Timothy's heavy snuffling. "Likely written by the Essenes," the scholar repeated in a mutter. "But see here — Greek letters are intermixed, and Greek loanwords, like the scribe filled holes in his ignorance with what he knew. Some words are block letters. Others are cursive. Most unusual."

Yosi and Hector leaned over the scroll, almost knocking heads in their zeal, while Adrien madly twisted his gold ring. Rollo drifted back to the wall and lounged there, head propped against the stone, eyes closed. Finn envied his detached repose.

A soft hiss and Yosi said something in Hebrew. Timothy skimmed to Yosi's fingertip, held on the first line on the scroll, and they shared a wide-eyed stare until Yosi broke away shaking his head.

"What does it say?" Finn waited for the answer that never came, then prodded. "Can you decipher it?"

"Would I be here if I could not?" Timothy mumbled something that sounded suspiciously close to 'dolt.' He propped two fingers on a stubbly chin. "The text is antique. Muddled. And Jews are fond of speaking in riddles. Most of their sentences begin with a question. All of which means the scroll must contain clues and metaphors only a Jew would recognize."

Yosi nodded in agreement.

"Our brief study suggests…" Timothy trailed off, fanned a hand. "Rare lore awaits. But we must proceed with care. Errors are likely. The process will be relentlessly argumentative. Debates many and lengthy. It will require time."

"How much time?" Emma asked, then amended, "For the first score of lines, or thereabouts."

Timothy glanced to Yosi, who paused from unrolling blank sheets of parchment to return a shrug which suggested anything from days to years.

"Weeks, at least," Timothy said. "A complete translation … months, if not more."

"Our work is done," Finn said. "The scroll is destined for the Scriptorium, where it will moulder to dust. We'll escort you there, and Timothy and Yosi can argue over the translation for years."

Emma fixed her gaze on Adrien. "We will translate here," Adrien said, slow and firm.

Finn scowled. "Why here?"

"Why not here?" Adrien countered.

"Because then I must tend you when I would rather be doing anything else."

Adrien and Emma shared a glance, until Finn growled, "Just say it."

Emma tilted a head to say, *As you wish*, and fluttered a parchment sealed with the red Templar sigil of two knights on one horse. Finn handed it to Hector while squinting at Emma. A dry crack as Hector broke the seal. The crinkle of parchment and Hector's lively brown eyes scanned the words.

"The Master commands we follow Adrien," Hector recited. "And protect Adrien and Emma. And seek what is named in the scroll. And to bring these things to him, where he will return them to the Temple of Solomon. These holy items must be recovered for they are sacred to God, Jesus, and the Order. Our souls depend on our success. Paradise awaits. God bless us and guide us in this most noble quest. Signed, Master Gerard de Ridefort."

"No big thing, then," Rollo said without opening his eyes.

Finn glared at Emma. In her stoney eyes glimmered the thrill of the chase and, perhaps, a morsel of remorse for keeping details hidden. He snatched his gaze away before harsh words could break loose from his feeble hold. He turned to the window, glaring at Mount Arbela. He sensed Rollo at a shoulder.

"This is folly. Men will die."

"Relic hunting is vile," Rollo agreed, his voice soft. "And I hate to ruin the surprise, Brother, but we all die someday."

Rollo's calm was contagious and Finn breathed out, low and long. An ache settled in his jaw, from clenching his teeth, and he waggled it side-to-side.

"Why does this task make you angry?"

"I don't like being deceived. Nor used."

"Neither of these is new to you."

Finn gusted out what nettled him. "What if we don't find anything?"

"Then we return to minding pilgrims and…" Rollo trailed off as he realized what Finn meant. He tilted his head back, preparing a lecture. "My da used to tell tales. Of monsters and heroes. Of magic swords and relics. As a lad I listened like a slack-jawed idiot. As a younger man I mocked them, said they're for weak-minded folk. But sometimes I ask if I'm the weak-minded fool for lacking faith? You ask the same."

Sudden doubt hooked a claw into Finn. *God tries me. What if I fail?*

Rollo seemed to read Finn's thoughts. "Many times, Finnláech of Struan, you have said, 'My faith is the miracle. I don't need relics to confirm it.' And yet here you stand, doubting."

"But what if we find no relics? Does that mean…"

"No. It doesn't mean Jesus abandoned you. Nor are you unworthy if he doesn't allow you to find this holy thing, whatever it be. He will lead us there, if he wants us to find it, or he will keep it hidden."

Finn gave a slow nod. Rollo's shoulders began shaking with mirth.

"Why do you laugh?" Finn growled.

"Me. Preaching. On faith." Rollo sighed in laughter, cuffed an eye. "I've doubted more than Old Hob himself."

"The blind leading the blind," Finn said.

They chortled like children misbehaving in church. Finn peeked at Emma, hunched over the table and staring back with an icy gaze.

Rollo took a deep breath. "The smart-mouth said he needs weeks to translate the scroll," he mused aloud.

"He did."

"So, we have ample time to go for a ride in the sunshine, to clear your mind, no? I hear the Road to Masyap is lovely this time of year."

"Masyaf," Finn corrected. "Aye. A ride would be nice."

CHAPTER 9

Thus and so did they ride to find the devil.

The Road to Masyaf looped its way through a series of low hills. The road was not much used these days and had become the haunt of brigands — though what was rumoured to travel the road this day had no fear of such men. Finn rode from Tiberias two days past. Rollo, Lugh, Waylon, and Uncle Jerol were with him, along with Elias and several Turcs. Hector and Serlo guarded Emma and the scroll. Hector was in charge during Finn's absence.

Finn picked a turn in the road. Slabs of rock lined both sides and gave places to hide — and shelter from the brutal sun. He had dredged up skills from his days as a *cateran*, a raider in his native Alba, and chose this spot because a traveller would be momentarily blinded by the curve.

Rollo, crouched in the shade, flicked a strand of hair from an eye. The Rule mandated short hair and a long beard — to blend its wearer into a culture that revered beards as a sign of strength. Rollo, restive by nature, wore his hair shoulder-length and unkempt in petty defiance. If the Rule mandated long hair and a short beard, he would crop hair his close to the scalp and grow a beard to his knees.

Finn fingered prayer beads, carved to resemble human skulls, to pass the time.

Worry seeped in as the hours passed. The Master would not take insubordination lightly. Being caught meant punishment. Penance. Demotion. Possibly expulsion. Worse, it was said the Old Man moved like a ghost, never travelled the same path twice — which could make the lash strokes for naught. Yet

Finn had to chase the ghost. Had to go on the attack. Shabh was a boil to be lanced, an ill needing mending, and the Old Man was the salve.

A soft whistle focussed Finn's ambling mind. Elias lay flat as a lizard on a high rock, hand held back in a holding sign. Finn tucked away the skull-head prayer beads as his heart began thumping a lively beat. Fear pounced like a demon leaping from a shadowed niche, and with sudden clarity he realized the stupidity of what he attempted — not just penance, but death awaited around the bend. Elias, after what seemed an eternity, waved the hand to say, *Go*.

Finn breathed out, staggered into the road, hands held out empty like a martyred saint. He glimpsed white flowing robes, silvery flashes of mail, shemagh head wrappings banding dark eyes and brows. The lead horseman reined in, eyes flared at the spectre that had just materialized in his path. A score of others were coming up behind.

In halting Arabic Finn said, "No harm. Friend. Peace."

The man heeled his mount, spear levelled, then Finn's words hit home and he reined in. "Move or die!"

Finn raised his hands to emphasize their emptiness. "Peace. Parlay."

The spearman spat his answer and jabbed the spear toward Finn's eye. Then a hand on a shoulder stilled him. A gracile man on a splendid black Arabian heel-tapped his horse forward. The man was hollow-cheeked with fierce eyes topped by delicate arching brows. His age meandered somewhere between thirty and seventy.

"I am he." The envoy wore a white robe with a red sash and red head wrapping. His attire was as flawless as his French.

Finn gestured to the shade of a large rock. "Conversation would be more enjoyable in the cool," he said, switching to French.

The envoy's eyes flicked there and back. "Forgive my hesitancy, but the last time Templars surprised us many of the faithful died."

"We are not those brothers." Finn dropped a hand to the red cross pattée riding over his heart. "I mean no harm. This I swear on the name of God, Jesus, and Mary."

The envoy quirked a lip at that. He tilted a head to the left, the right, and men eased from their hiding places with bows in their hands. "Arrows have been aimed at you from the moment you stepped into the road. Speak, so we may be on our way."

Rollo stepped into the road behind Finn, and Finn shot him a glance over a shoulder. "We seek an audience with Rashid ad-Din Sinan. Can you arrange it?"

"We treat with the Master of the Temple and you are not he."

"This is not business. This is personal. A favour, if you will." Finn confessed, "The Master doesn't know I'm here."

"Intriguing." The envoy's fierce eyes dissected Finn in leisurely passes. A grin twitched his lips. A slide off his mount and he was in the shade sitting cross-legged, palms spread invitingly. "There is no cause for peaceful men not to converse. Come. Sit."

The envoy moved with such grace it seemed he was on his horse, then sitting in the shade, with no sign of his travel. Finn ambled over and eased into a cross-legged seat, though to his shame he needed a hand to drag his leg into place. His thigh had been speared in Robert's camp and, months after, the leg remained stiff.

"Your leg aches when the weather changes and you will always walk with a limp," the envoy said. His voice was warm. Fatherly. "Though these are a modest price for settling the account with the Apostate, I am sure you would agree?"

"You've heard of this?"

The envoy nodded sombrely as if to say sneaking into a man's tent and knifing him, face-to-face, amidst his guards, was a deed ranked high among the sect of Nizari killers.

"Fighting free of the traitor's camp was the harder task, truth be told," Finn said.

"And yet, despite your valour and loyalty to your vows, you have not been elevated above your station. Your Master neglects you."

"Tread careful, friend," Finn said in a low voice. "How do you know of goings-on within our Order?"

"I have eyes and ears everywhere. There is not much I do not see or hear."

Finn mouth gaped, then snapped closed. "You are he — the Old Man."

The Old Man dipped a chin, a simple gesture equally full of charm and menace.

Finn stared. Before him sat death incarnate in the form of a smiling man with delicate hands and a serene voice. Here sat the demon from a thousand Christian nightmares, though the Old Man's radiant calm and ice-cold eyes frightened more than any demon.

"Why the deception of envoy?" Finn asked.

"What better guise than hiding in plain sight?"

The Old Man spoke with such modest charm Finn almost laughed aloud. The notion of the Old Man delivering the annual bribe while acting the grovelling minion before the Master was ... strangely amusing. Gerard would be livid to find one of Christendom's most feared monsters had, more than once, stood within reach of his blade. Yet to tell him would be Finn's undoing and the Old Man understood this.

"We have a similar saying back home," Finn said. "Sitting on fire."

Finn told how when hunting, man or beast, Scots build a fire and sit over it. White oak was best. A wee bit burned hot for its size and nearly smokeless. Dig a hole then layer in strips of bark. Pull a cloak over your head, to hide the sparks, and start a fire with flint and steel. When the bark is going, cover the hole, leaving two side shafts for draught, and sit cross-legged with a slow fire under your knees. Inside the cloak is warm even in the snows of winter. And if a man sits over a smokeless fire, swathed in a cloak, still as a rock, with the wind in his face, he can hide in plain sight.

The Old Man quirked a head to acknowledge the cunning in that. For a moment he said nothing, certes pondering the mysteries of snow and sitting where one could be easily seen, if a foe only knew how to see.

"You're not armed," Finn commented.

"I need no weapon," the Old Man gestured at his men, "for I am armed with loyal brothers and my faith in the one true God, Allah. What more does a man need?"

Finn, to his surprise, found he was beginning to like this killer of men.

He glanced to Rollo and their sergeants, standing opposite the Nizaris. "Indeed. We are blessed." Finn took a breath. "I'm here to —"

The Old Man's hand shot up. "Not yet. Please accept my offer of guest. You gave a vow of my safety; now I give mine. Let us set aside rancour and savour this strange moment, no?" He smiled at the absurdity of two foes conversing like old friends, then twirled a finger at a follower, who scurried to his horse and began plucking at the tie to his saddle bag.

Being guest offered a momentary truce and in the Muslim ethos his safety was guaranteed by the honour of the host. Local hospitality was the stuff of legend, and folk said to be well-fed one should dine with a Muslim. The spearman squatted over a fire made from branches. The fire grew; over it he suspended a delicate pot of red clay.

Finn studied the Old Man. He was older than Finn, he must be, and was charm itself, like a courtier from the Sultan's palace where protocol and manners were all. Yet darkness threaded all that elegance.

"You speak French well," Finn said.

"And you speak Arabic poorly." The Old Man smiled to soften the blow. "But I commend you for learning. Most Franks see it as beneath them."

Finn quirked a head to acknowledge the apparent compliment. "A man shouldn't spare an enemy, nor cease to learn his ways. Where did you learn French?"

"Here and there."

"Where were you born?"

"Here and there." The Old Man's bland expression said such trivial lines of inquiry were a bore. He steepled his fingers in a pose of contemplation and regarded Finn a while. "I see in you a man not so different from myself. You disguise immaculate skill within a shabby exterior. You have no fear, but Saladin fears you, as he fears me. You would kill or die for your God, as would I. And as reward the promise of paradise awaits us — though, alas, you will find you have been deceived, no?"

"All faiths contain truths," Finn said, "yet all faiths quarrel, for there is only one God, praise be His name."

The Old Man hoisted a hand at Finn, then swung it to his men to confirm some point made during an earlier debate. His devotees, crouched in the road, murmured their approval and beamed and nodded like children.

They hang on his every word, Finn thought.

One of the devotees spread a linen coverlet and on it arrayed salted almonds, dates, and honey cakes. Steaming tea came in petite clay cups.

The Old Man washed his fingers in a bowl of water, brought for that purpose, then bowed a head to pray. He blessed the food with a Du'a, in the name of Allah, and with blessings of Allah, while Finn murmured grace and finished by signing the cross. Each gave the other a moment with his god, and each allowed the other the notion his was the one true god.

The Old Man gestured to the spread. "Honey cakes are a weakness."

Finn, as guest, had been invited to partake first, and he did. The cake was dry but sweet; unused to such rich fare he chewed slowly. Cardamom tea was new to his palate, with hints of eucalyptus, mint, and pepper. He noted the Old Man never used his left hand, his impure hand, and Finn did the same. Neither did the Old Man use his lips much when he talked or sipped. But he used his eyes. They were ever moving, ever alive, and he rarely blinked.

They sipped and ate until a shadow shimmered over the road. Finn looked up to see a hawk riding the currents, tilting in relaxed, graceful circles. He glimpsed a barred reddish breast and charcoal grey wingbacks when the bird angled into a turn. The Old Man tracked the hawk's flight eagerly, with a look of reverence and awe.

"Time can hover, suspended in the hawk's trail, or time can collapse in a broken heap, like an unsuspecting hare struck from above, frozen in time by the stillness we mortals call death." The Old Man's voice was a soft purr, though his next words were cold and hard as ice. "We will all be stilled by death. Eventually."

Finn, lacking a wise retort, nodded instead. The wavering shadow returned, and he squinted at the bird as it tilted into a turn. "My da hawked. I think of him whenever I see a hawk. I fancy his hawk-self is watching me, guiding me, warning me of danger."

"Perhaps he is."

The Old Man had been serene. Mannered. Fatherly. But now he devoured Finn with those unblinking eyes. Finn had the odd but fleeting notion to throw aside his mantle and join him.

The Old Man broke the spell with a smile that stayed at his lips. "Tell me, foe and friend, why have you surprised me thus?"

"Shabh." The one clipped word was enough.

"Ah." The Old Man wiped his thin fingers on a napkin until they were cleaned to his satisfaction. "Templars come here to fight for your faith and to bury your bones here. An admirable practice, though sadly misguided. Others of your kind, more misguided still, come to defile. To thieve. To return home with spoils, souls unburdened by their multitude of sins."

Finn, with no argument to the contrary, sipped tea. The Old Man carried on.

"Shabh was a victim of Christian sins. Her family lost all. She lost all. Even her pride was taken — at least for a while. Her hatred of Christians borders on," he circled fingers in the air, "madness."

112

"What was done to her?"

"I will not speak of such things, for they are hers alone to tell. Suffice it to say loss and shame plague her — and you *Faranji* are to blame. She can be kind. Loving in her own way. But then ancestors inhabit her and talk with her mouth, see with her eyes, cut with her hands."

"You trained her?"

"I did. She proved adept. Quick of mind and body. Fearless. For a while her hatred was put to good use." The Old Man tilted a head to say those uses needed no explaining between two killers. "She displayed a rare kinship with death — which I also see in you."

The Old Man's voice was tender, but took a sharp edge when next he spoke.

"It is said there is no transformation except through Allah, and without faith she did not fight free of her demons. Her anger proved too much, even for me, and she no longer adheres to the foundation." The Old Man breathed out. "We took our leave of each other. Several of my pupils left with her. She has agents among you — even within your Order, I hear. Her other adherents are kin, or lunatics, or vagrants."

The Old Man sipped tea, then made a face like he had tasted something sour. "Shabh kills for pay — *for pay*! Not for God. Not for influence. For filthy coin."

Finn studied the Old Man and saw a parent, heart-sick at their child's failings. "She was paid to hunt me," Finn said. "The jig is up and still she hunts me. Why?"

The Old Man tilted a head. "You do not know?"

Finn twitched his head and the Old Man said, "She and Robert of Saint Albans were lovers. Together they made a child — a precocious boy, also named Robert. Young Robert is fierce, like his mother, and keen-minded, like his father."

The words struck Finn dumb and the Old Man twisted the blade deeper.

"Love, or her notion of it, healed a part of her. But losing it, again, broke her. You were the cause. Worse, her failure completing your contract pains her, for if you had died, Robert would have lived."

Finn closed his eyes. Clarity came sluggish, like a morning breeze driving away a clinging fog. The Apostate spoke fondly of Shabh, and of a son, though Finn had not dreamed the two were bonded as mother and son. The hawk-decorated saifs, used by Shabh's minions … and an image, clear as glass now, of Robert's metal-handled saif, decorated with a stooping hawk, laying unused at his side. *The sword was a gift to Robert, from his love Shabh, as she gifted similar swords to her adherents meriting it.*

The Old Man spoke when Finn opened his eyes. "Your recent fight cost her. I doubt she retains the strength to come at you again in force."

"Where do I find her?"

The hawk's shadow shimmered over the road again, larger now, the bird of prey gliding lower.

The Old Man fixed his gaze on Finn. "She ventures into cities for work. For supplies. To recruit from among the downtrodden. Her lair is in the desert."

"Which desert?" There are two in Outremer, the Judean and the Negev. The Old Man said nothing and Finn could not help but prod. "You claimed to have eyes and ears everywhere."

The Old Man scowled at that. "Judean. But where therein I cannot say. Regardless, she will find you before you find her."

Finn pondered and decided the Old Man spoke true. They chatted a while longer of things mundane. Finn found himself on his feet, where he praised the generosity of his host, in the

Muslim tradition, then touched fingers to his forehead and offered a short bow.

The Old Man replied in kind. "We shall meet again, foe and friend, though I fear it will be on less friendly terms."

"Aye, though I wish it otherwise." Finn breathed out as the Old Man rode away. His vigour drained, as if the Old Man had sucked it from him, leaving arms and legs atremble.

Rollo strolled close and Finn said, "I sipped tea with the devil in the bright light of day. No one will believe me."

And perhaps that was better.

CHAPTER 10

Night darkened the *casale* near Tiberias. Ingbald stood in the courtyard. Entry was simple. Most fortifications boasted a sally port, a small door used to make attacks in the event of a siege, and this *casale* was no exception. He had been chaplain here for years. In all those years the door had not been guarded at night. And in the years he had spent with Shanks — time ill spent — the skinny devil never met a lock he could not pick.

He stood under the stars, admiring their endless beauty, before shuffling across the courtyard. The swinging lamp in his hand painted the courtyard with dancing shadows. Vespers droned from the chapel. Further on, light and chatter flooded from the doorway to the sergeants' quarters. They were not beholden to prayer, unlike knights, and the mood inside was less … gloomy. Someone sang Marcabru's *Pax in Nomine Domini*, one of the many tunes in fashion across Outremer.

Jesus will be with us,
And the lechers, drunkards,
Eager-eaters, fireside squatters,
Rumps-on-the-road,
Will remain in their squalor.

"We're chatting here, shut your bread hole," someone yelled.

"My farts carry a better tune," another said.

Ingbald thought the singing not so bad, and the singer carried on undaunted.

In the lineage of Cain,
Of that first treacherous man,
There are many,

Not one of whom honours God…

The words cut straight to the bone and Ingbald nearly turned on a heel to leave.

"Go," Shanks hissed, like some malevolent ghost.

How am I here? Ingbald was not a man of action, nor dead-of-night dealings; he was a man of peace and learning. A priest had once told him, 'A man facing the new can never go back to the old.' How he hoped that priest was wrong.

Gaspar was angry to be deceived, and rightfully so, but bags of gold and silver salved the burn. Then Beau arrived with a pack of scowling ruffians and Freelances at his back. He wanted the Copper Scroll, knew where it was, and had a patron willing to pay handsomely for it. Problem was, he had no way to get the scroll, nor had he seen it before. Gaspar did — or better said, Ingbald did. The knowledge mouldering in the head of a disgraced chaplain, to his surprise, was now invaluable. For a fee, paid to Gaspar of course, Ingbald would steal the scroll for Beau.

Ingbald, foolishly, had vouched for Templar integrity. He owed Gaspar loyalty, for the Armenian extended a home where others offered only derision. Resentment of the Order and loyalty to Gaspar started him down the road. Images of his bones dangling from Mouse's beard had been the final shove.

Sandaled feet padded silently along stone hallways. Soon he stood in the Scriptorium. And there it was, sprawled in the middle of the table, parchments stretched out beside it. Shanks lurked in the hall as Ingbald ghosted in, stooped over the scroll. He squinted at the archaic words. *These might be unknown teachings of the saviour … or some ancient prophet.* His heart skipped a beat at the thought.

"Who are you?"

Ingbald whirled to a dark-skinned man with curly hair.

"Chaplain Benedict. Just arrived this fine day to assume duties here henceforth. Have you not heard?" Ingbald signed the cross and added, "My son."

"Benedict, you say?" The man spoke with a strange accent, like sticks clattering on rock. He tilted a head and stared through narrowed eyes.

Fool, go back to whatever hole you crept from.

He did not.

A shadow moved behind the man and a hand snaked around to cover his mouth. A grunt of surprise and something poked out the man's chest and disappeared. Again, the strange thing came and went, and Ingbald felt something warm and wet on his face. The man crumpled like God had yanked the bones from his legs — revealing Shanks, grinning wickedly.

"Go!" Shanks said and scooped the scroll and parchment into a shoulder bag.

Fear took over Ingbald's brain. He was dimly aware of his sandaled feet, now speckled with something dark, retracing the way. A trail of cold shivered down his back. At any moment the cry of alarm must go up. A glance at Shanks found him still grinning. Then they were at the sally port. A short scamper into the brush and they were on their horses.

And the evil is done.

Or has it just begun?

Being free from the Old Man's grasp, which might have consumed Finn entire, and free from the Rule, at least temporarily, was invigorating. Finn pushed hard for Tiberias, and they rode in the dark knowing a horse on familiar ground will find his path. Vigour fled and weariness settled. At some point he must have slept, for he dreamt the Old Man was a hawk, with finely boned wings and a beak made of steel, and whenever Finn neared Shabh the Old Hawk snapped his beak and fanned his wings.

Thickets of pine and eucalyptus lined the road to Tiberias; their fresh and sharp scent told Finn they neared the city. A while later the lights of Tiberias winked in the distance. Finn was half-asleep in the saddle, his weary mind pondering tea with the Old Man, and Shabh, and how to find her. The Old Man needled his thoughts; 'She has agents among you — even within your Order.' *Unlikely*. 'She will find you.' *Probably*.

"See that?"

Rollo's words brought Finn awake and he tracked the Norman's jutting finger to the Templar *casale*, glowing white in the darkness. Shadowed riders spurred madly away from it.

"Messengers?"

"Not at this hour."

The riders slewed away toward the mouth of the Arbela Valley, moonlit dust raising in their wake.

"After them!" Finn barked the command on instinct.

Fagan leapt to the pursuit with barely a nudge from Finn. Waylon and Lugh shot past, whopping in joy at the chase. Wind whistled in Finn's ears and he gave the destrier his head. Fagan was the fiercest horse Finn had ridden, as fond of a fight as Finn, though not the fastest horse in the stable. Within a hundred strides he was moving his head more than usual, blowing and overreaching his stride. Finn checked over a shoulder to find Rollo, Jerol, and the Turcs gone. The clatter of hooves and dust trailed back to him.

From the dark came two huddled shapes and Finn reined in.

Lugh crouched over something — no, someone. Waylon. Finn's guts turned to ice. He dropped off Fagan as Lugh staggered away. Waylon lay on his back, a gaping hole in his chest, wet and black in the moonlight. More wetness darkened the road.

"Cold." Darkness shone on Waylon's gapped teeth.

"Aye." Finn crouched, swept up Waylon's hand, gave it a hard squeeze.

"I'm a … goner … eh?"

Finn, not wanting to lie, managed a shaky nod.

"*Fils a putain.*" Waylon slurred the sergeants' pet phrase.

Rollo clattered up. "Rode to cut them off but…" He trailed off at the horrid sight; he and Finn shared a look of despair.

Lugh stood in the road, hand plastered to his forehead, then dropped to a knee to cradle Waylon's other hand. "Just a nick. You'll be fine, you damn whiny Englishman."

But Waylon was not fine, and no amount of wishing otherwise would stopper all the blood flooding from his chest. Finn watched the mist drift into Waylon's eyes as he opened and closed his mouth, gasping for air.

Finn held the hand and stared into those misty eyes until the opening and closing stilled.

They carried Waylon to the Templar cemetery and laid him down in a hacked-out grave.

Lugh led the procession and keened a mournful dirge in his Irish tongue as he walked. A chaplain, resplendent in a green robe, scowled at Rooster but dared offer no complaint to a man of war. The chaplain commenced as the keening died away.

'O God, by whose mercy the faithful departed find rest, bless this grave, and send a holy angel to watch over it. Comfort those who mourn. Sustain them with the hope of eternal life.'

The prayer fell on deaf ears; Finn's mind was busy replaying the night before.

Waylon and Lugh had been closing on the riders when men hurtled from the dark — mates waiting for the riders, no doubt. A lance took Waylon back-to-chest before he knew he was attacked. Lugh ducked a lance aimed for his neck. The attackers spurred away.

Waylon had come far. Orphan. Wolf's head. Sergeant. He had once saved Finn's life with an arrow, and on another occasion had dragged a wounded Finn to safety. Now all Waylon was, and all he could have become, was snuffed by a spear in the back wielded by a lowborn cur.

Finn took in the group — faces sunken, insides as hollow as a burned-out tree stump. Hector and Serlo and their sergeants, not knowing Waylon well, stood to the side. They stared into nothing and said nothing.

Uncle Jerol crouched and spoke to Waylon as though he were alive. Jerol's thinning hair was yellow-grey, beard more grey than yellow, his voice as grey as his hair. He spoke in a just-between-us tone before stepping back. "Order did him well."

"Well and ill. It's like the moon — waxes and wanes, depending on the week." Rollo ran a hand through long, grimy hair. "Most people discard something functional by seeking something better, only to find something worse. This was Waylon, tossing aside a crossbow to shoot with a fancy lacquered stick. Never did figure it out. But never quit trying."

Finn's mind was numb. It flailed for scripture, for holy words, but whatever it landed on felt trivial. He settled for a kiss on Waylon's linen-wrapped cheek.

Lugh squatted at Waylon's side. Rooster and Waylon, Irishman and Englishman, enemies at birth, brothers at death. They abandoned sinful pasts. Shared a joy for fighting. Hard times bonded them — deeply, and to the amused surprise of each. Lugh tugged bread and wine from a sack, hovered it over Waylon, then chewed and drank, staring intently at the linen-shrouded face as he did.

Rollo nudged Finn's elbow, nodded toward the grave. "Is now the time for a nibble?"

"Sin-eating. An Irish tradition. Waylon died unshriven. Lugh is eating his sins, absorbing them into his soul so Waylon avoids damnation."

"What do sins taste like, I wonder … chicken?"

"Brimstone." Finn dashed away a tear. "When a sin-eater dies, his soul is dragged to hell, weighted by the sins he's eaten. What Rooster does is not a thing to mock."

Rollo dipped a chin at the rebuke. After a while, Lugh heaved himself up, and tossed a handful of dirt into the grave. He strolled toward Finn with a grin and in Irish Gaelic said, "Let's give the English shite a proper send-off, eh?"

A proper send-off, for an Irishman, meant getting pissed. A Templar was allowed wine in moderation, but never to drunkenness, though how could Finn say no? Honouring a death was Gaelic tradition, shared by Gaelic folk of every stripe.

"Haven't been pissed in years," Finn said in the native tongue. "But Waylon is worth celebration and sin."

Lugh spoke Irish Gaelic and Finn spoke Scots Gaelic, and each understood the other well enough. Somehow Rollo also understood both and said, "I'll bring the elixir."

CHAPTER 11

Finn hunched in a high-backed wooden chair, heart and head as battered as the aged wood. Folk back home have a saying, 'once a year one is allowed to go crazy,' and they had. Lugh's eyes were red-rimmed and his hair, normally proud as a cock's comb, was plastered to his head. Rollo and Jerol looked no better. Drink drove off darkness, for a while, though now gloom roosted, black as a winter crow.

At least they were done with the cursed scroll and could leave Timothy behind.

Except they no longer had the scroll. Nor the translations. Nor Yosi, who lay in a fresh grave beside Waylon. Timothy had been cropsick while his friend died. He was cropsick now — would be for days, Emma said. They huddled in the Scriptorium around the now empty table. Hector laid out what had happened. The theft. The murder. Ill news worsened Finn's misery. Bad luck comes in threes, his ma often said, and he dreaded what might come next.

Adrien twisted his gold ring and stared into nothing.

The silence was crushing until Finn asked the obvious. "How? It was here. Guarded by us."

"Stolen!" Serlo said, then explained in two clipped words, "*Le Scélérat.*"

Heads came up, for Serlo speaking was such a rare event as to merit the attention of all.

"I led here. This is my fault." Hector spoke with a hint of the confessional. "*Semper vigilo*, yet I was not."

Nods and sniffs of agreement. None offered words of comfort, for failure is a bitter taste and naught can be done to better it. Finn tilted a head at Rollo as he realized something priceless had been stolen from under their noses.

"We must get it back," Finn said, despite a desire to do anything but.

"And kill the bastards that filched it," Rollo growled.

"No. We do not." Hector tore his gaze from the floor, where it had been nailed. "Well, kill them, aye. But we do not need to reclaim the scroll."

Finn waited expectantly and Hector said, "I read it — the translated parts, anyway."

"You can read?" Emma's words came out like an accusation rather than a question.

"Catalan. French. Latin. A bit of Greek and Arabic. Timothy, when he found out, put me to work transcribing."

Hector shared what had been done.

Yosi had translated the first three lines in a day. The remainder proved troublesome. Timothy and Yosi spent days debating the meaning of this or that word. Traditions. History. Meaning was enigmatic for some words and, after much bickering, these were set aside for another day. Most of the scroll was fragments; some refit, others did not. Rejoined pieces were translated when long enough to prove fruitful. In the end, Timothy pronounced they had more than half the original and, alas, to reliably translate all would take a year or more.

"You transcribed. Then you know where the gold is," Adrien said, sudden life in his voice.

"'In the ruin in the Valley of Achor, under the steps, with the entrance at the east a distance of over forty cubits, a strongbox of silver and vessels. Seventy talents by weight.' Yosi also argued it read, 'The Great Tabernacle and all its treasures,' though Timothy did not agree." Hector glanced up, sifted his memory, and recited the second line. "'In the sepulchre, in the third course of stones, one hundred ingots of gold.'" Then the third line. "'In the Mound of Kohlit, votive vessels, all flasks, and high priestly garments. And votive offerings. And the seventh treasury.'"

The words 'seventh treasury' flared in Finn's mind, then his thoughts crumbled to dust. A moment passed before he fixed an icy glare on Emma. "All this for a treasure map?"

"Treasure list," Hector corrected. "The scroll is a list of hoards. Each line describes a hiding spot, the amount, and instructions to recover it. Holy relics are also listed. Sometimes the coin and relics are together, sometimes not."

Emma tugged at an earlobe, then raised a palm to say, *There you have it.*

Finn often pondered what secrets the aged copper might hold. Esoteric teachings of Christ? A trove of obscure doctrine to bring peace between the faiths? The location of the Ark of the Covenant, perhaps? His hopes were many. Silver and gold were not among them.

"The Temple was a place of wealth," Emma said, as if reading his mind. "Vaults stored gold of the wealthy. And the Temple reserves. All Jews made an annual donation. Taxes. Tithes. Over the years it tallied up. And the relics of the Temple itself. The gold menorah. Bowls. Vessels. The gold Table of Shewbread. The treasure is enormous — measured in tons, I'd wager, and enough to make a man king many times over.

"Timothy said the text was chaotic, likely carved by an illiterate who simply mimicked words someone else wrote. The carver unknowingly took the secret of a thousand fortunes to his grave." Emma shook her head at the thought. "All done to hide the treasures from Rome. Rome had an insatiable appetite for gold — and death. Their greed —"

"You said the scroll was to be placed in the Scriptorium," Finn said, cutting her short. "That it held holy teachings. The histories of the Jews. But all along you knew what it held — boundless riches." His lips pulled back to bare teeth. "You lied."

"No. You said those things. Though I am guilty of not correcting false assumptions and withholding certain … facts." Emma stared unflinching into Finn's glare. "Besides, the scroll will reside in the Scriptorium, eventually, after we reclaim it."

Finn and Emma glared. Adrien, wisely, stayed out of the fray and toyed with his ring. Finn's head thumped a livelier tune now, if that were possible, as memories stomped their way through his foggy brain. As a near illiterate, he assumed what the scroll held, where it was bound. He felt shame for his ignorance, and for flinging the word liar, though not enough to render an apology.

"Why the … secrecy and misdirection?" Finn had almost said, *lies and deception.*

Emma offered a patient smile. "Because rumour, if spread, would have every idiot with a shovel at our heels. Fortune hunters. Scholars. Christians. Jews. Muslims."

Finn nodded to say he should have seen the obvious. Images of Beau battered his mind — the man running greasy fingers over the scroll, scowling at the ancient words. Days past Emma had explained all relic masters have scholars in their pay. No doubt Beau had planned to take it to such a scholar; Yosi and Timothy saved him the effort.

Hector seemed to read Finn's thoughts and said, "*Sapientia melior auro.*"

"Enough with the Latin, you arse," Rollo growled. "Speak a respectable tongue."

"It means wisdom is better than gold," Emma said.

"Is there a Latin saying for some folk need killing?" Rollo eased into a ray of sunlight and his face, scarred from cheek through lips to chin, was more livid than usual. "The bastards that backstabbed —" he corrected course, not wanting to dredge up the fresh pain of Waylon's death — "the bastards last night spoke French. Beau's Freelances, I'd wager. Cowards fled up the mountain, too, which means it's time to scour Arbela."

"Beau's not there anymore," Finn said.

Rollo blinked at that, then realised that none of the folk needing killing were at Arbela. Instead they were traipsing into the desert, no doubt carting shovels and picks and levers, seeking the hoard the Order commanded Finn to find. Lines remained untranslated but Beau would not waste time finding a scholar to unwrap them. No. Greed for the seventh treasury would drive him on.

Rollo spat on the travertine floor. "Bastards," he said, though it was unclear if he cursed the Order or Beau and Gaspar.

"Could be a bastard among us," Finn said, taut with anger and despair. He had dealt with traitors before, Robert of Saint Albans and Ulmer of Rothenburg, and the notion of sniffing out another was another kick to the gut. "But who?"

"Not us." Rollo jabbed a finger at Baret, then Watt. "Must be one of these laggards."

Baret, having heard it all before, shook his head wearily. Watt tried his best to look offended. Emma nudged Adrien and he leaned to slap a palm on the table. "Not so! These men have been loyal to me for years. Many years. I trust them with my life."

Fire was in Adrien's voice — fire not there before. Finn studied him, dull of mind and soft of body, and wondered what Emma saw in such a weakling. Then a wry grin flashed on Adrien's lips and his eyes moved with sudden purpose. Both fled quick as hares.

He thinks this is a game, a grand adventure, thought Finn.

Hector cleared his throat and gestured toward a window. "I examined the walls. Drains. Gates. Spoke to the guards. Nothing suggests an inside man. But several clues suggest a thief snuck in. Tracks near the sally port. More along the outside wall. *Le Scélérat* employs at least one ruffian skilled at breaking into well-guarded places, I should think."

"You are skilled at speculation, Brother." Rollo made a scoffing sound. "Tell me how a thief skulked his way to the Scriptorium without help? Blind luck?"

"Ingbald." Finn spat the name. "Nadal said Ingbald was chaplain here, years ago, before expulsion. He'd know the way. Beau rented him from Gaspar." Finn made an amused sound. "Gaspar had no notion what the scroll contains. Thinks it's just tedious old sermons. Considers himself a fox to be paid twice for the same useless relic."

Hector nodded to cede Finn's points. "Probably. But for sure God would not bring us this far only to deny us now. He tests our faith and we must not be undone."

Jesus was undone by thirty pieces of silver.

Evil has not one name but many. Greed is one. Betrayal another. And often such sins walked hand-in-hand with riches. Wealth did not matter to Finn — one cannot serve God and gold. But greed-sickness afflicted many. Too many. The notion words scribed on copper had loosed a plague burned; he shoved it aside knowing his mind, battered by Waylon and wine, lacked the vigour to work it through.

Cold lingered, despite the warm day, and Finn shivered. *Evil hides in all this.* He signed the cross and sat up straight. "Where do we seek?"

"In the Valley of Achor." Hector rolled a wrist to say the riddle was unwound. "The scroll describes three hoards. In ruins. In a cistern. And a sepulchre. I patrolled Achor when riding with brother Fulk. We steered clear of the lauras. Hermits are lonely folk. They'll talk your ear off. But there are the ruins of a fortress, Hyrcania. Saint Sabas built a monastery at Hyrcania — Castellion, now called Marda. There are cisterns. A sepulchre too."

"Visited Marda once … I think." Jerol frowned, struggling to remember.

"Wonderful story, Uncle," Rollo said, after it became apparent the tale had been told in its entirety. "Endlessly entertaining."

Finn pondered what he knew of Achor — which, like Jerol, was not much. It was near the Judean Desert. Bedouins roam there. Bandits too. Lauras, clusters of caves, scattered here and there. Hermits seek God in the solitude. He realized everyone was staring at him.

"Rooster," Finn shouted. "Get your lazy arse in here."

His sergeant hustled in and snapped to attention. "Brother."

"Pack kit for the desert. Water. Food. Fodder. Spare mounts."

Emma shifted to Baret. "Ensure we also carry what is needed."

"We? No." Rollo shook his head, setting his chest-length beard asway. "You've been escorted and now we ride into a dangerous place on a new task. You will be an anchor around our necks. Leave hard things to those who can do them."

"I will not leave off," Emma snapped. "I will care for myself, as always, and will 'anchor' no one. Besides, you have made a muddle of the 'hard things' so far. You might need a woman to sort them out for you."

Rollo snorted. "Somewhere I hear the lonesome cry of needlepoint in need of needling."

Emma glared at Adrien, who answered with a bemused smile, then she leaned to stab a finger at Rollo. "I will not suffer your —"

"Cease — both of you," Finn said. He recited the Master's command. "Follow Adrien's direction. Protect Adrien and Emma. Seek what is named in the Copper Scroll."

Rollo stared before muttering, "God's bones, not into the Judean with a woman."

Finn gave a sympathetic nod, then to Lugh said, "And bring shovels and spades."

"Good idea," Rollo said, tone still bitter. "We'll need them to dig Beau's grave — and to dig ourselves out of whatever mess we make."

"*Semper in excretia sumus solim profundum variat.*" Hector smiled at Rollo in defiance. "It means we're always in the shite, only the depth varies."

They laughed, short and sour, though at least it hinted of a turn toward better days. Few wanted to blunder around a sun-blasted desert chasing myths and rumours. But neither did they suffer theft lightly, nor would the death of a brother go unpunished. They would hunt Beau and pity the ugly bastard when they caught him. To succeed they would trust in their wits, their meanness, and in God — as always.

The Judean was a harsh place. A place where mad or holy men seek spiritual richness in the sparseness. Enlightenment through hermitage is a long tradition going back to the ancient prophets. Elijah. John the Baptist. Jesus spent forty days and nights there, and on the Mountain of Temptation found the Devil waiting to try him.

First, a trial of a different sort awaited — a trial on the Temple Mount.

Does God want this?

Finn dropped to his prayer bones at the edge of the Foundation Stone. Thereon, in days gone by, the prophet Abraham had stood and the Ark of the Covenant had rested. He knelt at the junction of heaven and earth to pray. Mingled aromas teased. Incense of sandalwood, wisteria, and agar. Musty rock. Old wine. But words eluded him. Meditation was no salve.

They had ridden from Tiberias to Jericho in two days. The Jordan River, a ribbon of green surrounded by browns and tans, meandered a sluggish path from the Sea of Galilee to the Dead Sea. The ride was pleasant. Days in the saddle. Nights camped along the river. They passed where John baptized Jesus, and Finn called a halt. Rollo sat in the shade of a white poplar and waved Finn on to his strange habit, which Rollo saw often enough to indulge.

Alone, Finn walked the river's edge until he found a spot, away from the pilgrims and gawkers. He stripped. Waded in. Revelled in the warm, muddy water. Welcomed the mud between his toes. He floated a while. Pondered recent days, and why he had come to Outremer, and what remained to be done. He arose with a spirit renewed by the simple ritual.

They weaved their way through the herds of sun-burned pilgrims migrating to-and-from the Jordan and Jericho. From Jericho it was a short ride to Jerusalem, where he now knelt within the Dome of the Rock.

The detour seemed sensible. Fresh mounts were needed. Finn also assumed it wise to apprise the Master. He was wrong. Gerard arrived red-faced — so red that Finn wondered if the man had fallen asleep in the sun. He grew redder still when Finn told him the scroll was stolen. To Finn's shame, Gerard cut him off, berated him for being in the city rather than in the desert. Failing his task. Wasting precious time.

So much for a renewed spirit. Gerard's rebukes battered him further; "Recover the scroll. Find what it describes. Fail and you will spend the remainder of your days chopping wood, perhaps milking cows, but certainly labouring somewhere lonely and cold and miserable."

"Saint Mary, intercede for me…" Finn sensed someone and the prayer dribbled off.

Brother Urs of Alneto stood there. Urs was new to the role of Seneschal, the Master's right-hand man, but he was a salt of the Order. Templars showed a humble mien. Sun-browned faces and unwashed bodies were marks of a salted man. Urs took this practice to extremes. An eye had been misplaced somewhere along the way. The puckered hole was uncovered, worn with pride, and he dared others to look away or complain of his stench.

Urs sat on the edge of the stone. The abyss into the Well of Souls yawned near his hip.

"Priests say that hollow," Urs jutted his chin at a dent in the stone, "was made by the Angel Gabriel. He held the stone when it tried to rise to heaven. And that," he nodded at a gash, "was made by a pilgrim, who hacked out a chunk and carted it home to decorate his mantel."

"Arse."

"Gabriel or the pilgrim?" Urs chuckled at his lame jest, then fixed Finn with his sky-blue eye. "You try the Master's patience, Brother."

Finn made no reply and Urs smiled, likely to soothe the humiliation of Finn's recent arse-chewing, though the gaps and few remaining brown teeth made the smile anything but soothing. "Have Gerard's rebukes eased?"

"Eased?" Finn made a scoffing noise. "I came to the stone to cool my head. But as I ponder his *rebukes*, I think I shall go mad — madder. The Master scolds me yet says nothing useful. I'm told nothing. Know nothing. Yet the Order's prospects, evidently, depend on my ignorant deeds." He breathed out, then with a burst of bitterness said, "I cannot abide it."

Urs gave a sympathetic nod. "Those above assume those below are dullards. Always have." He eased closer. "Gerard says field brothers are like mushrooms — best kept in the dark and fed shite. But I don't savour the taste of shite. Nor do you, I see. So. I will share what Gerard refuses you, and you in turn will feign ignorance in Gerard's presence. Agreed?"

Finn nodded once, tried not to stare at the pink chasm where Urs's eye had once resided.

"Gerard holds a wet finger to the breeze. And it tells him change is coming." Urs glanced over a shoulder, though from habit Finn noted, for he checked the side lacking an eye. "King Baldwin will not see ten years, I fear, and Guy manoeuvres to catch the crown when it falls."

"King Guy?" Finn shook his head in disgust. "We're Templars. We don't grovel before kings, nor need their favour."

"There is advantage in favour, much as there is advantage in change. He who shifts course quickest wins." The Seneschal sighed to say how much he longed for the simpler days as a field brother. "We guard pilgrims. Defend Outremer. But Gerard would make us more about the land, less about the pilgrims."

Finn held his tongue; Urs carried on in a wooden tone.

"Guy and the Order made an allegiance. Baldwin and Raymond oppose us and the Hospitallers are in league with them. There is a truce between Christians and Muslims, and Christians ready for war among themselves. Lord against lord. Order against order."

Christians came years past, and with sword and spear, and united in the cause, carved out the Kingdom of Jerusalem — the Kingdom of Heaven. Now they fight over it rather than fighting to preserve it, snapping at each other's throats like wolves fighting over the better bits of a carcass.

Memories prodded — Guy, his pointy boots, the haughty sneer. Jean's tight-lipped misery. A scheme had been afoot in Saforie; now it was unravelling in Finn's lap. Guy, with Gerard's hand on his back, sought allies to heft him to the throne.

The Order would make an arse in pointed boots King of Jerusalem.

And the kingdom will crumble. Finn signed the cross at the thought.

Urs said, "Brothers, bankers mostly, support the alliance. They, like Gerard, seek more, and to a banker *more* means putting coin into the purse that gives the largest return. And there is no better return than dancing cheek-and-jowl with a king."

The Seneschal fixed his one-eyed gaze on Finn.

"But here is the rub — making kings is not our charge. The Holy Father would censure Gerard. Force the council to replace him. Father spies on the Master, as always, and Gerard must walk a knife's edge between Father and Templar factions. The warriors, as I call them, would inform on Gerard just to put his mantle on one of their own."

"Bankers. Warriors." Finn spat, remembered where he sat, and rubbed off the spittle with the sole of his boot. "There are two orders, then?"

"There are orders within the order. There are rituals, rites, you are yet to see. I have just seen some myself." Urs wagged a hand to say he had said too much. "Much is at stake, is my point. War looms. The kingdom teeters. Do you grasp your role in righting it?"

"No, Seneschal. I'm a lowly field brother. What do I bring?"

"Gold! Kings are made with coin but Guy has none. The bankers could loan him, of course, though such a grand sum would catch the Holy Father's eye — and his wrath. Thus the money must be untraceable." Awe softened his tone. "Then manna fell into Gerard's lap. God showed us the way. The Master took the scroll as a holy portent, which certainly it is, and enacts His will."

Urs stared into the Well of Souls. Finn could hear the soft hiss of oil lamps. In the near silence he imagined the prophet Abraham scowling from the shadows.

The Seneschal patted the Foundation Stone. "Grandfather fought to take this in '99. Jews and Saracens stood side-by-side to defend it. Can you fathom that?"

"Need makes odd bedmates," Finn said, and Urs nodded in agreement.

"Thousands died. Men. Women. Children. Heads piled in pyramids. Streets ran with blood. A dark stain on Christendom, though Grandfather said darkness was needed to bring the light." Urs's voice was cold. "Hunting gold is a stain on us, I grant you. Pairing with Guy is another. But sometimes we must do ugly things. And you are a doer of ugly things. Things that bring notoriety but not acclaim."

Finn thought, *I understand my role now, and I preferred being kept in the dark and fed shite.*

Pieces clicked into place in his head, like the gears of some mysterious machine aligning. The Order was in union with Guy the Arse. Finn, the doer of ugly tasks, hunted wealth to fund the new King of Jerusalem. Guy, not sharp of mind, would be the Order's puppet and the puppet master, Gerard, would pull the strings. Gerard came to Outremer seeking land and now he would have it, all of it, and carve out a slice of gold pie too.

Change is coming, Urs had said.

The notion turned Finn's insides sour. Life before the Order had been chaotic and brutal. When he joined, he found a home, with purpose, and stability. It was like he was a rough stone, chiselled and shaped into a block and mortared into an immovable wall, where he would stay until he died or retired. But it was unsettling to find the new not so different than the old, to again have unsavoury tasks placed before him. Being a bone hunter … the agent of change … was more unsettling still.

Urs heaved himself up with a grunt. "Brothers tell me you are quick — snake quick. You will need quickness to see this through."

"Quickness means life," Finn said, climbing to his feet. "A Bavarian swordmaster taught me speed is gained by mastering a move gently. Feed skill with practice. Let it grow with training and use and it will grow quicker still."

Urs tapped his temple. "I meant quick here."

Finn, not used to thinking of himself as deep-minded, dipped an embarrassed chin.

"Now that I ponder, the notion of blade work appeals, and I should like to spar when you return. See what mayhem a one-eyed old man and a swordmaster can make." Urs spoke wistfully, perhaps because of age, maybe because his dance partner might not meet the date.

"I would enjoy a bout," Finn said. "But don't wait for me if I'm late."

CHAPTER 12

Sun and heat and dust.

A short ride from Jerusalem and they were at the lip of the Judean Desert, riding toward what Hector assured them was the Valley of Achor. The landscape was naked of green, mountains worn to bones by eons of wind. Once-in-a-decade deluges carved runnels off the bare, brown slopes. Furrows gouged their way down until merging with the deep wadis that wound across the land in endless loops. Drought ruled here, more so lately, and it was hard to imagine enough rain ever fell to carve those ravines.

Rollo took it in and spat. "What a hellhole."

"Hellhole?" Baret fixed Rollo with an outraged stare. "This is Jesus's land!"

"It's a dead land. Hot. Barren. Spiders the size of your fist. My only joy is the work."

"Which is?"

"Killing heathens."

"Might get some joy soon." Finn pointed toward a swirl of black crosses riding the sky beyond a distant ridge. The birds wheeled in a revolving column. He shook a head. *Birds … always birds marking trouble…*

Finn squinted over a shoulder. Emma and Adrien rode amid Baret and seven guards — Poulains, local-born Franks. Adrien had hired them in Jerusalem while Finn had taken his lumps from the Master. They were a cruel-looking batch, men-at-arms, and a semi-reformed brigand or two. One was Jeph, Watt's brother, a burly man with a reputation for violence.

Elias and Nik waited in the shade of a boulder. They chewed saltbush leaves, salty and savoury, and Elias pointed at the wheeling birds with a stalk. "Bit of a mess over yonder."

Knights and sergeants, unbidden, dismounted and began tugging weapons free. They formed into a loose line — except Rollo, who stood by his horse, muttering and bobbing his head in apparent indecision between great sword or axe. Every knight carried a great sword, arming sword, and mace or axe, and every knight was effortlessly adept with each.

Finn watched, bemused. "You're like a lady dressing for a ball. Can we get on with it?"

"Don't rush me, arse." Rollo waited a defiant moment, then yanked free the great sword. The blade measured three fingers wide at the guard and was as long as a man's leg, the handle built to fit both of Rollo's slab hands. "A craftsman needs the right tool for the task."

They waited and sweated while Watt and Baret spanned crossbows. Adrien's toughs did their best to look the part.

With a nod from Finn, his group prowled forward, slow and smooth, like a cat stalking a bird. They crept up and onto the ridge. On the other side, a splash of green marked a spring, burbling up from the base of the rock. Beyond lay a scatter of tents. A creak of wood echoed mournfully. The dead lay scattered or heaped. Skin-necked vultures hopped and hissed over the banquet.

Finn made a fist and held it out from his side to say, *line abreast*, then signalled *forward* with open and splayed fingers. They ghosted through the empty camp, slowing to peek inside a tent, to shift a hump of this or that with a boot tip. Flies swirled up in droning black clouds. The stench of rotten fruit and rancid meat seeped through Finn's shemagh. The creaking wood came, faded, and he twitched at the noise. Ahead, a brown foot poked from a tent, conspicuous for the pale bands marking where silver bangles had once beautified the ankle.

He shuffled to Lugh, who fought a losing battle with a buzzard. The bird defended its supper by flaring its wings and clacking a gory beak.

"Careful, Rooster," Finn said. "When threatened a buzzard will projectile vomit its last meal."

Lugh grunted to say he wanted none of that and wheeled to Finn. "Bedouins. Old men. Women. Children. Butchered, all of them." He nodded toward the ridge. "Hoofprints in a line. They charged in a conroi. A few Bedouins made a stand but died all the same. Others…"

Rollo used the tip of his great sword to lift aside a tent flap, peered within, then recoiled from whatever he saw.

Finn gazed over the bloated corpses. Bedouins came here for lifegiving water, as had generations of their ancestors, but found only death. Their ghosts flitted about, even now, no doubt wondering where the heat had gone and why the sun had dimmed.

"Beau," Finn said in a low growl. "Has to be. What would make him turn his dogs loose?"

"Distempered." Rollo tapped a finger to his helmeted head. "Up here."

Protecting pilgrims is why Finn came to Outremer. To gain absolution through service. It did not matter, to him at least, that these tent-dwellers were not Christians — they had done him no wrong. Some men, perhaps after too much time steeped in war, grow obsessed with slaughter. Men or women. Young or old. Made no difference when the head sickness took hold. These predators of common folk needed to be snuffed out, before their illness spread and more innocents died.

But a Templar took a vow not to lay a hand on a fellow Christian, which made snuffing rabid Christian dogs … complicated.

Rollo seemed to read Finn's mind. "Killing Christians is a sin."

"Then we sin and ask forgiveness later." Finn spoke calmly, like a dinner guest asking someone to pass the bread, though his voice was cold and hard.

Hector and Serlo came up and Serlo said, "We fight Christians only in self-defence."

Rollo huffed, which made Serlo scowl, then the four knights shared a dismayed look as a realization came upon them — no one could be left alive to spread the tale of temple treasures, Christian or not. That dark thought settled a while.

Hector spoke softly. "*Caedite eos. Novit enim Dominus qui sunt eius.*"

"More God-damned Latin," Rollo said, and jabbed a finger at Hector. "I'm going to beat your arse —"

"It means kill them, for the Lord knows those who are his."

Hospitallers waited further down the road. Circling buzzards had drawn them to investigate, much as the dead had drawn the birds. Two knights led a pack of sergeants and Turcs. Knights sat on their mounts, dark and sombre in their black cappas marked with white crosses.

Hospitallers and Templars camped rope-to-rope when on campaign. They quarrelled often, as siblings do, and there was as much bad blood between them as good. The Holy Father gifted Templars his blessing to guard pilgrims and fight God's enemies; Hospitallers were founded to provide medical care to pilgrims and only later took up arms. Finn often jested the

Templars, as the older and favoured sibling, suffered Hospitaller jealously.

The lead rider scowled at the knights, affronted to find them riding his road. The man was squat as a boar and wearing a battered nasal helmet wrapped with checkered linen. He pasted a hand to the swaddled rim. "God's blessings, Brothers. I am Brother Bernard."

"God's blessings to you. I'm Brother Finnláech."

Bernard's bushy brow arched, and the brow said Finn's reputation was known among the Hospitallers. Hunting an apostate brother was a hard task and the task itself bloody beyond measure. Such a deed made other knights scowl and rub their chins, pondering what they would have done in Finn's place — and how their skills matched with the man that snuck into an enemy camp, knifed the boss, then strolled away with the camp in flames.

Finn jigged a thumb over a shoulder. "Bedouins. Camped at a spring. All dead."

Bernard grimaced to say he was not surprised, though fretted all the same. He flipped a weary hand and sergeants and Turcs rode on to investigate for themselves.

"Who did it, do you suppose?" Bernard studied the rocky ground around them, as if expecting to see the fiends peaking over a hill.

"Other Bedouins? They're always biting and gouging for the best watering holes. Some nurse decades-old blood feuds." Inwardly Finn cringed at how greasily the lie came off his tongue.

"Bedouins creep north, as of late. Tribes shove other tribes out of the Negev Desert and the displaced shift into the Judean." Bernard stared before shrugging to say, *No matter, we will sort out the details.* "We are not far from the House. Will you accept our hospitality for the night?"

Campfires lit the courtyard of Bait Jubr at-Tahtani — called the House. The House sat on an outcrop south of the road from Jerusalem to the Jordan River. It boasted a fortified tower and walls made of rough-hewn ashlars enclosing a central courtyard and two-level keep. A rock-cut moat, dry as a bone, surrounded the walls. The rock hacked out to form the ditch was used to make the walls. Two banners of Hospitallers were stationed here.

Templars huddled near sputtering fires of camel dung and ate air-dried meat and horsebread washed down with water from the castle's cistern. Adrien and Emma sat away from the firelight, foreheads close together, conversing in whispers. Emma's eyes narrowed to slits; Adrien slid a hand to her cheek and murmured "Lambkin."

The sight fuelled an irrational — and unexpected — surge of … what? Anger? Jealously? Finn looked away.

"This is the famed Hospitaller hospitality." Rollo spat. "I find it lacking."

A shadow weaved through the fires toward Finn, and he nodded toward it. "We may be in for a treat." The shadow was a squire come to invite Finn, and when he stood Hector grumbled about Hospitaller generosity not extending to everyone.

Finn and Rollo found the Hospitaller banner leader in the lower keep, head dipped in prayer over a scarred table. Bernard sat at the man's side and nodded amicably at Finn. They waited while the balding head prayed. Its owner raised up and signed the cross in a crisp flurry born of decades of habit. He was lean, fiercely bearded, with a face hardened by sun and war.

"I am Eudo of Yvoire," the man said, raising to his feet. He gestured at empty chairs. "You are Brother Finnláech, I assume, and you must be Brother Rollo."

Finn returned a half-nod to say Eudo had it right. A battered pitcher stood on the table, and Bernard did Finn and Rollo the honour of pouring watered wine into equally battered cups.

"You are a Scot," Eudo said, a statement rather than question. He angled his face to study Finn. "I heard Scots paint their faces blue. Before a fight."

"We do?" Finn said, amused. For the first time in years he was conscious of the Gaelic lilt in his French. "Why would we do that?"

"To frighten your foes. Not true?"

Finn, grinning now, shook his head, and Rollo said, "Finn is more frightening without face paint — just look at that scarred pan!"

They laughed, and Eudo shot Bernard a look, confirming a wager had been settled. Eudo, the loser, sighed heavily. "The Bedouins," he said. "What a nasty business, no?"

Finn made a show of sipping his cup, hoping silence would say he had no opinion worth sharing.

"Our Turcs reported the brutes wielded lances. Charged in a conroi. Took no prisoners. Not the way of bandits or Bedouin." Eudo was musing aloud, expecting Finn would chime in, and when he did not Eudo asked the obvious, "What do you make of that?"

"Rogue Saracens sometimes cross the Jordan. They'd have a go at Bedouins."

"Could be. But we hear rumour of Freelances in the area. I wonder if they would do such a thing?" Eudo rolled out the bait and let it dangle. Finn declined and Eudo shifted course.

"Not often are we blessed by visitors, especially our brothers from the Temple. What brings you to the Judean?"

"Escorting a lord, Adrien of Acre, who seeks passage to the monastery at Marda." Finn had concocted the story, and though it was not the entire truth, neither was it an entire lie, and in that he took a measure of comfort.

Eudo nodded as if he suspected as much. "His wife too?"

Emma was swathed in Bedouin robes of blue and the Hospitallers had not given her a second glance — or so Finn thought. "Aye," he said. "Taking a woman into the Judean. Can you fathom it? What a pain in the arse."

Eudo cinched his eyes at Finn's crassness, and if he thought it odd a woman travelled with Templars, he did not press it. A squire brought a pitcher of wine, unwatered, and Finn raised a cup to Hospitaller generosity. They chatted. Swapped tales of arrogant nobles, ignorant pilgrims, and the woes of keeping either from harming themselves or others.

Finn, after touching the cup to his lip several times, made a show of slurring the odd word. Eudo and Bernard shared side glances when Finn interrupted his own sentence about the virtues of destriers to start another about his preference for heater shields.

Rollo slapped the table with a palm. "What do you say?"

"We say the Temple obtained a priceless relic," Eudo said, striking like lightning from a clear sky. "True?"

Finn gave a low sigh and used a finger to push the cup away, wine sloshing untouched. It was as he feared. Rumour spread like a plague on the air. In Eudo he saw something he was beginning to detest — the devious eyes of someone trying to parse out if the whispers of the Copper Scroll were true, and if so, what secrets it held. Eudo, in a bid to ferret it out, had even resorted to unwatered wine in an attempt to loosen tongues.

"We recovered enough of Saint Peter's bones to rebuild the man," Finn said in a flat and sober voice. "Oh, and the Holy Grail, and the Ark of the Covenant."

"They are glorious to behold," Rollo said.

Eudo's stare was icy, then he smiled wide enough for teeth to show.

Once, in the bazaar in Jaffa, Finn had teased a monkey with an apple. The monkey smiled to show teeth, which Finn thought strange. Then he realized a monkey smiles when it is angry. Eudo's smile was a monkey's smile.

"God is not mocked, Brother," Eudo said.

"Sometimes He is. The Lord and I share a playful relationship, at times." Finn gave a monkey grin of his own. "But for sure Templars are not mocked. Not by you. Not by anyone."

Eudo eased back and raised a hand in a gesture of peace. "Forgive my impertinence, Brother. I forget how testy you Templars get over questions of relics."

Finn nodded sombrely. "Just so, Brother. Our testiness is not without cause, you see, for we are vowed to holy duties and bone stealing is not among them. Tales of relics are just that — tales. But such gossip, repeated often enough, becomes a false truth."

"A false truth." Eudo nodded to say he had heard a false truth or two himself, a few this very night, then looked to Bernard. "I like that. Well said. Don't you agree, Brother?"

Bernard gave a brisk tip of the head but his unflinching gaze never left Finn's.

They talked a while longer about things banal. Every so often Eudo fished for answers he was not going to get. In the end, Finn and Rollo went back to their sputtering fires of camel dung, leaving Eudo and his monkey smile.

"Bastard tried to loosen our tongues with wine. Wasted his grape though."

Rollo's swaying gait said not all of it had gone to waste. "You're getting good at lying," he said with only a slight slur.

"Being less than honest, I call it. For a good cause. Do you think they swallowed it?"

"No. Though Eudo's none the wiser for trying."

"Wonderful," Finn said in a dull voice. *Coming here was a mistake. Now Le Scélérat lurks somewhere ahead while suspicious Hospitallers linger behind.*

In the morning they rode on.

Neither Eudo nor Bernard offered blessings of safe travel.

CHAPTER 13

A soft clacking of a wooden spoon on a wooden bowl. A shadow shifted in the darkness — the Traitor.

"Hungry?" Robert asked, and from habit Finn understood he was being proffered a wooden bowl half full of pottage.

He accepted their shared bowl and tasted bitter ash.

"I killed you," Finn said, and Robert nodded.

"You killed Sigric and deserved the same," Finn said, and Robert nodded again.

Silence but for the soft clacking of wood on wood.

"What is Jesus like, and Mary?"

Robert shifted and his eyes glowed in the dark like burning blue embers. "Never met them. I hear good things, though."

The wood in Finn's hands turned cold and heavy, and he looked down to see the Copper Scroll. And in his palm shimmered a mist, and therein a man, lean and dusky, hunched over a table chiselling at a sheet of copper. The chiselling went on in a rhythmic tick-tick-tick. The hand of the scribe was firm and sure.

"It was made to save the covenant from impure hands," Robert said. "You had it. You must find it. You must protect it from those who would misuse it."

"The treasure?"

"Not that."

"Then what?"

Robert's blue ember eyes were unblinking and Finn recoiled from them.

"The law, fool," Robert said. "It is holy to God, and to His people, and shall not be revealed until the day of the coming of the Messiah. These things will be delivered into the hands of the angels Shamshiel and Michael and Gabriel."

The blue embers glowed.

"What is impure shall be made pure, what is risen shall fall, and in the last days the earth will raise the Mishkan to meet the heavens."

Finn asked, "Why do you, a grievous sinner, speak of holy things?"

"Who better?"

Finn fell silent. His hands were suddenly free of wood or copper.

"Tell me, sinner, what is hell like?"

"You will find out yourself, someday. Who am I to ruin the surprise?"

Robert laughed and was gone.

Finn jolted awake with Lugh crouched at his side. The sergeant stared and Finn jutted a chin for him to speak.

"A Bedouin came. He seeks a word with our chief. That'd be you."

Finn sat up in his bedroll, twisted at his waist to work out the kinks, then climbed to his feet. Yellow and pink coloured the horizon as he staggered to the smouldering fire.

Rollo glanced up. "Morning. I see Shabh failed again."

Finn snorted his reply, and his gaze swept their camp, tucked against a spine of rocks.

Uncle sat near the fire kneading coarse flour mixed with salt and water. Nik slapped dough back and forth between his palms to flatten it, then dropped it to hot stones to bake. Adrien's men-at-arms lazed in their bedrolls, and beyond sergeants tended horses or dressed for the day. Mail hauberks were shrouded in flowing robes to cover the metal from the sun. Linen wrapped their heads and their helmets hung from cantles.

Lugh plopped warm bread into Finn's palm and tapped pieces of meat from the tip of a knife to the bread. "Elias and Nik shot hares last night. Cooked them the Bedouin way."

The Bedouin way was to cut the hare into pieces, stuff the pieces back into their own skins, and bake them overnight in a pit filled with hot embers and covered in sand.

"Where is the Bedouin?" he asked Lugh.

"Outside camp. Elias says he is being polite, waiting to be invited in."

"And why hasn't he been invited?"

Shrugs and blank faces answered, and after wolfing down his breakfast of bread and hare, Finn trailed Elias to where a robed figure sat cross-legged. Two other robed figures stood a dozen paces behind, holding flea-bitten camels. The largest beast glared at Finn, measuring the distance he could spit and daring Finn to come closer.

"That one wants to put his teeth on you, Boss." Elias nodded toward the glaring beast. "There are one-hundred names for Allah, men say, but only ninety-nine are known. Camels are the only creature who know the one-hundredth name, and therefore they wear haughty faces and look down their noses. I say —"

Finn caught Elias's elbow to silence him.

Adrien and Watt and Jeph sat before the Bedouin, their backs to Finn. He listened a moment, ear cocked, and to his surprise heard Adrien speaking fluent Arabic. Adrien and the Bedouin chatted in a smooth flow augmented by the occasional hand wave. The Bedouin sketched a map in the sand with a stick before smearing it away. Watt, sensing eyes, peeked over a shoulder and his hand went to Adrien's wrist. Conversation staggered to a stop. Adrien arose, swiped dirt off his arse, then ambled toward Finn.

"What did he say?" Finn asked.

"Alas, I hardly understood a word," Adrien said. "Thought he might speak French. Some Bedouins do. But not this one."

Finn dipped a chin at the poorly told lie as Adrien sauntered past.

The Bedouin was swathed in sky-blue robes. A sun-faded head wrap framed a face taut and brown and creased as old leather. Blue swirls and dotted lines marked his hands and face. Ink marks showed on Finn's wrist, and seeing them the Bedouin beamed like he had met an old friend. But fierceness dozed behind that smile.

Finn nodded amicably and sent Lugh to bring salt and bread, the symbols of earth and life. It is impolite to sit with the soles of your boots facing a Bedouin because soles are unclean, so Finn sat cross-legged, and the Bedouin nodded once to acknowledge the simple courtesy.

"*Marhaba*," Finn said, the Arabic word for welcome.

"*Marhaban bik*," the old man said with a grin that showed more gap than tooth. He launched into a stream of Arabic. Finn, drowning in the flood of words, held up a hand and tilted a head toward Elias. The Bedouin shifted to Elias and the flow resumed.

"His name is Saleh Mehedi Saleh abu-Tayi al-Huwaytat," Elias translated.

The first word was the Bedouin's name, the others the names of his father, grandfather, clan, and tribe.

"Saleh," Finn said. He offered a solemn nod at Saleh's lengthy name and tapped his chest. "Finnláech of Clan Donnachaidh, son of Ewen MacDuncan of Struan, who was son of Duncan MacEanric."

Elias rolled his eyes. Saleh laughed and said, "Finn," then ambled through a speech of some length.

"He says this spring is warmer than most," Elias said after a while. "Soon the hot season will be upon us, the time when travellers must lay up in the shade by day and move in the evening, when it is cool. To do otherwise invites disaster."

Finn nodded courteously while Saleh ploughed on.

Elias listened, nodded, translated. "He sees we hang water skins from our horses. This makes the water warm. He advises we bury skins in the sand. The desert grows cold at night, as you know, and by morning the water will be chilled."

Finn kept the smile but tilted a head toward Elias, "Why does he speak of weather and water?"

"He is being polite. And he fears you."

Saleh chattered politely, working his way toward whatever had brought him here, like a sailor edging around a hard wind in an endless series of zigzags. They ate bread and drank tepid water from wooden cups. After many a nod and smile, Elias finally said, "He asks if we saw children of *Al Khamsa* in the camp of the dead."

Al Khamsa. The Five. Even a Faranji like Finn grasped the meaning of *Al Khamsa*, the five mares of Mohammed, and the mythical founders of the five breeds of Arabian horse.

Finn scrunched his brows at Elias. "He asks after horses?"

Elias's curt nod said there is no better cause than a horse, and Finn said, "Tell him hoofprints led away but we saw no animals."

Elias spoke and Saleh rattled off something through clenched teeth.

"He asks what else?"

The air grew heavy. Muscles bulged at the corners of Saleh's bearded jaw. Finn shared the ugly bits — the dead, their age, their gender.

Saleh nodded sombrely, and when he spoke his voice was near a whisper.

"Kin of his lived in that band. Sister. Nieces." Elias flinched from whatever else Saleh said and checked over a shoulder.

"What did he say?" Finn prodded.

Elias came back with a flat stare, then whispered, "*Jinn*. One is at work here, Saleh says. Drove men to madness, for only madmen would murder women and children." He stared off a moment. "I knew a man driven mad by a *Jinn*. He ate sand like it were bread. Spoke in strange tongues. Lured my father into a cave. Tried to knife him."

"Who was the *Jinn*-madman?"

"My uncle."

Allah created angels from light, man from mud, and *Jinni* from smokeless fire. The people of the smokeless fire haunt desolate places and can shapeshift or possess the weak. A man can recognize them by their hooves and the fire in their eyes — literal fire burned there. Elias had an innate fear of them. Once, Finn might have mocked Elias's heathen foolishness, but now he gave a sympathetic sigh. Elias once thought Shabh a *Jinn* — and maybe he was right.

"Tell Saleh Freelances did the deed," Finn said.

Elias translated. Saleh fingered the curved *khanja* knife in his belt and spewed vitriol over a shoulder. The robed figures jabbered maledictions of their own. The words were muddled but their meaning clear — blood vengeance was demanded among the Bedouin, as it was among Finn's kin.

"Ask him the way to the Valley of Achor," Finn said.

Elias asked and came back with a scowl. "He asks which Valley of Achor."

"What?"

"He says there are three valleys named Achor."

Finn blinked, then groaned.

Saleh shared the ways to the Achors, even sketched maps in the sand, all while gesturing and flailing like a conjurer at a fair. For a while Saleh and Elias appeared to debate where the sun rose and set. By the end, Finn had a better lay of the land, but felt no better for it.

Bedouin and Templar thanked the other for his hospitality. Now Saleh stood by the glaring camel, a breeze tugging at his tattered robe, ink-marked face raised to the sky in a pose of bliss. A sudden notion filled Finn's head — a long line of folk like Saleh, each practicing an ancient lifeway, each living close to the ground in a way unchanged since time out of mind. The life-giving skills in Saleh's head were passed to him by generations before and those skills, ever at peril of loss, were more precious than gold.

"Saleh is master here," Finn said. "I thought this place a wasteland of dirt and stones. None wanted it, except for the rare good parts, and the tent-dwellers could have the bad parts without a fight. Now I see this ground is as noble as any. Barren and hot, sure, but with a beauty all its own."

"I'll take cool, green hills any day, I will." Lugh snorted a mirthless laugh. "So. Over which part of this lovely ground do we ride, and to which Achor?"

Sun and heat sucked the life from them. Shade was a precious commodity and they huddled in the lee of the rocky spine. Finn shared out what Saleh had told him — a Valley of Achor north of Jericho, so named by the Jews; a Valley of Achor near Wadi Qelt; and a Valley of Achor north-west of the Dead Sea. Some said Achor was one long valley extending from Jericho to the Dead Sea, though Saleh insisted that was nonsense.

Rollo's head shot up. "Wait, you're saying there are three valleys named Achor?"

Finn nodded and Hector shrugged an apology. "News to me."

"Names of places here are ever shifting," Elias said. "Depends on who controls the land. Jews. Christians. Muslims. Often, places have several at once, depending on the speaker. Most are on a third name — maybe fourth soon, if the Mongols invade."

"This quest is cursed," Rollo moaned, and others nodded in agreement — except Adrien, who smirked from the shadow of a rock and twisted the gold ring on his little finger.

"Missteps are expected," Finn said. "So. We'll ride to Dead Sea-Achor and poke around the ruins. See what they're about. If we don't find what we seek, we backtrack to Jericho-Achor and search, then to Wadi Qelt-Achor, if need be."

Hector nodded. "Seems simple, said like that."

"Let's go to work," Finn said, and made to rise.

"Ah, but you are forgetting something, Brother Finn." Adrien grinned and a mad light glinted in his eye not dimmed by the shadow.

"Aye?"

"I lead. Not you." Adrien waited until all eyes were on him, then made a show of slipping the parchment from his purse and waving it. "You are the muscle. Naught more. So says Master Gerard. And a slave must obey his master, no?" He gave a theatrical grimace. "Forgive my poor word choice. I should have said, *lackey* ... or perhaps *servant?*"

"Sod off," Finn said, the words sounding like a dog's growl.

Watt's hand drifted to the hilt at his waist; Adrien ignored Finn's feeble anger.

"You also forget we have competition — Beau, remember him? He has a head start, thanks to your bumbling. In our favour, if we do not know where to find the Valley of Achor, neither does he. Yet not knowing is the worst part. I fear he is digging in the correct valley as we dawdle here." Adrien nailed Finn with a scolding stare. "All of which means we have no time to, 'poke around the ruins,' as you say."

Adrien pointed a finger at Finn as though a thought had just occurred to him. "The Order seeks a priceless relic but sends one banner. Just one. Think on that a moment."

Finn, not liking the drift of things, held his tongue.

"You are expendable," Adrien said, and gave a mocking sigh. "The cost of doing business, like a blanket, or a sack of oats. Only proper leadership — my leadership, I mean — will bring you home healthy and whole." He pointed the finger at Finn again. "You need me more than I need you."

Need you? Finn quirked a head. If Adrien would utter such an obvious absurdity, well, what else would he lie about? Finn groped for a retort but, in the end, swallowed the burn of being rebuked by a fool. Yet as he glared at Adrien, toying with his ring, saw something new in place of bungling incompetence — the cunning of a wild dog.

Emma stared off through the whole back and forth, a dull look on her face.

Adrien glanced to her and nodded to say an understanding had been reached. He pointed at Hector and Serlo. "These brothers will search Wadi Qelt for ruins. I will ride to the Achor near Jericho." He nodded toward Finn. "You will go to the Achor near the Dead Sea."

"Dividing is unwise," Finn said. "We'll be vulnerable."

"A risk I am willing to take."

Finn forked fingers through his spiky hair, then flung up his hands in surrender. The plan, no matter how Adrien sold it, stunk of clumsy desperation. *And what kind of arse sends his wife into the Judean in the care of others?*

Adrien spelled out the other bits of his plan. Emma and Baret would accompany Finn to, according to Adrien, 'ensure my interests are considered.' Watt would stay with Hector. Jeph and the Poulains with Adrien. The Achors are two days apart, roughly, so riders were to notify other groups if something was found. If nothing was found within six days, they were to meet at Marda, where Adrien would decide their next move. Beau, if encountered, was to be avoided.

Finn stood by Fagan, brushing him, cleaning his hooves. Grooming a horse always soothed Finn's mood. Rollo leaned on his destrier. His mount was a brown chestnut, the same colour as Rollo's hair, and the two stubborn chestnuts were ever at odds.

"Thought I had a read on Adrien," Finn said. "But now I'm not sure if he is a fool or was playing a fool. By now Sigric would have his measure."

"Ah, Brother Sigric. Now he had a way of reading men. Could see straight into your mind. And I wager he got a terrible fright when he peeked into yours. Must have seen some horrid shite."

"In yours he saw nothing — nothing at all."

Rollo grinned; it died quick. "Adrien schemes. Head full of plans, eyes seek shortcuts, yet feet never find the way. Shows signs of gold sickness too, if you ask me."

"Adrien spoke to Saleh in Arabic. He learned of the three Achors but wasn't going to say anything. And he thinks the hoard is near Jericho, which is why he sends us elsewhere."

Finn closed his eyes and breathed Fagan's sweet earthiness. "Know what we should do with him?"

"Chib him. Toss the knife. Bury his carcass in the desert."

"What? No." Finn shook his head, appalled at where Rollo's mind landed with so little prompting. "We let him go. Follow his plan. He'll fail and we'll pick up the broken pieces."

Rollo gave a weak nod to say he liked his idea better but accepted Finn's.

Finn ran a hand down Fagan's neck. "What other choice is there?"

CHAPTER 14

The Salt Sea, so named by the Jews, glittered in the distance. Arabs call it the Sea of Death. Christians call it the Dead Sea. The sea was really a lake, salty because it had inlets but no outflow. The reek of salt and sulphur tainted the air. The land around the sea was, to no one's surprise, a lifeless swath of brown nestled between the Mountains of Moab to the east and the Judean Desert to the west. The desert is a rock desert, Elias told them — no sand dunes, but an endless sprawl of peaks, plateaus, and escarpments. Wadis cut off the high ground, steep and deep, then meander the low ground in a series of twists and turns.

They had seen much of what Outremer held and all agreed this was a wind-blasted, sun-scorched place even on a good day.

Elias and Nik scouted ahead. Lugh trailed. The column rode through the scorched and dreary land. Finn picked a mark on the shimmering horizon and focused on the mark. When he reached it, he picked another, and the whole thing started over in a mind-numbing loop.

A figure wobbled toward them through the heat haze — Nik.

"Elias says come, you must see this," the Turc said without preamble.

Finn tipped back his wide-brimmed hat and poured water over his bearded face. "What is it?"

Nik scowled at the foolish waste of water, dripping from Finn's moustaches, then kneed his mount around. "Bad things at a church," he said over a shoulder.

The church sat near a fork in the road. One fork led to the Dead Sea and the other to the Valley of Achor. Elias's horse was tethered outside. The church was a lone bump in an otherwise flat land. It was like many scattered across Outremer — one room, stone walls, battered wood door, narrow entrance. Finn eased through the door, blinking at the sudden shift from eye-blinding brightness to sight-robbing darkness. The space was cool, cooler than outside anyway, but the air oddly moist and thick.

"Tread careful." Elias's gravel-harsh voice came from a dark corner, where he leaned. The Turc swung his arm out. "Floor is nothing but holes."

As Finn's eye adjusted, he saw the floor was pocked, scarred by recent mutilations. Narrow bridges lined the spaces between. Mosaic tiles, which had decorated the floor in older times, littered the room in colourful piles of green and red and silver. Stumps marked where the altar once stood. At the far end a hole in the roof let in a single ray of light. Two figures bathed in its glow like martyred saints in a painting.

Elias tilted a head toward the light.

Finn picked his way through the maze of holes, the jingle of spurs and the crunch of tiles making a strange, vulgar song in the once-holy place. A figure sat cross-legged at the edge of the ray of light, back to Finn, and another sprawled in a pool of brownish crimson, head cradled in the lap of the first. The sprawled man had died hard. Skin was sliced from his face and arms and torso. Cream-coloured bone gleamed in a patchwork. Eyes gone. Teeth gone. Fingers twisted and canted. Scores of fat flies dotted the pool of congealed blood.

The seated figure twitched at the click of spurs. Finn squatted by his side, careful to avoid the sticky crimson, and took in the man's face. Young, lean, blank. A Jerusalem cross had been inked into his skeletal forehead. An oval pilgrim's flask lay by a knee. A fly, iridescent black, was ensnared in the pilgrim's hair — though he either did not notice or did not care.

"What happened here, Brother?"

"Bad things." The man's voice was a croak. "I hid. Craven, aye, but what could I do?"

"Hid from what?"

"Them. Abandoned Brother Jude," he nodded at the head in his lap, "to them."

"Why'd they hurt him?"

"Wanted to know where the sepulchre was. And the gold."

"Is that why they dug up the floor?"

A nod. "Tore up the cistern too." A sigh. "We didn't have gold. We came to pray to Saint Sabas. But they called Jude a liar. Thought he was the priest here."

The smell of blood and death was excruciating and Finn resisted the urge to pull up his shemagh. He wanted out of the church, and what he had seen cleansed from his head, though such sights tended to settle in for a while.

The man shifted and the fly fell from his hair, landed in the pool of blood, legs churning. "All I could do was pray…"

"Who did this?"

The man stared into nothing.

"Who did this?" Finn repeated, louder this time.

"Demons. Who else would break a man of God and desecrate a holy place?"

Gold-mad men.

"They asked if this was the church of the Valley of Achor," the man said.

"What did Jude tell them?"

"The Valley of Achor is east of the Dead Sea, of course. Everyone knows that."

Finn chuckled, despite the horror around him, for the Valley of Achor was not something everyone agreed on. The hardest part of finding the hoard was finding the valley where it lay. For sure the scroll's authors knew which Achor they wrote of, and now, from beyond the grave, laughed at the packs of blundering Christians.

Finn left the pilgrim and stepped into the light. Elias and Rollo were waiting. The others were tending the horses.

"*Le Scélérat* earned his name." Elias made the horn sign by raising his first and last fingers and covering the middle fingers with the thumb. "Curse him and his sow of a mother too."

"Ugly troll," Rollo said. "When Beau was born the midwife slapped his ma."

Finn spat, then spat again, trying to get the coppery tang out of his mouth. "Get the pilgrim a horse."

"He won't go," Elias said. "Says he's going to bury Jude. Carry on alone. His penance."

"Fitting." Finn told them what the pilgrim said about Beau and another candidate for the Valley of Achor.

"Beau is lost." Rollo's throaty chuckle died away. "Wonder how many good folks will die while he finds his way?"

Images arose like a flock of startled crows — a sacked monastery, corpses of monks, columns of smoke. "We must get to Marda," Finn said.

A horse gives his back and limbs to carry man. The companionship of a horse, to Finn, was an honour and a pleasure. Steady hooves, tail swishes, and snorts were on most days a lullaby. Not today.

They pushed hard from the crossroads church. Now Fagan's head drooped at the end of his neck like a rock hanging in a sling's pouch; Finn called a halt for water and rest. The Stable Master said destriers were cross-bred with Arabians, among several breeds, and a drop or two of Arabian blood gave them resilience to the heat of Outremer. Finn did not believe the brother, at the time, though Fagan plodding on where lesser horses would founder gave truth to the claim.

Elias roamed ahead and Nik behind. Rollo, Lugh, Jerol, Malik, and six other sergeants fed and watered the horses or themselves. Emma cared for her mount; Finn hoisted brows at Baret and he shrugged to say, *She would shoo me away if I tried to do it for her.*

Rollo was eating air-dried meat rolled in a pitta. He made a sudden sucking sound and started into a coughing fit.

Finn whacked him on the back. "Easy, Brother. Chew slow, swallow fast."

"Trouble," Rollo wheezed and pointed ahead with the stub of half-eaten pitta.

Elias was riding in hard and holding up a fist — the sign to hold in place.

Finn's hand died on Rollo's back. He scanned the surrounding ground. Nothing — not even a bird. But the sky looked ill. Wrong. A yellowish smear glazed the sun. Far off, the eastern hills shimmered strangely, then disappeared into a blur. A wall of dust billowed up behind Elias.

Lugh shaded his eyes with a hand and studied the cloud. "Saracens?"

A breeze sighed like a hot breath over dry ground. A sudden gust stirred the hems of their robes, kicked up dust swirls that danced around their boots.

Finn's thoughts also stirred and he muttered, "Storm."

Violent storms build and drop with no warning. Alkaline-laced dust is scoured from the salt flats around the Dead Sea and carried along in a rolling wall. They happen in the fall and spring — some fierce enough to carry sand from as far as Damascus. Savvy men waited them out in shelter, or if none were available, huddled with their backs to the wind, wrapped in their robes.

Finn watched Elias, nearly to them now, and fussed with his shemagh, as if the scarf alone might ward off the storm.

Elias slewed in and blurted what Finn feared. "Sandstorm," then almost as an afterthought added, "And riders."

"What kind?"

"The angry kind. At least a score."

"Freelances?" Jerol asked, and no one answered.

Rollo spat half-chewed meat. "Whoever they are, they'll be here soon."

The wind gusted, shredded the ragged hems of their cappas, threw grit in their eyes. Finn's shemagh flapped, threatened to unravel, and as he fought it back into place his gaze landed on Malik, who scrubbed at his hair in a flurry of frustration. The sergeant frowned at the incoming tide of sand, spat, then pasted on a confident air when he saw Finn's eye.

Finn cast about for a place to hide and defend. They had crossed many a wadi, but now the nearest ravine was a thin line at the horizon — a line they would never make. Nothing but salt flats to the east, and to the west ridges and hills climbing toward low mountains. A solitary rise beckoned nearby, somewhat flat-topped, and with a lip. Exposed, but defendable, and with any luck the storm would not be as severe as it threatened to be.

Finn gave a chopping hand motion, then a horizontal splay-fingered palm saying, *Rally there, hold there.* They filed across a dust-choked land under a darkening sky. Horses stomped up the slope, side-terraced along a trail, and burst to the top. A stone wall staggered across the flat like a mouthful of jagged teeth half-hidden in the dust. Piles of rubble dotted the flat.

Made by man.

Finn waved the banner close. "Pray the storm blows out. Pray the riders pass. Defend if need be," he yelled, and flapped hand signals to mime the plan.

Miming was not needed — they were salts and savvied what needed doing. Only a fool would stand at the lip. Your legs were naked to thrusting steel and it was further to cut or stab down. The sweet spot was several paces behind the lip, where the man coming up would be easy feed. They arrayed in fighting pairs, huddled against the wind, while gusts shoved their shields like sails.

Elias grabbed Finn's elbow and mimed shooting a bow and the arrow whizzing off.

Wind will make bows useless. Nik? Finn mouthed.

The man was watching their backtrail and yet to show.

Elias shrugged with a palms-up gesture.

Finn tapped Baret's shoulder, then chopped a hand at the wall. The man nodded and hopped off his horse, and with Emma and Malik began trudging toward the refuge. Sergeants wrestled horses to the wall and hustled back to Rollo.

Rollo spread his arms and hollered into the wind's maw, "Come get us, bastards!"

Finn laughed, the sound a dry rasp, then gave Lugh a clenched fist sign to say, *hold.* Finn scuttled along, scouting the flat. Every so often he moved to the edge and peered over. Swirling dirt. Something flickered in the dirt-fog. He swiped stinging salt from his eyes with a sleeve and tried again — nothing but eddying dust.

He checked behind, and with a lurch saw Lugh trigger his crossbow point-blank into a black-robed figure trying to claw his way to the flat. Jerol shot a second as Lugh threw his empty crossbow at a mounted man looming from the murk. The man batted aside the crossbow with a shield as Jerol pounced and stabbed with a spear. The horse went down on its front legs. Lugh loomed over the rider and his blade fell. A splash of gore came up.

The fight lacked sound — which in the shifting murk gave it a dreamlike quality.

Finn squinted into the dirt haze as a gust hit, flinging grit in his eyes. He dipped a head and scrunched his eyes to wet them. When he opened them, a mounted warrior was there, like a wraith summoned from the air. He was garbed in black with brown eyes glaring between the folds of his scarf. They gawked at each other a short, surprised moment, then the man spurred the pony up the slope.

They met as the horse surged over the lip. Finn slashed at the rider, got a hoof in the thigh for his trouble. The kick sent him staggering. He rolled and came up spitting dirt. Man and pony were gone. Another shape drifted out of the dark in their place and Finn limped forward to meet him.

A silver blur came at his face, silent in the gale, though he imagined the hiss of steel. Finn flicked the cut aside with his board and stabbed for a foot. A crunch and the man hopped like a demonic rabbit. Finn juked low and thrust high. Blood spray gusted away.

He spun back to his brothers. The scrum was a jumble of mute and half-seen images. Horsemen see-sawed out of the mirk. Templars surged to meet them and send them off.

Rollo wielded the great sword like a staff — windmilling slashes in elegant loops, choking his grip to the ricasso to stab, sliding back to scythe vicious two-handed cuts. He was fearless and mad and carved a man from the saddle. Whirled the blade up and hacked off a man's hand, then flowed into a thrust that took him through the chest.

Jerol stabbed and darted back; Lugh tucked behind his board and lunged past Uncle. The Irishman's combination was a blur — cut out of the high guard and a stab at a leg. A horse made it to the flat and Rollo chopped its legs out and dumped the rider in a sprawl. Elias flitted in and knifed the dazed man. The Turc skipped back as Jerol covered him by chopping a shield and using his own to knock a man back.

A blow thudded Finn's shield — he had not seen the man that gave it until almost too late. He shield-shoved the man and signed the cross with steel — stab at the face, slash down, slash across. Watered steel bit and the man staggered back to be swallowed by the dust.

A bellowing roar and Finn shuffle-turned, dragged up shield and blade.

Only the roar was not from a man. He glimpsed a roiling wall above like a rogue wave breaking over a doomed sailor. The wind took a breath, a brief silence, then screamed like a thousand banshees.

Heat hit like someone had opened the door to a blast furnace. Salt grit scoured his face and his world was reduced to flaying sand and howling wind. Pebbles clattered on his shield. Something heavy tonked off his helmet. He leaned into it, hunched behind the shield, and staggered blindly toward where he remembered the wall.

Then his step hitched, like one leg had shrunk shorter than the other, and the ground went out from under him. A moment of weightlessness. Panic as he fell. A sickening hit that smashed the air from his lungs and the wits from his head.

And blessed silence.

"Awake, Brother Finn. Awake." The voice was warm. Angelic.

He pried open an eye. A circle of light radiated above. A head floated in a halo, and he smiled like a simpleton. *I'm called to Mary's side … and if ye are summoned, ye must go.*

Something slapped his face, snuffing the idiot's grin, and he squinted at coils of a rope. *Why does Mary need a rope?*

"Take it. I will pull you up."

The voice was familiar.

Finn rubbed a dirt-crusted eye. Emma peered down.

"Damn. Thought I was…" His voice came out as a croak. "What are you doing?"

"Rescuing you," she said. "We stumbled upon ruins. Doubtless an outpost from the Roman era. You fell into an old cistern."

A column of light stabbed into the space and Finn peered into the dark corners. He lay in a stone-lined pit some six or seven paces across. Dirt piled like sea wrack. Bones of animals, fallen in and starved, littered the stones. The hole was too deep, its walls too slick to climb out.

"Take the rope. I will haul you up."

"You? Would need a miracle…"

"God will give me strength." She wagged an arm over the hole, apparently in an effort to show the muscle there. "Do you not believe in miracles?"

"Go for help."

"Take the rope. And believe."

With a groan, he sat up, and worked arms and shoulders and legs. The pony-kicked leg throbbed. His head thumped a beat along with it. Skin, where exposed, was red and burned and raw. But nothing was broken or out of joint. He staggered to his feet, looped the rope, gave a tug.

"Show me a miracle."

After a wait, he was hoisted up with a sudden lurch, then again until his arse hung off the floor. A steady pull until he spun in a slow twirl, shield hanging from its *guige*. Another heave and he was at the lip. With a mad scramble he fought over it and out to daylight. From his belly, he gazed up to Fagan's arse. The rope ran from Finn to the horse's saddle. Emma stood near the destrier's head, an impish grin on her face.

"See? Miracles can happen."

Finn coughed, intended as a laugh. "You're a strong woman."

She crouched and held out a canteen. "Keen-minded too."

He nodded as he drank, neck working, before lowering the canteen and giving a gasp. Helmet and coif came off; he poured water on his face; scrubbed at the dirt. "The others?"

"Not certain. Malik and Baret were with me." Emma glanced over a shoulder, as if hoping to see them. "And then they were not. The horses bolted. I kept hold of Fagan."

Finn climbed to his feet and leaned on Fagan. "Surprised he followed you."

"I grew up with horses. My father bred them. I have ridden as long as I could walk." She slapped a soft hand on the horse's neck. "Fine bit of horseflesh, this one."

"Fagan is a brother as much as any man." Finn hefted Oathkeeper, ran a hand down the watered steel. He brushed a palm over the face of his shield; the black-and-white paint nearly scoured away by the storm's fury. "How long was I in the hole?"

"A few hours. It took a while for the storm to blow out."

Finn took another swig of water.

"The day is pleasant," Emma said. "One would never know we just suffered hell on earth. Jews call the storms *ruaḥ qadīm*, east wind, and consider it the wind of God. I think I agree."

"Aye," Finn said, mostly just to say something. He surveyed the area. The bodies of eight enemy sprawled where Rollo had made a stand. Blackrobes — *Fida'i'n*, upon a closer look. Blood trails, baked dry by the heat, marked where the wounded had staggered off. No Templars lay dead, God be praised, though a knot in Finn's gut said not all the bloodstains belonged to Blackrobes.

"Where did they go?" Emma asked.

"Can't say. Wind swept the tracks." Finn mused aloud for Emma. "Our plan, if separated, was to meet at Marda. The others should be there. Water and food too."

They started toward the wall, Finn limping in a lopsided hitch. Dirt-covered clumps scattered along the flat. One groaned. Finn handed Fagan's reins to Emma and rolled the clump to its side, revealing a young, dark, fiercely bearded face. A leg skewed unnaturally.

"Who do you serve?" Finn spoke in halting Arabic. No response. He tried the *lingua franca*, then French, and the man twitched.

Finn studied the man for a moment, then spoke. "Emma, take Fagan to the wall and wait for me."

"I will stay," she said, her voice soft but firm.

"Perhaps I was unclear." Finn stood at the edge of the abyss but saw no need she should follow. "I'm going to carve this fool, then slay him. Better if you don't see it."

The man made a mewing sound and hitched forward, futilely dragging himself on scrabbling fingers.

"Knew you understood French." Finn yanked the long knife, stomped on the man's broken leg, dropped a knee in the back to pin him. The man bawled as Finn clamped a forehead and levered up his face. He caught Emma's eye as if to say, *Last chance.*

The firm set of her eyes replied, *I will not flinch from violence done in my name.*

Finn shrugged and cropped the top of the man's ear with a deft slice. A fountain of blood followed. "You serve Shabh, eh? So where is she?"

The man's reply was a garbled howl of pain followed by manic laughter.

"Answer, dog, or I'll crop your balls and stuff them in your mouth."

More manic laughter.

Finn glanced over a shoulder and saw Emma standing firm. He took the ear entire. "Where is Shabh?"

The man bit on a lip and Finn growled in his ear. "Where do I find her?"

"Find her where the dead monks sing. Where the dead monks sing!"

He lit into a lengthy speech in Arabic filled with spitting, curses, random laughter.

"Now he spews nonsense." Emma's words were soft, and Finn glared over a shoulder as she spoke. "He is a zealot. Carve him to bloody bones and you will get only laughter and curses."

The long knife hovered over the man's remaining ear, then Finn angled it and drove steel into the hollow of his throat and straight down, to his heart. The man clawed the ground and thumped a foot as Finn levered the knife handle side-to-side, ribboning the heart.

"But you saw what he was."

Finn yanked the blade and stropped it clean on the man's robes.

"So why?"

"Why not?"

Finn stared at the corpse but felt no remorse.

"Why, you ask? To protect myself. A madwoman haunts me — Shabh — and I will not cower."

Finn rambled through the story. Robert and Shabh. Her murder of Templar brothers. How, according to the Old Man, she carries on some twisted blood feud. He did not mention how being stalked by the woman shook his spirit. Unnerved him.

Emma listened stone-faced. "A beast is not frightening because it is male," she said softly, "it frightens because it destroys."

Finn almost said he did not fear Shabh. Not even one bit. Instead, he fanned a hand to say he was done speaking, then glanced at the corpse.

Find her where the dead monks sing…

They ambled in silence until reaching the wall. Three haversacks were piled there. Finn slung them over Fagan, then caught Emma's eye and nodded at Fagan.

"I assume you would like me to mount?"

Finn nodded.

Emma climbed into the saddle, patted the crupper. "Room for two."

He ignored the temptation of proximity, took the reins, and began limping south.

CHAPTER 15

Finn's limping gait and the failing light meant they did not get far. They made camp in a low spot ringed by rock. Finn unsaddled Fagan then rubbed him down. Fed him from a dwindling bag of oats. The fading sun brought a chill and he tossed a wool blanket to Emma.

"A fire would help," she said.

"And would draw bad men to us like drunkards to wine."

Emma bobbed a head to grant the point, then wrapped herself in the blanket and nestled against a rock. She plucked off the Bedouin head covering, ran a hand over her hair. The ivory hairpin had come loose and she clenched it between bright white teeth as she fussed with her hair. The monkey end of the pin faced Finn, and in his weary mind it seemed to caper and leap in mockery.

"Food?" she mumbled around the monkey.

Finn rummaged in the haversacks and came out with strips of air-dried meat and hunks of crusty horsebread. He handed some to Emma. A waterbag lay on the ground and Finn thought of burying it, to cool it, then decided he was too tired and settled instead against the saddle, Oathkeeper and the long knife propped by his elbows. Night was falling fast — as it does in the desert.

He chewed air-dried goat but did not notice the salty flavour. Thoughts drifted through his head. Idle talk was a chore. Whatever his brain cooked up was misplaced or bordered on insulting. *Raided many tombs? Stolen any relics of note? What is it like being married to a fool?* Her proximity bothered. Sweat mingled with the scent of rose, myrrh, and marjoram. He had not been alone with a woman in many a year.

Emma broke the impasse. "Tell me of Montgisard. Did you truly route a horde?"

"We did. They were mired in a muddy riverbed. Fools made it worse by trying to rebuild their line." Finn wiped a hand over his scarred face, recalling the day he had been given the wound by a raging Mamluk. "We charged as they shifted. Broke them open in one go. Pure glory."

"Lady Rumour says you dispatched Ahmad al-Taqi."

"With a lance strike — pinned his shield to his chest. Earned me the eternal hatred of his clan. They offer a bounty for my head."

"How much? He was kin to Saladin and the bounty is certes not a token. With one score I could leave relic hunting…"

Finn laughed. "A helmet full of gold. Men have tried to claim it but, as you see, I still own my head."

"Perhaps the task requires a woman's touch."

Finn laughed again. Fagan nickered with him.

"And you chased Saladin — alone?"

"I did."

"You are either very brave or very foolish."

"There is a difference?"

It was her turn to laugh.

Darkness cloaked them. The moon was waning gibbous and its feeble light cast inky waves over the hillside. A carpet of stars winked crisp and silver from the heavens.

"Did you knife Robert of Saint Albans?"

"Aye. We didn't get along, the two of us. I didn't like the way he trimmed his beard and he wore his sword wrong. English porkwit."

"Ah," Emma said in mock surprise. "I heard he murdered a brother knight. Joined Saladin. Tried to sack the Holy City."

"That too."

Finn did not remember those he killed. Most blurred into one generic, bloody face. Some haunted his dreams with distinct clarity. Robert was one.

"What of the Lord of Ibelin?"

"Balien? At Montgisard?" Finn sifted his memory. Secular lords lined up to the left of the Templars. Dust clouds arose at the charge. A knight could not see past his arm. Corpses piled like winter wood. Looters cut rings from the fingers of dead men — and sometimes from the wounded. Flies so thick it sounded like being trapped in a giant beehive. He blabbered all this before realizing he should have trimmed the uglier bits.

Emma said nothing and Finn asked, "Why'd you ask of Balien?"

"My brother, Emeric, was one of Balien's oath men."

"Was?"

"He died at Montgisard. I know little of his last day and wanted … something." Emma's voice grew thick. "We were twins, and twins are of two types — knotted soul-to-soul or bitterly at odds. We were the former. I felt something wrong the day he died — like an invisible blade had sliced my heart. The wound refuses to heal."

Emma went on to say she had lost her first husband too, from the coughing illness, and two cousins from the same disease.

She has known sore loss … but haven't we all?

Words of comfort failed him. In their place, the dark proffered temptation, seclusion proffered more. An image slipped into his head unbidden — him, sliding close, wrapping an arm over her shoulder.

The echo of his own voice, repeating his vows, shattered the image like glass.

Every fighting man observes rituals to preserve his life. Good luck charms. A lock of his lady's hair. A lucky piece of kit. Finn had his. A simple iron cross on a skull-beaded prayer cord; Da's long knife; kissing the flat of his sword. These rituals married to his vows. If he followed habit and obeyed vows, God held a protecting hand over him; if he failed at either, maiming or death awaited. These simple beliefs kept him rooted.

A clumsy change of subject was the best he could offer. "Your father bred horses?"

"Aye. Destriers, for the fighting orders, and for counts and lords. My eldest brother assumed father's estates. Emeric found his way to Outremer and took oath with Balien. Hendrick, my husband, passed not long after and I followed Emeric." She shifted against the rock. "Hendrick was a good man. Kind. My father was too. He treated me as a third son."

"Which explains how you're learned and lettered."

She laughed softly in the darkness. "A lettered woman ... is that outrage I hear?"

"You hear envy. I don't read well — hardly at all, in truth."

"I could teach you," she offered, perhaps to amend for her laughter.

"Too kind." Finn's reply was intentionally vague. Illiteracy was a source of shame; learning from a woman would only add to it. He could already hear Rollo's mockery. "Why relic hunting?" he asked instead.

"I am a gentlewoman, which means I have time and resources to pursue passions, such as relics and history. And with time, I found my hobbies profitable — very profitable." The soft rustling of Emma's shoulders shrugging. "Besides, I am childless, and not beholding to a family — well, at least not as much as other ladies."

Nor are you a woman easily told what to do, thought Finn.

It was Emma's turn to ask a question. "Why the Templars?"

"To be less like me and more like Jesus. To better myself. Join a higher cause. But I learned the Order, and war, are swords that cut both ways." Finn's voice took on a calm detachment. "I lack patience. Empathy is dead. Trust is gone. Whenever I enter a room, I keep my head on a pivot, my back to a wall. I'm comfortable only when with brothers; everyone else is an enemy."

There was silence. Fagan chewed oats. Somewhere a jackal barked.

"Emeric," Emma said haltingly, then ploughed on, "Emeric once said, the tyrant comes with swords, and to burn, and the sword and the torch are brandished by those who have no code. So the knight hefts a sword for those who cannot. And he takes vows knowing that which he seeks to protect in others — joy, goodness, love — are traits he sacrifices in himself."

Finn knew that some Templars also took vows for selfish reasons — serving God opened the gates of paradise, and this lure drove Finn as much as any vow. He came to Outremer to cleanse a sinful past, though it seemed the longer he stayed the more sins he gained, and the more he sinned the further paradise seemed.

Emma shifted in the dark and Finn imagined her leaning forward as she spoke.

"Trust … now that is something a knight should not sacrifice. Hold it dear, for trust is a fragile thing. Misplaced often. Broken easily. But nearly impossible to rebuild."

It was a fine lecture. Finn, with nothing to better it, grunted in agreement. He gazed at the stars, marvelled at their brilliance, while Emma's words, *misplaced often*, echoed in his head.

Not far above, a hawk glided an invisible trail, eyes on the endless sprawl of desert. Somewhere in that barren waste hid his meal. From so far below, the plumage was faint, the hawk but a dark silhouette against a cloudless sky. Finn held Fagan by the reins, his other hand shading his eyes as he squinted at the bird.

Morning, Da.

Finn's face was a mask painted with dirt and sweat and grime. He pinched Fagan's shoulder and the horse's skin stood for a beat, then dropped flat; he would water him in an hour or so with what little water remained. The trail was a hard tan ribbon — clear of rock, clear of tracks. He studied the barren ground and at the distant wind-blasted hills; for the hundredth time he wondered how much further the monastery was.

Night had been spent listening to Emma breathe, soft and slow. Finn, used to the farting and snuffling and snoring of men, found the sound soothing. The night sounds reminded him of Agnes, his old love, and fond memories filtered through his mind. Agnes, sitting under an aged apple tree, the hem of her kirtle tucked under her pale ankles. She took a bite of an apple, flashed a toothy grin, kissed him. Agnes meant chaste — though after a day among the apples he was not sure how well the name fit. God, but he still loved the taste of apple.

"Something in the trail," Emma said, bringing Finn back from the apple trees of Alba.

A man-sized lump lay on the ground ahead. Heat waves blurred it. A wadi cut just behind the lump and the shape seemed to hover at its lip.

"Wait with Fagan," Finn said, then prowled forward.

The lump was a man but, God be praised, not wearing Templar white or black. The body was stocky and, when he rolled it over, heavy and stiff. He fanned away a horde of flies. Stab marks pocked the man's chest. His throat gaped ear-to-ear; Finn recoiled from the dead man's contorted face.

"Baret."

"God, no…" Emma had come up, despite Finn's command. She propped her head on Fagan and sobbed. Fagan stared with ears pointed stiffly forward in a horse's pose of nervousness. Finn gave Emma a clumsy pat on the shoulder.

"Brother Finn, Emma," a familiar voice rasped.

Finn whirled to Malik's grit-blasted face, grinning from the other side of Baret. His sergeant's tunic was tattered and filthy. A boot was holed. Malik's countenance, as always, nettled Finn.

"Malik — how are you here?"

Malik held a shovel and he used it to point at Baret. "We… Baret and I, I mean, escaped the sandstorm. Sheltered in the wadi. Then Blackrobes attacked and … and Baret died. Fought and died." He grimaced in despair. "I am sorry. I tried to save him."

Finn swept the ground with his gaze. No boot marks. No bloodstains. No bodies, other than Baret. How had his throat been sliced ear-to-ear in a straight-up fight?

"Come, Brother," Malik said, and waved the shovel. "Help me bury him. I've gouged out a crevice in the wall of the wadi. It will do, for now, and we can return to give him a proper burial — a Christian burial with all God's blessings."

Finn glanced to Fagan, who stared toward the wadi with ears pinned back, then sucked in a breath and leaned to grab Baret's arm.

Malik, still grinning, slammed the shovel's pan into the side of Finn's head with a loud clang, then kicked him in the ribs. The blows were sudden and brutal and Finn, half-folded over, kicked feebly at Malik's knee. Malik danced back. The shovel clanged again and a cascade of stars exploded before Finn's eyes. The world tilted and the trail came up to meet him.

The last thing he heard was a babble of Arabic and Emma cursing.

CHAPTER 16

Awareness returned in fits and starts. Memories flitted — a shovel to the head, a kick to the ribs, rough hands binding him. His chest over a horse's arse, his head dangling.

Finn pried open his eyes but saw nothing. *Am I blinded?* Panic threatened then subsided as he became aware of an orange glow to the left. Other senses grew acute. The drip of water. Soft chatter in Arabic. From somewhere nearby a man howled and whimpered like a dog, and Finn flinched from the frightful outburst. The smell of damp rock. And a faint reek — acrid, salty, metallic. It was familiar. And unsettling.

Stone was cool against his bare back, though it was not unwelcome after suffering the desert's heat. Manacles bound his wrists and he yanked at the chain until Emma whispered.

"We are chained to a wall. The chains are solid."

"Where are we?"

"A cave. Used to be a laura, I think."

"Are you well?"

"I enjoyed every courtesy imaginable." Emma sniffled at her jest, asked the inevitable. "What will they do to us?"

"Nothing good, I fear. Torture probably." Finn saw no reason to lie, though he refused to be cowed by the prospect.

Finn hurt. His skull felt like it had been sawed away, his brain stirred with a stick, the skull reattached with nails. Thoughts drifted. He pondered the teachings of Jesus, and those of prophets aged and wise, and in them took solace. He considered God's grace. Weighed his deeds, good and bad, large and small, and found the balance tilted against him. Fret paid a visit but he denied it a place at his table, for it served no useful purpose.

Hours passed. Perhaps many. Time was measured by the rhythmic drip of water. He became aware of light bouncing toward him, and footfalls, and closed his eyes to play asleep. Ice-cold water doused him and he sputtered from the shock.

"Wakey, wakey, Brother Finn."

Finn squinted into painfully bright torchlight and there was Malik, grinning. Sudden heat filled Finn and he lunged in the chains. "Malik, you shite," he croaked. "What've you done?"

"Tsk, tsk, *Brother*. Wrath is a sin." A twist-key hung around Malik's neck. He tilted his head at Finn. "What have I done? What is long overdue. Been with the Order too long. Played the part. Licked Lanfrid's arse. Gained his trust. Then you became my task — capturing you, I mean. Could've put you down a hundred times." He half-shrugged to say that pleasure was for another. "My brethren awaited in ambush but the sandstorm saved you — at least for a moment. I shifted course. Knifing Baret was an easy play, and he made such good bait, no?"

Emma made a low sound in her throat, and Finn coughed and spat. "You knifed Yosi in the back. Stole the scroll for Beau."

"No. I didn't. Nor do we care for gold. We are driven by a greater purpose — to purge our home of filthy rodents. You Faranji ruined this land, polluted the water, foul the very air. You steal what is ours and stuff your purses with our prosperity. You are why the people of the one true faith suffer. *You*!"

"You murder for gold, if you serve who I think."

Malik flung up a hand and turned stiffly away. He used his torch to light lamps set in wall niches. Light gradually filled the space.

Emma sat with an ankle tethered to the wall. Her head wrap was gone, which made her ears more prominent, her cinnamon hair more striking. They sat in a room a dozen paces across. Chisel marks showed where it was enlarged from a natural crevice. A corridor led out. Chain ran from Finn's manacles to an iron hook in the wall, and from there to a second hook, where it was wrapped off. Dark smears and blotches marred the stone. The faint and familiar stink came to him again.

Fear and pain and blood — they're in the very stone.

Kit was piled in a corner. Oathkeeper, long knife, mace, mail. And his shredded cappa.

Finn was suddenly ashamed of his nakedness — and from being duped. Fagan's stiff ears and stare at the wadi screamed danger but Finn, worn of body and mind, had missed it. The Old Man's words echoed, *She has agents among you — even within your Order.* Something about Malik agitated Finn, always had, but in his wildest fits of paranoia he had not imagined this.

A peal of manic laughter rang out. A figure ambled from the corridor. Drool dribbled to a black-bearded chin. He had the vacant stare of a simpleton and a lopsided body — fat and round in places, hard and muscled in others. Fingers were missing from a hand. He was like something drawn by a child.

"Skulls are stars," the creature said, and slapped meaty hands to Finn's head.

"Aziz, no, no," Malik said, in the tone of a father scolding a misbehaving son. "No touching without permission. No action without direction. Remember?"

Aziz bobbed a head in apology, shuffled aside to leer and drool at Emma.

Then the ghost strolled from the dark — Shabh.

She had dark hair, dark skin, a dark smile. The smile was warped, forced, like she learned to smile by watching normal folk do it. She was broad-shouldered and sinewy as a boy. Hair cropped short. Cheeks sharp and jaw sharper. Full lips and doe eyes. Feminine, yet not, like an angel that is neither woman nor man but has the most attractive parts of each. Finn first met her disguised as Brother Sancho. Over the years he chided himself for not seeing *her*. But now, rapt by her strange allure, saw she could both captivate and confound.

He expected a monster. Here stood a woman. Deadly, aye. Perhaps mad, perhaps not, though for sure a brokenness lurked beneath her mask. Wrongs can break a person and breaks take years to repair, if they repair at all. Experience taught this. He had given vengeance, though carried no guilt or shame for it; breaks, temporary for him, were scarred over. But such a baleful stare said vengeance would bring her no healing — it would only gouge the wound deeper.

She stared, head tilted, and Finn understood an act of contrition was expected.

"Is it day or night?" he asked.

"Afternoon, and what a pleasant morning it was," Shabh said, cordial as you please. Her voice was like velvet, her French accented and melodic. She clicked fingers at Aziz, who hauled on the chain, hoisted Finn to his toes. It was effortless — Aziz had the kind of strength to wring a man like a wet rag and leave crushed bones. He looped the chain around the hook and stepped back.

She sidled close.

Finn studied her, then Malik, and the resemblance was uncanny. Threads of Shabh wove through Malik and these threads were what had nettled him, he realized.

"Siblings?"

"Cousins. Though Malik is dearer to me than any brother." Shabh glanced toward Aziz, shaded her mouth with a hand to cover her words. "The others are like children. Easily frightened. Gullible. I tell them I am half *Jinn* on my mother's side. They believe me, and fear me, though in truth I am more … fitful? Is this the word?"

"Cruel, I think," Malik said.

"Ah. More *cruel* than a *Jinn*."

Finn noted a shift in her voice — amity fled, shifted to something hard and husky.

Shabh slapped a palm on the wall. "Monks carved this from stone. Lived here alone. Until I carved them to pieces in this very room." She lifted a chin, closed her eyes to recall the scene, then her eyes flared open. "Their ghosts remain. This place they loved, and the place loved them, and their loss saddened it so deeply it trapped their spirits. Their ghostly chants form a choir now and then, and come sun or storm, I find them the finest of company."

Images swirled like dust; the storm, Finn slicing an ear from the Blackrobe, his manic laughter. *Find her where the dead monks sing…* Finn gave a brittle grin at the memory.

Shabh grinned too. "Death. Men never expect the doer to be a woman. The monks did not. Your brother Templars did not. Expectations are what kill men. I am but the tool." Her gaze appraised his pale, muscled body in leisurely passes before settling on his manhood. She nodded in apparent decision. "I will slice your cock first."

"Bad idea. Victim faints or bleeds to death — or both." Finn spoke in his best casual voice. "Better to start small. Fingers, toes, whatnot. Work up to the big parts."

Malik snorted at the jest. "He doesn't use it anyway. Won't miss it."

Shabh ignored Malik and leaned close to Finn's ear in a waft of musky sweat and sandalwood. Anise, sweet and strong, flavoured her breath.

"You are fearless," she whispered. "I will give you that."

Not fearless, just good at pretending. Dread and horror threatened to unpluck his nerve. Shoulders were hoisted high, but he twitched them in something like a shrug and said the expected. "God will protect me."

"Hmm. Just what the monks said. Yet despite their endless prayers God did nothing as they died. No avenging angel. No lightning. No floods."

From somewhere, maybe in his head, drifted spectral psalmody, *Even though I walk through the valley of the shadow of death, I will fear no evil … and I will dwell in Your house forever.* Calm suffused him. Fear drained away.

Someone without fear cannot die, and he smiled.

Shabh tilted an ear, perhaps heard the singing, maybe read Finn's mind. "Jesus offered just one person paradise. Do you know who? The thief on the cross next to him. Not apostles. Not prophets. Certainly not you. Eternal misery shall be your reward." She stroked a finger along his naked thigh. "As the crone, I pronounced you a wanderer of hell and all the dark places between. Remember? I do."

She dragged a finger over a bare hip, up his stomach, to his chest. It stopped at the spiral inked there and traced the spiral to its centre.

"Pretty. I want it."

She laughed at his vulnerability, his nakedness, and held out a hand to Malik. A knife slapped into her palm. The blade was no longer than a thumb and stained dark; lamplight danced along its shiny edge.

Aziz's eyes flared, then he clapped flabby hands and capered in a circle, bare feet slapping and shuffling on the stone.

Shabh held the knife to Finn's face and he fought the urge to flinch aside.

"Small, no? I call it, 'Sadiqi,' which means, little friend." She dragged it over his cheek and hairs fell away. "Sadiqi and I will take you gentle. One piece at a time."

"In my experience, the deed is best done quickly and savoured later."

She pursed her lips to make a show of pondering Finn's advice, then shook her head. "No. Your passing, and your suffering, will take days. Know Robert laughs at you. He awaits — and others you murdered. Walter. Andrew. Malin. They will shred your soul. There will be no peace in the next life."

Fire shimmered in her eyes; her nostrils flared rhythmically — the broken thing beneath her mask showed itself.

Aziz stopped capering and walked toward Finn with slow, exaggerated tiptoe steps, like a villain sneaking up on someone in a play. Shabh said something in Arabic and the simpleton leapt to the chain. Towed on it. Yanked Finn up until he swayed above the ground.

Malik wrapped his arms around Finn's waist.

And the horror began.

Shabh proved a cruel torturer with a crooked smile. She hummed softly as she slice-sliced Sadiqi in a quick beat. Each slice burned hot as fire.

Finn bellowed, despite himself, and from down the corridor replied a chorus like a pack of jabbering monkeys. Pain would break him, eventually, but now it made him frenzied. Rabid. He bucked in the chains — cursed, spat, bit at her. He was powerless to defend his body and all that remained was defiance. The pain deepened. He bled. And as he hurt and bled, he yearned to taunt her, lusted to dig at her more than he wanted life.

She came away with a yip of triumph and a patch of ink-marked skin.

"Murdering Robert was bliss," Finn hissed. Pride and wrath were irresistible sins. "Pure glory. My blade piercing his heart, his cries, pathetic tears. I relive it every night as I nod off to sleep."

In a blink her triumphant face contorted to something inhuman. She screamed, bit his arm like a dog, made quick slices over his chest and arm and stomach.

"Leave him be, bitch!"

The scream came from Emma. The slicing stopped, mercifully, and the burn of a dozen cuts merged into one torso-wide scalding. Shabh tilted her head to fix Emma with a wintry stare.

"Leave him." Emma spoke in a pleading, bewildered tone. "How can you be so cruel?"

Shabh's gaze flicked from Emma to Finn. Back to Emma.

"No…" Finn said.

"How did I not see it?" Shabh shook a head in mock reproach. "She loves you. You love her. And what better torment than watching a loved one die in agony, powerless to stop it."

"I murdered Robert." Finn's laugh was short and dry. "Spat in his face. Pissed on his corpse. And I'll do the same to your slack-witted boy!"

Shabh laughed at his too-plain attempt at diversion. "You are precious. Truly. Besides, young Robert is safe with an old friend."

She kissed Finn on a cheek. Soft, warm lips lingered until she whirled toward Emma.

Emma stared, entranced by Sadiqi's gleaming edge, then her eyes flared and her head drooped. She rolled into a ball like a woodlouse, arms over her head, and thrust trembling fingers into her hair. She spoke without looking up. "I am sorry. So sorry. I have silver. For you. Just do not hurt me."

Malik let go of Finn and stepped toward Emma.

Shabh waved him off. "The woman is mine. After she is broken, and after the murderer is broken by her screams, we will finish him."

Emma prayed, her rapid whispers loud in the stoney space, and fear made the words as garbled as a foreign tongue.

Shabh crouched and poked Emma's shoulder with a bloody finger. Emma flinched but stayed frozen in a ball, rocking, hands pushed into her hair.

Then the screaming began.

The man was buried to his neck.

Rollo stared. He, unlike most brethren, was not one to assign all things to the provenance of God, though even he could not help but wonder at finding a man's head in this trackless waste.

The storm fight had been chaos — glorious chaos. Sandpigs came from the murk and he cut and hacked them down until no more came. Templars huddled like a pack of cold puppies until the storm blew itself out. Sunlight showed them several arrow shots from the hill and backtracked to it. Found three horses. Buried four sergeants. Searched for signs of Finn or Emma. Most of the tracks were scoured away. A pair meandered into the hills and they trailed them — and when they found Nik and Yousef realized they trailed the wrong folk.

Somewhere in the chaos of coming and going they missed Finn. They searched until water bags grew perilously thin. Rollo made the hard choice to ride to Marda for water, then return to resume the search.

Marda was a bore. Toothless hermits, babbling about God, visions real or imagined. Then a fool said something and the air went out of the chatty hermits. After some prodding the fool explained they should search the Wadi of the Dead. A laura once thrived there. A demon lived there now, and snared and slaughtered and ate Christians. A boulder dropped in Rollo's gut — it must be her. Shabh.

The Old Man said she laired in some dark corner of the Judean.

The hermits refused to guide them — despite repeated coaxing, even upon threat of a beating. But one gave directions. Drew a crude map. Now Rollo was here — lost. They passed a score of ravines fitting the description of the Wadi of the Dead, seen the same cow-shaped outcrop for the third time, seen their own hoofprints. Elias, who claimed he could track a lizard over rock, scowled and cursed in his beard.

Rollo studied the ground, seeking signs of a trap, and seeing none stalked toward the head in the sand. The metallic jingle of spurs brought a shout.

"Bastards!"

The sun was at Rollo's back, and to the man he must appear a long, wide shadow with a halo at his head. A moustache, massive and drooping and black, covered his lip. The hair on the man's head was braided into small ropes that dangled by the sides of his sunburned face.

"Greetings," Rollo said. "We're seeking lost friends. A man with black hair. Scarred face. Mumbles like a simpleton. And a woman … comely, but grating. You'd know if you saw them. Have they passed?"

"Haven't put eyes on anyone to my front." The man snorted to dislodge an ant, then jiggled his head to demonstrate his limited point of view. "Bit of a blind spot behind."

"Why're you buried?"

"Borrowed a horse — two actually, and hadn't the chance to return them."

"Bedouins?"

"Weren't the Templars."

Rollo's laugh was dry. "Damn Templars, eh? So full of shite."

"Hate them. God-mad catamites. Ball-lickers." The man snuffed at the ant, which made its way back to his nostril. "How about a hand for a fella in a tight spot?"

"What can you offer?"

"Offer?"

"In trade. Digging a man out is hard work."

The man curled a lip in thought. "Got nothing. But I wager you've something in mind?"

"By your look, you're some species of bandit, eh? Must know the way hereabouts."

"Samaritan by birth. I live here now and could walk these hills blindfolded."

"We'll dig you free, bad Samaritan … if you take an oath to guide us."

"How long?"

"Ten days."

"Three. I've other tasks to attend."

Rollo heaved a sigh. "Farewell, my sunburned —"

"Ho, friend, not so hasty." His lip curled again as he made a show of thinking it over. "Upon reflection, I find your offer fair, and I give you my word as a gentleman."

Rollo chuckled at that, then flagged a hand at Jerol and Lugh, who started scooping away dirt while Rollo stretched out in the meagre shade of a rock.

The man's gaze froze on the red cross riding Rollo's breast. "Ah, shite, and bastard, and son of a —"

"Careful. I've been told, often and sternly, God doesn't look kindly on foul mouths." Rollo took a pull from his canteen. "What shall we call you?"

"A God-damn fool."

"God-Damn Fool is a mouthful."

"Funny man, for a Templar." His arms came free and he swiped dirt from eyes and ears, stuck a finger into a nostril and blew out the ant with a snuff. "Bastard."

"The ant, or me?"

"Both." The man wriggled out of the hole, stood on wobbly legs, then patted his chest. "Ashar."

"So tell me, Ashar, are you Christian?"

"I am." To prove it Ashar signed the cross, right to left, stomach to chin.

Rollo's eyes narrowed but he smiled. "Is it customary among Samaritan Christians to sign the cross upside down?"

"Out of practice, is all."

"Do you give me your word, as a Christian, to serve us for ten days?"

"I do."

Rollo stared, scarred lips pursed. "I believe you, strangely." He pushed himself up. "And now your first task is guiding us to the Wadi of the Dead."

"Ah, shite, and bastard, and son of a bitch. Why in God's name would you go there?"

CHAPTER 17

Finn's gut was ice cold — from the horror come to them both, and him unable to defend either.

Shabh crouched, face leering in Emma's. Then a flurry of slapping and stabbing. A hiss. Screaming. Shabh reeled away, the monkey end of an ivory hairpin jutting from an eye. She pawed at the monkey but only managed to snap it off. A stub of ivory gleamed in her eye as she staggered into the wall and fell.

Emma leapt to her feet, hair flowing free, and lunged at the pile of weapons in the corner. The ankle chain wrenched her back and her hand fell a finger length short of Oathkeeper.

Malik gawked at the sudden turn of events and Finn's legs shot out and wrapped him — a leg under a shoulder, the other over, shin tucked under his chin. His man parts squashed against Malik's ear.

Pain erupted in Finn's torso but he embraced it, for with pain came anger, and with anger came power. Stomach and leg muscles bulged and Malik writhed like a rat wrapped in a snake's coils. Malik was strong but Finn stronger, his strength and stamina built by endless training and hardship and warfare. Malik punched Finn's back with his free fist until Finn crushed tighter. Something popped, slipped, and Malik screamed.

"That'd be a shoulder," Finn hissed.

Aziz held them aloft while Malik jigged his head and gurgled at the simpleton.

"No action … without … direction," Finn grunted through clenched teeth. "Remember?"

They thrashed in the chains, panted like dogs, until Malik's flailing slowed to a tremor. Finn bore down until Malik went limp and heavy. He let go and Malik dropped like a sack of gravel.

Emma shouted in Arabic, "Aziz, lower him."

Finn crashed to the ground, gasping, muscles trembling. Training and instinct brought him to hands and knees. He crawled to Malik, yanked his dagger and plunged it behind an ear, just to be certain. Then rummaged his corpse for the twist-key. Freed himself. Freed Emma.

Aziz gawked at all the back-and-forth and sucked on a wet lip, waiting for someone to tell him what to do. He was still sucking when Malik's dagger pierced his heart.

Shouts jerked Finn around to Shabh, who yelled down the corridor in Arabic.

Shabh wept bloody tears from both eyes. Her head twitched left, right, eyes seeking but not finding. Sadiqi followed in rhythm with her head. Then she levered herself up the wall. Gingerly, she pinched ahold of the pin, plucked it from her eye, let it drop with a soft clatter.

"Even blinded, as I am, I could walk from here." Rivulets of tears and blood made her face grotesque. "But I will not flee. I ran once. In Jerusalem. And vowed to never flee again."

She laughed madly and waved Sadiqi in invitation.

Finn came in a low shuffle. She lunged and slashed at the shuffle of bare feet on stone. He took a cut to the hand. Dropped Malik's dagger. Managed to snag her wrist. A hard twist and he punched her elbow and broke her arm. She howled in pain and he shoved her to the wall, pinned her there, where she thrashed and kicked. Sandalwood filled Finn's nose as he glared into the ruins of her eyes. She went suddenly limp, aware what must come next, and began chanting something tribal and eerie.

He took hold of her slender throat, dug in, and all that remained was choking the life from her. His fingers froze. He had schemed, braved Gerard's wrath to find her, to kill the monster stalking him. Now he had her. But all he could hear was Da's hard voice, *Never harm a woman, boy. Never.*

A rustle at his side and Shabh grunted, puffed a gust of anise-flavoured breath. Emma hissed wordlessly and stabbed the long knife again. And again.

Finn shuffled back and Shabh slithered down the wall, leaving a bloody smear in her place. A spasm racked her arm and she was free to join the ghostly choir. An invisible yoke, heavier than Finn had realized, floated from his shoulders.

"What have I done? Never killed before…"

Emma's whisper rose to a shout before trailing off. Long knife trembled in her hand. Finn settled a palm on her shoulder and she flinched. He said nothing, gave a gentle squeeze, and with his touch she let out a long, shuddering breath. A firmer squeeze said, *We're not out of this yet.*

Five staggering strides and Finn scooped up Oathkeeper and the mace. A mace is a simple tool, a flanged iron head on a wooden handle, and a brutal mace and a sleek sword make a wicked pair. Weapons in hand put fire in his heart.

Footfalls thumped down the corridor. Finn pivoted on a heel as two bearded youths barged into the room — come to Shabh's aid, though too late. They held saifs high, stiff, like farmers wielding sickles. Then one shifted his grip; heel of the palm and little finger on the pommel, top of the hand flush with the guard, knuckles in line with the blade's edge.

Finn grinned like a wolf. "Recently learned the blade, I see."

They did not understand French but were shrewd enough to shuffle at him together.

A high feint of Oathkeeper lured a parry from the first tough and Finn chopped the mace into a knee. A crack of bone and he screamed and fell. Finn skipped away from the second man while deflecting a slash with Oathkeeper. Naked, he was ludicrously exposed, and he gave a brittle laugh at how absurd he must look.

A hiss of anger at the laughter, and the second tough stomped and lunged with his slit-eyed stare pinned on Finn's chest. The blade came for Finn's heart, as expected, and he twisted aside. Short-chopped a shoulder with the mace. Back-slashed Oathkeeper over his throat. He leaned aside while the tough sprayed and spattered, lurched and toppled.

The knee-busted youth was crawling and groaning until the mace ended him.

Another youth burst into the room and staggered to a stop. He took stock. Saw his mistress dead. His brothers dead. And a naked, blood-slathered demon leering at him. A garble of Arabic and he wheeled and ran back the way he had come.

Finn laughed, a mixture of relief and disbelief, and found himself staring at Emma. She stared back unflinching. The gaze spoke of shared things, hard things, the kinds of things that bind two souls. And so bound they would be friends for life — perhaps more, if each were not sworn to another. Her eyes, blue as a summer sky, shone in this dark place. Strands of hair, a mess of cinnamon and chestnut without the hairpin, flashed in the light. Her gaze wandered his body and, to his surprise, he did not mind.

Emma broke the strange spell. "Well. Now. Shall we get some clothes on you?"

Finn nodded in embarrassed agreement.

They bound his wounds with strips of his cappa. Dressed him in Malik's clothes. Tugged on his boots and wiggled into his mail. Thus fortified, they strode down the long, dark corridor and into the light.

A cave awaited — longer and larger than the one they had escaped. Water dripped from a seep into a cistern. A firepit smouldered. A natural cleft in the roof let smoke out and light in. Cubicles pocked the walls like cells in a honeycomb, and from one a naked, wild-haired madman leered. He clacked his teeth and barked like a dog. They shuffled past, daring the mad dog to challenge them. He declined.

The cave mouth was shaded by a deep overhang. Dust hung in a cloud, marking the flight of some number of less-than-loyal adherents. Horses stood further up the overhang in a makeshift corral. Fagan strolled toward Finn, bobbing a head in welcome, and Emma began saddling her Arabian mare.

Finn mounted Fagan and said, "Shabh said men never expect the doer to be a woman and die in their arrogance."

"As she died, by a woman's hand." Emma finished the thought, and they laughed — though it was the grim mirth of folk having stared a beast in the eye and lived to tell the tale.

"Where are we?" Finn looked to the sky, seeking a sign.

"Somewhere north-west of Marda," Emma said. "If we ride east, we will find the road."

Down the wadi they rode. The gorge narrowed, widened, meandered into an S-turn, narrowed again, widened again. Thrill was fading, leaving Finn bone-weary, limbs softly trembling. Sudden pain folded him over. He eyed his mailed chest in a stupor, admired the shiny blood oozing through the links, then listed dangerously to starboard.

"Can you make it?" Emma grasped an arm, steered him.

"Just scratches. I'll —"

"Riders," Emma said.

Finn jerked up to see two riders. Black braids dangled from the head of the first. The other was familiar.

"To come this far … and fail…" Finn's voice was a faint rasp.

For the third time in as many days he fell into darkness.

Elias was one of the riders.

Finn had come to encircled by grim faces and much stroking of beards. The wind-blasted remains of his band were there — Rollo, Nik and Yousef, Lugh and Uncle Jerol, and two other sergeants, Bili and Loic. Ashar, who Finn did not know, brought a confused scowl to his face. They propped him up. Gave him water and words. Lugged him to Marda.

Women were barred from entering Marda's compound. The Templars therefore resided in an outbuilding with Emma. A window, covered with a thin layer of opaque horn during chilly nights, was open to let in sunlight and a breeze. A fire burned in the hearth and over it hung a pot of pottage. The stink of burning camel dung filled the space. Emma, silent and staring, sat against the wall, knees hugged to her chest. Finn had an urge to touch her.

"You look like something a goat ate and shat," Rollo said, and laughed at his own wit.

Finn lay on his back on a cool, stone-tiled floor, with a blanket propped under his head. His skull throbbed, his ribs ached, and his chest burned. One of his wrists throbbed so bad he feared he might lose the hand. Everywhere hurt — though his pride hurt the most. Being cut by a woman stung the same as being cut by a man, he found, if not for the shame.

He gave a throaty groan. "Seen better days. Though at least I've cause for my appearance; what's your excuse for looking like you do?"

"Ah, there's my feisty Finn." Rollo smiled his mangled-lip smile, though it died quick. "Judean is a hell of a place. All looks alike. Got lost. Stumbled on Asher," he flapped a hand at the man, scowling from a corner, "and he led us to the Wadi of the Dead. Damn lucky to find you riding out ... wouldn't have made the monastery alone. Rooster was sick with worry."

Lugh shrugged, embarrassed. He was protective and proud of Finn, as were most sergeants of their knights, for a knight's reputation was shared, in part, by his sergeant.

"What an adventure, eh?" Rollo smirked. "And you two. Traipsing about alone."

Finn ignored the smirk. "I'd be a dead, skinless man if not for Emma." He spilled out their story — the cistern; Baret's murder; Malik's betrayal; Emma luring Shabh close to lance her with the hairpin; Shabh, blinded then dying by Emma's hand.

The Templars pondered the brave damsel rescuing the knight in distress. That tale was yet to be sung by a minstrel — and would no doubt raise a few brows if it were.

"God's bones." Rollo studied Emma a moment, gave an approving dip of the chin. "You can ride with me anywhere."

"No, but I will allow you to ride with me," Emma said, with a touch of venom. "You misjudge the fire and fortitude of women. We are not weaklings."

Rollo raised hands in mock surrender.

Lugh was suturing Finn's cuts. Pain came in waves. To manage it, Finn focused on breathing — in and out, deliberate and deep. Then Shabh's velvety words sliced through his trance; *She loves you. You love her.* He flinched. Wondered if it were true. And if the heat flushing his face was evidence for it or, perhaps, was just from the pain. His eyes flipped open and he caught Emma staring; she glanced away, as did he.

Emma climbed to her feet and strolled outside; at Finn's nod, Bili and Loic followed.

"Bad." Lugh waved the bloody needle at where Shabh had sliced away the ink mark. "Skinned you like a hare. Too wide to suture."

"Burn it," Finn said.

"Burn it?"

"You heard me."

Rollo and Lugh stared at each other until Lugh mouthed, *You do it*. Rollo puffed out a breath. Trudged to the fire. Tugged his arming sword out.

"Not your blade," Jerol said. "Heat'll ruin it. Won't hold an edge after."

"Forge heat traps spirits in the steel. Reheating lets them out." Lugh nodded confidently and handed Rollo a sword carried by one of the sergeants lost in the storm fight.

Rollo huffed at Lugh's ignorance. "Any fool knows bone and fire make iron into steel. Swordsmiths put bones into the fire. From a virgin are best. Tough to get your hands on virgin bones nowadays. No easy task. Why, once I —"

"Get on with it," Finn said.

Rollo thrust the blade into the fire. Jerol used a poker to pile hot coals around it. Steel was magic; a timeless mystery; holy for those who live and die by its edge. They watched, entranced, as the steel heated to light straw, to dark straw, to orange, to red. When it transformed to apple red Rollo wrapped the handle in a rag and pulled the sword out, then strolled to Finn, who lay with an arm draped over his eyes.

"Ready?"

"Distract me first. Then surprise me."

Rollo farted, loud and sharp, and the tension died in a chorus of juvenile laughter.

"Not like that," Finn said.

Rollo stared a moment. "You've noticed everyone gets a byname. Uncle. Rooster. Cackhand. Hector is Archimedes. Serlo is Chatter."

"Sir Chatter," Jerol amended, and Rollo ploughed on.

"You've one too, Finn, though none dare say it to your face. Ever wondered what it is?"

"No. Though now I confess a minor curiosity."

"Saint." Rollo hefted the sword and appraised its pulsing glow.

"Saint?"

"It's ironic. Like calling a huge man Mouse."

Finn laughed and Rollo gave a satisfied nod. Lugh and Jerol and Elias pounced, pinned Finn's legs and arms, and Rollo pressed the sword's flat to the wound. He waited a few heartbeats, face a rictus of concentration, then flipped the blade over and pressed down again. Finn thrashed and kicked and cursed.

The pain was beyond measure — worse than any suffered before. For a time, agony owned his mind, and he was aware of naught but the stink of his own charred flesh. Rollo and Lugh swapped nervous glances. Finn stared at the rafters and rhythmically thumped a heel as the agony eased. At least the pollution of Shabh's touch was burned away. Purified by flame. Wounds made him wiser too. Scars were symbols of what he survived — and reminders of the negligence that caused them. *Old scars say you're not learning fast enough, fool*, he thought.

Lugh smeared a remedy of garlic, onion, cow bile, and wine on the wounds. The ingredients, in measured quantities, were steeped in a copper pot while monks chanted prayers. The

201

medicine fought wound rot and everyone packed a vial of the blessed balm. Rooster held Finn up while Jerol wrapped him with strips of clean linen.

"So." Finn nestled his head into the balled-up blanket, shifted his gaze to Rollo. "Any word from Hector?"

"Nothing."

"How many days since we went our separate ways?"

"Four."

"Send Elias and Nik to the meeting place. See what they see." Finn gave a long sigh. "We clawed free of one trap. Why does it seem a nastier one looms?"

CHAPTER 18

The rising sun drove off the tide of shadow. Dark pools lingered in the low places until they too fled the light. The Mountains of Moab, distant to the east, were lit up tawny as lions. Finn took it all in from the window while pondering the solitude.

Something tingled his arm — a bee, just landed and righting itself in his hairs. Shiny eyes stared back smartly; black and yellow stripes glowed in the soft light. It was the most beautiful thing Finn had seen in days. *Strange how men don't see beauty until it intrudes unbidden.* He prodded the bee to a palm and tipped it on the sill, where it buzzed away.

"A killer of men, caring for one of God's smallest creatures. How surprising."

Finn turned to a man at the door — lean, like a bird-shooer that had lost its stuffing. His face was brown and much creased, his eyes large and kind and gentle. Dirty feet wore even dirtier sandals. A dark-haired child hovered in his shadow.

Finn had no witty retort and nodded once.

"Bees." The man gestured toward the window. "Brother Antero tries to domesticate them. Wild is wild, I say. As God intended. John the Baptist ate locusts and wild honey, and if locusts and wild honey were enough for him, they are enough for me." The man paused, smiled politely. "Forgive my ramblings. You must be Brother Finn. I am Cyran."

"Abbot Cyran," Finn said, and Cyran gave a humble nod.

"I oversee the monasteries and lauras. The monks and hermits."

Cyran stared, lips pressed, and Finn sensed a lecture forthcoming. He was not wrong.

"Templars are called monks — wrongly, for you are not ordained as such. The word monk is based on the Greek *monakhos*, meaning solitary, and from *monos*, meaning alone. Yet you are never alone. Far from it. By rule, and tradition, you share the company of others. Always."

Finn smiled politely as the lecture veered into the differences between a monk and a hermit, then on to the virtues of hermitage. The child hovering around Cyran shrugged skinny shoulders in mute apology.

"This arse blathers worse than Hector," Rollo muttered.

"Brother Cyran," Finn said.

Cyran stopped, mouth open. "I rabbit on — again. Forgive me. Jabbering is a vice common to old men, especially old hermits living alone. We get excited by strangers." He shook a head in self-reproach. "To the point then. Ask, and it will be given; seek, and you will find."

Finn and Rollo shared glances to say, *I thought he was getting to the point…*

"From Matthew. In the Bible. Do you read it?"

"Wonderful book, the Bible," Rollo said. "Hate your enemies, love your neighbours, and whatnot. Wish I had more time for study. But fighting heathens is damned hard work."

"Our chaplain reads to us from the Bible during each meal," Finn said, more tactfully. "But we don't devote much time to study ourselves."

"Pity." Cyran sighed in disappointment; his lecture had fallen flat and Templars were no biblical scholars. "Point is, Matthew tells us to seek, and if we seek there are wonderous things to be found. And you are here seeking things."

Finn said nothing and Cyran spoke into the silence.

"Hospitallers came here seeking things."

Inwardly Finn cursed. "Two Frenchmen? One built like an ox, the other with a beard to his belt?"

"Just so. Brothers Bernard and Eudo."

Finn and Rollo scowled in unison, and Finn asked, "What did they find?"

"Find? Nothing. Rumour sent them sniffing about like hounds, though whether they seek the scent of boar or hind even they could not say." Cyran stared a moment before beckoning. "Come. I will show you what I showed them."

Cyran led them from the outbuilding and into blindingly bright daylight. Emma fell in behind and a scowl hitched the Abbot's lip — though he voiced no complaint.

Marda stood on a lone rise nudging up from the desert floor. A cobble wall ran around the edge of the rise. A second inner wall surrounded the refectory, chapel, and baptistry. Several outbuildings, including the one the Templars occupied, scattered between the walls. The ruins of two towers jutted up to either side of the walls.

"The towers are from the old days," Cyran said. "Hasmonean kings built Hyrcania, along with others like it, to protect the Jewish Kingdom against the Edomites. Hyrcania was reinforced by King Herod but later abandoned. Monks rebuilt and repurposed and called it Marda. What you see is a mix of old and new. Hermits live in cells at the base of the cliff." He tipped a thumb over a shoulder, in Emma's general direction. "We are ... mixed company, and therefore shall walk a lesser used path to avoid distracting the brothers."

Cyran trod on, then heeled in like he had just remembered a forgotten task.

"Brother Finn. We, the brothers and I, wish to thank you for cleansing the Wadi of the Dead. Violence is an evil I would

205

rather not ponder. I abhor it. I also detest God's church sending men, such as yourselves, to shed blood in His name." Cyran took a breath. "But on rare occasions it is merited when fighting evil. The brothers at the wadi … their souls were trapped in that dark place. We pleaded to God to send an avenging angel — and He did. Now they are free."

Finn dipped a head at Emma. "She was your avenging angel. Thank her."

Cyran shuffled toward Emma and half-bowed. "We thank you."

Emma smiled or frowned, behind the face scarf only she knew, then returned Cyran's half-bow.

"I mean no offence," Cyran said and, for the first time, fixed Emma with his kind gaze. "The last time I saw a woman, a Christian woman, was … eleven, twelve years ago? And a hermit, to remain sane and celibate, must not only avoid the fairer sex but convince himself they do not exist." He smiled patiently. "Now then. To the task at hand."

Cyran strode off, the child trailing like a loyal hound. Finn gave a wink and the child beamed in reply.

"Samuel," Cyran said without looking back. "Away now. To your studies."

The path worked down the slope in a series of switchbacks before branching. They took the left-hand path, angled around the hill, and as they walked Cyran explained Samuel was found as a babe, abandoned by an unknown mother. Cyran had named him Samuel, who in the Bible was adopted by the prophet Eli, though now he thought Lazy might have been a more apt name.

A door in the hillside awaited. The stone lintel was pocked and scarred in a rough square.

Cyran nodded at the scars. "This was the sepulchre of a Kohen, a member of the Jewish priestly clan. Their sepulchres are marked thus —" he held his hands side-by-side at the thumbs, palms up, fingers of each hand splayed to form a V — "though this marking was chiselled away. The Jewish tomb was empty and we converted it, if you will, into a Christian chapel." The old man snuffled at his lame jest, gestured at the door. "This door, the sepulchre it guards, this is why you came to Marda. It is open. Examine it for yourself."

"For what?"

"Do you think monks live here, at Marda, not knowing the legends surrounding this place? Of course we do. And of many other supposed hiding places."

"Don't know what you mean," Finn said, stiffness in his voice.

Cyran smiled, implying he knew an evasion when he heard one. "I think you do." He stared off then said, "In the ruin in the Valley of Achor. In the sepulchre, in the third course of stones, one hundred ingots of gold."

Finn's mouth dropped open and Cyran said, "Copper scrolls were hidden and Templars found one. But the original parchment, the source parchment, was also hidden. Bedouins recovered it in a cave, not from here, and traded it to us for leather. This was many years ago. Before my time. Much of the parchment was mangled by rodents or decay. But what little remained was passed from abbot to abbot. Maintaining knowledge is part of my duty. So, Brother Finn, I know what you seek."

Cyran raised an inviting hand, and as the hand raised so did Finn's heartbeat. *Was it here?* He breathed in to calm rising nerves and pushed the door open on well-oiled hinges. A short flight of stairs. A rough-hewn room awaited at the bottom. An altar stood at one end. Oil lamps sat in niches.

Those aren't burning by chance... Cyran planned this.

Finn shuffled around the room seeking clues to something. Anything. He studied the altar. Examined the walls. One was painted with faded frescoes — of hermit saints, if their long beards and bedraggled robes were any indication. Crosses had been carved randomly, and chi-rho, and ichthys, and other Christograms. Symbols of arcane provenance intermingled with those Christian.

Finn crouched to run a hand over the floor. Limestone pavers. The stone was grey and smooth. Tan-red stones, rough surfaced, caught his eye and he hopped a few paces to study them. Sandstone — three of them fitted together at the base of the wall. He peered up, and on the wall was a mark. What had been there was chiselled away, like that on the lintel, but a fractured finger showed at one edge. *The sign of the Kohen.* He studied the mark with a tilted head.

"Latin," Rollo growled. He passed a hand over the wall near a sputtering oil lamp.

Finn stood as Emma leaned past Rollo's shoulder.

"*Veni, vidi, clepsi* — meaning I came, I saw, I stole. A play on Caesar's saying, *Veni, vidi, vici* — I came, I saw, I conquered." She tapped the inscription. "A Roman came to this spot, saw something, and stole what?"

"Griffonage. Carved by a Roman legionary, no doubt. Like a dog raising a leg to mark what it claimed." Cyran had come down the stairs, quiet as a spider, and stood with hands tucked into the sleeves of his robe. "Have you been to Rome? I have. Horrid place. Dirty. Loud. Reeks of garbage and excrement. Romans are obscenely rude. Could not wait to be gone." He studied the ceiling while corralling rambling memories. "But there is an arch in Rome. Constructed on the Via Sacra after the death of the emperor Titus. The Arch of Titus, as it is called, commemorates the Roman victory over Jewish rebels. Do you know what it shows?"

"The emperor marching in triumph?" Finn guessed.

"And parading spoils taken during the Jewish war. Artefacts stolen from Herod's temple, most likely. A solid gold menorah. The Gold Trumpets. The gold Table of Shewbread. Fire pans for removing the ashes from the altar." Cyran glanced from Rollo to Finn. "Have you read Josephus?"

"Not lately," Finn said, and Cyran honoured the jest with a smile.

"Josephus witnessed Rome's war with the Jews," Cyran explained. "His history tells us a man named Phineas, a treasurer of the temple, was captured by the Romans and put to the torture. Phineas, you see, led the Romans to the treasures, which were dug up and carted to Rome. Much of it funded the Colosseum — says so on the building itself." He gave a moment to let all that sink in. "Josephus also wrote the standard of gold throughout Syria fell to half its value, so great was the hoard stolen by Rome."

"Fascinating history, Brother, but why tell me?"

"Because, Brother, Romans were here. Beat you by, what, one thousand years?"

"By a thousand years," Finn repeated. He scrubbed a palm over his bearded jaw as the scraps in his head, half-formed, drifted together to make something whole.

They stood at the bottom of three courses of stone, in the sepulchre, in the ruins in the Valley of Achor. The hoard had been in the vault. Just above, on the wall, the markings of the Kohen, which to a Jew must plainly show the hiding place. Romans came and prized up the stones. The rent was later repaired with stone of a different species. Romans chiselled away the mark, and in its place left graffiti to mock what an empire stole.

"You are on a fool's errand, I am afraid," Cyran said, his voice soft with sympathy. "What was here is gone and the treasures, if any remain, should be sought in Rome, not here."

The words were a whisper but felt like clashing cymbals against Finn's eardrum. "What next?" he asked, mostly to himself.

"The Hospitallers asked the same, after I showed them this room and told them what I told you. I counselled them to leave off this foolishness." Cyran gave a soft shrug. "They ignored me and rode to the ruins of the Essenes, not far from here, convinced something must be there and desperate to find it. They waste their time. Possibly their lives."

Finn said nothing.

"Do you know, this valley might not be the Valley of Achor in the Holy Book?"

"Three possible Achors. Aye."

"Then you also know the very name *Achor* means trouble." Cyran's lip's pressed tight, as they did when he was readying a lecture. "The book of Joshua tells us Israel won a great battle. But a man, Achan, kept the spoils for himself and his display of greed angered the Lord. Achan was stoned to death. Then burned. And over Achan's ashes they heaped rocks. That barren place has been the Valley of Achor ever since — the Valley of Trouble, Jews call it."

Cyran shuffled closer. "Nothing good ever happened in Achor. I advise you, like the Hospitallers, to let it be."

"I hear you, Brother Cyran." Finn forked fingers through his hair, black and spiky with sweat. "But I cannot. A command was given and a vow of obedience means I carry on."

Even though obeying may be the end of me.

Images of red-faced Master Gerard filled Finn's head, and of himself, banished and bitter, milking cows in some dreary barn.

Marda had many cisterns — eight, that Finn had inspected. He rubbed his scarred face, brooding over the cistern before him, as though brooding would drain the thing.

Water ever flows from rain to earth, to plant, to animal, to the streams and to the sea. Monks of Marda trap it here, for a time, for without it they could not live in this harsh place. Winter rainfall was stored in the cisterns and an aqueduct moved water from Jabal Munttar, the Mountain of the Watchman.

Cyran told them Jabal Munttar was also home to the Biblical scapegoat. The story went that two kid goats were to be sacrificed but one, the scapegoat, was released into the wilderness, taking with it the people's sins. The second was sacrificed. Finn could not decide which of the kids he most felt kinship with but found the tale fitting all the same.

"Can't search this unless we grow gills and learn to swim," Rollo said, and nodded at the cistern. "And I'd wager the hermits would get riled if we drained their supply of water into the dirt. What would they bathe with?"

"Mmm," Finn said.

"You're especially cheery today, Brother."

Finn wheeled on Rollo. "What do I have to be cheery about? We had the scroll. Lost it. Now here we are. In the middle of … nowhere. Jews speak in riddles and we're not certain we hunt in the correct Achor. Worse — what we hunt, if it ever existed, was likely hauled away long ago."

"At least we have this charming landscape in which to share each other's company."

"There is that." Finn sucked in a cleansing breath. Puffed it out. "Silence and solitude appeal to me. I would like to return, when all is said and done, and live out my days as a hermit."

"I'll retire to a nunnery," Rollo said.

"You mean a monastery?"

"Nunnery. Sisters need a strong hand. To pull weeds. Cut wood. Carry things. And they get lonely." Rollo sighed, pursed his scarred lips. "There was this young woman in Caen."

"Stop talking," Finn said.

"She was blessed with huge paps. Round as pies too."

"Don't want to hear about paps, nor your past loves."

"Love? Never said I loved her."

"Even talking about women is… God's bones, do you know any of the rules?"

A voice harumphed — Cyran had again crept up on them and was now pretending not to have heard their impious chatter. Samuel hovered behind and gave Finn a grin.

Cyran proffered Finn a linen bundle. "For Emma. As a token of our esteem. A hairpin, to replace that which she lost. Brother Alfons carved it from the bone of a gazelle. Brother Toros engraved it. Together we blessed it, prayed it will bring her peace."

Nowadays Emma wore a shemagh, ever hiding her face and thoughts, a habit formed since the Wadi of the Dead. Her sky-blue eyes seemed dimmed. This was not how Finn remembered her when all this had started. Then she was all smile and savvy, cunning and confidence. He said as much to Cyran.

"Women, most anyway, find cruelty an appalling mystery," Cyran said. "What she suffered and did caused injury. Inside. And inner wounds take time to heal." He flashed a look of pity. "Though certes you know this."

Finn dipped a chin to say he did, and to say he would give the gift.

Cyran made a show of peering into the cistern and said, "You found the treasure, and under our noses all these years."

Finn scowled at the ridicule. "Brother Rollo and I were thinking of draining the water, to have a proper look, and your jest makes me think the idea has merit."

Cyran's mouth dropped open. "Brother Finn. I must object. The cisterns were in disarray when Saint Sabas came. Cobbles were pried away. Sabas rebuilt them, even built a kiln to make burnt lime to coat the insides. So. Obviously anything in them, if ever there was, is long since removed. Certes you see emptying the cisterns would be a waste of precious…"

Cyran's lecture ploughed on but fell on deaf ears. Finn stared over the abbot's shoulder at Ashar, who was hustling up the slope towards them, black braids asway.

"Yer Lordship," Ashar panted.

"Brother," Finn corrected, and Ashar waved a hand to say, *Whatever.*

"Uncle says to come to the south wadi. The one below the hill. Found something."

They left Cyran and Samuel, both frowning at the prospect of losing Marda's water supply. As they walked, Finn glanced to Ashar, then to Rollo. "Is it wise to let a bandit linger?"

"Ashar," Rollo said over a shoulder. "You won't chib us in the back and steal, will you?"

"No, yer Lordships."

"See?" Rollo said. "Ashar is a good Christian and a reformed man."

Finn snorted.

The something, when they got to it, was a hole. A wadi cut along the base of the hill; the bottom was a jumble of boulders;

one wall was earth and rock; the opposite wall was bare cliff face below Marda. The hole yawned in the rock the height of a man above the wadi's flowline.

Jerol and Lugh stood below the opening. Jerol held pebbles in a hand and he tossed one at it. "Rocks were piled in the mouth and seemed out of place. Pulled them down and had a peek. Stairs drop into blackness."

"Bring light," Finn said.

Jerol flung another pebble past Finn, and Finn tracked the pebble's flight toward Loic, who trod toward them with unlit torches in hand. Finn's gaze tracked up from Loic to the hill above. The sepulchre was there, on top of the hill, and the tunnel opening was beneath it. If the tunnel was of any length it would, more or less, pass under the sepulchre.

Finn's gaze was nailed to the opening as he stripped his belt and handed it, along with Oathkeeper, to Lugh. Cappa and mail came off. The belt went back on and the long knife with it. Sweat coated his wounds, still raw and weeping, and he tried to ignore the sting.

"Explored caves before?" Jerol asked.

"No."

"Four things." Jerol held up his fingers for emphasis. "Don't panic if you get wedged in; only makes it worse. Bats bite but they don't kill — unless they carry the raging disease, in which case you're humped. A torch doesn't burn as long as you think; carry a spare, and flint and steel. And if you can taste the air, or it stings your eyes, back out quick."

"What if I don't come back?"

"Then Cyran will say nice words over the hole and we'll share a drink in your memory."

Lugh hoisted Finn's sword. "And rest peaceful knowing I gave Oathkeeper a good home."

"Too kind." Finn clambered up the rock until he squatted in the mouth of the hole.

Loic used flint and steel to ignite a torch and handed it and a second unlit torch up to Finn. He tucked the unlit torch into his belt. A heave and he shouldered his way through the narrow opening and to the first stair.

Stone dust and old air lay heavy. Darkness enveloped Finn. Torchlight illuminated a flight of steps that descended into inky black. Nightmarish images of trowes, and goblins, and an endless fall into nothing flooded his brain. He cinched his eyes and shook his head to drive them away. He sucked in a lungful of air — clean air, he noted — and started down.

Hack marks showed where the tunnel had been carved from the bedrock. The passage was just wide and tall enough for a man. He stepped lightly, and deliberate, like the stairs would crumble beneath his boots at each step. He counted as he went. So intent was his focus it took twelve steps before realized he was not alone. He twisted to Rollo's grinning face.

The Norman waved his torch in greeting. "Not a good place to take a tumble. Besides, I'd never forgive myself if you found a stash of ale and succumbed to temptation."

Finn rasped a nervous laugh and took another twelve steps before slowing. Black fled orange flame. The notion occurred his might be the first feet to touch these stairs in a thousand years. "Straight as an arrow," he said under his breath.

The tunnel carried on straight for another sixteen steps until the walls fell away and the stairs opened into a black hole. He stood in the entry of squarish room maybe seven or eight paces across. His heart stomped in his chest as he hefted the torch and squinted into the darkness. A ceiling was just visible there.

"Tall, for such a small room," Finn said in a cracked whisper.

"I'd wager we're underneath the sepulchre," Rollo said, and Finn nodded.

They set off, shuffling around the walls, probing and patting for … something, anything… They found nothing. No markings. No signs of digging. All seemed as pristine as the day it was made and, presumably, abandoned. They met again at the stairs. Finn fanned his torch close to the wall, seeking the priest's mark, and slid a hand along behind the flame's light.

"No mark of the Coven," Rollo said.

"Kohen," Finn corrected.

Rollo said something smart but Finn did not hear it. His was staring at a flat rock propped at an angle against the wall, forming a small lean-to. In a burst of excitement, he plunged a hand under, groping for what, he was not sure. Something shifted in his hand and he felt cold scales. He jerked back and dropped to a knee, held the torch to the recess, and glimpsed a dark coil. Black flickering tongue. Filmy eye slits. Chisel-like head. He blurted a curse and found himself on the other side of the room without recalling how he got there.

"Snake."

"Sir No Shoulders?" Rollo crouched to peer, then laughed. "The famed swordsman, Finnláech of Struan, pissing his breeches because of a snake."

"Unnatural. Crawls on its belly. Licks the air."

Scaled creatures were rare in Alba and Finn had not laid eyes on one until Outremer, nor touched one until now. He had not gotten used to them — and never would.

"Poor thing. It's cold. Sluggish." Rollo reached in, slid it out. Uncoiled, it was as long as a man is tall. "Viper, by the look. Want to hold him? Best way to conquer fear is to face it."

"Who said I'm afraid? Startled me, is all."

"So I see."

Rollo heaved Sir No Shoulders to a corner, where he hit with a slap, rolled to his belly, commenced flicking a tongue as he pondered what had ruined his peaceful repose.

"There. Better?"

Finn glared at Rollo, then the snake, and hoped the tremble in his hands did not show as he crouched to stare under the rock. Empty. He stuck the torch in and peered again. No marks on the wall, nor the floor. No hidden levers. No signs of looting — nor signs of anything.

Finn frowned in disappointment. "Empty … can't be, can it?"

Rollo tipped the rock over with a boot tip, then rapped a heel on the floor where it had rested. Finn did the same, and the two moved around stomping and tapping the floor. The strikes of leathered heel on stone was muffled, like the stone extended uninterrupted to the centre of the earth and devoured the sounds of feeble men.

Rollo gave one last frustrated stomp on stone. "Solid. Bastards hacked this rat warren from bedrock, and bedrock makes for tough digging. Lot of work for no reason I can see. Unless the loot was just stored here, sitting all pretty for the taking, and Romans obliged?"

"Could be." Finn glanced to the ceiling, oddly tall, then double-checked the snake was still in its corner. It was. "Though that seems … too easy."

"We're chasing our arses in circles," Rollo muttered.

The tunnel seemed like something important. Hope had blossomed. Now all Finn could feel was the darkness tightening.

CHAPTER 19

Finn hurt. The cut-burn had split open and was weeping and stinging. Climbing the stairs from the empty room sapped his vigour, to his shame, and he lay on the floor of their house weak as a kitten. Monks bustled around outside the house; several peeked in on Finn every so often. Rollo and the others searched Marda while Finn's body rested and his mind worked.

Questions circled and wheeled like birds. *Le Scélérat*; what other mischief had he done? Beau, already vicious as a stoat, was driven mad by greed-lust. Murdered Bedouins for fun. Killed a man of God. Had he found the hoard and hauled it away? The thought made Finn's guts boil with worry.

And Adrien? He was late. Likely he had been scattered by the storm. Or murdered by Beau and left to rot in the sun. *Would serve him right*, Finn thought, then crossed himself. Memories nettled him — Adrien twisting his fancy gold ring, grinning the smug grin Finn wanted to smack off his face. Might he have gone mad, like his shite-eating father, and be roaming the desert eating oats and sand? Or maybe he had gone rogue and played a game under rules he invented. This notion haunted Finn the most.

A shuffle of feet yanked his mind back to the present.

Samuel stood in the door, steaming bowl in hand. "Brother Antero sends goat stew. Meat to replenish your blood and strength, he says."

Finn levered himself up to slump against the wall, then studied the boy. Twelve years old, or thereabouts, and so lean Finn doubted he could throw a shadow. His feet were too long for his body; a growth spurt loomed and he would be taller by next summer. Black hair and olive-hued skin, darkened by the sun, made his bright hazel eyes striking. Part Saracen and part something else.

Finn waved the boy over and took the bowl. Famished, he tucked in like a wolf, suddenly obsessed with meat. Samuel licked a lip.

"Sit, Samuel. Eat. There is enough for two."

"Sam," the boy said.

"Eh?"

"Sam. My name. Only Abbot Cyran calls me Samuel. And Brother Toros, when he is angry, which is often."

"Same here," Finn said, and tapped his chest. "Finnláech. My ma called me that, and Master Gerard calls me that when he is piqued, which is often. Brothers call me Finn."

They ate in companionable silence, swapping the bowl back and forth, until the stew was gone. Finn expected humble fare, bland as mud, but the stew was layered with parsley, onion, and peppercorn and proved savoury. Sam licked the bottom like a gorged cat. Finn leaned to grab his purse, tugged it open, and dumped dried apple slices into Sam's hand. The boy inhaled the treat but kept his gaze nailed on Finn's sword and long knife.

"Yours?" he garbled around a mouthful.

"Aye. Oathkeeper. The long knife is called, well, long knife."

"I want to be a knight but first I need a sword, and a dagger, and probably a helmet and shield." Sam gaped at Oathkeeper in a trance. "Cyran wants me to be a monk. But monks just pray. And babble. And stink."

"Templars pray and babble too. And you've caught a whiff of Brother Rollo?"

Sam made a disgusted face to say he had, and Finn laughed.

"Don't want to be a monk," Sam said. "Boring. I'll be a Templar. Maybe a Hospitaller."

"Not a Hospitaller." Finn slapped a palm to his forehead in feigned outrage. "They pray the most. Stink the worst. Besides, they're no good at fighting and you want to be the best — a Templar."

Sam nodded sombrely to say he did. "Are you a Saracen? Born a Saracen, I mean." The question was given with childish sincerity.

Finn snorted at the notion. Yet, after a moment's reflection, saw how his sun-browned skin and black hair and dark eyes might lead some to think him native-born.

"No. I was born far from here, in Alba. At the edge of the world. Rains most days. Dark lochs and darker forests abound."

"Brother Toros says I'm half Saracen, which is the same as being half demon. I'm not half demon, am I?"

Finn stared at the boy, who stared back with watery eyes. "You're no demon, boy. Far from it. Next time remind Toros good Christians aren't mean to children. And sometimes Templars punch bad Christians in the mouth and knock out their last two teeth. If Toros wants to keep his teeth, which certes he does, he should be a good a Christian. Tell him I said that."

Sam, half listening, nodded to say he would. His gaze twitched back to Oathkeeper. Finn tugged her free, put the handle into Sam's palm. Her tip dipped, almost nicked his foot, and his eyes flared as he struggled to right her. She was watered steel, crucible steel, and Sam ran a finger along her fuller, tracing the blue-grey swirls.

"Careful, she's sharp as sin. One must be strong to wield her," Finn tapped a brow, "and wise enough to use her at the right time." He took Oathkeeper and leaned back to study the boy. "Know what? Methinks you should learn all Cyran has to teach. Grow clever. And strong. Then decide which type of God's warrior you will be."

Sam rolled his eyes to say he had heard this same advice a time or two.

Finn offered a compromise. "You'll meet Hector. He's learned. Studied to be a priest before he took the vows of a Templar. Maybe you could be a learned warrior, like Hector?"

Sam pursed his lips, considered the idea, then bobbed his head side-to-side to say it was not entirely daft. "Does he curse like Brother Rollo? Knights shouldn't curse."

"Hector cursed. Once. But only because a bastard bee stung him on the arse."

Sam scrunched his face at the cursing, then saw the jest and laughed.

Keen-minded … and not a pouter.

Knives littered Finn's body. One in each boot, one hanging on a cord around his neck, one tucked under an armpit. He lifted the corded knife and handed it to Sam.

"Every lad should carry a knife. Even monks own a blade for trimming quills, or whatnot. But take care Cyran doesn't confiscate it, and promise not to use it on Toros, aye?"

Sam nodded solemnly and tugged the blade free. Its handle was wrapped with hemp cord, the blade dark with age and much used, but the lad gawked like it was the flaming sword of Genesis. "What is her name?"

"Uh, Spike," Finn said, inventing the name on the spot. He tapped his boot tops. "Stabby and Slicey ride here … and here."

Rollo loomed in the doorway. He propped himself against the doorframe, nodded at Sam. "Things so desperate you'd arm a boy?"

"No. But you never know when he might need to chib some smart-mouthed laggard."

"Laggard … says the man who spent the day sleeping." Rollo stared a moment before raising a brow. "Found another stairway. In the north wadi. Like the first but filled with rock about halfway down. Put the lads to clearing it." He smirked. "Didn't see Sir No Shoulders, not yet, though the sneaky bastard could be lurking anywhere."

Finn glared and Rollo's smirk died.

"Adrien rode in. Got worked up about the stairs to the empty room. I took him down, showed him there's naught to it, but he only got more riled." Rollo hawked and spat and Sam scooted away from the spray. "Fool accused us of finding something, taking it, hiding it. No sense to an empty room, he said. He rambled. Talked shite. Reminded me a lunatic I met once, back in Caen."

Sam squinted at Rollo's profanity.

"I'll profane as I please, boy," Rollo said. "And the more you squint the more I'll swear."

Sam said something smart but Finn did not hear. Old stories needled his mind. Tales of Isnard of Ribeauvillé, the Templar Draper, and Adrien's elder brother, and how the toll of counting things broke his mind until one day he was found eating horse manure for the gold-laced oats therein.

"Pray we don't ever find Adrien eating oats," Finn repeated to himself in a mutter. He puffed out his cheeks and said to Rollo, "I'll speak to Adrien. Where is he?"

"Gone."

"Gone?"

"Said he was going to the ruins of Qumran, to dig, and he'd be back in a day or two. Chatted with Emma for a bit; left Jeph with her and rode off with the Poulains."

Finn shook his head at the unexpected news. Adrien reminded Finn of a diabolo on its string — frantically running back and forth, back and forth. All for gold.

Folk back home said the faerie folk, the ancient folk that lived on the land before man, hid away their treasure. When folk came digging faerie magic made the hoard wriggle away or burrow deeper into the ground. Finn's da told a story of a man who found a hoard at Abernethy and set to digging it out. Goblins, called redcaps, tasked with guarding the gold, drove the man away. Or was it dwarves? *Doesn't matter.* What matters is hoards are rarely found, if ever, and few treasure hunts succeed. Some said faeries hid their wealth because of greed; others said God kept man from finding it because of man's avarice.

Maybe God doesn't want us to have his temple hoards?

Dust clouds hung in the dry air. Finn and Sam stood in shade near the second tunnel. This tunnel, like the first, was hacked into the sidewall of a wadi. Fast floods had filled it with debris. Clearing it was gruelling work, at least for the sergeants, who formed a human chain in the stairway and passed baskets of rock up hand-to-hand. Rollo tugged at his beard in thought, though what he tugged over Finn could not say.

Finn's wounds ached, though less sharply. He had taken many a dunt in his day, always healed from hard licks, but since Shabh's handiwork felt weakened. Like she had cut away some secret healing ability. Meat was the remedy. He ate enough of

Toro's goat stew he was beginning to bleat — though, to his surprise, each bowlful brought back more vigour.

Lugh dumped a basket of rock from the opening and fanned a hand at the dust.

"Wear your shemagh," Finn said. "It'll keep grit out of your beak."

Lugh grumbled, "Sod off, you lazy eejit," and Finn pretended not to hear.

"You've grown a second shadow."

Finn turned to Emma and Jeph, who had come up behind.

"You as well," Finn said, and dropped a hand to Sam's bony shoulder. "Though I'd wager my shadow is better company."

Jeph scowled at that, then squinted at Sam, seemed to notice him for the first time.

"Samuel, is it not?" Emma asked, and the boy nodded. "I hear the Templars have taken a shine to you. But be warned — in my experience they can be a surly lot."

Sam nodded, awed to silence by the presence of a woman, so rarely seen at Marda as to become myth. He idly fingered Spike, hanging on its cord under his tunic.

"I regale him with tales of the learned warrior-monk Hector de la Roca." Finn ruffled Sam's hair. "He is yet to meet the great man but wants to be him, eh boy?"

Finn wanted Sam to have what he never had — book learning, thus steered him toward Hector as the model knight. The mantra became, *Wait till you meet Hector*, or, *Should have been there when Hector…*

"I would imagine Rollo grows more jealous with each passing tale," Emma said.

"Jealous of Hector?" Rollo feigned an offended face. "Piss on that."

"You'll never make friends being surly," Sam said.

"Had friends once."

"What happened to them?"

"Knifed them for pestering me about being surly."

Sam narrowed his dark eyes, pondering the truth there, then giggled as only a child can. The sound was pure innocence and charm, and Finn smiled.

Emma smiled too, though it never made it past her lips. "How goes the work? Looks backbreaking."

"It is," Finn said. "They've a ways to go before reaching the room, by my count, at least if this tunnel has the same number of stairs as the other. Doubt we'll find anything though."

"I have dug in ruins. In caves. In valleys. Never dug in solid rock." Emma mused in a dull voice while Finn nodded along. "But a savvy bone hunter must look in every crevice."

"Aye. But to be a savvy bone hunter one has to, I assume, have an urge to hunt bones. I have no such urge."

Emma did not hear Finn's goading — or chose to ignore it. She watched sergeants labour with a gaze gone vacant, as though some neglected thought had crept up and stolen her focus.

Things had been cold after the Wadi of the Dead. More so after Adrien's visit. Finn's ma once said conversation, if done well, is a fluid dance. If not, you are alone, and slink off and pretend it never happened. Time with Emma, at first, had been a chore. Dealing with a woman after years of shunning them proved a harder challenge than fighting a score of Mamluks. But with time they tolerated one another's company, then enjoyed it, even teased and jested. Now conversation was again a chore. Something warm still lurked in Emma, though, and Finn wanted to bask in her warmth again.

"Where is the ugly Turc?"

It was the first time Finn recalled hearing Jeph speak, and he stared at the man before replying. "Elias? Sent him and Nik on a scout. Why do you ask?"

Jeph grunted a reply just as Lugh dumped a basket and waved Finn over.

"Cleared the blockage. Uncle says no room. Nothing."

"Ask Jerol to tap the wall for hollow spots. And search for a mark. About waist high." Finn hastily said, "And check for Sir No Shoulders before poking hands into dark places."

Rollo laughed.

They waited, holding a collective breath, until Lugh stuck a head out of the hole. "Nothing. Stairs end unfinished, Uncle says — like most of the dotard's thoughts."

Finn and Emma swapped glances, and she exhaled in lingering frustration.

"No, no," Jeph said, and spat. "Can't be. You bastards are hiding something." He made to climb into the tunnel but Lugh held his ground. Jeph growled, "Move."

Lugh glanced to Finn with a bemused grin, then back to Jeph with a snarl. "You calling me a liar? Shite on that."

A shove sent Jeph staggering back. Jeph righted himself and came back hard. Lugh dropped out of the hole and strutted up nose-to-nose with Jeph, like two boars readying to tussle.

Rollo wedged in, shoved them apart. "Now, now, lads. All on the same side here."

"Are we?" Jeph mumbled.

"What did you say?" Finn's hand slid toward long knife. Jeph smirked his reply and Finn stabbed a finger at him. "Speak as a man or don't speak at all."

"Jeph, leave," Emma said, granite in her voice. "Leave. Now."

Jeph raised hands in mock surrender, then stomped his way down the wadi.

"Temper, temper," Rollo said drily.

Finn stared unblinking at Emma, demanding an explanation, though she offered naught but an unblinking stare of her own.

CHAPTER 20

Finn found Hector and Serlo trudging up the road to Marda. Yousef and two sergeants led three horses, heads hung like boulders at the ends of their long necks. Of Hector's other sergeants and Turcs there was no sign. Hector's face was sun-blasted. Lips cracked and sore. His cappa torn and dirty. The others fared no better.

A warm smile split Finn's beard. "You're a day early."

"Aye? Thought I was late." Hector's voice was the dry rasp of the undead.

Sam gawked at the fabled Brother Hector de la Roca, the learned warrior-monk. Myth became real. Finn introduced the boy, then laughed at his fly-catching gape while Sam's ears bloomed red as an apple.

Hector spilled out their tale. They, too, had been scattered by the storm. Hector and Serlo sheltered in a wadi with their sergeants, Ruben and Amic. Watt, their minder, stumbled in and together they waited it out. After, they spent days searching for horses, bolted by the gale, and lost brothers. Only four horses and Yousef were found. Watt rode in search of Adrien, to report, but never returned. The five Templars took turns riding and walking. Came to the meet place. Found no one. Carried on to Marda.

Two sergeants were swallowed by the storm.

"I pray they find a way out." Hector signed the cross. "Though I fear someone will stumble upon their bleached bones and wonder who they were and how they were lost."

"And years from now someone back home will say, 'I wonder whatever happened to old so-and-so?'" Rollo said in a drawl.

"Did you find ruins?" Finn hated to ask but knew he must.

"None. Caves and overhangs aplenty, though. Poked around a few. Found broken pottery. Old bones. But no sepulchres or cisterns." Hector wagged a hand to the west. "Bumped into Saleh and his Bedouins."

"What was he about?"

"Hunting Freelances, I think."

Throughout Hector's woeful tale, Serlo threw in the occasional nod, a grimace or two, ran a tired hand over his stubbly pate.

"You're more talkative than usual, Brother Serlo," Finn said.

Serlo scowled, then hitched a brow to ask, *And you?*

Finn shared their story, leaving out where he was trussed like a pig and hung nude in chains by a simpleton. Rollo, ever a nit-picker for a good tale, amended it to include all the salacious bits.

Hector stared up at Marda, plain-faced, not even showing amusement at Finn's embarrassments. To Finn he said, "Did I ever tell you the Rule allows brothers to partake of bread soaked in wine? As an indulgence, though only before compline. Read that a while back."

"Yet never shared it until now?"

"I was waiting for a special occasion."

Wine-soaked bread was Hector's way of saying he needed a strong drink — and Finn agreed. By his reckoning any time after sunrise was before compline. Dreams of wine-soaked bread filled his head. He prayed Cyran had both at hand. Then added another that Rollo would show restraint with the wine.

Cyran stood rigid as a board, hands hidden in the ends of his robe, and seeing Finn he slid a hand out and flapped it toward the door. Finn scowled, then dipped a sharp chin and nudged Sam toward Cyran. He stepped over the threshold with the long knife tucked behind his back.

Inside, Emma was cornered with Watt, the pair conversing in mutters and whispers. Emma's blue eyes were flinty slits; Finn had seen those eyes before — in the Wadi of the Dead. Two of Adrien's toughs scowled at Bili. The sergeant leaned on the wall, arms folded so they half-hid a naked blade against his breast.

"Watt," Finn said, the name dripping with ice.

The man wheeled and the deep creases in his face went smooth. "Brother Finn. Why, I was just asking where you might be. There is news."

Finn raised a chin to say, *Share it.*

"We found it!" Watt blurted. "Gold and silver — too much for our few men to recover! Adrien commands you come. Lend a hand."

"How exciting," Finn said, his tone flat. "Where?"

"The Valley of Achor." Watt snuffled at his jest. "The Achor near Jericho, of course."

Watt, like his brother Jeph, was not much of a jester or talker, but the excitement of discovery let loose a torrent of a tale. He told how he rode from Hector, found Adrien, and together discovered a mountain of coin and bar buried in a sepulchre and old cistern. The treasure was just where the scroll said it should be — hiding all these many years. They hastily reburied the hoard; Adrien and his Poulains stood guard over it like a troop of redcap goblins. Watt began recounting how, at one point, they dug through a layer of boulders and despaired of finding anything until Finn cut his gibbering off.

"Any sign of Beau?"

"None. Rumour says he hunts to the east of the Dead Sea — apparently, a fourth Valley of Achor is there." Watt breathed out, clapped a hand on Finn's shoulder. "Make haste, Brother, and we will haul the treasure to the Temple before *Le Scélérat* learns he searches the wrong Achor. Take the Road to Jericho. Then the Road to Naatah, which leads into the valley. The ruins are but an arrow shot further east." Watt eased past Finn and said, "Emma knows the way."

Finn dipped a head in false humility. "Tell his Lordship Adrien we'll come forthwith."

Finn leaned on the windowsill. Outside, Watt and Jeph were laughing and back-slapping, no doubt deciding on which whores they would spend their new-found wealth. He spat, then dragged a finger along a lip. *Temple treasures wasted on whores and kings.*

He had placed Cyran's gift, the pin, near his bedroll but in his bodily weakness had forgotten it. He gave it to Emma now with an apology; she took it without a word in return.

Sergeants brought bowls of horsebread steeped in red wine. The bread was stale, the wine vinegary, but it tasted like manna from heaven. Salty, with a bit of tart, and this was a habit worth adding to their routine. They grunted and snuffled like pigs at a trough.

"So. The sacred treasures were near Jericho." Hector dabbed bread into his wine bowl. "Doubtless I walked over it a time or two back in the day."

"The chances," Rollo said. "A host of university types, armed with quills and parchment, couldn't calculate the odds of finding it."

Emma turned the pin in her hands, rapt by the engraving.

"What does it say?"

Emma glanced up, brows bunched tight, making a creased canyon between them.

Finn jabbed a finger at the pin. "The engravings; what do they say?"

"'He healeth the broken in heart'." Emma's voice was a whisper, eyes moist and staring. She rolled the pin to show the other side. "'Ye shall know the truth, and the truth shall set you free.' Scripture. From Psalms. And the Book of John."

Cyran prayed the hairpin, simple in its execution but heartfelt, would bring Emma comfort and meaning. Finn prayed the same. Her hollow stare said it brought meaning but not comfort.

"So." Wine and bread slopped Rollo's bearded chin and he swiped a hand over it, managed to smear it into the beard. "Ride to Jericho in the morning?"

"Aye. Too late to depart now." Finn was in no hurry to rush to Adrien's side.

"It is a trap," Emma blurted, and peeked over a shoulder toward the doorway.

"Trap?"

"A trap, Finn. A ruse. I am to lead you into it. They seek to lure you from Marda and expect the promise of gold will bring you running." Emma held the pin aloft. "The truth shall set you free. Lies threaten to own me. But no more — I shall be free of them."

Finn gave a half-dazed laugh. "Adrien thinks to kill us?"

"With Beau's help. Adrien and Paulus made a pact over the spoils."

"Spoils from Jericho?"

"A lie. Nothing was found. The pact is over future spoils." Emma's tone turned sour. "Adrien thinks the hoard is here, at Marda, under your nose. There is naught, I told him. Romans hauled it off. Empty sepulchres. Empty cisterns. Stairs to an empty room. Yet greed deafens him. He is certain it is here because nothing was found in the other Achors."

Finn realized he was dumbly holding his bowl of wine-bread and set it down. Emma ploughed on.

"Adrien convinced Beau the empty room is not so empty. Things are hidden under a false floor." Emma inhaled a breath. "They need you gone to search and in exchange for … eliminating you, Adrien will give Beau half of what they find. Beau will give Adrien a quarter of everything else."

"Such generosity," Finn said, and spat.

"Marda is just the first. From here they ride for the Mound of Kohlit. The problem is no one, Timothy of Yorkshire included, knows where or what Kohlit is. Paulus employs no scholars — none as good as Timothy, anyway. Yosi was murdered. So, Timothy will research Kohlit, then they will dig there, wherever *there* is. Then on to another place, then another, and another. They will —"

Finn held up a hand to say Adrien's plan was made clear. "Idiocy and madness," he said, voice full of sorrow. "There is no honour among thieves. They'll gut each other for a few coins."

"Not just a few coins," Emma shot back. "The seventh treasury. And others. Do you fathom how much wealth that is?"

Finn flapped a hand to say he did not care. "How long have you known?"

"Watt told me all just before you came in. Before, I feared Adrien would do something foolish. Now he has."

"Dumb bastard," Rollo growled.

Emma shared the rest of the sordid tale. Adrien first broached the idea of turning on the Order during the ride from

Tiberias to Jericho. She balked; he persisted. Much of it, at the time, seemed foolish chatter. Then Adrien, unbeknownst to Emma, sent Watt to find Beau and arrange a meeting. They met. Haggled. Struck a deal. Now Freelances wait on the road to kill the Templars.

Gold sickness brought two rivals together, though no doubt each schemed against the other. Their pact would not last; betrayal and bloodshed awaited. And Adrien hiring Jeph and the Poulain men-at-arms was not done on impulse; Finn had been in the city but a morning and Adrien came out with hired men at his back? It had been arranged — well in advance. Finn imagined messengers riding the roads, to-and-fro, to set all this up. *Christ's blood — the whole game played out under my nose.*

Finn realized he was glaring at Emma, as if she were to blame, then hoisted a hand in mute apology. "Why?" he said.

"Because why take a portion when you can take it all? The score would be … immeasurable. Templars would claim it and we —" Emma paused to correct herself, — "Adrien, I mean, would get the pittance of a broker's fee." She scooted across and took Finn's hands in hers. Her eyes welled. "But I cannot, will not, be party to lies and betrayals. You and I … we shared a moment. A dark moment, certes, but in the darkness we were bound. Forever, I fear. I will not betray you. Not for gold. Nor anything else."

Hector looked away; Rollo was suddenly interested in a skinned knuckle and began picking at it; Serlo climbed to his feet and shuffled outside.

Finn fought the urge, engrained in most Templars, to scamper away from her. Her hands were petite and soft in his own big, calloused hands. He gazed into her bright blue eyes and there saw honesty.

Finn nodded dumbly, managed a lame, "Thank you for your candour."

Thick silence. Emma waited, then let go of his hands. He flicked a tentative finger toward her hand but did not take it back.

"Can't be easy turning on your husband," he said, mostly just to say something.

Emma nodded, lips pressed tight, and Finn blundered on.

"I thought Adrien a fool. Either gold lust sharpened his wits or he hides skill behind a mask of stupidity."

"I never said he was a fool. Just rash. Reckless. But the temptation of boundless wealth…" Emma tapped her chest, "broke him. In here. Me too, in a way."

After a moment she said, "He broke the holy orders too."

Finn quirked a head and Emma said, "Have you not wondered who Paulus worked for?"

Finn stared a heartbeat or two, then said, "Hospitallers."

"Aye. Your brother order was his client. They also sought the scroll."

"Sought?"

"Why would Paulus sell it to them now?"

"Aye," Finn said, seeing it all for the first time. Paulus and Beau stole the scroll thinking they dealt in yet another fusty relic but, after learning what it really was, reneged on their deal. Christians opposing Christians, through surrogates, when they should be united. He shook a head at the bad cess.

"Where's the trap?" Rollo asked.

"Not far up the road. They want you here, in the Judean, where none will come to your aid. No witnesses to place blame. No survivors to carry the tale." Emma's gaze hopped from Finn to Rollo to Hector. "Yourselves … your bodies, I mean, will be buried in the desert."

"How kind to give us a proper kist," Finn said, voice cold. "Do the Freelances know what is at play?"

"No, nor they have they been involved in the planning. Their contract is to guard Beau and destroy you."

Serlo shuffled back in and spoke in a low rumble. "Adrien is a dead man walking."

"Mayhap." Emma glanced at Serlo. "Should it go wrong, Adrien plans to blame Paulus and *Le Scélérat*, both villains of repute, then paint himself as the victim. And who will refute him if you are gone?"

"And Adrien's brother Lanfrid, Commander of Acre, will protect him," Finn said slowly.

They pondered. The scheme was diabolical, they had to admit, their options few.

"We could hide here … or make a run for Jerusalem," Emma said, and Finn huffed. Hide. Run. The words put his teeth on edge. A Templar never fled — or almost never. *I will never shun combat, nor fly from an enemy.* Besides the vow, which was no trivial thing, fleeing was not his way. Never had been. Never would be.

"We won't walk into the trap," Hector said.

"Certes not," Rollo said. "We're not idiots. Are we?"

Finn said nothing, sipped wine, dragged a fingertip over a lip.

His wounds ached; lesser wounds were at the itch-hurt stage of healing; larger wounds still hurt. He idly rubbed the wound on his chest, meditating on the hurt. A piece of him had been carved away — literally. He gave much for this idiotic quest. Now he would likely give all.

Outnumbered. In the middle of nowhere. They could try for Jerusalem, as Emma said, or send Elias to fetch help and huddle at Marda. The Turc had done it before. But sending him to snake through the Judean, man-hounds at his heels, was a death sentence. No. Attack was the best way. The Templar way. But Finn led more men than horses — which meant a hard charge would not be so hard.

"*Semper in excretia sumus solim profundum variat.*" Rollo flipped a chunk of bread at Hector. "Always in the shite, only the depth varies. Isn't that what you said?"

Hector feigned a shocked face. "Latin. My, my, would you look at the brain on this one?"

They laughed, though it was the grim laughter of the doomed.

Then a notion settled, desperate but deadly, and Finn's laughter died. He dragged a palm over his scarred face. Grinned.

"He gets that nasty smirk when he's planning mayhem," Rollo said to Emma.

Finn spelled out the bones of it. The others added bits until the bones took on flesh.

The thump of horse hooves outside — Watt, leaving.

"What of my shadow?" Emma asked in a whisper, and Finn quirked a head.

Emma grunted, then mimicked a man with a vacant, slack-jawed stare.

Jeph.

Finn flurried hand signals to Serlo, who nodded once, put a hand on the wheel pommel of his heavy dagger and strolled outside.

Emma held a few heartbeats, gaze locked on Finn's, before shouting, "Jeph. Attend me."

A moment later Jeph appeared in the doorway and grunted — then grunted again when the pommel of Serlo's dagger slammed into the back of his head.

"Ouch," Emma said, as Jeph staggered into the doorframe, fell to the floor.

They eyed Jeph, laying in a heap, and swapped glances while considering if they had forgotten anything else.

After a moment Finn gave a satisfied nod.

"Easy," Hector said with a toothy grin. "Back in time for bread and wine before compline."

CHAPTER 21

Morning began like all the others — hot, dry, the sun rising on a landscape long since scorched barren. There was little life here except for skittering lizards and droning insects. A lone hawk glided above and seemed to tilt a wing at Finn. He saluted it.

Two days had passed wherein they readied to leave Marda. They departed on the third morning, knights riding, sergeants walking. Emma, wrapped in blue robes, led the way — though she did not handle her Arabian mare with her usual ease. All was well until Elias, scouting ahead, spied something and rode back. Templars milled, confused, then wheeled and beat feet toward Marda. The Freelances, seeing their prey running, and mostly afoot, gave pursuit.

Now Finn sat on Fagan at the top of a low mound. Alone, by all appearances.

A breeze tugged at the tattered hem of his cappa and, thankfully, drove off the sand flies pestering his nose and ears. He counted skull-head prayer beads, meditating as he counted. Deceit. Greed. What drove a man to betray promises and friends — though, admittedly, Adrien was no friend of his. Something about the empty room nagged; the oddly tall ceiling; the second unfinished stairway in the north wadi. Why had Adrien honed in on them? Waylon was also on Finn's mind; he grieved the gap-toothed Englishman and, like Lugh, longed to settle the score.

Fagan stomped a hoof and powdery dirt puffed up. "Patience, Brother," Finn said. *Tic, tic, tic,* went the beads. He touched the iron crucifix at the end of the cord and began anew. *God will favour me,* he thought, and angled his face into the rising sun to bask in its warmth.

Dust clouds marked distant men. After a time drifted the murmur of voices and jingle of gear. Freelances rode in a double column up to a wadi and snaked into it; the head climbed up the other side.

"Crossed the wadi," Finn said, and squinted at the riders.

A figure bounced up and down on a horse, showing his lack of horsemanship with each strike of the arse. Beau. Must be him getting his bollocks battered black and blue. Finn felt savage glee — petty, aye, but still. A handful of his toughs bounced along behind him.

To Beau's right rode a beast of a man, huge and bearded and glaring. Had to be the Lance Captain, a leader of thirty men. Freelances, seen up close, were scowling and scarred. Their armour and weapons were a mishmash plundered from a hundred battlefields — well-made arms, though, Finn admitted. Blue and cream-coloured tabards covered mail hauberks or brigandines. Many were festooned with trinkets. Sun-faded scarves. Rings glittered on fingers or in ears. Gaudy as peacocks, as men-of-arms often are, yet lethal for all the vanity.

Finn spat. How he loathed the swagger and the stink, the cruelty and crudity of Godless men like these.

A scout rode ahead. Seeing Finn, he rushed forward, made a sweeping turn, then reined in. The two glared a long, edgy moment before the man yelled in French, "Who are you?"

Finn gave back a flat stare to say, *Who do you think, fool?* The scout spurred back to the Captain. After much pointing and flailing, the column lurched forward before staggering to a stop a stone's toss from Finn. The Captain checked over a shoulder, then the other, keen enough to know things were not always as they seemed.

Finn's gaze swept the column — in the middle rode Adrien, unshackled from his deception and grinning like a fox. Watt gave a mocking wave.

"We are seeking you, and to my pleasant surprise, here you are." Beau grinned his snaggle-toothed grin. "Do you know a bounty is offered for your head? I shall take care not to batter it, when I cut it from your body, then I shall preserve your idiot face in salt gathered from the lake. Send envoys to Taqi al-Din…" He trickled off and his grin shifted to a confused scowl. "Manners dictate I should thank you for such a windfall, yet it also seems … awkward. What does one do in such an unusual situation, I wonder?"

Finn made no reply. *Tic, tic, tic,* went the beads and Beau said, "Here to make a valiant stand while your brothers scamper for Marda?"

"I'm here to do God's will, gain His blessing, kill His enemies. Nothing more."

Beau ignored that, shook his head in mock sadness. "Fleeing. Such cowardly brothers you have — or had, I should say. Aren't Templars supposed to be brave?"

"Aye. God will not welcome them into his bosom. Though they're not as craven as hedge-born curs that murder women and children, I'm certain you'd agree."

The Captain smiled wide enough to show his one brown tooth. "Oh, the Bedouins? Got to keep the lads happy." He rubbed thumb and fingers together to say, *And loot is the only way.*

Finn stroked the last skull bead and kissed the crucifix. "The jig is up, Adrien," he bellowed. "Gerard will know of your betrayal. Templar vengeance will be fierce. You will hang. Burn at the stake. Break on the rack. Probably all three."

Adrien smirked his retort and Finn spoke on in a voice sharp as fresh-knapped flint.

"Your doom is upon you; the slayer is here; sinful men will be destroyed, their blades shattered, their souls sent screaming to hell. Ye verily, shall they bleed from their eyes and ears and mouths, and their stomachs shall be cut open, and their guts pulled to the light of day for all to see, for great is the fury of the lord thy God."

He badly meshed bits of half-remembered scriptures into something part sermon, part eulogy. But the effect was evident. Silence — thick enough you could have heard a mouse cough.

Then someone said, "God-mad lunatic."

Freelances shifted uneasy. Some grinned dumbly, others gabbled nervously, but all had the air of creeping fear. The Captain, sensing it, barked commands and the column shuffled into a five-wide, three-deep formation.

"Time to die, lunatic." The Captain lifted a flat-topped helm from his saddle. Such pots were all the fashion in Christendom, Finn had been told, with an attached face guard and coif to protect the neck. The guard had eye slits for vision and perforations for breathing. The pot came down and the man's head jerked up, right, left.

Slits cut your vision, eh? Finn smiled cruelly, began tugging on leather gauntlets.

Beau slapped a knee in amusement, flailed a hand at Finn. "You're a madman."

"Aye, well, that is true. Though at the moment I'm an angry madman." Finn pulled Oathkeeper and propped her over his lap, flipped the shield from his back, slid an arm into the straps. His voice grew cold. "This angry madman gives you one chance: surrender or die."

Beau laughed. One of his toughs shrugged to confirm, *Mad as a pox-ridden whore.*

Beau was ruthless but not salted in war. The Captain was, and his helmeted head twitched to and fro as he sought something, anything, to make sense of this. The hills were far off. Bare but for rock. Nowhere to hide folk. The rise Finn held was not enough to conceal men — at least not men upright on horses. The Captain paid no heed to the ravine at his back.

Beau laughed, forced now, and said, "You'll slay us then … all alone?"

Finn pulled up his mail coif, thumped a battered nasal helmet down, but paused before tying the ventail over his face. In the pause he appeared to consider Beau's question. "But I am not alone. I have this fine horse. And my sword, Oathkeeper. And my long knife." He finished tying the ventail in place, threw his arms out and roared, "And I have these!"

Finn nodded, fierce and sharp, at the ground behind him to say, *Time to go, brothers.* Rollo and Hector and Serlo were there. Destriers are trained to lay on their sides — and they were, hiding behind the crest of the rise. With a kick of spurs, horses shot to their knees, then their hooves. Knights held tight as they rode up in pillars of dust, like dead men raised from the grave.

Within three heartbeats they formed a wedge and hurtled off the rise bellowing, "For God and for Waylon!"

A flicker at the edge of Finn's vision and something clanged off the Captain's fashionable helmet and knocked his head to the side like an invisible fist had punched him. Another flickering thing and the second-in-command toppled. Beau's horse took a bolt to the shoulder and reared, Beau flailed, and the horse bolted with the flailing fool still attached.

Fagan's ears flattened to his neck and Finn knee-steered him at the Captain, struck dumb and lolling in the saddle. At the last a Freelance spurred in front of his boss — Fagan lowered a shoulder and the Freelance's horse went over in a blur of legs and arms. A bulge-eyed tough waited on the other side and Finn chopped at his mailed arm. Felt it snap. Glimpsed it flop unnaturally. Fagan burst through the press. A quick glance at the wadi — no one.

Four Templars wheeled in unison. Dust billowed in their wake.

Freelances scrambled to reform around their Captain, who was now upright.

Oathkeeper flashed forward. "Again! For Waylon!"

Templars tapped spurs. Charged. Hit with a medley of screams and cracks and thumps.

Rollo was fury unchecked; his great sword hit and skidded over a shield to gouge the face behind. Hector was cold to Rollo's hot — the Catalan slayed with precise strikes, blade flowing from one combination to another. Serlo, silent as ever, hacked right, wrist-rolled to slice left, and a Freelance fell.

A man loomed, sword running back along his draw arm, teeth bared in a snarl. A combination from the high guard carved splinters from Finn's shield. The man flicked aside Finn's counter and thrust at his leg. Finn dropped his shield, felt steel gouge into wood, then slammed the rim up into the man's chin. Teeth cracked together. Another shield slam, corner to temple, and the man folded like an empty water skin.

A Freelance hurtled at Serlo's back and Finn spurred Fagan, who short-hopped and blindsided the man's horse with a shoulder. The horse grunted, stumbled, and Finn leaned and thrust. Oathkeeper punched through brigandine and the man fell away, mouth an O of surprise and pain.

Half-seen shapes danced in the dust haze. The four knights were upright but hemmed in — the momentum of the charge was dead, and they would be too if the plan failed. Finn spared a glance at the wadi — still nothing.

What the hell are they waiting for?

Something slammed Finn's shield. A blow rang his helmet. A dropping cut broke rings from his mail and knocked the breath from his lungs. Fagan reared and kicked at something and Finn clenched his knees and scrabbled to stay seated.

A blur of blue and cream in the corner of Finn's eye — Rollo's blade flashed and a man fell away clutching a ruined face. Rollo whirled to cut another and the man's sword flipped away hilt over tip, an arc of crimson droplets trailing the sword. Finn regained his saddle just in time to shield-parry an overhead cut — the man who gave it blurred past.

Hector slipped free as his mount went over. Serlo, also afoot, wraithed to Hector's side. The two shuffled back-to-back. Rollo ploughed his destrier into the Freelances, driving them back, then stood in the stirrups to hack down and cleave a shoulder like a man chopping wood.

Fagan tailed Rollo as Finn slashed and hacked with Oathkeeper, battered and bludgeoned with the shield. Hits from an axe pounded Finn's shield. The man's arm came up and Finn thrust low — Axe Man gave a surprised, "hoo," at cold steel biting into his gut. Finn twisted her free and cut at another, missed, but Fagan's head snapped out like a snake to bite a man's face.

The man held a mauled cheek and stared past Fagan. Finn leaned out and Oathkeeper sent the horse-bit head away in a lethargic, lopsided twirl. He laughed at the sight — then laughed bitterly at the notion he would die here, hemmed in and dragged down by a pack of low-born curs.

And as the thought came, Saleh came, riding up and out of the wadi in a stream of blue robes. Bedouins followed, more than a score, with Finn's sergeants and Turcs on Bedouin horses.

Two nights past, Elias and Nik and Yousef had slipped away from Marda, each heading in a different direction, each on a quest to find Saleh. Elias had found him. And explained how vengeance lay within the man's grasp. They hid in the wadi. Now Bedouins and Turcs poured arrows into Freelances.

A man took a shaft in the spine and another arched up with fletching sprouting between his shoulders; both died without seeing who sent them on. Freelances shattered into knots of rearing horses and shouting men.

Finn knee-shoved Fagan full around and raked spurs as a shaft burred by his ear and into the throat of the Freelance before him. He slashed the man for good measure as he thundered past, charging at the Captain, whose head twitched left seeking the thundering hooves. He never saw Rollo, coming from the right, nor his great sword as it cleaved his arm from his body. Nor did he see Oathkeeper until the moment it plunged under the mask and into his gullet.

"Mine! I got him!" Rollo hollered.

Freelances, those still alive, witnessed their Captain die but battled on in vain. Bedouin shrieked and yipped with rage, loosed arrows into men until they tottered and fell like bloody hedgepigs. Beau's toughs broke, Bedouins at their heels, hounding any who fled or hid. The fight splintered into isolated islands, where Freelances fought in ones or twos, then faded to cries of the wounded or screams for mercy.

No mercy was given.

Finn let Saleh and the Bedouins do their savage work, for there was no reining in the bloodlust now. These murdered their people and would themselves die in ugly ways.

Lugh strutted the bloody ground with mace and sword, bellowing challenges and maledictions and taunts. A Freelance staggered at him and he parried the man's cut with the sword and broke the man's shoulder with the mace. The man collapsed; Lugh stooped over him and worked the mace like a smith pounding iron.

"Lugh," Finn said, then whistled. "Heya, Rooster. He's blood pudding."

Lugh glanced up, teeth bared and face splattered in blood and bits of something gungy and white. "I'm working here, can't ya see?" the Irishman bawled.

These were Waylon's killers, one of them anyway, and would pay. Finn slumped over the cantle, as weary as Fagan, and left Lugh to his grisly work. He would come around, spent and hollow, but for now nothing could be said or done to rein him in.

His mind trudged through these last days of scheming.

It had been a grand play — full of actors, staging, and misdirection.

Brother Antero, not a large man, nor a man skilled with a horse, dressed in Emma's blue robes. He was she, at least for a time, and led faux Templars toward the trap. Hermits and monks wore Templar robes and tunics and played the part of knights and sergeants. Monks ran for Marda as bait while Finn took his place on the rise, knights hidden behind, sergeants and Turcs hidden with the Bedouins.

Robert of Saint Albans had provided the seed. So often he had said, "Show the enemy what they want to see. The expected swells confidence. Reduces suspicion. And an enemy, so lulled, is easily crushed." Beau expected them to leave Marda and his expectation was his undoing; Templars broke the Freelance trap and lured them into one of their own.

Jerol was trudging up leading his mount.

He tugged off pot and coif to rub at a sweaty head. Hair fell out by the fistful and soon he'd be as bald as Serlo. Three arbalests hung from his horse. The monsters need windlasses and ropes to span their steel arms, and with steel arms they can shoot an awful long way — and with an awful lot of force.

"Well done." Finn tipped a head at the arbalests.

It had been Jerol firing the bolts. He hid among the rocks and shot to kill the Freelance leadership, to leave them rudderless at the moment of attack. His accuracy bordered on mythical and Lugh, no novice himself, was yet to best him in their competitions.

"Three for three." Jerol shrugged, then confessed. "Hit the Captain by mistake. Shot at the ugly Frenchman but a breeze nudged the bolt off target."

"Sowed chaos all the same," Finn said. "They fumbled about while we smashed them open." He looked over a shoulder at Lugh, who stood stiff as a board, sword and mace hanging at his sides. Blood and gore slathered the weapons and on up to Lugh's elbows.

"You've rejoined us," Finn said.

"Freelances." Lugh's tone was wooden, gaze pinned to the horizon. "Where I'm from, Ireland, we never forgive. Never forget. Save the chatter, kill the bastards — Uncle always says that. Didn't know which of them speared Waylon. So I gave them steel. Every one of them."

Finn scanned the littered ground, then remembered why he was here. "Find Beau! Bring him to me. Search every Freelance. Every horse."

Templars scurried to the tasks, and Finn bellowed, "Find the scroll!"

CHAPTER 22

"Where is it," Finn growled. He waited as sergeants searched dead men and sweaty horses.

Templars rummaged every corpse, horse, and bag, then let the Bedouins claim the spoils, as was their agreement. Ashar claimed a bauble or two. Templars had no use for loot except a handful of horses, which replaced those lost to the storm. Finn and Saleh parted with sombre nods of respect.

They did not find Adrien. Nor the scroll. But they found Beau.

Rollo nodded at something behind Finn and he turned to Beau, being led in by Bili. Elias and Nik tailed with shafts on their strings.

"Found the turd cowering in a hole," Bili said, grin wide as a slice of melon.

Images flashed in Finn's head — Beau's horse hit, rearing and running, Beau fighting to stay mounted. Dirty clothes said he lost the fight and been tossed like the novice rider he was. Beau was just as ugly as Finn remembered. Still as long and skinny as a spider's leg, too.

"You ran off in search of a sewer drain," Finn said. "Like the rat you are."

Beau ignored that. "You are here. So who were we chasing?"

"Monks. Dressed in our cappas. Gave them a bit of fun in an otherwise boring life. I'd wager they're back at Marda and on their prayer bones by now."

"Crafty."

Finn tipped a head at the apparent compliment. "Your toughs?"

"Dead or fled."

"Adrien?"

"Gone."

"Where?"

"Couldn't say. Horse tossed me, the bastard. Climbed to my feet to see Adrien riding away, easy as you please, with my horse limping along. Adrien turned north. Watt to the south."

"The scroll?"

"Was in my saddlebag."

Finn managed not to curse.

"Fights done. Adrien ran. Scroll is stolen." Beau gave a laugh that ended in a theatrical sigh. He was trying his best to appear unworried. "Paulus will pay ransom. Name your price."

Rollo said something about no one wasting good coin for a churl like Beau, a man so ugly that when he sits in sand cats try to bury him. Finn did not hear the taunts. He was remembering Acre. Beau had come at him there, first with blades and violence, then with mockery and intimidation. Such disrespect was never tolerated — never. Finn tried to turn the other cheek. He did. But he found righteous anger at the proper time, at the proper place, can be a good thing.

"No point being hostile," Beau said.

"I disagree." Finn's voice was hard. He hitched his lips high enough to bare teeth. "You attacked me. Threatened me. Said you'd teach me manners, remember?"

"Ah. That. Nothing personal — just barking, playing the mean dog."

"A dog shouldn't bark if he's not willing to bite."

Beau and Finn locked unflinching glares; some unsaid agreement was soon reached and Beau flashed a smile that showed crooked teeth. "First blood or death?"

"Death. Yours."

"After I kill you, will I be freed?"

Finn snorted at that and began tying the sword knot around his wrist.

"Figured as much." Beau flapped a hand at Finn's shield, propped against his knee. "But I have no board. Not good with one either, I confess."

Finn gestured at Bili and he tossed Beau's sword and dagger at the man's feet. Finn handed his shield to Lugh and pulled the long knife. "Better?"

"Much." Beau scooped up sword and dagger and gave the sword a hard cut that whistled through the air. His blade was thinner, lighter than Oathkeeper, and tapered to a needle point. He finished by slashing an X in the air, then flared nostrils and eyes in a look meant to frighten. "I killed a swordmaster once. In a duel. You're less than that man."

"I nearly killed a swordmaster in my youth and a youth nearly killed me not long past. A lesson I've never forgotten." Finn hefted, pointed Oathkeeper. "Time for your lesson."

Finn advanced in a style taught by Catalan swordmasters — Oathkeeper extended, knife back, knees bent, back straight. He lingered, then pressed with a probing thrust. Beau parried and the ring of steel brought sergeant heads up from searching the dead.

Beau traversed like a scuttling spider and thrust outside. Oathkeeper batted it aside, and as Beau scuttled back Finn went for an arm with a tip slash. Beau parried and riposted and Finn counter-parried and cross-cut at a thigh. Each regarded the other for a moment, then circled, came in, swapped blows, flowed back.

"Ah, good to warm the muscles," Beau said, tone cheery. "Now we can begin in earnest."

He shuffled in, and back, and sideways, cutting and thrusting and slicing. Movements were unpredictable. Erratic. Finn's movements were precise and methodical. Their feet were ever moving — engaging, disengaging, gliding, pressing; their hands feinting, parrying, cutting, countering. Blades flashed silver in the sunlight.

On they went — round and round, in and away, grunting and huffing.

They broke off, Finn dropping into the low guard, but Beau came on, trying to force Finn's blade high and refusing him rest or reflection. Steel rang and sparks flew. A stiff blow shuddered Finn's grip. A tip slash raked his chest but the mail held.

A juke outside and Beau stepped right to left and thrust inside at Finn's sword arm; Finn was forced to parry with the long knife and almost took Beau's dagger in an eye.

Finn pressed hard and fast but with fluid combinations that, for a moment, put Beau on his heels. Oathkeeper stabbed a shoulder but Beau's mail shrugged it off.

"Cut his ugly bollocks off," Lugh bawled.

Finn spared a glance. A ring of Templars had formed. Hector and Serlo wore blank faces. Rollo rubbed a scarred lip in silent contemplation. Sergeants cursed and goaded and gestured. Elias and Nik, just agreeing to a wager, spat and gripped hands.

Beau had tracked Finn's nomadic gaze — swordmasters always do — and attacked from an inside left guard. He stabbed for Finn's throat and he swayed aside to let the blade hiss past, shifted, and sliced at Beau's knee. Then a flurry of cuts and thrusts, parries and counter-parries. Their blades moved in sinuous rhythm with their feet, and to those watching the dance was a blur of motion in a cloud of dirt.

The dance went round and round until Finn broke away. He cuffed sweat from an eye with the back of a wrist, and was slow to raise his guard.

"Ha!" Beau grunted, and flitted through the dust, sword leading and dagger held back. Finn parried his thrust, barely, and his riposte came late.

Beau pressed and Finn stumbled. A feint from Beau and a lunging thrust, and Finn planted and swung Oathkeeper in a fluid arc. Rather striking for the man, he struck Beau's lighter blade and knocked it down with a sharp *clang* of steel-on-steel. The long knife blurred in and slashed Beau's forearm; a glimpse of pearly bone; his dagger clattered to the dirt.

"First blood," Finn said, and winked. "But not the last."

Shadows dimmed Beau's face — doubt, for the first time, and realization Finn was not so tired after all. But boldly was his style and he pounced and thrust. Finn blocked and riposted without lunging. Beau misread, parried to the outside and took an inside stab to the thigh.

"Second blood." Finn pointed Oathkeeper. "See how your blood flows?"

A low and throaty growl — then Beau wagered it all on a hard dropping cut.

Most men, no matter their training, close their eyes at the impact of steel. Not Finn. His eyes were pinned wide as the blade arced in. He took the edge at an angle to his and flip-rolled his wrist to sling it wide. His counter was a blur. Beau flinched right, too late, and Oathkeeper flayed cheek and jaw. Blood sprayed. Then streamed.

"Cut…" Beau's hand went to his face to confirm his good looks had been ruined.

Beau bled and shuffled back; Finn trailed like a stalking wolf. Oathkeeper slapped aside a feeble poke, then rolled into a hard thrust that split mail and rib as easy as if they were woven of straw. A garbled grunt, probably as a curse, and Beau wobbled and dropped to his knees.

"Bastard," he wheezed, and coughed a spray of crimson.

Finn knelt before him, Oathkeeper's tip propped in the dirt, hand on her hilt. "Your lung is pierced, Beau. I can only offer a prayer for the dying. Will you accept it?"

Beau cinched his eyes to hide surging fear, then remembered he was *Le Scélérat* and flared them open. Blood shone on his crooked teeth as he sputtered in defiance.

"Spit … on your prayer. Shite … on your —"

Finn gripped Beau's shoulder and pulled and thrust in one motion. Beau hunched over long knife, gurgled, slumped against Finn and rolled off. He regarded the twitching corpse with a tilted head; eyes were open, and Finn left them that way. *So he can see the Devil coming.* He sighed at the mean thought and flurried the sign of the cross.

Rollo hoisted him to his feet.

"*Le Scélérat* wasn't so scary after all, eh?" Rollo pursed his scarred lips and unable to resist critique said, "Though you were a dupe for his plunging cuts; couldn't you see his set up? And your Thrust of Wrath lacked wrath."

"Your Nimble Crooked Cut was crooked and not so nimble," Hector added. "His crosswise thrusts were deadly; surprised you didn't lose an eye; next time try parrying those."

Finn huffed, glanced at Serlo, who mimed quick-stepping into a half-thrust to counter a cut from above, then a man wading in mud to say Finn's half-thrusts were too sluggish.

"Mother Mary, you'd think I lost," Finn muttered.

"Rider coming."

Finn tracked Lugh's pointing finger to a blue-robed monk — Brother Antero, bouncing toward them on a sway-backed mule, flailing the reins high, bony white thighs clinging for life.

"Why, it must be Emma, come to congratulate you for besting *Le Scélérat*."

Rollo beamed at his lame jest.

No one else did.

"Tracks leave the Road to Jericho." Elias crouched, hand hovering over tracks like he spoke some arcane tongue shared only by dirt and trackers, then he nodded west. "Head into the Judean."

Finn swung a leg off Fagan, to give him rest, and squatted by Elias's side. He pulled the wide-brimmed hat and forked fingers through spiky hair. Thoughts waged a war in his head, fighting between what to do and what had happened.

Brother Antero had brought news — but not good news.

Emma wanted to lead the Templars toward the trap, as Adrien expected. Finn argued it was too dangerous and, after much debate, and more than a little arguing, he won out. She stayed in Marda with two guards, Umar and Loic. His plan was to return to Marda, if he lived, and if he did not, they were charged with seeing to her safety. Emma was no fool and had good odds of finding her own way out of trouble, if it came to that.

But trouble came to Marda.

Watt and several of Adrien's Poulains had ridden hard from the skirmish. Stormed into Marda. Ransacked the Templar's house. Fought and slew Loic and Umar. After Serlo's blow to the head, which perhaps was a bit too vigorous, Jeph spent two days in a stupor, calling Emma 'ma' and asking if he could go outside to play. A mending Jeph was rescued from a dry cistern, where he had been kept, and when freed threatened to gut Cyran and the monks in his rage. But even a cruel ape like Jeph did not want the blood of an abbot on their hands, so Cyran and the monks were roughed up a bit and dumped in the cistern. Brother Antero climbed out on the shoulders of the others and rode for Finn.

Emma was taken.

Sam was missing and, Finn assumed, also taken, though the why of it eluded him.

What's Adrien about?

A rush of cold spread through Finn, snuffed the fire of triumph, turned victory to ashes in his mouth. He chewed on the ashes a while. And in that while realized he had been so intent on foiling the trap, then setting one of his own, he had not considered Adrien. It came to him, clear and sharp — he had used Beau and the Freelances. Either they killed Finn, which was good for Adrien, or Finn killed them, which was good for Adrien. Men fought for their lives while he snatched Emma and beat feet.

"Crafty bastard," Rollo had said.

"After her." Finn made to mount Fagan.

"Don't you mean, after the scroll?"

Finn fanned a hand to say, *You know what I meant*, though in truth even he was not sure what he meant. Getting hands on the scroll was his task. Yet, strangely, Emma drove him on now. The notion of chasing after her felt stranger still. *Why am I chasing a woman to, supposedly, rescue her from own husband?*

Elias had backtracked, found Adrien's trail, and followed it.

Now Finn knelt in the road, trying to make sense of it all.

He rubbed a palm over the scar on his face, like some men rub a lucky talisman, and stared at the tracks. *What is Adrien up to?* He stepped back in his head, to let himself roam, to think like Adrien, to see like Adrien. The fool had given up on what he thought was at Marda and schemed for the Copper Scroll, which was the more valuable thing. Now he sought refuge — somewhere to lay low, gather allies, make new plans. It is what Finn would have done.

"A brigand's path," Ashar said, nodding toward the Judean. "The Ghost Trail, we call it, on account of all the ghosts made along it. Follows a wadi. Stays close to it because there is water trapped in wadis, if you sniff and dig the right places. Must be a fella among them — a hard fella, if you catch my meaning — with some sechel and chutzpah."

"You're still here?" Finn asked over a shoulder.

"Gave my oath for ten days of service to this one," Ashar jigged a thumb at Rollo. "Got three to go."

"Blessed are we," Finn muttered. He levered himself up, dusted his palms. "Adrien can't stay in Outremer. We'll run him to ground and he knows it."

"He'll go to Acre," Hector said, finishing the thought. "Then take ship abroad."

"Then we must catch him before he does," Finn said, "because I hate ships."

Rollo called Adrien crafty, which he was, but he stunk of desperation too. Leaving the road to Jericho for a bandit's trail was risky. The path was shorter, sure, but steep and gruelling. A hard ride was needed to come out the other side. Only a man not versed in the wilderness or desperate, like Adrien, would attempt it.

A morning's travel between here and Jerusalem, as the raven flies, but three days of climbing and sweating for man and horse. And us wringing our hands through it all.

The Judean rose like a wall of rock and dirt. Ridges slashed down to the valley floor. Wadis and gorges abounded. To

Finn's eye it seemed an impenetrable maze of water-cut and wind-eroded ground. The land back home was deep green forests and lush valleys, and even blindfolded and twisted in circles, the map chiselled into his brain would lead him home. But staring at the trackless waste he knew within a day he would be lost, if left to find his way.

Somewhere in that wasteland rode Emma. And Sam. And the scroll.

"They beckon," Finn said to himself, and they moved into a dry wind, leaving behind the road and Marda and what they had thought to gain there.

Dusk was falling when Jeph and Emma and Sam rode into camp. The raid on Marda had caught them by surprise, and Loic and Umar, God rest their souls, died trying to stave off Watt. Emma was shoved on her mare and, with Watt at her side, led from Marda.

Adrien's camp hid under an overhang at the end of a winding side track; she could not find her way out alone if given the chance. It was an old brigand's haunt, the path well-worn but recently used — by Adrien. More men here than she expected, too; Freelances and toughs glowered nearby.

My husband has become a brigand…

Emma dropped from her horse and staggered from stiff legs. She stared into the rapidly darkening sky and wished she were somewhere else.

"Wife. You look well."

She twisted to Adrien's smirking face and blurted, "What have you done?"

"No kiss for your husband?" Adrien's smirk morphed to a mocking frown. "Testy, I see. Often you say, 'One score and I could leave bone hunting behind.' Well, you will have your score — thanks to me. We will be set for life. Off to Acre. Then Cyprus. I arranged a villa, where we will stay while the dust settles. We will translate more text — with Timothy's expertise, of course. And then, when the time is right, we return and find it. Each hoard. Every coin."

Emma arched an eyebrow at that. "Why Sam?"

"Assurance. Jeph said the Templars are fond of the boy. We can use him as leverage, if the cause arises. Not that I want to. Only if need be, is my point."

Adrien was rambling, as he did when fretted.

"The treasure at Marda — bah, the fools can have it. We have the scroll. And on it are another sixty hoards, each spelled out, each waiting to be recovered. And we will. We will. The Order will say they are blessed by what was at Marda. With time they will forget the rest."

Adrien glanced away, watching Sam, who was being led to the overhang by Watt. Emma regarded Adrien in the lull. His face, unshaven when last she had seen him, now sprouted a patchy beard; his usually fair hair was darker, stuck to his head with sweat and filth. The reek of unwashed body, like sour onion, wafted in the night air. Whiffs of something undefinable too — sweet, like overripe fruit. He brought to mind a beggar-madman.

Inwardly Emma recoiled, yet, to her surprise, found herself stepping closer.

Adrien started, like an unseen person had whispered in an ear, and turned to Emma. "Do you want to see the scroll? It speaks to me; I speak to it. It is alive."

"You are at it again."

"It?"

"Saying foolish things, my dear." Emma gazed into the night sky and back to Adrien. "Brothers were killed. The scroll stolen. Sam abducted. The Order will not forget, nor forgive, nor can Lanfrid save you. Agents will stalk your every move. There will be no reprieve. Finn…" she flailed a hand toward the darkness, "Finn will hunt you like a dog."

"Don't you mean hunt *us*?" Adrien mumbled something unintelligible, then laughed at whatever he had said. "Finn might be God's favourite simpleton but he is a simpleton all the same. We will be in Cyprus while his bones rot in the desert."

"You underestimate him."

"And you seem fond of him. A less assured man might grow suspicious. Jealous, even."

She almost said Finn would track her, find her, go to the end of the earth for her. Instead she made a vague, agitated sound.

Thoughts bubbled like boiling water. Adrien is dead. And me with him. But perhaps… Perhaps if Adrien gave the scroll to Gerard, pled for forgiveness, all would be well. If soft words were spoken, and spoken well, they might yet keep their lives. Maybe even claim their commission. Lanfrid would not abandon kin — would he?

Emma breathed in but the words stuck in her throat and came out as a weak sigh. *It is too far gone…*

A distant flash of lightning backlit Adrien, and for a moment he seemed like a demon. Darkness returned, the imprint of forked lightning still seared on Emma's eyes, and the rumble of thunder jarred memories loose. The pin. The scriptures. The horrors of the Wadi of the Dead. And Finn — sworn to God, in love with Mary. Yet hope lived. *Always hope for love.* Her heart skipped a beat at the thought.

To be loved just for one's strengths is wrong, she decided. Weaknesses ignored or, worse, exploited was no way to live. Only loneliness there. Yet loneliness was not what broke her

— no, daring to outshine Adrien and being shamed for it was the cause. Love should be accepting. Supporting. Only then do masks fall away and true warmth emerge. She shared maskless moments with Finn. Saw him for what he was. And he saw her. Both Emma and Adrien were layered in masks — more with each passing day.

She must be free.

"You are changed, husband. But not for the better. Greed has warped you." Emma huffed out a breath, the sound surprisingly loud in the gloom. "I would run through fire for those I love. You know that. But our love was burned by manipulations and lies. Turned to ashes. And a bit blew away each day until none remained."

"How poetic."

"I am leaving, Adrien," Emma said, a cold edge in her voice. "With Sam. Tonight. Now."

Adrien snorted — dismissive, not surprised. "I don't think so, my dear. Wouldn't be safe. Besides, no ashes have been made, naught has blown away. Wealth will repair all. You will see."

Adrien half turned away, then came back as if something just occurred to him.

"A last … issue, lambkin. I saw you at the trap, in your blue robes, though now I see it was not you in your robes."

Emma said nothing. Adrien grabbed her elbow.

"I assume Finn learned of our plans by beating them from our loyal servant, Jeph. The fiend must have forced you to stay at Marda? Perhaps bound you. Abused you."

Still Emma said nothing and Adrien's grip cinched until she bit a lip.

"No doubt you longed to tell me a trap was set but, alone, feared for your life."

The painful grip lasted an eternity, then Adrien eased off.

"You mustn't fear for your life, lambkin," he said in a broken whisper, breath hot in her ear. He shifted suddenly and barked, "Watt! Guard my wife and our new friend, Sam. Ensure they stay with us."

You mustn't fear, Adrien had said. Yet now Emma's stomach fluttered like she swallowed a bird whole. Her mouth was abruptly dry but palms slick with sweat.

Trembling fingers went to her hair. She fumbled, slipped the pin, and let it fall. The soft clatter sounded like an avalanche and her heart, already racing, surged anew.

A flicker of lightning.

And she glimpsed Adrien, bright as day, staring at her with unblinking eyes.

A flash of light lanced the darkness. Finn held his breath, waiting for something, then thunder boomed in the distance. *Been so long I'd forgotten what comes after.*

"Do not fret for tomorrow, for tomorrow will fret for itself." Rollo had been listening to Finn chew at a lip, and in a brighter voice said, "The trap, the fight. That was some mad shite."

"Mad? So why follow my mad plans?"

"God loves madmen. Figured he'd care for you and we, as your brothers, would be cared for in the bargain."

"How happy you must be."

"Brother, you need to laugh more or all this stupidity will drive you mad — madder, I should say. I tell you as a friend. No meanness intended."

Finn's voice was hollow. "Ceaseless angst, day after day, night after night, leading to madness … that's like saying leprosy makes your skin itch a bit."

"See? You're getting the hang of it."

Finn said, "What if Adrien gets to Acre or beyond?"

"You'll do penance. Might be booted out of the Order as the ill-tempered half-wit you are. It'd be a bore without you, so I'd leave too, and willingly. I reckon we could start an export business in Acre — always thought there was coin to be had in olive oil. Maybe hire ourselves out to guard wealthy pilgrims? Same work as now but we'd get paid."

"Is this supposed to console me?"

A shushing sound of mail as Rollo shrugged. "It's all I have."

Elias's ugly face loomed from the darkness and Finn flinched.

"They camped up yonder. Firepit ashes were warm." The Turc slipped something slim and smooth into Finn's hand. "Found this."

It was a white sliver in the darkness — Emma's hairpin. Finn looked to the heavens. *Emma and Sam are near, praise God.*

Lightning flashed again.

"Dry storm, I'd wager," Elias said. "But we're humped if it's not."

For folk used to the desert, and to years of bone-withering drought, he need not say more. Storms can happen miles away, be dry where you stand, but runoff from the distant storm can scour the dry place with a deluge. In the blink of an eye wadis can become deathtraps — fast floods, folk call them. Novices can be swept away, never seeing the storm that claimed them. Finn had wanted to ride through the night. Elias argued a misstep in the darkness would be ruinous, thus they settled in to await the dawn. Now prudence forced them to higher ground.

"God tests us," Hector said.

"God is as mad as a drunken monkey, if you ask me," Ashar muttered.

"No more of your blasphemy."

"Apologies, yer Lordship."

Finn heaved Fagan's saddle to a shoulder but stayed rooted with a sudden thought. "Ashar?"

"Yer Lordship?"

Finn started to tell Ashar, again, that his proper title was *Brother*, but decided he did not care. "The Ghost Trail … where does it come out of the Judean?"

"The plateau between Jericho and Jerusalem."

"Trail crosses rough ground to get to the plateau. Doubt they have spare mounts. They'll be slow." Finn was musing aloud. "But I'm thinking a fella should be able to get ahead of slow movers. Should also be places a fella could lay in wait."

"Yer Lordship knows banditry," Ashar said in a low voice. He was quiet, appraising Finn with a new eye. "Aye. Side path not far ahead. Hard ride, it is, up and over the mountain rather than around it. But if all goes well, it'll put us on the other side, snugged up in a hiding spot I know."

"Elias?" Finn prompted.

"They'll be turtles, as you say." Lightning flashed and in the bloom of light Finn saw the Turc twisting his beard, forming it into a long, black spike at the end of his prodigious chin. "But if they take another path…"

"We'll lose them and not know it," Finn said, finishing the thought. He swiped a palm over his hair. "I'll take the shortcut, try to get ahead." To Hector he said, "You take Nik. Stay on their tail. God willing, we'll trap them between us."

"And if I catch them before you do?"

"Kill everyone."

"*Novit enim Dominus qui sunt eius*," Hector recited softly, then, louder, "And take the scroll to the Temple, if we recover it?"

"Aye." Finn gave the command easily — too easily. He felt lessened, man and monk and knight, by all the cruelty. *I commit new sins to scrub away old sins, though at least the new sins are ordered by God.* "Kill everyone not named Emma or Sam," he amended.

Hector was praying, soft and fast, but Finn made out Hector's shadowed head nodding to say he heard.

And so it was decided.

Finn stared into the flickering darkness and wondered at the wisdom of trusting Ashar, a brigand found buried in the sand waiting to die. Was this Samaritan sent by God? Or by chance? And, if chance, could he be trusted?

Ashar seemed to read Finn's doubts. "I could have slipped away a score of times, yer Lordship, but I didn't. I'll be good for another three days."

"Saint Mary," Finn said, and began leading Fagan, "bless Ashar with moral fortitude, and aid us in a quick and safe climb."

CHAPTER 23

Half-seen figures wraithed in the darkness. Finn refused to see them, for he knew them, and kept his gaze on the stairs. They dropped into the gloom, steep and narrow, and he descended toward the empty room. There stood the Master, scowling, and he knelt to buss his ring. When he looked up, the Master was Robert, as Finn had last seen him — face pale, body crimson. The dead man gestured Finn should rise, which he did, and Robert raised the first three fingers of one hand in mockery of a saint.

"I killed Sigric for pleasure," Robert said, voice a gravelly rasp. "Payback was but an excuse. Truth is I did not like Sigric — not one bit."

"Murderer."

"Hypocrite. You, too, murdered for the joy in it."

"I killed you in righteous vengeance, as mandated by the Holy Father."

"Not what I meant and you know it."

And there, in the nonsensical way of dreams, was Tomas. Glaring. Accusing. The stub of Finn's broken blade jutted from his ribs. Other gashes marked the flurry of stabs Finn had given him. Tomas was a MacDougall, the first to pay the hard price, and the one who came to him most often. Three others crowded around. Each lacked eyes and ears and tongues — just as Finn had left them. They flailed and stared and moaned things unintelligible.

"May you forever wander deaf and dumb and blind," Finn growled, as he always did.

"See? We are the same, you and I. On the inside."

"We are not alike," Finn said, though with little conviction.

Robert chuckled, the sound echoing up like cold from a bottomless well.

"Are you going to murder Adrien? His wife might not take kindly to it … or maybe she would?" Robert seemed to flow and shift and melt, then

he was a skeleton, leering with empty eye sockets and speaking with a clatter of yellow teeth. His cappa hung in rags. "I took lovers when I was a Templar. You were my bowl mate and never knew. Nor did the Order, and they spy incessantly. Married women are especially … wanton." His skeletal mouth opened and closed in a vulgar imitation of a laugh. "Psalms says the liar's mouth shall be filled with gravel. Yet I found fruit gained by deceit tasted twice as sweet."

Finn's gaze darted to a corner of the room, seeking the snake, and trying to ignore the stares of eyeless men.

"You could taste it too, if you could find a lover that stirs your soul…"

Robert's cold laughter echoed.

Morning.

The darkest hour, just before the dawn. Finn awoke from restless sleep and dreams he would rather not have. The world seemed muted, after the dream, and him skittish and surly.

Shapes shuffled in the dark. Voices murmured conversations about nothing important. Jerol warmed pottage in a sergeant's kettle helmet, much-abused and now used as a pot, and Rollo stared into the food in a weary trance. They were but five now; Finn and Rollo; Jerol, Lugh, and Bili. And Ashar.

The Samaritan guided them in and out of wadis, over barren ridges, over shifting talus slopes. Always up. The mountain loomed, and just when Finn thought they had reached the summit, another rise beckoned. In places, they dismounted and led the horses, fought and clawed over ground and wished for nimbler feet. Occasional flat terrain gave respite before the climb started over. The sun was at their back and Finn, weary of mind, watched his shadow try to outrun him and wagered with himself if it would.

They pushed hard. Ate in the saddle, pissed from the saddle, and by mid-morning horses dragged their hooves. They stopped to take water from a pool, protected in the deep recess of a wadi that never suffered the sun.

Finn gazed out at the Salt Sea. Seen high above the sea was a green-blue dollop between brown mountains and salt-white hills — like a huge washbasin with no drain. Nearer, the Judean was a camel-coloured wilderness, a place of prophets and messiahs. Yet the place, for all its bareness, possessed an aura. Ancient but ageless. It defied the laws of nature — nothing grew here, so nothing died; no death, no decay.

The thing he dreaded happened in the early afternoon. They were terracing over a side slope when a grunted curse rang out followed by a crash and clatter of rock. Finn twisted to see thrashing limbs, man and horse, then Bili rolled clear. Came to his knees. Backslid in the scree and staggered to his feet.

The horse did not.

It sat, trembling, eyes wide and white. A front leg canted unnaturally.

"God's bones," Rollo cursed.

They slid from their mounts, getting their weight off them whenever, wherever they could. Finn propped a head on Fagan and stared at the rocky ground. He had a soft spot for horses and their kin — for all creatures, truth be told. Animals are guileless, trust man to meet his unsaid agreement to care for them, and betraying such trust was a torment. He glanced to Lugh, trying to keep the pleading from his eyes.

Lugh waved a hand for them to go on and Finn nodded his thanks. As Finn climbed, Lugh clucked and cooed at the horse, and in Irish Gaelic said, "There, there, friend. Pain'll be gone soon." Then the slither of steel leaving the scabbard.

Finn clambered around a turn and held. The Irishman came up a while later, saddle over a shoulder, sack of provisions slung over the other. He drummed the saddle with his fingers.

"Draper will knock me with a pan if I return without it, he will."

Fretting over kit. In the Judean. With all else at stake. Finn stared, then despite the exhaustion, or more likely because of it, began laughing. The others joined except Ashar, who scowled, not seeing the jest.

Rollo's laughter trailed into a sigh. "Remember the time Master Odo sent us back to find the sword Hector dropped? Three days from Jerusalem. Just to look for a sword."

"Bavarian steel, as I recall," Finn said. "Well made. But Petrus dropped it. Not Hector."

"If you say so."

Finn clapped Rooster on a shoulder, nodded at the saddle. "Pile some rocks on that, maybe leave some breadcrumbs, so you can find it when the Master sends you back."

"Us. Sends us back."

"If you say so."

They laughed more. Ashar's scowl deepened. No doubt he questioned his decision to guide Templars that, apparently, had lost their minds.

They rode on.

While he rode, Finn ran a thumb over Emma's hairpin in an endless loop. Weary of mind, as he was, he did not realize he had landed on what fretted him until he balked at the notion. He fretted over neglecting the Order, breaking his vows, failing his brothers. Always did. But now — and here was the surprise — he also worried about failing Emma.

She had drifted into his soul like a breeze. Silent. Warm. But unwanted.

Unforeseen friendships were to be expected. But life as a Templar fated they were often severed by war. Bonds, by necessity, grew at a snail's pace, if at all. A bond with a woman more so. There was his vow of celibacy, certes, but also fear of rejection and loss. When love beckons, when he sees braids twining, an inner voice warns naught but pain lays at the end of the braid. Actions are taken to break it.

But feelings had taken root.

Now what to do?

"And noo, for His name's sake, I'm dune wi' a' fearin'. Though cloods may aft gaither and soughin' win's blaw. 'Hoo this?' or 'Hoo that?' Oh, prevent me frae spearin'. His will is aye best, and I daurna say 'Na'."

Finn was trudging up a winding path, leading Fagan, and singing softly. The tune was Psalms Twenty-three, in Scots, which is how he learned it. He could not sing it proper if asked.

"The valley o' death winna fleg me to thread it, through awfu' the darkness, I weel can foresee. Wi' His rod and His staff He wull help me to tread it, then wull its shadows, sae gruesome, a' flee."

"Melodic, certes, but pure gibberish," Rollo said. "Might as well be Latin."

To annoy Rollo, Finn recited the only Latin he, or Rollo, could speak. Every Templar knew at least this much: *Non nobis, Domine, non nobis, sed nomini tuo da gloriam.* Not unto us, O Lord, not unto us; but to your name be the glory. Rollo laughed at the attempt.

By early afternoon the ground began to lessen, almost imperceptible at first, then more noticeably. Wadis still confounded their progress, though they were fewer, and shallower. They found a spring and partook of the cleanest, coolest water to pass Finn's lips in weeks.

Somewhere in the late afternoon the Samaritan reined in, swept a hand over the ground before them, then thumped a chest with a palm. "See? I'm a man of honour."

Rollo shook his head. "Another bastard trap. All we do is set traps. When can we have a stand-up fight? Like proper Templars."

Finn studied the terrain with a hunter's eye.

Before them the trail passed into a low valley, and along the valley ridges were rocks — many rocks. Perfect for mayhem. Travelers would stop at the water hole to drink, likely to feed too, and friendlier terrain from here made an easier walk to Jerusalem. They would be content. Then the trail subtly funnelled the complacent sheep into a slaughter yard.

"The valley of death," Rollo said.

"Thought you didn't understand my gibberish?"

"Aye, well, the word 'death' has a way of catching one's ear."

Finn studied his dwindling band — just five fighting men and one semi-reformed bandit.

"Aye, the valley of death," Finn said. "But is it Adrien's or ours?"

CHAPTER 24

"Careful with your shots," Finn called out. "Emma and Sam will be there."

Rollo and Jerol were trudging toward the ridge at the left.

"You're the one who needs to take care," Rollo said over a shoulder. "I've seen you with a crossbow."

Elias rode ahead and would be the stopper in their bottle. He strung his tirkesh, plucked the string as if it were a lute, then gave a nasty smile. The bow was a graceful recurve and shorter than the bows of Christendom. Yet a tirkesh was lethal, despite its wee stature, for its draw was equal to lifting a lad using only one arm and it sent shafts in a deluge.

Bili hid near the mouth of the valley and would watch for their prey, then bottle up the rear — or try to. Hector, hopefully, was coming up to lend his weight. It was a pitiful trap — only one man in front and one behind. Ashar would hold their horses around the bend.

Finn shaded his eyes with a hand over his brow, seeking a perch.

Lugh pointed. "There. The boulders that look like a pair of dog balls."

They climbed the slope, treacherous with loose rock, and perched behind the Dog's Balls. Finn set out two crossbows and an arbalest while Lugh opened a leather cannister holding bolts. He picked through them, muttering to himself as he did, and arrayed the better ones across a ledge. Several were warped, or lacked a vane, or were otherwise not their best selves.

Finn counted eight good bolts. The faces of Adrien's nine men paraded through his mind, and he cringed at such slight margin for error. Rollo and Jerol took up places on the opposite ridge, each hunkered behind an outcrop separated by a dozen paces or so.

"Loaded." Lugh handed Finn a crossbow, then used a fingertip to steer the bolt's point away from his face. "Don't want to accidentally shoot old Rooster now, do you?"

"Course not. Who'd cook my meals if you were gone?"

"That's the spirit."

Lugh was a savant with the crossbow. Finn was not.

As a lad, Finn had missed every deer, boar, or man he shot at. Practice did not improve his skill. Memory skipped back to the street fight at Arish, not long ago, where he suffered Lugh's mockery for every bolt that went wide, low, or high. Weapons with strings were his curse — always had been, always would be.

Finn studied the ground below. "What's the range, I wonder … should we move closer?"

"Are you being serious?" Lugh stared a moment, then eased the crossbow free of Finn's hands. "On second thought, maybe I do the shooting, you do the reloading?"

"Mmm. Good idea."

They waited. Time passed. The day was warm. Drowsiness nudged Finn toward a nap; to stay awake, he freed the skull-head prayer beads and began ticking through them. The rhythmically clicking beads lulled him into a trance, though he was not sure how much was trance and how much was sleep. For the hundredth time, he pondered the empty room, the tall ceiling. And chasing Adrien. Had he chosen correctly — did the fool head their way? Had he already passed by or, God forbid, backtracked to Marda? And what would Finn do if he had? The thought brought a surge of dread to his gut. Failure was no option.

"Someone coming."

Bleary-eyed, Finn tracked Lugh's pointing finger to Bili, who was waving a hand to the south-west. He held up both hands; flashed all his fingers, did it again, then just one hand. Bili hustled around the bend. Finn kept an eye through a fissure in the stone. A while later a scout rode into view and reined in to study the valley. The ridges. The rocks. His gaze lingered on the Dog's Balls. Finn's breath stuck in his throat.

He sees me…

The scout tapped his horse on and Finn eased out the breath. They let the scout pass unmolested; Elias would see to him. More came around the bend in a ragged column, heads hung, salt rings marring their brown tabards. Some wore mail, most wore brigandines.

Still more came — eleven, twelve, thirteen.

Worn of mind, as Finn was, it took a moment to realize more were joining the party than were invited. A twinge of alarm livened him — Bili had flashed eight fingers twice, plus another four. Finn looked to their meagre row of bolts and cursed under his breath.

"Some of Beau's eejits must've escaped the fight and joined Adrien," Lugh whispered, and Finn nodded.

He glanced to the opposite ridge and Rollo gestured with an upturned palm to say, *What is this?* Finn shrugged and gave back a clenched fist to reply, *Hold*. Finn squinted through the fissured stone. There was Adrien, in the middle, rather than leading. Watt and Sam rode at his side. Just behind rode Emma. Finn's heart, already thumping with the promise of a fight, skipped a beat at the sight of those blue robes.

Not yet. Adrien dithered — even Finn could see he was close enough for a crossbow but far enough away to escape. *Closer, you back-stabbing bastard.*

"Shoot Adrien?" Lugh mouthed.

Finn blinked at that. *Kill or capture Adrien?* He was still blinking when a curse echoed below.

"Bastard."

Finn flinched, almost gave the command to shoot, but saw Jeph's horse stumble to the side.

Adrien held up a hand. "Hold."

The column staggered to a halt. Those already past Finn reined in, milled a moment, then angled their horses back. Toughs dismounted while Jeph examined his horse's hoof. Finn wanted Adrien below him, like a fish lounging in a shallow pool, but he hopped off his mount and began tugging at girth straps.

Adrien said something and Jeph yelled, "Lame."

Watt meandered over to two of the Poulains, who yanked crossbows from their mounts; one trudged toward Finn while the other climbed toward Rollo.

"Taking watch, while the others take rest," Finn muttered. *They'll find us.*

Finn caught Rollo's gaze, then pointed toward the man climbing and mimed shooting. Rollo gave a finger and thumb in a circle to say he understood. Finn tapped Lugh's elbow, nodded toward the man huffing up the slope toward them. He held to give the fool a moment to get closer — a short breathless silence fell, and in it the blood thumped in his chest, swooshed in his ears, flared his vision with each surge.

Lugh's palms came together in prayer. "Blessed Mary, who art in heaven, blessed is thy name. I beseech thee to guide Uncle's shooting this day, because he is shite, nowhere as good as me, and also bless his failing eyesight, that he might be able see his targets. Amen."

Finn ignored Lugh's sacrilege and said, "Do it."

Lugh propped the arbalest on a rock and took aim at someone Finn could not see.

The sergeant murmured in lilting Irish, "Heya, fat man … want this bolt?" He squeezed the trigger and the bolt was gone in a blur. A meaty thud and the *shish* of a body sliding in scree. "There. Yours."

He laughed at himself, handed Finn the empty, scooped up a loaded crossbow. Finn began reloading the first.

A babble of yells and shouts erupted below, amplified by the rock walls.

The *spang* of another shot.

"Ah, had to hurt," Lugh said, bored, as if discussing the proper way to gut a fish.

Finn spared a glance at Rollo and Jerol, who fired in an alternating beat, one reloading, the other firing. Below, three men were down, another hopped with a bolt in his thigh. Several ran this way or that, like a pack of mice unexpectedly exposed to sunlight.

Two men that had been riding back now lay face down, the shafts in their backs apparent even from where Finn sat. Elias stood, loosed, dropped back to let a bolt whiz past. Arrows flowed to his string and off to the target in a steady stream. He pulled, held, then released just as a man popped up from behind a rock — the arrow seemed to sprout in an eye like magic. Another scampered for cover; an arrow stuck through his hand and he fanned it as if it were aflame and him afraid to touch it.

Where's Bili?

Lugh aimed and squeezed the trigger. "Bolt in the neck makes breathing tough, I wager." To Finn he said, "Feed me. Keep them coming."

Finn switched between loading the crossbows and the arbalest. Winding an arbalest was hard work, fighting the windlass, elbows all-a-blur. Crossbows were loaded with a wooden prong, used to pull back the cord, and a boot in the front stirrup for leverage. He rotated the twin cranks on the windlass or fought the prong, then loaded a bolt, handed the weapon to Lugh and took his empty. Again. And again.

Finn craned a neck over the Dog's Balls as a bolt flashed out and thumped into a man's chest. He counted the dead or groaning men — Lugh had missed once.

"Uncle Jerol hasn't missed."

Lugh snorted, "Old bastard's eyes will fail him, you'll see."

Shouts below. Someone yelled, "Adrien, they're shooting! What should we do?"

No reply from Adrien but Rollo mimicked his voice. "Stroll up and introduce yourself, fool."

Several fools took the challenge and charged up the ridges. Jerol and Rollo shot at something out of Finn's sight. A man cursed. Another groaned. The *shish* of rocks cascading. Rooster scuttled forward and aimed down the ridge. "*Suuup*, I'm hit," he said, mimicking the sound of a bolt in flight and an imagined reply.

Finn handed Lugh a loaded crossbow and said, "Such shooting … how do you do it?"

"Easy. Aim for the middle. Widest part of a man."

"It's cowardly to kill from far away."

"That's what I'd say, too, if I was no good at it."

Finn ignored the jibe and poked up a head to count the dead men. A live man fired a bolt. The thing blurred toward Finn, obviously too high, and he grinned defiantly as it whirred overhead.

"Aim for the middle, I've been told," Finn yelled. He scanned their row of bolts, dwindled to a shockingly small few. He picked a crooked bolt with one vane and loaded it.

Rooster took the weapon. Marked. Fired. The bolt whizzed off, spiralling in a circular flight. He laughed. "Wild one. Scared 'em at least."

Bolts came back now, random but steady, and cracked and rattled off the Dog's Balls. Men fired timid — firing when they had no target, and only because it made them feel like they were doing something useful.

Lugh hunted targets, crossbow skimming over the rock, then settling and firing. "Another bad bolt," he said, and cursed. He snatched up the arbalest.

Finn and Lugh craned their necks for a look — something buzzed between them like an angry hornet but neither paid it heed. Finn scanned the valley, squinted into the shady recesses, and there was Adrien huddled behind a boulder. The top of his pale head peaked above — a head so like his brother Lanfrid's that Finn laughed. The fool seemed to be arguing with someone out of Finn's sight.

Sparring with Emma, most likely.

"Adrien! You're trapped. Surrounded." Finn waited a moment before throwing out a lie. "We've enough bolts to shoot until the Second Coming — enough for all your foul hides. But surrender and you'll live. Gerard will grant mercy."

Silence. Then Adrien's hoarse laugh.

"No. You come down here. Or you won't like what happens next."

Sam.

He was held in Watt's hard grip, the man's dagger pressed under a quivering chin. The lad's face was pale but firm. Finn closed his eyes, breathed out a long shuddering breath, then looked back hoping the sight was different.

It was not.

Adrien, emboldened by the notion of hiding behind a child, beamed and spread his arms in a *Well, here we are*, gesture. Poulains and toughs formed up behind Adrien. Three held crossbows.

Watt's head showed above Sam.

"Can you hit Watt?" Finn asked, and Lugh squinted down the arbalest.

"Probably."

"Probably won't do. Hold your shot."

Lugh nodded once but kept the arbalest trained on Watt.

"Give up the lad." Finn's mouth was suddenly dry, tongue pasted to the roof of his mouth, and he managed a weak, "Give him up Adrien, you arse…"

Adrien shook his head in mock disappointment. "I tried to work with you, despite your bumbling. I gave you several chances to share what you found, too, but avarice muddled your simple mind. Made you a liar." He jabbed at Finn with his sword. "You found gold and hid it from me. I know you did."

Finn growled at the accusation of treachery. Rollo found his tongue.

"I'll gut you cock to chin, arse-face, and dance in your guts while you die."

"You paint a heart-warming image, Brother Rollo, as only you can." Adrien strolled forward; Watt shoved Sam in staggering steps. "I have our friend, Sam," Adrien said, and leaned to ruffle the boy's hair. "And he will give me safe passage to Acre."

Adrien stared up at Finn's glare. The fool wore a sweat-stained aketon and had, Finn assumed, removed his mail to save himself from the heat and weight. His eyes were bulging and unblinking — the feverish stare of a man teetering at the edge of sanity. Greed had driven him to that edge, cooked away pretence and left bared innards. The old Adrien was gone. Consumed and replaced by someone else — no, *something* else.

Finn tried for reason.

"We found nothing, Adrien. Abbot Cyran reasons, and with good cause, the gold was hauled off by Romans. Marda is bare. I swear on God and Jesus and Mary."

Adrien waved a hand to say he did not care for Finn's vows. "Marda doesn't matter now. I will have all the hoards."

"You broke an oath. Betrayed us. Made allies with an enemy." Finn spat. "All for coin."

"A pat on the head for our clever brother," Adrien replied, then hollered, "I want to hear weapons hitting the ground."

"What will you do with Sam?" Finn asked, mostly to delay while his mind galloped through various futile schemes.

"Keep him close until I get your vow no harm will come to us." Adrien squinted and gave a hard smile. "The death of a boy would mean little to most folk, especially with so much at stake, but it would mean everything to you. Protect the weak and innocent, remember?"

Adrien knew Finn's mind — and a Templar's heart. Protecting defenceless Christians was a sacred duty. And if Adrien got them to swear oaths on God and the Virgin, and on their honour, it meant he would ride out of the valley of death.

All wagers were off after that, of course, but by then Adrien would be in a refuge surrounded by toughs paid to guard him.

Adrien gestured, just a twitch of two fingers, and Watt slid the blade ever so slightly across Sam's throat. Sam gasped. A bead of blood dribbled down his neck.

"Watt keeps his blades well-honed, as you see," Adrien said, feigned friendliness gone. "I say one more time: drop your weapons."

Finn whispered to Lugh, "Toss the crossbow. I'll drop the other. Hide the arbalest."

He held up a crossbow, let it fall. Lugh toed the arbalest close to the edge and made a show of tossing aside the other crossbow.

"Blades too," Adrien said.

Finn held up Oathkeeper and long knife then let them fall. Echoey clatters told him Lugh and Rollo and Jerol had done the same.

"Now come down and give me your vow of safe passage." Adrien fluttered a ringed hand like a lord. "You will kneel and kiss my ring to seal the oath. After, we will take your weapons, your horses, and leave you to walk to Jerusalem in disgrace."

Bastard liar. They would die here, Finn saw with sudden clarity. Him. His brothers. Sam too. No amount of ring kissing or reasoning would change that. With a wooden nod to Rollo, they started down the slope, sliding and skating on the talus until they stood in the valley of death.

There was no sign of Emma.

But there was Hector and Ruben. They strolled around the bend with hands on hilts. Hector gave Finn a cordial nod, like they were old mates who had by chance met at the market.

Watt shifted to face Hector and yanked Sam to his toes. "Another step, arse-humper, and I'll slice his neck to bone. Drop your blades."

Hector slid his sword out — a fine blade, made in Toledo, and carrying the rearing lion mark of a famed smithy. She was Hector's one vanity, and he laid her reverently at his boot tips.

"You disrespect your wife," Finn said, still seeking time to hatch a plan.

"It was more business arrangement than marriage, truth be told. She gave me expertise. I gave her connections within the Orders. Neither was dissatisfied. But the usefulness ran its course." Adrien shrugged. "Besides, lambkin is not much longer for this world, if she is still here at all."

Adrien spoke of Emma in a flat, calm voice, and Finn spat at the obvious lie.

"Your brother, Lanfrid, will suffer for your sins. Did you think of that?"

"I did. And decided Lanfrid's career was an unfortunate casualty."

"You'll never make it, dumb-arse," Finn snarled, anger rising. "I'll chase you like a hound, place to place, hidey-hole to hidey-hole. I'll kill your hired toughs and lay their bloody heads at your feet. There will be no rest for the wicked."

"How ominous. I will lose many a night's sleep to worry, no doubt." Adrien half-waved a hand and a grinning Poulain came forward with a crossbow levelled at Finn. Adrien tilted a head at Finn's scowl. "Climbing down to me sealed your fate. But take consolation Sam will live."

Rollo glared, then grunted, the closest he came to voicing fear.

Sam shook like he had the ague. A trembling hand went under his tunic and crept up his chest. The knife. On its cord. Finn cringed and gave a near imperceptible shake of the head. Sam forced a smile.

Hector shifted, took a step, readying for a leap to save the boy, though everyone could see it would be futile.

Watt lifted the dagger from Sam's neck to point it at Hector. "Try. I dare you."

"Hold…" Finn said, seeing the situation spiral away from his grasp.

Sam moved — yanked Spike and backstabbed her into Watt's groin. A screech pitched high enough only dogs could hear it, then Watt dropped to his knees, groping at his pierced twig and berries.

Finn crouched and scooped and threw a rock at the Poulain. It was poorly done, but done well enough the Poulain flinched when he triggered the crossbow — the bolt buzzed over Finn's head, close enough it tickled his hair in passing.

"Death!" Rollo bellowed.

And Death answered the call.

Serlo and sergeants stormed around the bend and charged. Nik and Yousef trotted behind, picked targets and loosed, then scuffled forward and loosed again. Elias came forward. Now the rats were penned between three bowmen, who ruthlessly sent shaft after shaft into their midst.

Serlo ploughed in swinging a great sword in two-handed, scything cuts. Men fell or scampered back from each pass. Jeph held his ground, then ducked and stomped in, trying to get inside the big blade. Serlo short-gripped the ricasso and smashed the pommel into an arm, deftly reversed the blade and put it through an enemy neck. Men swarmed and Serlo bobbed and slithered, agile for such a broad man, and a sharp *tang* rang out as his blade snicked away a mailed arm.

Dust billowed up from running and stomping feet.

Hector deftly hooked his blade with a boot tip. Flipped it up. Snatched it from the air and leapt at Jeph. He tried to parry but the lion-marked blade but it was not where it was supposed to be — it had shifted from a cut to a thrust that went in Jeph's mouth and out the back of his head.

Bili and Amic shoved and hacked and thrust their way into the press. The *spang* of a crossbow. A scream. A curse. The clang and thump of steel and wood was deafening. A man reeled away, clutching the gushing stump where he used to keep his hand.

Sam stood in the middle of it all with the darting eyes of one seeing more than he wanted. Adrien lunged for the boy — until Hector sliced at a hand and sent Adrien scampering back with a yelp. Hector hauled Sam in.

A Poulain came at Hector's side but Ruben's thrust took him through the neck. A spear took Ruben in the back and he arched and shrieked and fell.

All this chaos in a dozen heartbeats.

Something blurred past — an arrow, from Elias — and the man coming at Finn's back stumbled into him. Finn shoved the dying man aside. Crouched and yanked Stabby and Slicey from his boots. There was Adrien, sword low, head twitching left and right.

I'll gut you, bastard. Finn ran at him in a crouch, blade in each fist.

A whip-lean man cut him off, brown teeth bared and sword slicing in at an angle. Finn, with no shield to block or blade to parry, swayed aside to let the slice *siss* past, then slashed for an arm. Lean Man laughed at the feeble attempt, thrust, and Finn dodged the point coming at his throat. *Only a fool brings a knife to a sword fight — get inside his guard or die.* Finn charged and his shoulder-slam knocked loose a grunt. The unexpected blow upended Lean Man, and he lay sprawled and struggling in his mail like a turtle flipped to its back.

It was Finn's turn to grin until something silvery flashed in the corner of his vision. On instinct he went down. Rolled. Came to his knees with Adrien looming over him, grinning triumphantly, sword tip hovering over Finn's eye.

I'm done for — stabbed in the eye by a bland-faced madman.

An echoey crack, like dry snapping wood, and Adrien lurched back like he had been shoved. A puff of cotton drifted from his aketon and he fell to his arse, a confused scowl on his face. Finn checked over a shoulder — Lugh crouched on the slope, empty arbalest in hand, grinning like an imp. Finn flourished a hand in thanks.

The fight did not go on much longer. The riot of sound died with the last Poulain. The dull silence was punctuated only by the occasional groan or curse. Sergeants and Turcs weaved through the carnage, using knives or maces to give mercy, until none but dead remained.

Caedite eos. Novit enim Dominus qui sunt eius — kill them, for the Lord knows those who are his.

Serlo yoked the great sword over his shoulders and stood wide-legged, taking in the mess he had made. Rollo staggered to his side, panting, bleeding from a dozen cuts. He clutched a blood-slathered dagger in each fist. Jerol took a drink, sloshed the waterbag to get Rollo's attention, then squirted a stream into his mouth, open and gaping like a baby bird.

Nik had gone on. Bili was bleeding from a gut wound but putting on a good show of nonchalance. Ruben lay on his back gasping like a fish dragged to land. Hector kneeled, signed the cross over him, murmured, *Per istam sanctam unctionem et suam piissimam misericordiam…*"

Finn took Sam by the shoulder and steered him away from sights a lad need not see.

Sam glanced up as they walked. "No fear, in me, none," he said through chattering teeth. "Used my thinker, too." He tapped a trembling finger to his temple. "Like you said, a knight should be wise enough to know when to use his blade."

"You did well, Sam." Finn squeezed a shoulder and pointed at Rollo. "Go to him."

Someone was mewing pathetically. Watt — on his knees, slumped like a lump of melted wax and still clutching his ruined nuggin and nutmegs. His braes were soaked crimson, face white as a freshly laundered sheet.

"Help me, for the love of Mary."

"Ah, Watt." Finn grimaced and made a floundering hand movement. "You're pierced bad, and in a bad place."

Lugh ambled up, Oathkeeper and long knife tucked under an arm, mace propped on a shoulder. Finn took his weapons and nodded at the mace, tipped a head at Watt, then turned away. From the corner of an eye, he glimpsed the shadow of the mace raising, falling; heard the blow, crunchy and wet. By the time Watt's body crumpled, Finn stood over Adrien.

Adrien sat in the dirt and panted like a heat-worn dog. A puff of cotton stuck to his aketon like a red snowflake. *No sign of the bolt; passed clean through.*

"Didn't end the way you'd planned, did it?"

"Rarely does," Adrien said, and sniffled like a toddler.

Seeing the man brought pity; Finn was surprised by that. Making foes of friends is the art of an idiot, wise men said, and Adrien had proved adept. Such folk lack loving bonds strong enough to counter the instinct for self-enrichment. Madness and greed were the embers under it all. Deceit puffed the ember into fire — nurtured it, made it seem a noble trait. Folk, so deceived, will say or do anything to enrich themselves, even at the price of their soul.

Finn glanced to Sam and thought, *Better to have the soul of a child, giving and forthright, but with the nobility of a warrior, loyal and honest.*

Adrien rasped something unintelligible, gestured for Finn to come closer. He crouched and Adrien stabbed with a dagger that had been hidden behind his back. It was a pathetic attempt and bounced off Finn's mailed chest. Adrien dragged the blade up again and Finn, annoyed and tired, swatted it aside.

The dagger rolled from Adrien's hand. He was shivering and sallow. Finn fought the sudden urge to stab him in the neck with his own dagger and leave it stuck under the corner of a scraggly jaw. Then Robert's ghostly laughter echoed; *'Will you murder her husband?'* Finn would not. Neither did he raise a hand to save him. Instead, head tilted, he stared as Adrien glared and huffed and trembled.

"The dust shall return to the earth, from whence it came, and the spirit return to God, who made it." Finn signed the cross. "Can't say if God will receive you, Adrien…"

By then Adrien was gone.

He lifted Adrien's hand and tugged at the gold ring on his little finger. It was stubborn, clung on, but after several twisting tugs came free. Finn palmed the ring and levered himself up, turned away and strolled toward Rollo.

Rollo ran a palm over his matted hair and said something to Jerol, who hustled away. He shifted to Finn. "We have the scroll. It was in Adrien's saddlebag."

Finn closed his eyes and breathed in. The Copper Scroll. Recovered. He breathed out. *But so many lives, so much pain, for something so small.* When he opened his eyes, Rollo was staring, scarred lips pursed in worry.

Finn jerked a chin to ask, *Aye?*

"Emma is hurt."

CHAPTER 25

Adrien had not lied. At least not about Emma.

Finn found her propped against a rock with a bolt in her right shoulder, just above her breast. The bolt had one vane and a warped shaft. He blinked slowly at the memory of that bolt careening in flight, wild as a blind hornet.

Lugh was blinking too. "I've killed her," he said in Irish Gaelic, then wheeled away, hand plastered to his forehead.

Finn crouched by her side.

"Knew you'd come. Just didn't think you'd shoot me." Emma smiled at her jest, normal enough, but there was no humour in her pinched lips. Her arm trembled like she was having a fit.

"Your fault," Finn said. "I'd wager you were standing, ordering folk about, when anyone with common sense would be crouched behind a rock."

Her laugh came out as a wheeze and she settled for a nod. Pain dimmed her blue eyes but pain-pale skin made the sun-kisses over her nose brighter.

Jerol knelt by Finn's side. "Barbed?" he asked, and Finn shook a head.

Removing a barbed point, or trying to, would likely kill her.

But Finn knew it was not barbed because he had loaded it.

"Hurts," Emma said, huffing shallow breaths. "Am I dying?"

"No, you mouse." Finn spoke light-hearted and calm, to show confidence he did not feel. He had been shot there and lived. But he had also seen men shot there and die. "You've a broken rib or two is all. Lung isn't pierced, God be praised."

"How can you be certain?"

"You're not wheezing for air. And no blood in your mouth."

Jerol rummaged through a haversack and took out pads and balls of linen, then three clay vials. He nodded at Finn to say, *Ready*. Finn laid hands on Emma, one on each shoulder, and Jerol put both hands on the bolt.

"What are you doing?" Emma rasped.

"Checking your heartbeat."

He pressed down and Jerol pulled, steady and hard. Emma screamed. The bolt, dark and dripping, came free with a soft sucking sound.

"Liar," Emma hissed, and tossed her head from side to side. "Liar, liar, liar."

She rattled off curses that made Jerol and Finn sit up with arched brows of appreciation. Finn dropped back to press a pad of linen to the wound, to staunch the flow, which made Emma curse more. Jerol laughed, and Finn started laughing, which made Emma curse louder.

Jerol slit a hole through her robes and chemise, working around Finn's hands, then tapped Finn's wrist to say, *Move aside*. The bleeding had slowed to a seep. Jerol unstoppered a vial and used its contents — a brew of vinegar, garlic, and oregano — to wash the wound. From a second vial, he smeared a blob of the blessed ointment over and into the gaping hole, then covered the hole with honey-sticky linen.

Emma was beyond cursing now and could only stare wide-eyed. Her face, white to begin with, was a shade of pale Finn did not think possible in the living. Jerol hoisted her, groaning, to a sitting position and motioned Finn should wrap her in a strip of linen.

He gawped at the linen, then at the swell of her breasts.

"After all that…" Emma panted, "and now you fear bumping my paps?"

She started laughing then trailed into a pain-filled moan. Finn wrapped her chest, breasts, and over the shoulder. He tied it off and gave a yank as payback for the mockery.

"Open up, tongue out," Jerol said. He tapped several drops from a vial into her mouth.

Emma swallowed, then bobbed a head to say it was not as vile tasting as she expected.

"Poppy juice and willow bark," Finn said. "To dull the pain."

"Pray God heals her," Jerol whispered into Finn's ear. "But getting her to the healers, and soon, is a damn fine idea too."

Lugh dropped to Emma's side. He confessed and begged for forgiveness until she said there was no point asking forgiveness for an accident — unless he meant to shoot her, in which case he needed to improve his aim. Everyone laughed. Except for Lugh; it was too soon and he could only stare at the dirt with the face of a guilty dog.

After a time, the pain seemed diminished, and Emma closed her eyes. Finn sat with her in companionable silence.

Ashar hopped among the dead like a sharp-eyed crow, stooping every so often to pluck rings and coins and pendants. He sorted weapons and armour with an appraiser's eye and piled the better bits in a pile. Finn left him to it — as a bloody reward for his loyalty and service, and because Finn did not care enough to stop him. Freelances and toughs would receive no Christian burial; they would be feed for buzzards and other eaters of the dead. Templars suffered losses too. These they tied to horses, to carry back to Jerusalem, to be buried in the Templar boneyard.

Adrien was tied over the rump of his horse, though where the fool would be buried Finn could not say, nor did he care. A sudden thought came, *What will I tell Lanfrid?* After a moment's contemplation he decided not to twist history to soften the blow.

Emma seemed to read Finn's thoughts. "Adrien?" she murmured, eyes still closed.

"Dead."

There was no way to break the news gently and, besides, Adrien was not at her side.

"Did you kill him?"

"I did not." Finn breathed out. "He was wounded. Died after."

He did not say Adrien's wound was likely mortal, though he had not tried to treat it and would never know. Neither did he say, *I am sorry for your loss and may God bless and keep you in your time of need*. Somehow the words felt stale.

Emma was silent and he waited for her rage, for tears, for keening. He saw no signs of grief, thought she had drifted off with poppy delirium until she spoke in a low rasp.

"He was not always thus. He was sometimes bumbling, often rash, but always had a good heart. Until the scroll corrupted it."

She spoke of other things. Love. Loyalty. Grief. Business arrangements. Hollow unions. The future. Finn was half-listening until she asked, "Now what?"

"We ride to Jerusalem. Get you proper care. Then do what the Master commands."

Emma opened her eyes, fixed a stare on Finn to say, *Not what I asked.*

She had meant, *What of us?*

He ignored the question.

Finn idly regarded Bili, wounded in the gut, being pushed onto a horse. He sat hunched and pale, but when he saw Finn's eye gave a confident nod.

"Ready?" Lugh came up with Fagan and Emma's mare.

"Can't ride with one arm." Emma grimaced. "Need someone to hold me."

Finn shot Rollo a glance and gave a nearly imperceptible shake of the head. After all that Finn and Emma had shared, he could not be close to her, for closeness might unravel him.

"Brother Rollo will attend you," Finn said, stiff, and Emma frowned.

"He stinks."

"I stink —"

"Less than him. Besides, Fagan has a gentle gait, for such a big beast."

Finn shook a head while Rollo smirked. Together they lifted Emma gently onto Fagan. Finn climbed to the crupper and reached around her to take the reins. A heady scent of myrrh and marjoram greeted him. It was intoxicating. Emma snuggled into his chest and the feel of a woman's body, after so many years, was almost lurid.

"God's bones it hurts." Emma breathed, ragged and laboured, then smiled. "Finally got you to share Fagan with me, though, which is a victory."

Finn shook a head and heel-tapped Fagan into a walk. Ashar tucked something shiny into his belt, grinned like a jackal, then hoisted a hand in farewell. Finn tipped a head in gratitude, and under a dusty, pale sky they rode out of the valley of death.

"Took an arrow once," Finn said. "Same spot you're wounded. It'll take a while to heal. Broken ribs are a bear." He was unnerved to have played a hand in maiming her and fretted for her injury — more than he let on. He made small talk to settle his nerves. "After, you'll do exercises to break up the scar, or your movement will be limited. It'll ache too, when the rain builds, which fortunately isn't very often."

Fagan stumble-stepped around a stone and Emma gripped Finn's thigh with her good hand. Finn flinched but said nothing. Neither did he remove her hand.

"Would you have?" Emma's voice was a hoarse whisper in his ear. Her breath was warm and tasted of willow bark and too many days spent in the desert, but he did not mind.

"What?"

"Killed Adrien."

Finn closed his eyes while he mulled a lie. How can you tell a woman you had gone at her husband with knives, that he was dark-souled, and not deserving of mercy? Lugh had saved Finn's life, aye, but he had also saved him from the messy aftermath of killing Adrien himself. In the end Finn could not lie.

"Aye. I would have." Finn spoke with a hint of the confessional. "Instead, I watched him die and withheld my blessings, for I had no patience, no charity to offer. My heart was hard."

Emma said nothing and Finn asked, "Does that make me a bad Christian?"

"No." The word was thick with anger and hurt. Emma fell silent and was likely pondering whose corpse was carted along somewhere behind her.

Adrien's pale face flashed in Finn's mind and he remembered the ring.

"For you," Finn said, and reached around and wedged the ring into Emma's palm.

She held it to an eye and quirked the moonstone to capture the sunlight ... then flicked the thing away with a sigh.

They rode in silence. The Ghost Trail came out of the Judean grudgingly, then eased onto a plateau. After a time it joined another, which not long after merged with the Road to

Jerusalem. Somewhere along the way plant life began dotting the land. Islands of green-brown were a welcome sight. They passed a herd of raggedy pilgrims, who gave them the road and waved like simpletons.

"I made inquiries," Emma said, jerking Finn from his musings. "Found out folk in Alba called you … *queue see*, I think it was. Meaning Black Dog? Because of your hair?"

"No. Not that." Finn made a scoffing sound in his throat. "Cù-Sìth," he said, pronouncing it as *coo she*, "is a devil-dog. Night hound. Bringer of mayhem."

"What deeds earned you such a horrid name?"

He stared ahead but it was not the Road to Jerusalem he saw. Dull images of vengeance and violence filled his mind but he did nothing to sharpen them, let them fade.

"Bad deeds." Finn breathed out. Shades of Tomas MacDougall and his sons paid a brief and unwanted call. "But I turned my back on darkness. Came here to wash my sins in the Jordan. Still do, whenever I'm near it, and think of muddy water when I'm not." He held tight as Fagan worked up a slope. "Despite all the washing, though, I am still that other man. And fear I always will be."

"Stop beating yourself up for what you have done. It is in the past. Leave it there. I was wrong to ask of it." Emma turned her head against his chest. "You are a knight. Yours is a noble profession."

"Doesn't feel noble," Finn said. "Templars are sinners trying to make amends. Or like Parsifal, the innocent and devout fool. One or the other. Little nobility in either."

Emma shook a head at that and Finn carried on. "I've more work to do, on not being that other man. Perhaps the work will never be done. I don't know. But I must see it through."

"Would you seek a wife? After the work, I mean."

"I would — if any would have me."

She smiled like a child in a dream. Or from the poppy.

It's not the poppy… He knew what was making her smile, or thought he knew, and could not humour it — must not humour it. Marriage. Family. These were indulgences, but he did not allow indulgences. Certain things become real only if you allow them to be. His heart began rattling in his chest strong enough she must be able feel it. He filled his lungs and puffed it out.

"But I would tell my prospective wife, should by chance I find myself speaking to her, that I'm sworn to another. Mary Magdalene. And what is broken in me might be healed by Mary. Or made worse. So, don't wait for me, find another."

Silence except for the plod of Fagan's hooves.

Jerusalem shined in the distance; a thin pall of smoke hung above her like a cloud. Nearer, a hawk wheeled in the sky, serene and timeless. There had always been hawks; there will always be hawks. Finn took comfort in that thought.

"Men," Emma said, more to herself than to Finn. "Why do they so often choose wrong?"

"Practice?" Finn offered, though she did not seem to hear him.

"Next time I will follow my heart."

Finn did not know what next time she spoke of, not exactly, and dared not press for more.

CHAPTER 26

Bili died. Emma lived.

They had dragged into Jerusalem a tattered remnant of what they had been. But it seemed the sergeant might recover, for he managed the hard ride to Jerusalem. Surgeons sniffed and prodded his gut but their inaction to treating it said much — the wound was rotten. Bili passed on three days later, sweating and groaning and rambling as the fever claimed him.

Emma was carried to God's House too, despite the glares and mutters from Christian healers. The barber-surgeon, a pasty Frenchman, said God's House was no place for a woman and demanded she be taken elsewhere. Finn threatened to break his delicate fingers, one by one, if she was not given care. Miraculously, the surgeon vowed Emma would receive prompt ministrations and a full recovery was expected, God be praised. Rollo and Jerol would visit each morning and night to ensure Emma's care — and to break the surgeon's fingers, if it be God's will.

Sam stayed with her. He seemed … older, aged by what he had seen and done.

Finn walked to Master Gerard, knelt before him, and laid the scroll in his hands.

"The gold is gone, Master."

Gerard grunted at the weight, brushed fingers over aged copper, set it aside. "Gone?"

"Taken by the Romans," Finn said. He told Gerard about the looted sepulchre, the griffonage, the Arch of Titus, the stairs to the empty room.

Gerard closed his eyes and began kneading his forehead in measured passes, as if struck by a sudden headache. Finn shot the Seneschal, Urs, a weary glance. Urs winked his one eye.

After a moment of kneading the Master said, "We learn from our defeats, Brother, not our victories." He raised Finn from his prayer bones with a wave of fingers.

"Wise words, Master. Yet I think our defeat is not entire. Upon reflection it seems unlikely the Romans recovered each of the sixty-something hoards. Some must remain hidden? Therefore, scholars should carry on translating the scroll then, fortified with knowledge, brothers could be sent to search each location one-by-one?"

Ideas ebbed and flowed. Finn played the part of humble brother; Urs added the occasional, "Well-said, Brother," while Gerard stroked his chin or nodded slowly. And in the end it was decided Finn's plan had merit — brothers would carry on the sacred quest.

"Certes we must carry on," Finn agreed, though to him the words were equal parts statement and question.

Finn and Rollo visited Emma in God's House. Paleness lingered — though she could raise herself up without aid and, though weak, walk about the cell. On the third day Finn arrived to find her staring at the ceiling and tapping a heel in pain — a look he knew well.

The bonesetter had come and done his vile work. Bright blood marked the fresh linen binding her right breast and shoulder. When wounded at Montgisard, Finn thought the ribs would never heal. But they did and with training, painful though it had been, he regained use of the arm.

"You must move it," Finn said, and mimed stretching an arm.

"So they tell me. I do the exercises, though it hurts and I curse — a great deal."

"But you must do it," Finn insisted.

"Curse?"

The jest brought a smile, though it fled quick.

"I'll be sent away soon and will no longer visit," Finn said.

"Sent where?"

"The field, I imagine. There are pilgrims to escort and roads don't patrol themselves."

Emma was silent and he asked, "Where will you go? After healing, I mean."

"Acre. Home." She attempted to shrug, but remembered the pain it would bring. "Cannot say what I will do after."

"I shall visit, when I can. We could discuss relics? I confess a growing interest."

"Liar," Emma said, then flashed a teasing grin.

"No, I will come, I do what I say … though, now that I think on it, maybe this is why I say so little."

Emma smiled and Finn stood and leaned. She raised an arm to accept his embrace and, remembering the Rule, he clumsily squeezed her good shoulder instead. They departed, her body hurting, him aching inside. He desired seeing her again, in his heart, though his head scolded and said it would only prolong the misery.

Perhaps I don't mind more pain.

From God's House Finn and Rollo strolled to the Scriptorium, where Timothy and a gaggle of scholars laboured at the translation. They had been at it several weeks now. Bits of copper sheet spread over the table. Pieces rested together, where they re-fit, and larger sections aligned across the middle of the table.

After exchanging greetings, Rollo fell asleep in a corner of the room and Finn found himself gazing out the window, half listening as Timothy gibbered about some inane scrap of Jewish lore. He realized Timothy had stopped gibbering and stared with an arched brow.

"Hmm, you don't say?" Finn said, and hoped he had guessed right.

"I do say." Timothy hovered a finger over a fragment. "Says so right here."

"Fascinating," Finn said, perhaps a bit too zealously. "Though I'm not certain I agree without further supporting evidence."

The scholar huffed to say he knew a bluff when he heard one. "I will begin again. Please remove the wool from your ears and listen this time."

Finn bowed his head, like a chastised pupil, and Timothy ploughed on.

"As I said, more time refined the translation. One must be well-versed in local history and rabbinic language — which, I confess, required time to unravel. Recall the first line." Timothy gave Finn a moment to sift his mental stores before continuing. "It was altered thus: In the desolations of the Valley of Achor, *under the hill that must be climbed*, hidden under the east side, forty stones deep, is a silver chest, and with it the vestments of the *Cohen Gadol*, the high priest, and all the gold and silver with the *great tabernacle*, and all its treasures."

Timothy stared expectantly; Finn offered a weak shrug.

Timothy pasted on a false smile. "The great tabernacle; the Hebrew word for it is *Mishkan*, or so I believed. Yosi, however, argued Mishkan more accurately means 'wilderness tabernacle'. Debate remains, of course, over the word and its meaning — ask a room of scholars their opinion and you will get a roomful of opinions." Timothy steepled his fingers in a pose of erudite contemplation. "But with time, and with further study, I am now sure Yosi's was, and is, the correct interpretation."

Finn had heard the word *Mishkan* somewhere and stared off as his mind chased the fleeing word.

"The Mishkhan was the portable Temple. Do you not see?" Timothy rolled his eyes. "It transported all that was holy during the Jews' forty years in the desert. Held the altar for sacrifices, the Menorah of gold, Ashes of the Red Heifer, vessels used by the priests. And within the Mishkan's inner chamber, called the Holy of Holies, resided the Ark that held the Ten Commandments — the very tablets carried by Moses. The Mishkan was pure. Utterly sacred. So pure and sacred the *Shechina*, the Divine Presence of God, rested therein."

"The Ark," Finn mumbled after a moment.

"Aye. You hunted the Ark of the Covenant." Timothy glanced from Finn to Rollo, then snort-laughed and slapped a knee. "It was there! At Marda. You were near it — so near!" He waved a dismissive hand. "You sought the wrong treasure, Brother Finn. Gold … silver … naught but silly baubles in comparison to the Ark."

Thoughts swirled and swooped like swallows. Eventually they landed. Shock shifted to denial and Finn ticked through the argument — tired by now. Looting Romans. Inscriptions on the Arch of Titus and the Colosseum.

"Josephus."

"Josephus." Timothy snorted. "He was a Jewish commander, named Joseph ben Mathias at birth, who turned traitor to save his skin. After the rebellion, he took the emperor's family name, Flavius, and changed the Hebrew name Joseph to the Latin name Josephus. Born a Jew but died a wealthy Roman.

Some think Josephus recovered the gold himself, and perhaps he did, but certes he is reviled by Jews."

Finn opened a mouth and Timothy held up a hand to stall the counter brewing there.

"Aye. It is likely much of the treasure was plundered by Rome," Timothy said. "But remember the Zealots, and Masada, and how they defied Rome to the bitter end. Rome found enough to deflate the gold market in Syria, I grant you, though a few hoards should be enough to account for that. No. Finding all the hoards is most unlikely."

Finn had said as much to the Master — though he spoke the words to give the man hope, and to save himself from a milking barn in some dreary corner of the Order's holdings. Certainly, he did not speak the words because he believed them.

Timothy fixed Finn with a fevered stare. "Certes they did not find the Ark, for if they had, the capture of such a priceless artefact would be widely celebrated, thus widely known. It is not engraved on the arch, mentioned in the histories, and so on."

Finn quirked a head to acknowledge the truth there.

"Emperors bragged of their victories — to the gods, to the classes, to the plebes. But Jews are not Romans." Timothy tapped at the fragment of scroll with an ink-stained finger. "Jews fought rebellions with the Persians, then Greeks, then Romans, and by the end of it all learned to say the opposite of what was intended. Joy is sorrow, day is night, down was up, and so on. Obfuscation is woven into the very culture —"

"Christ's bones," Finn blurted, and Timothy feigned shock at hearing a Templar curse.

Rollo flinched awake and pried open a sleepy eye. "What?"

"Down was up."

It was not enough to translate the words. One must translate the culture itself. Robert's dream words, half-forgotten the morning after, came to him like a slap to the cheek. *What is impure shall be made pure, what is risen shall fall, and in the last days the earth will raise the Mishkan to meet the heavens.*

Finn knew where the Ark of the Covenant lay.

Three months later they rode to Marda on the Ghost Trail. Thereon they passed the battle site. Only tatters of cloth and dog-gnawed bones remained. Adrien's ghost, if it haunted there, made no fuss. Someone had piled rocks to make a shrine — or perhaps to mark the spot as a place of woe, as the Hebrews had done to Achan.

From the hills, the vista was bleak and brown and endless. The sun blazed where hawks soared and hares hid, where nothing grew and water was priceless.

The stairway was still there. They pulled down the rocks used to block the entrance. Now Finn and Rollo stood in the empty room. Their torches burned yellow holes into the darkness.

Down is up.

Those who crafted the text set out to deceive. Deception was the point. They had not buried the Ark, as any bone hunter would assume, they had raised it up to hide it away.

But raised it under a hill.

In the desolations of the Valley of Achor, under the hill that must be climbed...

The tunnel cut into the hill and extended under the sepulchre — Finn saw this when standing back, away from the hill, and studying the sepulchre's position relative to the tunnel. All which meant the hiding place was not *within* the sepulchre but *under* it — under the hill that must be climbed, as the new translation said. Adrien had accused Finn, said gold hid under a false floor when all along the real treasure, the Ark, hid behind a false wall.

I might have parsed it out the first time, thought of searching the upper walls, if the damned snake hadn't scared the wits out of my head.

Rollo, in a rare moment of insight, once said God would lead them to it, if He wanted it found. And here they were. Finn gave a long, low breath and nodded.

Rollo interlaced his fingers to make a stirrup of his hands and hoisted Finn up to examine the oddly tall wall. Finn slid a palm over stone and high up felt a seam, not visible from below. It cut horizontal across the wall. Torchlight from his left hand shadowed a seam, straight as an arrow, where a stone had been cut and removed in a block roughly three paces wide by three paces high. The stone was re-fit with such skill the seam barely showed.

A mark, no bigger than his palm, scored the wall just under the seam — two hands side by side, palms out, middle fingers splayed into a V. The mark of the Kohen. A little to the right was a second mark of two angels crouched, facing each other, wings extended forward. Together the marks spoke in a dead tongue, like ancient picture writings from a cave wall, where the language was not readable to a layman but meaning was plain all the same. Finn yanked his hand away, as if burned, and dropped to the floor on shaky knees.

"It's there," he whispered, suddenly reverent. "Romans found gold but missed the Ark."

"Seems so," Rollo said. "Fetch prybars?"

Finn craved what lay behind those marks. More than anything. Curiosity to touch, to see, to know, cut sharp as a knife. But a still, soft voice in Finn's head said the Ark should be left in peace. Dragging it to light would unleash chaos. Christendom was not deserving, not yet, and not pure enough to bask in the presence of the Holy of Holies. Men would lie and steal and kill to own it. Nations would wage war over it. The Church would sell indulgences to see it, and sell even costlier indulgences to touch it.

"No good will come of it," Finn said, still whispering. "It would break the world."

Would it mend me? He leaned and rested his palms on the stone. For how long he stood thus he could not say. *It will not heal me … only I can heal me.* Calm suffused, soft as thistledown, and Finn knew, as sure as he knew each of his many sins, he was not worthy. Not yet.

"Prybars?" Rollo asked again.

"No. Leave it untouched. And never tell a soul."

"If a half-wit like you could unravel this, well, other half-wits could do so too."

"Aye. And that half-wit, God bless his soul, will be guilty for all the horror. Not me."

Besides, maybe he's a worthy half-wit…

Rollo stared at the wall and what must behind it, pulling his beard through a fist in slow, methodical passes. After a moment he grunted and extended a hand. Finn took it. They nodded but said nothing and began the long climb out of the empty room.

HISTORICAL NOTES

The Copper Scroll is real. It is on display at the Jordan Museum in Amman; one can see it in person. Much of the story in *Fortress of Crows* is inspired by this real artefact, though facts around it are much debated, murky, or stray into the realm of myth.

It was found with the Dead Sea Scrolls in 1952, in Cave 3 of the Qumran Caves, near the archaeological site of Qumran. The Copper Scroll differs from the Dead Sea Scrolls in several ways. It was inscribed on copper, rather than written on parchment or papyrus. It is in Hebrew, though in a style like Mishnaic Hebrew, and differs in orthography and palaeography.

Engraving with a hammer and chisel likely explains some of the oddities. Scholars also think the text was copied from an original by an illiterate scribe who, for secrecy, was used because he could not read (thus could not repeat) what he wrote. Not surprisingly, the ignorant scribe introduced errors that, in turn, confounded modern translations. Several translations exist and each differs from the other — not surprising given the antiquity and oddity of the text.

The scroll varies in its purpose, too. It is not a literary or religious work but a list of sixty-four places where gold and silver were buried. Sacred vessels and priestly vestments are also listed. Entries follow the same formula — general location, specific location (often with distances to dig), and what is buried there. One entry notes, "… a copy of this document with its explanation … and an inventory of each and every thing," which indicates a duplicate scroll exists containing details to unlocking the first. No such "key scroll" has been found.

The scroll's editor, Józef Milik, thought the scroll written by the Essenes, an apocalyptic sect, around the year 100 CE. He thought it folklore. Possibly a hoax. Subsequent researchers upended these notions. They argued the scroll was written 70 CE, or earlier, and was placed in Cave 3 after the Dead Sea Scrolls. Clauses in the text have parallels with inventories from the Greek temple of Apollo. Copper was also common for archival records. Collectively, these traits affirm the Copper Scroll is a temple inventory, thus an official administrative document.

Most scholars agree the scroll lists wealth from the Second Temple, hidden from invading Romans during the First Jewish–Roman War (66–73 CE). The Temple was razed by Titus's troops in 70 CE. Others think the treasure might be tithes accumulated after the First Jewish–Roman War, while the temple lay in ruins, and prior to the Bar Kokhba revolt of 132–136 CE.

Regardless its provenience, the scroll details an amazing amount of wealth, even by modern standards. The treasure is measured in tons. In 1960 the value was estimated at $1,000,000 U.S., or roughly $10,000,000 in today's dollar, though some place the value at $1,000,000,000.

Using such an intriguing piece of history as the bones for a fictional tale proved tricky. Translations are open to interpretation. Geographical references now carry multiple names or refer to places that no longer exist. Entries give internal or external landmarks, or hints that require familiarity with local geography, culture, or rabbinical vocabulary. One must "know the place to know it" and, for outsiders, picking apart these threads is a near-impossible task.

Deciphering the scroll with any degree of confidence would (and did) take years — which is time a novel does not have. Therefore, for simplicity and flow, only the first entry of the Copper Scroll was initially translated. The wealth listed in this one entry seemed sufficient, along with the promise held in the other entries, to set off an ill-fated quest. The fight to simply possess the scroll could drive one to sins innumerable — murder, theft, torture.

Locating the Valley of Achor also proved problematic.

Eusebius, bishop of Caesarea and fourth-century church historian, placed the Valley of Achor north of Jericho. Several nineteenth-century writers place it south of Jericho. In the twentieth century, the Hyrcania Valley, to the south-west of Qumran, was proposed, as was a valley to the north-west of the Dead Sea. Some argue it is one continuous valley from Jericho to the Dead Sea.

The "ruin in the valley of Achor" could be one of several sites, including the fortress Hyrcania, which was the location used in *Fortress of Crows*. Hasmonean kings built Hyrcania; King Herod later reinforced it, then abandoned it. Saint Sabbas repurposed and renamed it Kastellion, sometimes informally called Marda (Marda was used in *Fortress of Crows*, though it means "fortress" in Aramaic, and is also used to refer to Masada).

Rather than sort out the muddle of names and places, the story embraced it, even used it as a plot device. Modern researchers cannot agree on the Valley Achor, so why would folk in 1186 fare any better? Three candidates gave Finn a valley to search; the antagonist Adrien another; and the villain Beau a third. Eventually they collide in the Hyrcania Valley/Valley of Achor.

The layout of Marda is as described in the novel — including the tunnels. In 1960, archaeologist John Allegro found two stepped tunnels below the summit of Hyrcania, a few meters above the riverbed, and cut into soft limestone to the height of a person. The tunnels were excavated but yielded only Second Temple period pot sherds and a skeleton. No clear purpose for the tunnels was determined, so why not make them part of the Copper Scroll quest?

Timing was also an issue needing a solution. The Copper Scroll was found in 1952, too late for our story, though the scroll mentions copies. Finn obtains (then loses) one of these, while the Copper Scroll remains snugged up in Cave 3. A previous owner had pried open Finn's copy, though enough legible bits remained to allow translation. Scraps of the original papyrus scroll were supposed for the sake of story (though most researchers agree it probably existed).

So, what about all that treasure? Has anyone found it? The answer is a resounding *maybe*.

John Allegro led an expedition in 1962. Vendyl Jones and Jim Barfield, amateur archaeologists, spent decades sifting the scroll for clues, then digging for treasures. Other hunters come and go. Modern efforts failed, though, and came up empty-handed despite endless research, years in the field, and the application of cutting-edge technology.

Perhaps these fruitless searches are simple to explain: someone beat them to the treasure by two thousand years. As noted by Michael Wise, greed is a strong motivator, and if you know gold is hoarded, and it is within your power to take it, you will. Rome was greedy; gold drove their conquests; they pursued a formal policy to seek the hidden wealth of whatever nation they conquered. They held power in Judea. But did they possess the knowledge — the Copper Scroll? No sources indicate they did, though there is evidence they obtained the knowledge.

Flavius Josephus, a Jew who fought against Rome until changing sides in AD 67, wrote of one Phineas, a treasurer at the Temple, who was tortured and gave up numerous treasures and "sacred ornaments". Phineas, according to Josephus, led the Romans to the temple treasures, including some of those on the Copper Scroll. The Arch of Titus, in Rome, confirms Josephus. It celebrates the triumph in AD 71, after the fall of Jerusalem, and depicts looted artefacts. The gold menorah. Gold Trumpets. The gold Table of Shewbread. The combination of historic eyewitness and the arch suggest treasure hunters should search Rome, not Israel.

Another possibility is that the Jewish people waited and, after the Romans left, used the Copper Scroll to retrieve their valuables, as was intended all along. Conspiracy theorists also claim the Templars found the Copper Scroll treasure. Did they really? Probably not. If Templars searched, they, like modern treasure hunters, likely found nothing but frustration. The notion of a scroll quest was too enticing a story to leave lay, however, and off we went!

The Copper Scroll might also contain cryptic references to the Ark of the Covenant. Allegro's translation of the first entry notes: "… the vestments of the High Priest, all the gold and silver with the Great *Tabernacle* (Hebrew, *Mishkan*) and all its treasures." Mishkan is the Hebrew word for the Wilderness Tabernacle, which Israelites carried during forty years of wandering the desert. The Mishkan held sacred vessels and within its inner chamber, the Holy of Holies, resided the Ark of the Covenant. Dr. Albert Wolters also argues the last entry reads, "Cavern of the *Shekinah*." Shekinah, as used in the Bible, is the Divine Presence as it inhabits the Tabernacle. Such clues are tantalizing but, as usual, academics are far from agreed.

As for the Ark itself? Long-gone, most likely, or well-hidden and not likely to ever be found. The Ark is a relic of such immense importance perhaps it is best if it is left in peace.

Relic hunters play a role in *Fortress of Crows*. There was coin to be made in bones, thorns, nails — especially those from the Holy Land. The lust for relics spanned high and low classes; nobles owned them and commoners clamoured (and paid) to see them. Clergyman or nobles in Christendom gave "wish lists" to agents, who worked with bone hunters in Outremer to find the relics, then acquire them for a fee. Curios were also sold to pilgrims in Jerusalem. Many were fakes or forgeries — not surprising when coin is the driver.

There is no evidence Templars employed relic hunters, like Emma of Cherbourg, though it seemed plausible an Order with the interest and wealth might "sub-contract" out such expertise. Templars certainly venerated relics — they were devout Catholics. Finn did not discount them. However, after years in Outremer, he had seen the ugly side of the relic trade. Greed. Fraud. Looting. He became embittered by the relic trade and he, like other field brothers, wanted nothing to do with it. He led the Copper Scroll quest only grudgingly.

Assassins, or Nizaris, also played a role in our tale. They are a sect of Ismailism, a branch of Shia Islam. Devotees who wanted to be fighters were trained as Fidai. They fought as a military unit, but also as secret agents who hunted enemy leaders (Christian and Muslim), attacked them in public, and died in the attempt as a sign of their devotion.

Medieval Islam was rife with splinter groups — religious and political. Historians think the Nizari's Sunni enemies, then, began a smear campaign that the Nizari were hashish addicts led by a crazed cult-leader. The myth was spread by Christians, and Marco Polo, who claimed Fedayeen were given hashish to make them tractable. Thus emerged the term *Hashishins,* or *Assassins.* There is no mention of Hashishins in Persian sources, though, and founders of the Nizari called their disciples Asāsīyūn, or people faithful to the foundation. From Asāsīyūn grew assassin. Polo missed or mis-used this context — as have several authors of historical fiction.

Fortress of Crows, as well as *Brotherhood of Wolves,* avoided the term "assassin" because it was not used in the twelfth century (even though the people who inspired it were well known). Nizaris were not paid killers, either, and instead conducted assassinations for religious reasons. Thus the historical and modern meanings of the word also differed.

Assassins and Templars were much alike. Both were an enigmatic society built on hierarchy. Members gained paradise by killing or dying, were forbidden to flee a fight, wore white with red to symbolize purity and blood. Their relationship was also complex. Fluid. They were sometimes allies (strangely), sometimes enemies, but often left each other in peace.

Polo also began the myth of the Old Man of the Mountain, the name ascribed to the leader of the Nazaris. Though myth, it was too enticing to ignore. Finn meets the Old Man in a peaceful (or relatively peaceful) interlude of Templar-Assassin relations. The character Shabh was a devotee of the Old Man, though she had gone rogue and killed to chase off old demons (and for a bit of coin). No sources indicate women were allowed as Fedayeen; many would argue it did not happen. Yet Nizari teachings espouse social justice, independent reasoning, and the acceptance of ethnic, racial, and inter-religious differences. A woman adherent under these edicts, especially one wronged by Christians, might not be so far-fetched.

Attempting to frame a historical world requires copious research. References on the Copper Scroll were many and varied from sensationalized to academic. The most useful proved to be *The Dead Sea Scrolls*, by Michael Wise, Martin Abegg, and Edward Cook; *Copper Scroll Studies*, edited by George Brooke and Philip Davies; and Joan Taylor's *Secrets of the Copper Scrolls*.

Farhad Daftary's *The Assassin Legends: Myths of the Isma'ilis*, and Marhsall Hodgson, *The Order of Assassins; The Struggle of the Early Nizârî Ismâ'îlîs Against the Islamic World*, proved invaluable for understanding the nature of the Nizari assassins. *The Templars and the Assassins*, by James Wasserman, also proved handy. Several works informed all things Templar, including Malcolm Barber's, *The New Knighthood*; Helen Nicholson and David Nicolle's *The Knights Templar: God's Warriors*; Nicholson's *Knight Templar: 1120–1312* and *The Knights Templar: A New History*; and Paul Hill's, *The Knights Templar at War*.

Templar knights, or most of them, were noble born, which meant they trained in the knightly arts since toddlers and came to Outremer as fully-formed fighting men. There is evidence, as well as common sense, that tells us Templars trained extensively after taking vows. Templars fought as a cohesive unit, thus were an elite fighting force of their day — impeccably trained, well-armed, highly motivated. The Order's Rule instilled a discipline lacking among other fighting units of their day that, it might be argued, was the equal of any modern army.

Warfare was a Templar's primary job and several fights figured prominently in *Fortress of Crows*. The phrase 'medieval warfare' suggests muscled brutes, crude weapons, hacking. Knights were imminently skilled at arms, however, and erudite fighting systems existed in Europe for centuries. Techniques were time-tested, brutally effective, yet elegant. Armor was hand-fitted and comfortably functional, like a modern-day businessman's suit, and weapons were made by artisans with skills lost to the passage of time.

I own and make (or attempt to) period-correct swords. Holding a tool, feeling its balance, then giving it a swing is a first step to understanding medieval warfare. Several works were also used to craft lively but believable sword fights. These include *Medieval Swordsmanship* by John Clements; *Swordfighting* by Guy Windsor; and *Medieval Combat*, Hans Talhoffer's fifteenth-century manual on fighting. Ewart Oakeshott's *Records of the Medieval Sword* guided all things slicey and stabby. Hopefully these details are reflected in *Fortress of Crows*.

Modern readers might assume a Templar would not be tattooed. History suggests it not improbable. Isabella Fusillo's *Tracing Stigma: The Evolution of the Tattoo in the Middle Ages*, indicates Christian tattooing was common. Early edicts distinguished between secular tattoos, like those one might have before joining the religion, and religious tattoos, such as those worn by Coptic Christians or pilgrims. Legend also has it Hospitaller knights tattooed a cross on their wrist so, when killed in battle, they could be identified and properly buried as Christians.

Several characters are historical personages, like Gerard de Ridefort, and not the creations of computer and keyboard. Some of their traits have been given fictional flourishes, to varying degrees, or are fleshed out from what little history tells us.

Finn and his Brotherhood are invented, though threads of historic Templars were woven into each to make believable fictional knights. Not every Templar was a saint with a sword. Some had dark pasts but strive for absolution; Finn is one of these. Others, like Rollo, were strong-willed and struggled with the Order's rules, while the next brother is devout and obedient. Some are learned, such as Hector, while a few, like Finn, can barely read.

A disproportionate number of historic Templars hailed from Provenance, France, and from other regions of France, Normandy, Aragon, and Catalonia. Many of the fictional characters, to mirror history, also have roots in these places. A lesser number came from far-flung lands.

Historic name spellings vary; for simplicity, spellings followed modern conventions, such as Jakelin, not Jacqueline. Names for characters were gleaned from the Academy of Saint Gabriel and *The Dictionary of Medieval Names from European Sources*. These in turn draw names from medieval records, such as tax rolls and parish registers, and cover several geographies, including Normandy, England, and Jerusalem. Rendering Turkic or Arabic names into English is vexing, for several reasons, thus English versions were used for readability.

Place names attempted to mirror the time. However, a given locale often had a name ascribed by Jewish people, then Romans, then Arabs, then Christians, etc. For example, the Dead Sea was used by Franks, Jews called it the Salt Sea, and Arabs call it the Sea of Death. The name in Western sources was used here and this choice was based on ease of use.

Religion drove twelfth-century life and medieval peoples firmly believed in religious ideals. Belief, whether Christian, Muslim, or Jewish, drove a litany of deeds, many virtuous, others horrid. Killing and death were also viewed differently than today. Daily life included violence in many forms — wars, tournaments, murder, religious art. Knights were raised from birth in a culture of warfare, then, and were hardened to bloodshed by adulthood. No attempt was made to judge practices of religion or warfare, nor place them under the scrutiny of modern morals, but simply to show them as accurately as possible.

GLOSSARY

The definitions provided here are fine-tuned to *Fortress of Crows*. Words or phrases often have multiple meanings, spellings, or uses, especially when dealing with a melting pot of cultures, as was Outremer. Only those used in this novel are given.

AKETON — Thigh-length jacket worn under mail to cushion blows, reduce chafing, and improve fit. Fluted, stuffed with cotton, and quilted. Aketon comes from the Arabic word *al qutn*, meaning of cotton. In Europe, the jacket was usually stuffed with wool and called a *gambeson, haubergeon, or padded jack.*

ALBA — As in the Kingdom of Alba, the name for pre-eleventh-century Scotland. Scotia was also used at various times and places, but by the eleventh century 'Scotland' was mostly used to refer to the Gaelic-speaking Kingdom of Alba north of the river Forth.

ARMING CAP — Wool, cotton, or linen cap under a mail coif.

ARMING SWORD — A Templar carried an arming sword and a great sword. Here, arming sword denotes a sword wielded with one hand (what Ewart Oakeshott might classify as a Type X or Xa). Arming swords often had a cruciform guard and round (wheel) pommel. Blades averaged 30 inches long and were broad, double-edged, and tapered to a usable point. A fuller, or longitudinal groove, often ran down the blade to lighten it without sacrificing strength.

BANNER — A band of Templar knights. Each band carried their own black-and-white banner. Banner is invented and used here to avoid confusion with similar terms used interchangeably, such as *conroi* or *eschielle.*

BAUCENT — Templar war banner. Variously spelled *baucant, bauceant, baussant, beauséant,* etc. The banner was black-and-white, or *piebald,* and the origin thought to be the Old French term for a piebald horse. Black was thought to symbolize ferocity to enemies and white kindness to friends. Medieval frescoes show the upper half white, the lower half black, with a red cross in the white field.

BLACKCOAT — Slang term for Templar sergeant. Non-noble. Included tradesmen and fighting sergeants. Fighting sergeants were light cavalry, some the equal of a knight in training and skill. Not equipped as generously as a knight. Wore a black or brown mantle with a red cross.

BOLT, OR QUARREL — Projectile shot from a crossbow. Resembles an arrow, but shorter and heavier.

BOWL MATE, OR BATTLE COMPANION — Invented slang term for Templar tradition of two men sharing a bowl in compliance with the Templar Rule that a knight should never be alone.

BRAES — Men's knee-length pants made of linen. Tightened with a drawstring.

CACKHAND, OR CACKHANDED — Slang term for a left-handed person. Likely derives from the ancient tradition that one used the left hand for cleaning oneself after defecating and the right hand for everything else. *Cack* was an Old English term for excrement, thus the left is the cack-hand.

CAPPA — White robe, usually linen, extends below the knees and to the wrists. Hooded, belted at the waist, and slit front and back below the hips. Marked with a red cross, though when marking began, the size and design of the cross, and placement is debated. Also covered mail to keep the metal from heating in the sun.

CASALE — A type of rural farming village. Templars owned many, and usually had a small castle or fortified villa (walled with a tower or two) from where they supervised and guarded surrounding farms.

CATERAN — Scots Gaelic term for a Highland fighting man, but also raiders or cattle thieves.

CERTES — Medieval term for, sure, of course, or I assure you.

CHRISTENDOM — The wider Christian world, here used to denote Europe.

CHURL — A person of low birth, impolite, mean-spirited.

COIF — Mail hood covering head and neck. Often included a leather-backed chin guard that was laced in place or left open when not fighting. Worn over an arming cap and under a helmet.

COMMANDER — Below the Marshal in rank. Each land had a Commander who oversaw farms, castles, etc. in their jurisdiction. The Commander of Jerusalem was treasurer of the Order and shared power with the Master.

CONROI — A wall of cavalry, riding knee-to-knee in a charge (some sources use *eschielle*). Conroi is also slang for a band of knights that trained, lived, and fought together.

COURSER — Light horse for riding, hunting, or battle. Templars had a courser or two, perhaps a rouncy, and one or more destriers. Terms like *courser*, *palfrey*, and *charger* are also common. Here, only courser and destrier are used for simplicity.

COZEN — To trick someone, or deceive them.

CROSSBOW, LATCHBOW, ARBALEST — Family of weapon consisting of a short bow mounted horizontally on a wood frame. Held and aimed like a modern rifle. Reloaded using a wood prong or both hands to pull the string and re-hook it over the locking mechanism; feet were propped against the bow or placed in a stirrup. Arbalests were heavier; reloaded with a hand crank.

CROSS PATTÉE — Type of cross with narrow arms at the centre and flaring in a curve to be wider at the perimeter. Several variants are known.

DAGGER — Double-edge, straight knife used as a secondary weapon.

DESTRIER — War horse. Origins are murky, though argued they trace to the Spanish Jennet, an ancestor to the modern Friesian and Andalusian horse. The Jennet had Barb and Arabian blood brought to Europe after the First Crusade. A destrier was well-trained, fearless, as well as strong, fast, and agile. Costly to breed and train; valued at eight times the cost of an ordinary horse. Sources refer to the destrier as the *great horse* because of its size. However, a destrier was not more than 15 hands tall, or the height of a modern riding horse (though more muscled in the hind legs).

DONNACHIE — As in Clan Donnachie, later Clan Robertson. The clan system, as it is currently understood, such as each clan wearing its own tartan, was not firmly in place by the twelfth century. However, the clan tradition was emerging by the eleventh century, if not much earlier.

DRAPER — In charge of the Templar garments and linens. The Rule states that, after the Master and Marshal, the Draper was superior to all brethren.

FALCHION — A single-edged, heavy, wide-bladed sword. Often widens toward the tip. Can have a point, but meant as a chopping and cutting weapon.

FRANKS — As used in the Levant, means any European (Latin) Christian, whether French, English, Norman, etc. (the term *Crusader* was not used in the twelfth century). Frank originates from the Arabic term *Frangistan*, a Muslim and Persian term meaning *Land of the Franks*, and generally thought to refer to Francia, which gave its name to the Kingdom of France.

FREELANCE — Used to denote a soldier who fought for pay. Term comes from "Free Lance," meaning the lance is not sworn to any lord's service and is open for rent. Later called mercenaries.

GUIGE — A strap, usually of leather, on the inside of a shield. Used to hang a shield on the shoulder or neck when not in use or, when fighting, to wield a weapon with two hands without discarding the shield.

GREAT SWORD — The second sword a Templar carried. Comparable to a hand-and-a-half, long, or bastard sword. Called a 'great sword of war' in historical sources, its blade was around 46 inches and the handle long enough to allow a two-handed grip (a Type XIIa or XIIIa in the Ewart Oakeshott typology). Slung from the saddle; often used after the lance was lost or broken.

HAUBERK — Mail coat with integral coif. Reached to mid-thigh, included sleeves, slit front and rear below the waist to allow riding a horse. Made by riveting links in a four-in-one pattern, where each ring is linked to four others. Some archaeological examples show a six-in-one pattern. Knights also wore mufflers (mittens) and mail chausses on the legs. Sergeants wore only a hauberk.

HORSEBREAD — Form of medieval bread. Inexpensive, coarse, made from one or more of beans, legumes, bran, and/or seeds. Often fed to horses, but also eaten by people.

IFRANJI — Slang for Frank, or foreigner, from Christendom usually. Also Faranji, Franj, or al-Franj for *the Franks*.

KETTLE, OR KETTLE HELMET — Shaped like a brimmed hat, open faced with a metal rim all the way around, but made of riveted metal. Also called a war hat. Worn by sergeants.

LANCE — Close relative of the spear but heavier, more durable, and meant for a cavalry charge. Hardwood shaft measuring around 8 to 10 feet long; tipped with a narrow, spear-blade point.

LEG YIELD — Lateral movement used by a horse to travel sideways (or diagonal) in small hops.

LINGUA FRANCA — A pidgin dialect spoken in Outremer. Based on *langue d'oil*, the language of Normandy and France, but borrowed from many languages, including Arabic and Italian.

MACE, OR TURKISH MACE — Blunt weapon consisting of a wood or metal handle and an iron or steel head, usually flanged or knobbed. Simple, inexpensive, but wickedly effective.

MAHOUND, MAHOUNDS — Slang term deriving from the Anglo-Saxon word *Mahun*, a generic pagan deity Christians thought (incorrectly) Muslims worshipped.

MAMLUK — Slave soldiers serving the Arab dynasties (also mameluke, mamluq, etc.). Many were Turkic or Eurasian steppes peoples, but others came from the Caucasus Mountains, Greece, or the Balkans. Harvested young and sold to Egypt, where they were taught Islam and Furūsiyya.

MARSHAL — Primary role was military advisor and organizing the Order for war. Consulted with the Marshal on tactics. His retinue was four horses, two squires, a turcopole, and a sergeant. An Under Marshal oversaw the footmen and equipment.

MASTER — Grand Master of the Order, worldwide, and led the Order in battle, as well as in spiritual matters. Based in Jerusalem and answered only to the Pope.

NASAL, OR NASAL HELMET — Helmet worn by Templar knights during the twelfth century. Usually worn over a coif. The helmet was open-faced, rounded or conical, with a metal strip (or nasal) covering the nose. By the early 1200s, helmets had evolved to a flat-topped affair with an attached face plate. By around 1240, helmets were totally enclosed with eye slits and breathing holes.

ORDER — Used here to denote the Templars, as in the Order of the Templars.

OUBLIETTE — A dungeon with one escape route through a trap door in its ceiling.

OUTREMER — The Latin east and the four Christian states carved out by the first crusade. French, meaning beyond the sea (*outre-mer*, or beyond [*outre*] the sea [*mer*]). Included the Kingdom of Jerusalem (1099–1291); county of Edessa (1097–1150); county of Tripoli (1102–1289); and principality of Antioch (1098–1287).

PITTA, OR KHUBZ — Round flatbread baked from wheat flour. Called *naan* in Iran and the Eastern Mediterranean and Central Asia.

POTTAGE — Thick stew or soup. Made of boiled vegetables, grains, and, if available, meat or fish.

POULAIN — French slang for a baby horse. In Outremer, and in this book, used as slang for Frankish descendants of the original crusaders who captured Jerusalem in 1099 and remained in Outremer. Local-born Franks.

QAMA — Edged weapon from the Caucasus. Resembles the offspring of a Roman gladius and a dagger; distinctive for its wide, double-edged blade that tapers to a needle-sharp point. Handled with a single piece of horn, ivory, or wood, and lacks a separate guard or pommel.

RICASSO — An unsharpened length of sword blade just in front of the guard. Allowed the swordsman to place their index finger above the guard, which improved grip strength and torque. Could grasp the ricasso to shorten their grip, allowing a large blade to be used in a tight press.

ROUTIER — Term for a French brigand, or sometimes French mercenaries.

RULE, OR THE RULE — The Rule of the Templars, first put to parchment in 1129, outlined sixty-eight codes governing Templar life. Rules for penance were included. Eventually covered several hundred edicts in multiple languages.

SAIF, OR SAYF — Arabic word for sword; can refer to any sword, curved or straight (though early Islamic swords were straight and double edged; curved sabres developed over time). Here, saif denotes a straight sword with a wide, double-edge blade; reasonably sharp point; and fuller.

SARACEN — Used to denote any person who followed Islam. Originally applied to a tribe of Arabs living in the Sinai Peninsula. The term morphed to cover Arab tribes in general, and, after the establishment of the caliphate, to refer to all Muslim subjects of the caliph.

SERGEANT — See Blackcoat.

SENESCHAL — Right-hand man to the Master; acted as advisor, tackled administrative duties.

SGIAN DUBH — A small, single-edge knife (Scots-Gaelic, *skene-dhu*) commonly worn in a sock or boot, around the neck, or under an armpit.

SHEMAGH — Scarf, usually a long rectangle of cotton, wrapped around the neck and face as protection from sun and sand. Also called a *keffiyeh* or *ghutrah*.

SHIELD, OR BOARD — Templar shields were triangular and curved along the edges to a pointed bottom; flat across the top; convex across the face. Covered shoulder to mid-thigh. Usable mounted or afoot. Wood with a painted leather cover. A leather strap, or *guige*, allowed it to be slung over a shoulder or across the back. Frescoes from the thirteenth century show Templar shields as white in the upper half, black in the lower half black, with a red cross in the white field.

SQUIRE — Knights were allotted squires to see to their horses, gear, etc. Squires were often not members of the Order and were outside labour hired for a set period.

SWEETMEAT — More or less, medieval candy.

TIRKESH, WAR BOW, OR TURKISH BOW — Composite bow made of horn, wood, and sinew. Recurved, compact, and meant to be used from horseback. Draw weight of 80 to 120 pounds. Pulled with the index finger and thumb; a ring on the thumb aids the draw. Effective range of 300 yards.

TONSURE — Cutting, plucking, or shaving the hair on top of the head and leaving a ring of hair around the sides. Confusion exists about whether Templars tonsured. Some medieval paintings show tonsures, though others show long hair, curly hair, etc. A thirteenth-century account mentions Templars with shaved heads. The Rule states only that hair be regularly trimmed. Beards were fashionable in Outremer, where beards were a sign of manliness. In *Fortress of Crows*, short hair and long beards were the norm, though some might tonsure as a sign of devotion.

TURCOPOLE, OR TURC — Worked for the Order as archers, crossbowmen, light cavalry, scouts, etc. Local Christians; usually Syrians, Armenians, Lebanese, Greeks, often half-bred with Turks. Turcopole meant *son of Turk*, though over time the term evolved to denote a profession.

WATERED STEEL, OR DAMASCUS STEEL — Steel made in a crucible. Homogeneous content and high carbon with low slag (impurities) made watered steel tough, resistant to breakage, and able to hold a resilient edge. Shows banding, swirls, and mottling evocative of flowing water. Modern forge welding produces similar patterns, leading some to wrongly label welded steel as Damascus steel.

WHITEBACK, OR WHITEDOG — Slang term for a Templar knight.

WOLF'S HEAD — Term used in the medieval English legal system to designate a criminal, an outlaw, someone who could be killed without penalty.

A NOTE TO THE READER

Dear Reader,

Historical fiction, it should go without saying, is not history, no matter how well researched. This novel is entertainment. That said, I am a professional archaeologist (retired) and amateur historian, therefore care deeply for the past. Accuracy matters, but weaving history and fiction requires research and time. Effort does not ensure I get it all right. No author does. Errors are few, hopefully, and entirely mine.

The Crusades speaks to me in a way few other eras can. The notion of fighting monks, serving God with their swords, is a long-held fascination. Templars were the preeminent military order, charged with protecting pilgrims and God's kingdom, and one of the most revered military units in history. Recklessly brave. Utterly devout. Writers of the day praised them as, "formidable rather than flamboyant," and they chose to be humble in their mien, ragged in their attire.

Templars are often mythologized, painted as a secretive sect of Christian mystics, guardians of the Grail. In the Brotherhood series, they are presented as people, with the virtues and flaws unique to our species — pious, fearless, dedicated, but also scheming, ambitious, backstabbing.

I once vowed to never write a 'Templars hunt a holy relic' story. Those have been done — overdone, some might say. Yet the lure of the Copper Scroll proved too strong, the retired archaeologist in me too weak to resist it. Most folks are fascinated by the ambiguous and love a treasure hunt; the Copper Scroll is both. The fact it is a real artefact and describes temple treasures, holy and monetary, only makes it doubly fascinating.

I hope you found *Fortress of Crows* an entertaining read, and thank you for your time! Reviews are crucial to authors, so if you enjoyed the novel, please spare a moment to post a review on **Amazon** and **Goodreads**. You can also connect with me on **Facebook**, where you will find more information about upcoming books.

Thank you again!

Daniel Colter

Sapere Books is an exciting new publisher of brilliant fiction and popular history.

To find out more about our latest releases and our monthly bargain books visit our website: **saperebooks.com**

www.ingramcontent.com/pod-product-compliance
Lightning Source LLC
Chambersburg PA
CBHW071248250626
47163CB00002B/372